THE
READING PARTY

THE
READING PARTY

Fenella Gentleman

MUSWELL
PRESS

First published by Muswell Press in 2018

Copyright © Fenella Gentleman 2018

Fenella Gentleman asserts the moral right to be
identified as the author of this work

Typeset by M Rules
Printed and bound by CPI Group (UK) Ltd, Croydon CR04YY.

This work is a work of fiction and, except in the
case of historical fact, any resemblance to actual persons,
living or dead, is purely coincidental.

A CIP catalogue record for this book
is available from the British Library.

ISBN 978-1-9998117-2-3

Muswell Press
London
N6 5HQ

To my father, David, with love

Prologue

The other day I looked something up in a book and out fell that sheet of paper.

Whoooooosh! A rush of memories, as if a sluice gate had opened; my insides suddenly in free fall.

Which is odd. I mean, it was only the list of names. It's not as if it had been a photo or a flower – something evocative. It wasn't even handwritten; just one of those cyclostyled sheets we sent round in those days. And yet it conjured the Reading Party as if it had been the group photo, offering a glimpse of his face; or a pressed daffodil, with a vestige of the colours he talked about.

I must have been using the list as a marker when I was sitting in that room with him – the little library with the view through the pines to those Cornish cliffs. I'd have been trying not to look his way, trying to get on with my work. At Carreck Loose, you spent as much time reading the people and the situations as you did reading your books. Well, I certainly did.

To recover from the emotional jolt, I tried thinking about that year – my first as an academic – with the dispassion of a social historian. But every time the exercise made me cross. *Of course* it had been hard to read the signs correctly and behave appropriately; no need to have given myself such grief. Many of my difficulties were just a symptom of the times:

the balance of power was inherently unequal and what was at stake for men and women was simply not the same.

There were huge pressures on us – which naturally meant the women – to set an example; to show that 'going mixed' was 'a good thing'. The junior tutors were often very young: one minute strutting our stuff in the belief we were making history; another fearing the boot for failing to make the grade or for breaching one of those diktats that the men never bothered to mention. And a few of us hadn't even been there as undergraduates – we weren't Oxbridge types at all.

The first female Fellow in what had been a male college – in my mid-twenties and an outsider to boot! That says it all, really. How could it not be challenging?

I did my best. Did very well, in the circumstances. I'm proud of what they called my 'feistiness', even though it got me into trouble. Besides, if I hadn't been feisty, they wouldn't have offered me the job in the first place. But some of the men said it was precisely the feistiness that they found so very attractive, which rather proves my point: as a woman, you really couldn't win …

The Reading Party
12th–19th March 1977
Carreck Loose, Cornwall

Tutors

Dr Dennis Loxton: Senior Fellow and Tutor (Philosophy)
Dr Sarah Addleshaw: Junior Fellow and Tutor (Modern History)

First Years

Mei Chow: Law – Hong Kong Scholar –
(King George V School, Hong Kong)
Eddie Oakeshott: English (Westminster School, London)

Second Years

Jim Evans: History (Cathays High School, Cardiff)

Finalists

Hugh Chauncey: Classics – Exhibitioner (Ampleforth College)
Gloria Durrant: Modern Languages
(Roedean & Colegio Peruano Britanico, Lima)
Chloe Firth: Psychology, Philosophy & Physiology
(Camden School for Girls, London)
Rupert Ingram-Hall: Oriental Studies
(The Manchester Grammar School)
Lyndsey Milburn: English – Exhibitioner
(Walbottle Campus, Newcastle upon Tyne)
Priyam Patel: Law (City of London School for Girls)
Barnaby Quick: History (Gresham's School, Holt)
Martin Trewin: Geography (Truro School)
Tyler Winston: Philosophy, Politics & Economics –
Rhodes Scholar (Harvard University, Boston)

Glossary of Oxford terminology page 335

Michaelmas

'There's just one other thing, Dr Addleshaw,' he said, as I was readying to get back to the sunshine.

Here we go, I thought: not reprieved yet.

It was early October 1976, just before the start of Oxford's Michaelmas Term. I was in the Warden's Lodgings, having a meeting with the head of the College about matters on which, it seemed, he needed to put his stamp. From next door came the low throb of an IBM 'golf ball' and the occasional burst of electric typing. Through the windows was a view of the front quadrangle, the odd student or don passing by. On my knees flopped some paperwork, none of it referred to.

The Warden began explaining how it would be 'most helpful' if I accompanied one of the Senior Fellows and some undergraduates on that year's trip to Cornwall. A week at the end of the Hilary term, so they could revise for Finals during the Easter break – nothing onerous: a matter merely of deciding who should attend and then, once the group was at the house, taking a few walks and checking people read for seven hours a day.

It sounded straightforward enough, if archaic.

'The thing is,' he continued, the huge head turning back to its view of the Gatehouse, 'our Reading Party has yet to go mixed. For the first two years of female students, I could defend an all-male event, but I can't any longer, now they are Finalists. As our first woman on Governing Body, you will see that.'

'Of course.'

He looked at me – I had a habit of clicking the lid of my pen – before carrying on. 'Dr Loxton has been leading the Reading Party for two decades. He accepts it must keep pace with the times. He assures me he expected to include women this year, knows I'd like you to accompany him and says he's delighted for you to do so. So all the signs are in our favour.'

Not so straightforward.

There was a pause while he adjusted the green reading lamp on the vast mahogany desk: even on a bright day his study was gloomy, the sunshine blocked by the stone mullions or absorbed by the deep recesses of the window seat.

I realised my t-shirt was too low, too many freckles revealed. Mum would have told me the trousers were wrong too, but I liked my bell-bottoms. Only my patchwork handbag looked the part – real suede and no tassels.

The Warden affected not to notice me fiddling. 'We are a progressive college. We've done well so far with the admission of women, but ...'

It was all so circuitous. 'Let me guess. We have a reputation to uphold ...?'

'Quite.' He gestured towards the window and the life beyond. 'We have a duty of care for *all* our students, male as well as female, postgraduate as well as undergraduate, wherever they are. And we must keep Dennis on side: the Reading Party would not *be* the Reading Party without Dennis at the helm.'

He completed his circuit and stood by the chair again, arms still clasped behind his back, watching me over the glass lamp, twirling his thumbs.

My papers were slipping off my lap, soon to meet the floor. 'Whoops,' I said, rescuing our brief agenda and putting

2

it back on top. Stupid to look so unprofessional; Dad would smile if he knew.

'It is a corollary of being one of one, Dr Addleshaw,' he continued, regardless. 'I appreciate – we *all* appreciate – that it may be trying, having to set the standard. But the Reading Party offers an exceptional experience for our students. Hard work matched with fresh air, even some larking about, and *companionship* – the benefits are incommensurable. This year will be crucial. You'll understand the importance of getting it right.'

My Parker clicked again. There were stories about such traditions; historians like me were always arguing about why some survived and others did not.

'Absolutely,' I said. 'Anything in particular you have in mind?'

Perhaps he felt the need to convince. 'Oh, don't worry about the pastoral side, important though that is: the Dean will fill you in. You have an advantage, as a woman – it will come naturally. But there are other rewards: you will be able to get some work done – an article for one of the journals, or polishing your lectures. That's what we care about here: our Fellows should lead the field.'

Already I was exhausted by the endless tests. At least this one was blatant: no mistaking being volunteered – or put on notice to produce.

'I'll do my best,' I said, stuffing the pen in my bag. 'Why shouldn't a *mixed* party be a success?'

The Warden put his hands on the back of his chair and pushed it under the kneehole. The craggy face softened.

'Why shouldn't it, indeed! That's the spirit we need. I'm sure you will set an excellent example. And you'll soon get the measure of Dennis. Some of my colleagues bark a little harder than they bite. There's always a reason. He is not quite what he seems.'

3

Business done, he ushered me into the hall, dispensing pleasantries, even calling me 'Sarah', and then stood by the front door, his arm outstretched to indicate the exit.

I imagined his days punctuated by meetings like this, geeing people up or giving them a dressing-down. As a newcomer, I'd be in the first category for the moment. How little did it take, during that long probation, to move into the second? What kind of role model, or misbehaviour, did they have in mind? No one had ever accused me of being tame ...

'It will be another historic moment,' he concluded, which was clever of him. 'I knew you would appreciate that.'

He opened the heavy door and waited while I stepped down onto the flagstones and into the warmth of the afternoon.

There was a minor collision with someone on the path: an explosion of apologies, a helping hand. My papers were suddenly everywhere, my red hair flying, my cleavage again too visible. The man – film-star looks, all the trappings of the Ivy League – dropped nothing. He crouched down to help me gather my things, his knees touching mine. I noticed the sheen on the loafers, the very soft socks, the patch of honey shin, the miniature curls.

'Sun ...!' the Warden observed, as if nothing had happened. Then, while we each claimed the mishap as our own, he rounded off: '... nearly eclipsed by our scholar here! Isn't it glorious at this time of day?'

The American handed back the last of my sheets and the three of us stood for a moment, surveying the contrast of creamy stone, green grass and blue sky. From that angle the composition was almost a perfect trapezoid, the sides of the quad tapering away from the shadow. It was indeed lovely.

'The best light in which to see them,' the Warden pronounced, indicating the statues of the founders, a formidable husband-and-wife team about whom I'd heard tales.

He bent down as the American moved off, hand raised by

4

way of goodbye. 'He's the sort we need,' he said conspiratorially, as if it was obvious what sort of promising the man
was – older student or young academic, my peer or not.

Then he reverted to the booming voice: 'It was all down
to our foundress, you know: her vision and tenacity after her
husband died. So there is a very good precedent for women
here, as my own wife likes to remind me – even if it has taken
a few centuries.'

He gave me an indulgent smile. 'Come to see us if anything
troubles you. We are always here.' And he leant forward, hand
on the doorjamb, his massive body threatening to topple onto
my much smaller one.

'That's very kind,' I replied, and watched as he pulled his
weight back, swivelled and went inside.

Was he, in effect, my new boss? No one told you how it
worked.

As for the Ryan O'Neal lookalike, how much had he heard?

The early days were so exhausting that thoughts of the
Reading Party were easily pushed aside. I loved exploring the
College, the Faculty and the University, and was constantly
amazed at the beauty of the buildings and the grounds, the
intelligence of the people I talked to. The challenge was
working out how to behave.

The first hurdle was the ordeal by dining.

I come from a modest background: my family doesn't
use a phalanx of silver cutlery and no one serves you from
behind; as for talking over a meal, you can't hold erudite
conversations when my brothers are around. So the formality
of High Table in Hall, processing past the students to reach
the dais, where you sat surrounded by similarly gowned but
solely male figures, was intimidating. No one explained the
rules – when to start eating, how to pass the various decanters;
I was constantly worried about getting it wrong in front of

everyone. And the dons were all so learned, so fascinating on their subjects! When they turned to my own, it felt like one of their *viva voce* examinations. Even the social chat assumed you knew about the arts and required you to have views.

It was worse when we withdrew, again passing the students, for coffee, port and cigars in the Senior Common Room. With its careful arrangement of burnished leather seating, its polished tables of journals and newspapers, the SCR was how I imagined a gentlemen's club. And I sensed that the dons hadn't quite got the measure of 'the situation', as the Warden had called it in relation to the students: I – the sole woman – was being treated as a visitor rather than a new member. There was too much of the careful courtesy they might extend to a colleague's wife before resuming a more important discussion with somebody else. Either way, I was being assessed. It was utterly different from the slap-dash banter in the staffroom I'd just abandoned.

Interestingly, there was no sign of the American amongst the tutors. I began to think he might be a student, in which case there would be less scope for joking about the English and their arcane customs, which would be a shame.

Then there was the business of 'tutes'.

I'd never *had* a tutorial, let alone *given* one – it wasn't the way you were taught at York – yet suddenly I was expected to carry them off with aplomb. There was no guidance about what to cover or how, in that hour in your rooms; you were left to work it out for yourself.

My first went without a hitch. It was with a Finalist who handed in an essay he should have delivered the previous term. I suppose I could have put it aside, but I liked him – he, too, was from Norfolk – and the topic intrigued me: it was about the impact of a group of nineteenth-century reformers and who deserved the credit; those who campaigned for change or those who enacted the legislation. So I asked him to read it out. We had a sparky discussion about his argument that there was courage on both sides, and that historians were prone to glamorise a few highly visible protestors at the expense of the many people struggling to improve things from within. It was nice to see him looking so relieved when I reassured him that it had been worth the wait.

So far, so good – and Barnaby Quick went on my mental list of candidates for the Reading Party.

My second tutorial was more testing. It was with a pair of Second Years: one was a cocky guy who made endless lazy comments – about the topic I suggested they study, the books I recommended, my plan for the rest of the term; the other was a taciturn Welshman with eyes that noticed everything. I wanted him to contribute more. Perhaps Mr Smug felt the need to retaliate. As he went to the door he tossed off something else. He said it was 'groovy' being taught by a woman, especially a pretty one, but you could make too much noise about it: a female Fellow might be a novelty – it was certainly an amusing misnomer – but there'd been endless changes over the centuries; it wasn't such a big deal.

I was taken aback, having planned no less than transforming the character of an institution. I certainly hadn't expected a student to put me in my place – let alone with complacent flirting.

That was no fun at all, though a glance from the other student helped: *he* understood my quick retort; *he* was on my side. I made another Reading Party note: Jim Evans.

Worse, almost, than the fact of these difficulties, there was no one to discuss them with or to explain the many things that were hard to handle, like the intricacies of the collegiate system or the bizarre niceties of academic dress. Of course there were the two other historians on Governing Body: the diehard from the panel at my final interview, who taught Ancient History and had decades on me; and a nice man

7

approaching forty, who focused on the period up to 1500 and seemed a real supporter. But the older man wasn't the sort of person in whom you would confide, even though we were meant to be colleagues, and the Mediaevalist had a young family, which meant he wasn't around much.

As for my own generation, if it turned out that the American was not on the staff, then the youngest of the Tutorial Fellows would be two men a few years older than me: a scientist and a mathematician; perhaps unlikely to become confidants. That left the Dean, a free-market economist in his early thirties who seemed to relish the opportunity to keep, as he put it, a quasi-parental eye on the students and had endless extravagant stories about what they got up to. He wasn't really my type – the first thing he did was declare himself unashamedly right wing, banging on about Friedrich Hayek and that awful Thatcher woman – and he had a way of prancing around like a pop star, flaunting his tight jeans and ruffling his layered hair as if he were Rod Stewart, which made even a handsome man look slightly ridiculous. But the energy, the wit and the inside knowledge were very compelling, and he made you laugh. Besides, no one else had offered to get me up to speed.

Meanwhile I did my best to find out about Dr Dennis Loxton: important to be able to read him too, or we wouldn't pull off the landmark 'retreat'.

There was a portrait in the College prospectus – he must have been in the category of elder statesman to merit a picture – which showed a slight and not particularly tall man in his late fifties or early sixties with a gaunt face and sharp features, who might once have been called dapper. His cuffs peeped out neatly from his jumper, which in turn protruded just the right amount from the sleeves of his tweed jacket; his shimmering hood was neatly arranged behind his shoulders to show just enough of his academic distinction; his hands were loosely clasped, resting lightly on the crossed knee; everything was just so.

His books were similarly austere. There were two of his publications in the philosophy section at Blackwell's: a short study in epistemology, described as 'ground-breaking', which they only had in hardback, and a slim collection of essays based on a series of seminars, which was more manageable at £1.45. Both were written in a prose so taut, so precisely calibrated, that each line would surely snap if he put a word wrong. How would you survive, given so little room for manoeuvre, I wondered, thinking with relief of the disorderliness of my own subject. And what if you tried to *live* with such a person? But he was old, of the era of bachelor dons and their spinsterly counterparts; the issue wouldn't have arisen.

I was about to get Loxton's essays when I spotted the American: he was at the till just as I emerged between the bookshelves. Even from behind the College scarf was visible; that ruled him out as a fellow lecturer unless people were much more tribal in the States or it was part of his preppy look. Maybe the Warden had meant Scholar with capital 'S', in which case he might be a postgraduate? It was awkward not knowing, so I backed away. Buying Loxton's book went out of my head.

Instead of reading him in print, I tried my colleagues. Occasionally, I gleaned a useful nugget – a reference to the line Loxton had taken on a particular issue or an affectionate example of his foibles – but the Fellows didn't seem to gossip about each other, let alone get into a discussion of character; there was nothing about his home or the absence of family. Presumably reticence helped when living so closely together, or maybe men didn't swap notes about people as women did.

The Dean was the exception. He turned out to have accompanied Loxton on some of the Reading Parties, but said he'd found it hard being his sidekick; it was a role better suited to doctoral students, who were happy to defer. He promised to fill me in over a drink; meanwhile, he made do with a warning.

'Loxton is a difficult man,' he said. 'Solitary, reserved; a bit ascetic. Something of a conundrum.'

He gave me a teasing look, ostensibly hesitating about how much he should say, and then plunged in. 'I don't suppose anyone's told you, but it's probably the war: he abandoned his studies to help the codebreakers in Bletchley Park and was stuck there for years – not that any of us knew. He only confessed once that book on the "Ultra" intelligence came out. Do you know it?'

I didn't.

'No matter. My guess is that Dennis never recovered from the isolation and the habit of secrecy – or from losing people he cared for. But he has a brilliant mind and is devoted to the College: you can't fault him there. You just have to hold your own. I'd say, beware.'

None of this was exactly encouraging.

And then there Loxton was, one evening after dinner, asking if he might join me just as I failed to do the right thing with an engraved silver platter – the kind that has tiny curving legs – that was doing the rounds, carrying dark chocolates to the little tables perched by the sofas and easy chairs. It was an inauspicious start: feeling vulnerable always makes me combative.

Leaning against the curl of his armrest, he explained that it was one of their 'unfathomable traditions' that the dish should not be put down until all the chocolates had disappeared. The eldest amongst them remembered it from their youth, he said, but nobody could recall when or why it began: it just was.

This excessive courtesy seemed to me patronising and I resolved to stay alert, as the Dean had advised.

Loxton peeled foil off a Bendicks Bittermint. Then commented that he had been delighted – they had *all* been delighted – when I accepted their offer; had hoped for some time that, when there was an opening for a new Fellow, the best candidate might prove to be a woman; had been eager to meet the person about whom there were such high expectations.

This was faintly intimidating and a little pat: too perfect, like the immaculate fingernails and the polished shoes. A sign, as the Warden had indicated, that there was a difference between doing something because one wishes to and because one must.

I made an equally bland comment – felt like Eliza Doolittle watching her words: 'How kind of you to let me come' – and sat awkwardly between the cushions, riled. We weren't going to hit it off.

We turned to the arrival of female students. I asked, had that gone as expected? This should have been interesting – there were even links with my research – but he said it had been remarkably uneventful. Spreading the newcomers around had helped, although the sanitary arrangements weren't perfect. There were more staircase parties, but none of the lurid breaches of security for which the Dean, as chief welfare officer and enforcer of discipline, had been primed. Most noticeable had been the increase in civility: the college had never been a loutish place, but there was less egregious behaviour than before.

The Mediaevalist was smiling at me. We had talked about some of the older dons referring to the 'fairer sex' as a 'civilising influence'; perhaps he'd guessed what was being trotted out. I smiled back and asked Loxton how we were we doing academically.

'You won't need me to tell you,' he said, but he told me all the same, that there were 'some very bright women'. He had taught several from the women's colleges over the years, and he also had the highest respect for his counterparts. Perhaps the female undergraduates weren't quite as resilient as the men? They gave measured responses rather than shooting back; had to be encouraged, not provoked. It was not a matter of innate capacity, more a reflection of the teaching at school, or expectations at home. Still, their marks at College Collections and more importantly at the University Preliminary Examinations were promising.

I resolved to spar on behalf of my sex where Loxton was concerned.

'But there have been no women yet on your Reading Party?'

Loxton cradled the bottom of his brandy glass where it swelled, just as I'd seen him fingering the bowl of his pipe.

'Transitions are always difficult, are they not, Dr Addleshaw?'

The taste of mint fondant bursting into bitter chocolate must have emboldened me.

'Really?' I said. 'I find change invigorating. Did the women not want to come with you or did you not want them to come?'

That made him sit a little straighter.

'Ah.' He looked at me carefully with grey eyes, very pale. 'You must have been a pleasure to teach!' But it wasn't a generous smile. Besides, he hadn't answered the question.

'And . . .?' I asked, with a touch of coquetry, to liven things up.

'I felt we had a double difficulty. There would have been one woman, at most two, out of a dozen students, which would have been uncomfortable for everybody, and it wasn't obvious who would join me in accompanying them.' He sat back. 'But now we have female Finalists and you on Governing Body, there should be no problem. No problem at all.'

'So I'm to be their chaperone!' I glanced around to check how loudly this had come out, and dropped my voice. 'But the women might *not* have felt uncomfortable, Dr Loxton. I

12

wouldn't describe myself as uncomfortable and there is only one of me.'

He leant forward a fraction and for an awful moment I thought he might pat my knee, but instead he sucked air into his tobacco and damped it down. 'I am glad to hear it. But the comparison is not exact. We would expect you to be undaunted; we could not expect that of a first-year undergraduate.'

'Really? Is it so very different?'

'I felt it was, yes.'

'And the Warden?'

'The Warden was happy to take my advice.'

'I see.'

The mints came round again, depleted but not yet finished.

'What happens if no one eats them?'

'The chocolates? They disappear into the pot plants or various pockets, I suppose. It's a bit of a game.'

I imagined the American struggling to understand. 'It seems utterly extraordinary, viewed from the outside,' I said.

'Traditions often do, don't you think? But that doesn't mean they're wrong.'

'Surely this one may have had its day?'

He leant forward again, this time a little conspiratorially, with the same tight smile. 'Ah, Dr Addleshaw! You are – as promised – determined to challenge.'

That conversation seemed to epitomise what women were up against. It wasn't only the injustice of the numbers and the ratios – that after nearly a century of co-*education*, with men and women in their separate colleges, there was still so much to do on co-*residence*, through further colleges admitting the opposite sex, if we were to achieve anything like parity. It was also the emotional toll – the depletion of your energy in that wearying business of holding your own in a male environment – just when you wanted to focus on achieving all you were capable of.

The trip to Cornwall began to feel like one thing too many. So I may have been a little on edge when a missive arrived from Loxton later in First Week.

We collected our mail from the Porters' Lodge, a burrow of a room leading off the Gatehouse, which acted as post office, key depository and venue for inconsequential chat. The students and academics had separate banks of pigeonholes: the students' on one wall, arranged A to Z; the academics' on the other, individually named.

The spidery handwriting on the crisp white envelope had to be his. Superficially neat, elegant even, it was almost impenetrable, the ascenders and descenders minimally delineated, although, on inspection, all the defining features were there. A subtle barrier, just as the Dean had warned.

Fleetingly, I considered replying in similarly inscrutable script; the idea might be childish, but it made me feel better, as if the point had been made.

Perhaps I giggled. The figure standing by the other wall turned my way. It was the guy from the Warden's Lodgings. So he'd be a student – I might even be teaching him – and there was no escaping it. This was the price of being that rarity, a female tutor amongst male students, and on notice to set the standard: he was out of bounds.

'Pardon me?' he said, looking up from his mail.

It was still there: the all-American air of Ryan O'Neal as the preppy in *Love Story* – flecked wool jacket, soft crew-neck jumper, pale blue button-down shirt, those ox-blood loafers – without quite the actor's looks. But that might not be fair. The hair was the same near blond: it was just that I usually went for dark.

'Oh, hello,' I said and waved the envelopes in my hand. 'Just mastering Dr Loxton's handwriting.'

'Some of them seem determined to be obscure, don't they? His is notorious.'

This seemed remarkably frank.

'Really?' I said.

'Sure. We all joke about his indecipherable notes. But he's a great tutor: one of those who are clever but kind.'

What a strange take – and no deference at all! A good thing the Lodge was empty: someone might have overheard.

The flimsy blue paper of his letter crackled as he opened it. 'What the English call "a gentleman", I guess.'

'Yes, that's probably right. Still, a challenge to read.'

I wondered what behaviour was called for. He was being friendly, as Americans were, and he'd helped pick everything up.

'I'm sorry, I should introduce myself. I'm Sarah Addleshaw. The new Tutorial Fellow. We collided in the front quad a few days ago.'

'Got that. I mean ... not the colliding, but we all know who you are – you're easy to remember. The social historian – if you use that label here?'

This would have been flattering if I hadn't been the only female Fellow, and with hair the colour of a pumpkin; of course I stood out. But he'd remembered my subject too – that was something.

'No, the label's good – it's a different approach. Neither in the Marxist camp nor out of it.'

'Neat! And you like your tape recorder.'

A girl from my staircase collected a parcel and went out again, but the American wasn't to be deflected.

'Oral history. Your book on the suffragettes. It's on display in the Library. I dipped in.'

This was even more embarrassing. 'Goodness!'

'Yeah, all those stories from the ones who're still alive. "Ordinary" folk as well as Lady this and Lady that? I thought they were great.'

'That's a relief. And you?'

'Tyler Winston, Rhodes Scholar, PPE, final year.'

Confirmation: a student. But at least not a historian. 'So you're a postgrad undergraduate?'

'Yup. But we only do the second and third years ...'

'Of course.'

'... And there's nothing you'd call a social history paper, which seems odd to me.'

'Well, that's certainly a shame. You'll have to go to some lectures instead. Anyway, nice to meet you properly.'

I stuffed my post into my bag and went back to my rooms. It still unnerved me when people had read my book. Made me feel exposed, almost naked.

As for Loxton's letter, with its whiff of printers' ink and its elegant embossing, so formally offering a Reading Party briefing, what was I meant to do? Reply with another laid-paper note, in a tissue-lined envelope that rustled when opened? It was infuriating.

Our encounter a few days later renewed my apprehension about spending a whole week together.

Loxton was scrupulously polite – enquiring if we might relocate to the gardens, as it was an exceptional afternoon and the roses again in bloom – but he didn't go in for unnecessary chat. He led me to an arrangement of furniture overlooking the lawn, noted the obvious landmarks – the rear of the Warden's Lodgings, the side of the Chapel, the glimpse of the Library through the trees – and turned swiftly to business.

There were no concessions to the loveliness of the view or the comings and goings around us, let alone to the awkwardness of holding our first meeting in front of everyone – especially when I was still such an object of interest. Instead, he rattled through the basics as if talking to a tiresome student. It felt aggressive, despite the punctilious civilities; a bombarding with information to see if you kept up.

He explained the history of the Reading Party and why it took place in Cornwall, about both of which the Mediaevalist and the Dean had been hazy. The regime, he said, was inviolable. Breakfast, reading and lunch, of the bread-and-cheese variety; outdoors activity (here he gestured vaguely towards what looked like a netball team gathering noisily under a huge tree); reading and supper, which the students cooked in turn; board games and talk. As before, there would be twelve in all, only nine or ten of them Finalists – a sprinkling of other years mattered, or the atmosphere became anxious. The students would be chosen by the end of this term and briefed at the start of the next.

I scanned the expanse of grass. My colleague the Ancient Historian was ambling towards a bench with the cocky student; presumably an outdoor tutorial. The Warden's wife was showing someone round. Even Tyler Winston was there, with a female student. He gave us a wave and, after a backwards glance from the woman, disappeared out of sight. Friend? Girlfriend? They weren't touching, but they walked in step...

Loxton wasn't to be distracted. Could he assume I had reviewed this year's 'bible' on the members of the College? A useful checklist, especially of the schools and bursaries, but 'we' – 'that is, you and I, if you are agreed, Dr Addleshaw' – would also take soundings. The Dean must be 'on side' too in case of disciplinary or pastoral issues, though happily both were rare.

'May I?' he asked, pulling his pipe out of his pocket and resting it on the table, where it rocked in the breeze. It was very hard to concentrate. Across the grass came a drift of Bowie's 'Aladdin Sane'; there were gaping windows everywhere.

I asked about the selection. Was the Reading Party open to all disciplines? Yes, but it had become, *de facto*, an event for those studying the humanities. Judged on past performance or the potential to do well? More the latter, or preferably both. Were we to consider postgraduates, like that American? Only if they were taking undergraduate degrees; theoretically he was eligible. Presumably students could put themselves forward? There was nothing to stop them, but it didn't happen. So the Reading Party wasn't advertised? Ah, now that was an interesting one. Naturally it could be done, but a self-selecting student might not be suitable . . .

We were back to the gentlemen's' club and another little impasse buried beneath the courtesies. A phrase of the Warden's floated into my head: 'We rarely know where Dennis stands unless he's chosen to tell us.' Too true.

'In that case,' I said briskly, 'Could you describe your ideal candidate?'

Loxton settled his glasses back on the bridge of his nose, even though he had nothing to read, and appraised me carefully over the top of them. 'One cannot list the qualities that make for "a Reading Party sort of person",' he said, 'but one recognises them immediately if they are there.'

This sounded far too cosy, like the Warden's verdict on 'the sort we need', even if it meant a Tyler Winston might get through on the nod.

'Best to trust our instincts and leave it at that,' he said.

Hmmmm, I thought: 'instinct' will favour the men.

He sucked on his pipe – it looked like a habit honed in tutorial with recalcitrant students – and then added that the arrival of women made no difference: the same considerations would apply.

The sun had moved further across the garden. Loxton asked if I was warm enough. Such a fussy man! I ignored him, gesturing towards the gaggle of women in their College colours, setting off for their ball game. 'So how many women should we aim for,' I asked, 'given the experience of going mixed?'

His reply came laced with history. The College had taken

more women than it was meant to; proof that the talent was there. By analogy, we should longlist for Cornwall on *merit* – arbitrary quotas set limits.

At last we agreed on something! I probably beamed.

Then he took me by surprise again. 'Lest we pass anyone over unfairly,' he said, standing up and brushing his jacket free of the odd petal, 'we could encourage people to apply. A message to the Junior Common Room or a notice on the Gatehouse board, perhaps?' He held the lip of his pipe a few inches away, to reveal again that tight little smile. 'Would you like to make the overture to the JCR President and do the necessary with the Warden's secretary?'

I'd known there'd be a catch somewhere.

I had much more fun talking to the Dean about practical arrangements now the Reading Party was to be mixed. Not a subject for a stuffy meeting, he said, with a knowing look; it demanded a certain amount of levity. He took me to the pub and bought me a double.

The main concern, from a pastoral perspective, was who should sleep where in Cornwall. There weren't enough rooms for everybody to have one, but clearly we couldn't have men and women sharing. How should this be resolved?

Unsurprisingly, given his politics, his argument was remarkably black and white. He suggested it was simple enough, if we wanted to avoid 'a love fest': put the women on the first floor and the men on the second.

'But that's not what you did in College,' I countered, clinking his glass. 'Dr Loxton said you made a point of not segregating; you spread the women around the staircases.'

'And look where that got us: there's bonking all over the place!' The Dean licked the froth from his lips, gave me a little dig with his elbow. 'Unfortunately, it's not so simple. There is also the matter of the facilities – which is where things always come unstuck. The bathrooms are better downstairs – they're in the old dressing rooms. Dennis will want them reserved for the women.'

'But we're capable of sharing a loo with a bloke! Did you see that piece in *Isis*?'

The Dean nodded as he took another swig of beer. 'Though mostly I steer clear of the student rags. A student of Loxton's wrote it: Chloe Firth; she'll be on his list. He likes to surprise, you know. But it's not the *sharing* of the facilities we have to worry about; it's their *quality*. The top of that house was for servants: pokey attics, plumbing shoehorned in. Downstairs is more generous. Dennis will want the men to oblige.'

'Oh, for Christ's sake! Anyone would think ...' But I couldn't be bothered, resorting instead to my trump card. 'Besides, I've looked at that floor plan you gave me and on my count there aren't enough beds in the attic, unless Dr Loxton sleeps in the annexe.'

The Dean said Loxton always took one particular room on the first floor and that you couldn't give the suite over the kitchen to anyone else.

'Why not?'

'Because that would be asking for trouble. Anyway, much more interesting to leave it empty – demand is bound to outstrip the supply. Have you met Gloria Durrant?'

'Not properly.'

'You wouldn't forget: she's the one everybody fancied until you arrived, imagining a Renoir nude. She's always angling to go and joking about the annexe. Top-up?'

When he returned, we moved on to the allocation of rooms. I was all for letting the students choose, but the Dean said that wasn't the way it was done.

'The students have always drawn from a hat. Dennis will want that tradition to continue. For that matter, so would the Warden.'

'Sounds risky: danger of mixed rooms!'

'Nonsense: have you never drawn different colours?'

'Of course: stupid of me.' I scratched the inside of my wrist where I used to get eczema. 'And if they don't like the person they are with?'

'Same as the arrangements in College. They lump it or swap.'

I thought of Tyler Winston, whose name had already come up in the soundings. 'And does the same principle apply to the desks – we draw lots?'

'No, there you'll be pleased to know that Dennis allows you to choose.'

You couldn't help but smile. We chatted a bit about the students whose names had already been suggested – the Dean became tantalisingly unrevealing, I suspect on purpose – and then turned to our own work. He asked how my research was going.

'Ace,' I told him. 'I've found my way round the Bodleian; mastered that underground labyrinth – just how I imagine a submarine: all echoing metal – and got the hang of those little green slips for the book stacks. Research is a cinch compared to dealing with Loxton.'

As term moved on I began to go native, the sense of strangeness undermined, like a majestic cliff face back home in Norfolk, by the ebb and flow of the day-to-day.

Oddly, the Reading Party helped.

Canvassing opinion from the Fellows was revealing. Loxton's retreat had a reputation for vigorous walks and, depending on your point of view, equally vigorous or vacuous talk. How it would adapt, as a mixed party, was the subject of some speculation: a few doubted the students would get through their books; the majority assumed it would just be more relaxed. No one suggested it should be dropped: it was, apparently, a given. I began to think the same.

As for the students, most were happy to chat about their studies; many were equally animated about their passions – bands, sport, politics, religion, getting laid or getting high; and any number looked capable of 'larking'. A rare few – like Tyler Winston, who was disarmingly urbane whenever I came across him: hard to think of him as a student – offered the possibility of all three. Invidious to choose between them, but I knew whom I liked.

There was remarkably little take-up from my notice on the board outside the Lodge, which fluttered against the green baize until someone pinned something over it. As for the ministrations of the JCR President – male of course, but no way a toff – he seemed reluctant to help. He was more fussed about changing College terminology – students should be 'workers' and members of a 'union' – than about establishing the right to join a rarefied retreat. Our encounter made me feel old, as if I'd moved beyond the demos and sit-ins of my youth and become a symbol of bourgeois oppression, but the Dean said I was acclimatising; it was just the difference between being twenty-one and being twenty-six. That made me feel better; he was a real support.

When family and friends phoned to ask how things were going, I talked gamely about my colleagues, my students, my rooms; the butterscotch colour of the stone and the way it soaked up the autumn sun. When they probed for more, I found myself saying that Oxford was 'odd, but rather wonderful', citing the Reading Party as a typically absorbing anachronism.

Jenny, remembering our rebellious schooldays, teased that I appeared to be enjoying the place after all, which made me laugh: surely everyone was entitled to change – hadn't she once been dead against being a lawyer? She didn't answer, just said we'd see what happened in the Easter vac – the trip to Cornwall would be telling; I'd have to watch my step.

Andy, an ex-boyfriend who'd lingered on in my life, was predictably tart about what he called my 'about turn'. In another difficult phone call, the Reading Party became the conduit of the tension still between us – he ridiculing it as a symbol of all that he disliked about Oxbridge, while I stuck up for its oddities. Trying to be friends didn't work, I said, and asked him to stop ringing: over meant over.

That was the right decision, brutal though it felt; things were complicated enough, teetering between intellectual flirtation and flirtation proper with my various admirers, most of them married or otherwise untouchable, without allowing old lovers to prowl about. I went back to exploring the emptying gardens and meadows, the busy teashops and pubs, as a free woman determined to belong, while simultaneously going decorously into battle with Loxton.

For Loxton and I did have very different views about who should go to Cornwall, as became clear when we made our selection in Sixth Week.

We met in an uninviting room that lacked 'a woman's touch'. My mum, who is the archetypal homemaker, would have added a bowl of fruit – even Jenny's college, a mile up the road, had had its pot plants. Not that I commented; I was cross with myself for noticing. Why was one sex so *domesticated* and the other not? Society – no, *patriarchal* society – had a lot to answer for.

Loxton didn't waste time. He placed a typed list on the table – his names and mine – and watched while I read. Between us we had nearly thirty, including Tyler Winston, I noted, and a gratifying number of women. But how to choose?

Loxton suggested we start where it was easy to cull – with the undergraduates who were *not* Finalists.

This led to an uncomfortable discussion of the admissions policy and access for pupils from modest backgrounds like mine. Eventually we chose Jim Evans, the talented second-year historian from the Cardiff comprehensive, whom I hoped might emerge from his shell; Eddie Oakeshott, a bumptious Fresher from a London public school, reading English, about whom Loxton had extravagant reports; and Mei Chow, a first-year lawyer, one of the new Chinese scholars. That gave us three of our twelve.

What about the Finalists? We had twice as many names as we needed.

A few stood out academically and were swiftly decided. There were two Exhibitioners: Hugh Chauncey, in his fourth year of reading Greats – always useful to have somebody who knew the ropes, Loxton said, while I puzzled at the Norman edge to the name; and Lyndsey Milburn, reading English, recommended repeatedly as an extraordinary self-taught one-off. There was also the College's sole student of Oriental Studies, Rupert Ingram-Hall, and a diligent lawyer, Priyam Patel, one of the rare Asian students, whom I was pleased to see chosen.

Tyler Winston was not mentioned.

We moved on to our own fields. Loxton gave in on the historian from my first tute, Barnaby Quick, in spite of the shaky performance that had frustrated my colleagues. So I deferred to him on the journalist Chloe Firth, reading the trendy hybrid Psychology, Philosophy and Physiology, whose school had something to do with the suffragettes; if she was 'something of a handful', that would be his problem.

Still no reference to the American.

We were in danger of getting stuck, and there was no relief in that forlorn shell of a room, with its air of a neglected side chapel and its absence of refreshment, so I suggested phoning the Dean for his opinion. I'm not sure Loxton liked that, but he let me make the call. When the Dean offered to come round and 'rescue' me – not how I passed it on, of course – Loxton shook his head. Still, we dispatched a few candidates under the 'worthy but dull' rule, and Martin Trewin – 'maverick geographer with a light touch' – was through.

That left four people – Tyler Winston and three women – of whom we could take only two. If we dropped Tyler we'd have parity between the sexes; if we took him we would not. Did it matter?

Of course I had to argue for parity. Loxton, equally predictably, said an 'arbitrary' principle shouldn't override merit. Take Tyler, he said: extraordinarily rewarding to teach *and* suited to a career in academia, though he might need to be wooed; the women were not in his league.

We went to and fro, Loxton's low baritone contrasting uncomfortably with the high pitch I succumbed to when my argument was weak. Eventually Loxton suggested the Warden arbitrate; he was confident of the outcome. So I caved in. At least I had tried. We settled on Gloria Durrant, the linguist from my staircase, who was quick *and* had put herself forward. Ironic that he indulged me there, given that I hadn't warmed to her: too much of a county type.

Decisions made, we had a treacly sherry spirited from the sideboard – the indigo-blue bottle like a splash of stained glass amid the gloom – and tried to talk of other things, such as my coming series of lectures and Loxton's preference for seminars, but my appetite for jousting was exhausted. Within minutes the booze was back in its cupboard and the smell of caramelised apple had merged with the general mustiness. As soon as it was polite to do so, I escaped.

I may have worried about some of the choices, but the Warden declared himself happy with the outcome, bar a hint of irritation that both lawyers were women – what was it about the law, he asked rhetorically, that so appealed to the conscientious female mind? As for the process, he commended the principle of 'our' opening it up, though in practice we should keep an eye on our volunteer – Miss Durrant being somewhat 'testing'.

Still, I'd got through that hurdle.

Just before the vac began, the letters of invitation went out to the students, signed by us both, with an explanation about costs. I kept a file copy, pleased that we'd been given equal billing, and waited for questions. To my surprise, there were almost none: it was as if being chosen was reason enough to accept. No one suggested that they had other plans or preferred to revise to their own timetable; no one queried whether the days in Cornwall would be worth the travelling time, or what it would be like being stuck in the middle of nowhere with Loxton and me. Best of all, no one who had *not* been invited made a fuss.

Instead, my two historians used their last tutorials to check what the Reading Party involved before saying yes – Barnaby dubious about what he had to contribute, Jim warily interested but anxious that the £1 a day cap on costs should stick.

The two lawyers – Mei Chow and Priyam Patel – wrote prompt and correct notes to us both: Loxton was amused, suggesting such punctilious courtesy was without precedent. My volunteer, Gloria Durrant, had the nerve to say she hoped she'd have a proper desk, but the Dean said she'd contrived a waiver from the linguists' year out on account of spending her life 'holed up in Francophone this or Spanish that', and was known for making demands. The best response from the women was from the English Exhibitioner, Lyndsey Milburn, who found Loxton under the huge copper beech, gave him an astonishing address in sonnet form and then sent us a crinkled, longhand copy.

The other English student – the flamboyant Eddie Oakeshott, who had petitioned for an invite – collared me again to say he was glad to see 'democracy' at work. The orientalist likewise addressed his more formal response to me, even though we'd never met; the Dean said that was true to form – Rupert always had an eye on the main chance, and what did I expect from a boy with a name like Ingram–Hall? Hugh Chauncey, the classicist who'd been to Cornwall as a Fresher, gave his acceptance orally to Loxton, who was still teaching him, and the geographer, Martin Trewin, replied via his subject tutor, joking that he wasn't looking for another reading list.

As for Tyler Winston, he rattled a box of College stationery at me in the Lodge, teasing that he could now do justice to the occasion, and pointedly addressed his note to us jointly, which endeared him to me despite what the Dean said. Why not be well behaved? And I liked his handwriting: a confident flow – each word curling towards the next, the ideas entwined.

The last person to respond was the PPP-ist, Chloe Firth, but Loxton said we were lucky to have heard from a natural rebel. For that matter, we were lucky all twelve had accepted; occasionally someone did not.

How extraordinary, I thought, realising that the possibility had always seemed hypothetical: why would anyone ever say no?

Christmas

I marked the end of term by going to London for the weekend. A quick exchange of postcards showed that Jenny was up for a visit.

When she opened the door to her tiny flat, I nearly disintegrated into tears with the relief of seeing a real friend. We settled down on the thick pile of the rug that dominated the main room, propped against a Habitat beanbag and sofa, of which she was inordinately proud, armed with our cups of instant coffee, and talked about what she'd been up to since I saw her last.

'But this is all about *me* . . .' she exclaimed, after we'd been at it for the best part of an hour. 'I want to hear about *you!*'

So I told her about the College, getting to know everyone, trying to find a balance between teaching and research, the right and the wrong type of flirting. I made her laugh with my picture of Governing Body meetings – the men in their black gowns resembling what the farmers back home called 'a murder of crows'. She smiled when I thanked her for role-playing tutorials, which had allowed me to pass myself off as an old hand, and for answering my questions about the grading of essays, so I didn't embarrass myself. She tutted as I talked about being on my guard with some of my colleagues, nervous about getting things wrong, and about the oddity of having students defer to me, even when the age gap was small. I should have more confidence, she said: it had always been my Achilles heel.

'Oh, but I love all the attention,' I said. 'It's just that some-times it's a bit much.' And I mentioned eating custard tarts in the Woolworths tearoom because it was a treat to eavesdrop on *normal* lives, and bicycling out to Port Meadow on my own, because I missed the countryside.

'And what about missing Andy?' she asked. 'Where've you got to with *him*?'

Thankfully we agreed that was a whole other conversation; we needed a drink, should get cooking, before we started on that. So we grabbed our coats – she generously wore mine and I tried on a glamorous number of hers from Biba – and pottered off to the local shops. There we goaded each other into our favourite indulgences – slippery tinned peaches with vanilla ice cream for me and a dense slab of Black Forest gateau for her – laughing with the pleasure of spending more than we were used to. Even allowing for inflation, such treats were more affordable on a salary.

Back in the flat we opened a bottle of Valpolicella, emptied nuts into a dish bought on holiday together, put her favourite album on the stereo and settled back on the floor. When I'd had enough of *Breezin'* and her fondness for smoochy jazz, we crammed into the miniscule kitchen and stirred pots over each other's arms, teasing about who was getting in the way, fooling about companionably, and then took our supper – beef stroganoff on fluffy rice, with Birds' Eye *petit pois* by special request – and ate next door with legs outstretched, plates on our laps. And all the time we talked and all the talk, no matter where it began and what it was supposedly about, brought us back to the same preoccupation: men. Who had banished Andy from my head and why was Jenny dabbling without serious intent? I hadn't had such a conversation all term.

When finally we said goodnight, we were resolved. Jenny was going to stop footling with the guy she'd been seeing, who made her feel cheap; and I was going to make use of my freedom, not retreat into work. She stood by the door holding a glass of water and saying 'Promise?' – and I, unzipping the sleeping bag, promised back.

In the morning we took her acrid fag ends down to the bin, opened a couple of windows to create a through draught, and sat at the little table surrounded by breakfast things, enjoying the waft of proper coffee mixed with hot milk and sipped from a bowl, as we'd had it when we backpacked in France.

'You still haven't told me what it's *really* like,' she said, probing with the same subtext as before. 'What about being the only woman?'

So I told her about that too. To leaven the serious chat, I talked about the Dean, whom possibly I fancied, though he could be a bit of a prick, and about the student who had a certain nautical appeal – Barnaby Quick – though of course he was off limits.

It was stacked in men's favour, she said, judging from her own experience as an undergraduate. She remembered a don from one of the older colleges who used to feel all the girls up and was reputed to have bedded a few – was notorious for it in fact, not that that stopped him or made any difference to his career. He was married, needless to say. There hadn't been that kind of hanky-panky where she was – no talk of female dons, married or otherwise, having student toyboys. Little scope, because men so rarely had tutorials there; besides, it wasn't the same.

'But why not?' I asked, surprised at the force of the question. 'What held them back?'

'Oh, I don't know. Abuse of power and all that. The feeling that women, having fought so hard, ought to be above it. Besides, it's just so sleazy, isn't it? Older men and nubile chicks is bad enough, but imagine the roles reversed. Most of the women were such old crows. Anyway, would *you* bother with a pipsqueak of a student? They're so young and inept – there's nothing appealing about that in a man, is there?'

I thought of Tyler Winston and his air of sophistication. There was nothing of the pipsqueak about him; he was a cool cat. But she was right. You couldn't criticise men who took advantage of their position if you behaved the same way – and the Warden had warned about the duty of care, so I couldn't claim ignorance. Besides, a scandal involving a female don wouldn't be so easily dismissed, even if not a disciplinary matter. Some things were taboo – the gossip would dog you for years. And women had that ridiculous need for the moral high ground; we gave ourselves so much more grief. Those were the issues. Women might be just as capable of lusting, or being led by the heart not the head, but the damage was greater and we weren't good at brazening it out.

For some reason I didn't say any of that, and chose not to discuss what felt like a dangerous topic. Instead I described a seventeenth-century portrait of the College's first laundress, allegedly recruited because, being ugly, no one would want to molest her when she delivered the washing. It hung in Hall, at the student end, as a reminder to everyone. Jenny thought that was hilarious.

Eventually I got to the Reading Party and the discussion with Loxton about the students we should take in the spring. I tried to explain the mix of curiosity and exasperation it induced; my sense of being presented with a problem that should have been solved two years before, when the women arrived.

'He sounds a nightmare,' she said. 'Don't let him get to you.'

Back at Oxford, spared from marking the History Prelims and from the round of admissions interviews, spared even from thinking about Loxton, I revelled briefly in making my 'set' mine, pottering happily around the tiny College flat.

Men were extraordinary! My predecessor's students must have sunk physically as well as emotionally as they read out their essays, so low were the chairs: I bought dusky velour cushions so they could lounge at the same level as me. As for the bedroom, I swapped the heavy masculine drapes for cotton, which billowed if you opened the window; it made me feel carefree.

I dug out a colourful vase – a kind of tie-dye in glass, swirling orange and black – to soften the austerity and, with the help of the 'scout' who looked after my room – a man, as it happens, though the College now had female ones too – hung photos of the Norfolk coast and put up some Athena posters.

Best of all, I unpacked the rest of my books and rearranged my modest library: reference books, biography, history and historiography, feminist texts. My own volume on the women behind the Pankhursts, whose publication must have helped with my appointment, stayed immediately behind my desk. Part multiple biography, part oral history, it cut across boundaries and was hard to place – unusual for a work based on a thesis. Besides, it was comforting to have it to hand: a reminder of those good reviews.

Only once was I interrupted, late on a wet and gloomy morning when steps bounded up the hollow wooden stairs and seemed to hover the other side of my door, neither moving away nor mutating into a knock. I stared at the doorknob, wondering whether to open it, but before I could make up my mind the footsteps went away again, descending rather jauntily in runs of two, and splattered off onto the stone flags down below. Stupidly I hesitated again; by the time I got to the window, there was no one in the front quad. No note on the door either; only my own message from the day before, saying I was out for the day. Fool!

Gloria Durrant was on the landing below, talking to a friend of hers. I could have asked her who it was – she must have seen – but thought better of it and was annoyed that she might have registered me looking. After some fruitless conjecture about who the visitor might be – my various colleagues seemed to favour the phone; the Dean normally scrawled chalk across my blackboard; Loxton I couldn't imagine skipping anywhere; my students should all have returned home – I stopped speculating. In my teenage years my younger brother would wind me up with stories of friends who'd called without leaving a message: I'd learnt not to rise to the occasion.

In the afternoon, I put my pristine filing cabinet to better use, working out a logic for all that paperwork, labelling files and marshalling the contents. Teaching was in one mental box, lecturing in another, research in a third. Now, I created the physical equivalents by piling correspondence across the floor. There was a mass of papers about the tutoring of undergraduates; rather fewer for a graduate to be supervised; my lecture notes on the female reformers, mapped out over the summer; jottings for an article on a Dr Ivy Williams, an alumnus of Jenny's college, who'd thought the poor should have access to free legal advice; endless scribbles towards my research on other women pioneers. All disappeared into the files.

That left me with a messy residue, mentally labelled 'admin'. The Reading Party didn't belong there, or anywhere else. It was like a known family member whose relationship to the rest of the lineage was stubbornly uncertain. In the end I gave it a folder of its own.

At that point, when my taxonomy became boring and I ached from spending so much time on the floor, I stopped, ran myself a bath and luxuriated amid the warm suds, pondering those footsteps.

It was during this marshalling of my professional life that Mum rang to probe about the personal. I took the call in my study, surrounded by the evidence of my new competence, but found myself succumbing to old habits and getting tetchily defensive. It wasn't true that she'd been right about Andy 'all along': why did she need me now to concede it? And why fret so much about how I was meant to behave? Those were *her* insecurities about moving 'up' in the world, not *mine*.

34

That conversation took the edge off my sense of getting on top. What most annoyed me was her suggesting the Warden's wife could help me decipher the protocols: I'd only mentioned the Bittermints as a joke. That needled away at me as I discovered the rotund pleasures of the Radcliffe Camera and other, less harmonious libraries and, sitting in its upper gallery, got back into the rhythm of my research. Even when profoundly absorbed, lost amidst the generous circles of that sublime space, irritation about Mum's fussing would jab its way into my head and bring me back to the present. Nothing else undermined my concentration in quite the same way, although the notion of 'toyboys', and the absence of feedback on my performance as a don, were sometimes distracting. I felt doubly apprehensive about the trip to Cornwall.

The first concern might be hypothetical but, having failed to mention Tyler to Jenny, I wasn't about to mention him to anyone else; as for the second, which was all too real, I didn't know whom to talk to about how I was doing. I'd have asked the historian whose retirement created the vacancy – we'd chatted easily at the interview – but unlike the other Emeritus professors he rarely visited. The Mediaevalist kindly invited me to Sunday lunch, which should have created an opportunity, but his children were too noisy for a proper conversation. That left the Ancient Historian, but why show vulnerability to a blinkered old so and so who'd cheerfully conceded he hadn't wanted women in College in the first place?

I wondered about asking the Dean, but something stopped me, and I was too proud to make an overture to the Warden, let alone to his wife, after what Mum had said. Instead I waited: eventually somebody would comment on how I was doing, my fitness to accompany Loxton on that dratted retreat. And then, as the College emptied for Christmas and the Faculty failed to call me in, I realised that they would not. I was being left to muddle through again, just like the students.

Only *they* made me feel I was on the right track. Barnaby invited me to join him and his mates for a pre-Christmas drink in the bar, and we spent a friendly hour chatting over our beers under the blare of Showaddywaddy's ghastly hit before I left them to it. Another historian – a girl, the only one I'd seriously considered for the Reading Party – used a festive card to tell me how much she'd enjoyed our tutorials and what a difference it made to have a role model; a shame she'd been just that bit too bland.

Now it was Tyler Winston, walking with me one crisp but sunny day after we caught sight of each other on Magdalen Bridge, although it meant him pushing his bicycle for a good twenty minutes when he could have got back in five.

There was some brief chat about what we were doing at Christmas. I explained about the family gathering in Norfolk, which he thought sounded fun; he was flying back to the States, but it would just be him and his parents.

Then he asked about my career; how I'd come to be there. This was my cue for some wooing. I explained that the early part had seemed a natural progression: absorption as an under-graduate; doctorate efficiently done; further research and a bit of teaching. I conceded that there'd been a brief loss of faith when signing off the proofs of my monograph, seeing the areas of weakness and worrying about being discovered a fraud. And it had been extraordinary to find myself at Oxford, when I'd seen my application as a dummy run for other things and never imagined that, as a woman, there was a chance of being appointed; but it was proving wonderful.

I asked about him and he explained that, unlike me, he'd had a gap year – that American urge to travel. Then he too had read History, which he'd enjoyed, but he'd always assumed his path would be law, like his parents, though possibly he would teach rather than practice – he was considering a doctorate. The opportunity to come to Oxford was unexpected – and not something you would turn down – though, like me, he had never thought he would get through all the hoops. To be there when so much was changing, women having arrived at College the same year that he did, was a bonus, but – he said with a laugh – sometimes a little distracting.

That led to a lively conversation about which was worse – being a Rhodes Scholar, required to show 'moral force of character and instincts to lead', or being the first female don, about which there was such a welter of expectation. It was oddly intimate: we even teased that we might be taking our responsibilities far too seriously – life was far too short! In fact, the whole thing was full of banter and suggestion, and it gave me a fillip because there was no conceivable need: I could have carried on alone and, if he was being polite, there must have been a quicker way round.

He was the only person I knew with eyes that were different colours: one a blue-grey, the other brown.

Suddenly almost half the vac had gone. I packed my bags again – one for my clothes; another with presents for the family – and headed off to the station in a taxi, feeling as if another era had begun. When had I gone anywhere in a cab?

Arriving home, I was emotionally drained and physically spent. Dad carried my bags up to my old room, Mum brought out the cake she'd made, the dogs were briefly beside themselves with excitement – yapping loudly and bashing their tails against the upholstery – and I settled back into the reassuring shabbiness of the family home to be fussed over by both parents. It was just what was needed.

I was prescribed an afternoon nap and then sat in bed with newly fluffed pillows behind me, behaving like a patient while Dad cleared childhood knickknacks to make space for my mug and chatted inconsequentially about his work at the pharmacy. Later I sat in the kitchen on a chair with a dimpled cushion tied to the spindles, watching Mum prepare supper, listening to village news and her endless stories of family and friends. After we'd eaten I sank into my favourite spot on the sofa, tucked my feet under me, and joined them in a game of Scrabble.

The following day my brothers breezed in within minutes of each other in time to decorate the tree; then my uncle arrived and suddenly the house was its usual chaotic self again, full of habitual banter and noisy one-upmanship – exactly the kind of family life that Tyler had said he didn't have. The rest of Christmas Eve, Christmas Day and then Boxing Day came and went in a fug of family togetherness watching *Morecambe and Wise* and the like – the highpoint being Angela Rippon kicking her newscaster legs – interspersed with the obligatory drinks with neighbours. The whole house became properly festive, stuffed and glazed like a well-prepared bird: downstairs was heady with the scent of mulled wine – cloves, cinnamon and sliced orange, the peel stewed to pinkness in Dad's choice of plonk; the upstairs reeked of the bars of Bronnley soap kept by Mum for when we had guests; archways everywhere were bedecked with red-berried holly, my brothers having vied to outdo each other's ingenuity. Only the tiny conservatory escaped attention and smelt normal; I retreated there with my uncle for long conversations about what we were working on, the views across the salt marshes between us and the North Sea making up for the cold.

After three days of sustained raillery during which my brothers and I revealed almost nothing of substance about our private lives, the boys drove off again – the elder one back to Glaxo's research labs, the younger to the hospital where he was a senior house officer – shortly followed by my uncle, who was wanted in the newsroom at the paper. Dad and I did a favourite walk with the dogs along the length of the sand dunes at Wells, talking about the years when he was the junior chemist angling for promotion and drawing tenuous parallels with my own sense of being on probation. Mum, under the pretext of clearing old clothes from my cupboard, took me to task for not caring about my appearance when 'many a girl would have loved to have a complexion like yours'; all it needed, she said, was a little blusher and a bit of lipstick, but I knew that just wasn't me. The three of us chatted a bit about what Oxford was like, but I said nothing about my anxieties, still less about moral dilemmas. Rashly I mentioned the attentions of the Dean, but the Reading Party got barely a mention, attractive postgraduates none at all: such things were far too complicated to explain.

I stayed an extra day, knowing it would please them, and gave them the Faculty lecture list for the Hilary term as a parting gift. There was page after page of it, so I pointed out the entry for my contribution: 'Reforming women 1792–1918: suffragists and suffragettes, from Wollstonecraft to Fawcett and the Pankhursts (Part I); Dr S. Addleshaw; Th. II; Examination Schools'. Mum asked if it was about my book and I had to explain that these lectures took the argument a stage further; Dad got that straight away and said he'd have it framed and put in the loo, along with the pictures of our graduation ceremonies.

Perhaps I'd had enough of cosseting and scrutiny. There was also the latest Pink Panther to see with Jenny, and I had to get back to Oxford promptly – the Medievalist and his wife had invited me to their annual jamboree; there'd be lots of hip people.

The movie was fab, and Jenny was impressed with my plans for New Year's Eve. 'You deserve a blowout,' she said, 'given the pressure you've been under. Find a guy you fancy, have a good time, start 1977 the right way: you've been ducking the issue for too long.'

I didn't like the idea that I'd been 'ducking', letting the remnants of an old relationship stop me from having a new one. I thought we had different priorities: she put men first and

I didn't. Or perhaps it was just a matter of meeting the right person. Anyway, I determined to enjoy myself.

And I did have fun at the party, enjoying all the introductions and the recaps with people I knew. There was no one I took a shine to – mercifully no sign of any 'forbidden fruit' from the Reading Party, or indeed any other students – but the Dean was there, being outrageous. We gossiped naughtily in a corner and then boogied happily to 'I Wish', 'Isn't She Lovely' and other new tracks until even I'd had enough of Stevie Wonder. He was a good dancer – in his element when they rolled up the rest of the rugs and we jived – and it was fun fooling around. No surprise then that we kissed on the lips when Big Ben boomed midnight and danced again when someone put on the smooches. That was all fine – I mean, it was New Year's Eve and everyone was doing it. It was only afterwards, when I tried to slip away but he hauled me back, that I didn't know how to extract myself without being rude. In the end, we left together at about 2 a.m., supposedly to have a nightcap at his. Still I thought I could manage my exit.

The thing was, I hadn't reckoned on him having a pad of his own. I assumed we'd be going back to College and I could slip away to my rooms and he to his. But no: all those consultancy fees paid for a small terraced house, part of which he let in term time to visiting academics. Of course he had to show me round, tumbler in one hand, bottle of brandy in the other. It was nice enough, if you ignored how he funded it – all those people he hung out with on his trips to London who commissioned research, and whose op-eds and papers for the Centre for Policy Studies were strewn about the place. It was only in the bedroom that I fully realised my mistake, though by then it was already too late. His lair had the air of too many conquests: the purple sheets, all those cushions and joss sticks, *The Joy of Sex* by the bedside, 'Love to Love you Baby' ready to go on the stereo – even a red light like the ones in the windows

Jenny and I had seen in Amsterdam. It was how I imagined a knocking shop.

I tried to get out of it – said we really shouldn't, what with being colleagues and having to work together. But he had that way of teasing that made you sound a prude if you objected – he'd done it about politics too, always winding me up – and there was something infuriatingly sexy about him, about that outrageousness, that kept you laughing even as you were had. He might be playing you, deploying those extra years – what was it in my case, seven or eight? – to make you cave in, but he was very good at it.

'What's wrong with being irresistible?' he said with a winning grin, and, 'Cut yourself some slack' – all feminists were killjoys in his book – as if daring me to join in the fun.

It wasn't that, of course, or jumping into bed so quickly, which had never been my way. Nor was it the question of professional ethics, though on that count it was hardly wise. Even as he was peeling off that stupid slinky top of mine, I knew this was not for *me*. It was something visceral. His skin was wrong: there was a roughness wherever our bodies touched, like sleeping with sandpaper; he didn't have my kind of smell.

Of course *he* didn't notice anything. He was rather pleased, actually – impressed with my boobs and chuffed with our performance, as if it was all another part of his show.

The following morning I lay there next to him, enduring an extended postmortem on the party, wondering how to draw it all to a close. He was buoyant, full of stories of the various pairings, whereas I was beginning to chafe, not that I let on. It was his attitude that got me. He thought our hosts' set-up was ideal and claimed to envy my colleague, whereas I considered it an uncomfortable compromise, particularly for the wife, who was bright. Even likeable men like our Mediaevalist could only reconcile work and family, I suggested, jumping up and yanking the duvet off him, because their wives – often intelligent, talented women – put their careers second or wanted to be earth mothers anyway. Examples of it working in reverse were disappointingly rare, especially in academia, I said, wagging a finger as I wrapped myself in the duvet at the end of the bed; I'd only spotted one at that party, though the ground floor had been heaving with people. Of course the Dean didn't see it that way – tugged my protection off me; said I was being far too serious and should stick to being 'delightfully pneumatic' – and he was dismissive about the woman I cited, said she was a cliché of another sort, married to the man who had taught her.

So I didn't stay long. Made my getaway amid a cloud of casual repartee, as if a quick screw was just my thing, a mark of my sophistication. Skirted the Lodge, hoping not to be caught mid-morning in my party gear, my activities betrayed by my shoes. Dressing afresh for a New Year's Day lunch, I had a patch of worry about gossip – women comparing notes, men bragging about conquests – and then of crossness: the body made things so difficult; why couldn't feminists be flat-chested as a matter of course? Then I moved on – the previous night was nobody's business; no one else need ever know; the American had gone home.

Besides, I hadn't time to fret. After all, there were eight lectures to finalise and a paper to get underway before term began. For two weeks I immersed myself and made good progress, adding colour to my lectures with anecdotes about the more spirited women amongst my campaigners; typing up my paper about the exemplary Ivy Williams, who turned out to have fought not only on behalf of the poor but also for women's right to academic and professional recognition, to see how the narrative worked. Bar a couple of low patches in the early evening when the College was dark and empty and I was alone with my thoughts, I was happy enough. Anyway, the thoughts weren't about the Dean: you could like him or not, as the case might be, but he didn't prey on your mind.

Hilary

Hilary began. I hardly thought about the Reading Party, being caught up in all the other pressures – reasonably confident of helping my students, some of whom I was tutoring for a second time, but anxious about delivering lectures behind the huge doors of the Examination Schools when no one was required to attend. And when would I fit in the bulk of my research? The weeks free of teaching had whizzed by.

On the upbeat days I was buoyant, in demand at High Table and full of verve afterwards in the SCR, enjoying the banter and teasing about the sillier conventions.

On other occasions I missed the company of my own sex, there being only sporadic competition from female guests and almost never from wives, who were classed as guests but rarely came. Then the sparring became a strain and the hidden rules irked me. Even the kindness of the Warden's wife drained my sense of self.

I dealt with the lows by escaping College with one of the bachelor dons, someone from the Faculty or the occasional visiting friend; we usually went to the new hotspot, Browns, where you sat amongst ferns and ceiling fans and had a different kind of food. Tyler, I noticed, was often there too.

The background worry was that a mixed group of students would object to the sleeping arrangements the Dean and I had devised – at York we argued with the academics whenever we got the chance and no one took orders about sex. But then you never could tell. The whole notion of the Reading Party was so anomalous that it might appear above question: a throwback to be taken in its entirety or not at all.

Loxton had arranged for us all to meet in an unoccupied 'bachelor set' one evening in Third Week. (Why we weren't allowed to squeeze into his study or mine I couldn't fathom, unless it was that thing about the war and giving nothing away.) The students were all very prompt – only two latecomers: Chloe Firth, his PPP-ist, who was instantly recognisable in the vibrant Peruvian poncho she'd been wearing when the Dean pointed her out; and Eddie Oakeshott, whose voice I recognised before he even entered the room – one of those theatrical English students who, once you'd heard him, you heard everywhere.

Loxton moved around with a wooden tray, offering sherry and juice in delicate glasses that circled a rose inlay; clearly his but decidedly feminine. When everyone had one, he encouraged them to 'find a pew'. There were just a few housekeeping matters, he said; it was more a 'getting to know you' session.

We began by introducing ourselves with a supposedly personal detail. Loxton's was tagged to a black-and-white photograph of young men in shorts and long socks, one of them recognisably him, which he circulated. He explained that his predecessor, Godfrey, the older man in plus fours, had taken groups of students to a succession of 'hostelries' in the Lake District in the 1920s and 1930s, and briefly after the war, for long walks and a little reading. It was a legacy from this bachelor don that ensured the tradition continued, but Loxton had shifted the emphasis onto the reading and an alumnus lent the place in Cornwall.

The students were too nervous to reveal much, but the geographer, Martin Trewin, said that his family had a dairy farm near the Helford River, about an hour further on, and Tyler quipped that, being from such a new country, he was looking forward to seeing more of an old one. He also asked a question about Cornwall and the Tolpuddle Martyrs, which was a mistake – you can be too much of a cool cat. Jim, my ginger historian, had to explain that that was Dorset and we were going further west: touché.

Loxton picked up the thread of his own story. 'It's a remarkable house, as you will see,' he said. 'Built by the harbourmaster, then a substantial figure in the community, and added to in minor ways by his descendants, who shared his naval leanings. Large by our standards, though the heating is rudimentary: the men will do much laying of fires.' And he surveyed the room, taking in all the male students and resting his gaze on Martin, presumably earmarking him as a country boy.

I bridled, but my linguist, the Durrant girl, got in before me. Tossing thick auburn hair in the manner of flamenco dancer – that figured! – she said sharply that she'd made plenty in her time and didn't need a man to do it for her. Applause from Chloe; laughs from elsewhere.

Loxton was unperturbed. 'No doubt yours will be better than anyone's, Gloria. I look forward to being warmed.' He moved on to the matter of luggage.

Mei Chow, the lawyer on the Hong Kong Scholarship who looked so young, even for a Fresher, asked softly about the weather in Cornwall and was instructed to wrap up well. Poor girl, I thought, she might need looking after.

Otherwise, Loxton stressed – and it really was his show: I could only interject – we should take only modest packing, please: warm clothing, something waterproof, footwear for walking.

Barnaby, the elder of my two historians, stretched his arms at the talk of outdoor activities – an expansive gesture that set me wondering if he'd got his tan sailing. Behind him the

45

gangly man in the cord jacket, whom I took to be one of the fourth-year students, proposed guidance on the reading.

Loxton smiled. 'Yes, you will all enjoy deciding what to bring, but fresh air and a relaxation is important too. Even ardent classicists like Hugh shouldn't read into the small hours!'

A couple of students still looked uneasy. Tyler passed them the bowls of crisps, which was tactful; he was very considerate. And those lovely hands! They'd held me outside the Warden's Lodgings, just a fraction longer than necessary ...

I did my bit too, smiling at Mei, and caught Jim watching her face relax – perhaps he was taken with that oriental purity; the Dean, rather sharp with his verdicts, had labelled it virginal.

'We read from nine until one, and four-thirty 'til seven-thirty,' Loxton continued. 'Those hours are sacrosanct: library conditions and no wandering around.'

The other lawyer raised a finely boned finger. 'The choice is up to us – we don't need to get it approved?'

Loxton's glance softened. 'Correct, Priyam. Your decision and yours only.'

Lyndsey Milburn, the English Finalist – who'd been looking wan, like that poster of Ophelia drowning – tugged at her long skirt. 'How tempting! I'll never be able to choose. How many books may we take?'

'It depends, Lyndsey. Someone took Kant's *Critique of Pure Reason* and was occupied for the week, whereas the lawyers usually speed-read several tomes. I recommend a choice but not too much choice.'

'And where *do* we read in such a grand house? Does it have those buttoned leather chairs, like in old-fashioned clubs, with scrolly arms?' This would be Rupert Ingram-Hall, the rather arch student of Oriental Studies: he wore a crushed-velvet jacket, deep plum – just the thing for a smoking room.

'Oh, wherever we like, bar retreating upstairs, and you should move around – part of the pleasure is enjoying all the house has to offer. But "grand" is not the word I would use: indeed, I have heard it called shabby.' Loxton appeared to be lost for a moment. That, too figured, I thought: a codebreaker would be a stickler for meaning. But he couldn't crack it and gave up.

All in all, I thought, he didn't make it sound much fun.

'What about meals?' I prompted, and then regretted identifying myself with the kitchen.

It was indeed an own goal. Loxton said something about expecting 'culinary standards' to be higher than usual – his generation were such sexists! – and launched into an explanation about supper being cooked by the Finalists, in pairs, while lunch was prepared by the others, who shopped.

Eddie was in there straight away: 'So I'm fagging for my elders and betters? No way, Jose! But I might dogsbody for a fee. Or a favour. What do you say, Dr Addleshaw?'

'It's not a matter of rewards, Eddie,' I said. 'Anyway, we could do it together. Might even be fun: we decide what the others get to eat, or *I* decide if *you* get anything at all!'

I'm sure the burly Martin, all beard and curly hair, gave me a wink. He'd need his Morris Traveller at home, he said, so he'd be driving down; if anyone wanted to join him, he'd welcome company, especially female . . .

This must have been a standing joke. Chloe suggested the banger might not make it, while Barnaby thumped the arm of his chair: 'You are such an operator, Mart!'

Loxton put his glass on the side table and waited for the laughter to subside. 'You will want to know, also, about the allocation of rooms. Dr Addleshaw has discussed this with the Dean' – renewed titters – why? – 'so I'll let her explain.'

I spread my props on the rug – floor plan, bowl, strips of coloured paper – and rattled through, throwing in a recommendation that any bed-hopping be invisible. The students opted to draw lots straight away – one hurdle jumped – and cheerfully read out where they would be. The mood palpably eased.

Still, it was mildly discomforting to think of Tyler immediately below, if better than having him on the same floor. And there were odd combinations for my historians – the Celtic Jim matched with the cosmopolitan Eddie; diffident Barnaby with pushy Rupert. But no one complained. Another hurdle passed.

'There's an important rule about the bedrooms,' Loxton announced, prompting – I'm sure I saw this – glances between Gloria and Rupert; Martin watching. 'No smoking up there. The family dislike it and we respect their wishes, to the letter; we include the stairs.'

That was a bit of a damper, or perhaps the students felt awkward with us there. Apart from Tyler and Jim, who roped me into an animated discussion about West Country martyrs as one of the few who – my Welshman said – had a feel for what it was about, most of them didn't dally. Priyam Patel stood up first, rather sweetly thanking us both, and soon they all thundered down the wooden stairs, Lyndsey trailing at the end with Hugh Chauncey. We could hear a mass of talk with the occasional explosion of laughter, the sounds diminishing as they dispersed.

'A good mix, all things considered, and you have a good bond with your historians,' Loxton said, gathering up the floor plans and the photo. He reached out behind me to switch out the light as we left. 'It will be interesting to see what happens, Sarah, don't you think?'

He'd never used my name before – progress of sorts.

A few students clarified practicalities. Chloe Firth lobbed a question about the smoking rules into chat in the pub, which confirmed she might be hard to handle, and Gloria

Durrant wanted to know about locks on the bedroom doors, which seemed a bit of a giveaway. Eddie Oakeshott, who was becoming part of their gang, did his own bit of needling about having to share; I told him to sort it out with Martin Trewin, the only bloke getting a single room – it was nothing to do with me.

But Martin, who was having none of it, said he'd earnt his independence and had far too many plans for it. He was the perpetual joker: he ribbed me about the briefing and suggested 'the headmaster' would soften with such a fetching 'matron' to do his bidding – they'd never had the likes of me at school. I didn't mind the teasing – it made him feel like an ally.

Lyndsey Milburn looked the opposite. Where Martin was earthy and relaxed, she was thin and abstracted, as if bodily functions didn't count for much and she was engaged with her mind, which was elsewhere. I couldn't work her out; usually the wafty ones had money, which she patently did not. But when I suggested that she and I, too, were chalk and cheese, the Dean claimed that 'we see more similarity than you like to think', which was disconcerting – what else did my colleagues say about me?

I suspect he was getting his own back after my rebuffs. He did it again about Priyam Patel and Mei Chow, calling me naive to suggest that only friends in the making would talk in undertones the way those two did; he said the lawyers were known for sticking together and women could be 'thick as thieves' – what did you expect when you combined the two?

It wasn't exactly easy.

The Mediaevalist was much nicer about the group who were going, roaring with laughter when I told him that Rupert Ingram-Whatnot had asked why you'd do a commonplace subject like History when you could choose one that was utterly obscure.

'Yes, but how did he become so breezily challenging?' I asked.

'It's just male swagger,' he answered, 'of the kind you take so easily in your stride.'

I didn't know where that came from either – no notion that I might find such belligerence undermining – but felt equally unable to probe.

The Ancient Historian was more interested in Hugh Chauncey, whom he'd taught, and wasn't the least surprised he'd been invited again.

'An academic enthusiast of the best sort,' he pronounced. No one would dispute the first bit, I thought: Hugh so professorial with his corduroy and his leather-patched elbows. But the second? Hugh had that well-bred way of listening – bending his head to you, neck stretched and reaching down like a horse about to nuzzle – which could make you feel inferior.

'What's the *worst* sort?' I asked, to provoke.

'The meretricious variety – bells and whistles instead of substance,' my colleague bellowed, as if it was self-evident. Was that how he saw me? What did he think of the Dean?

But it was the historians whom the three of us discussed in most detail. I was shocked how little they knew about them; not even whether they were friends. They explained this away: Jim Evans wasn't around much – it being his second year, he was 'living out', far away up the Cowley Road, where it got industrial and 'possibly cheaper'; and Barnaby Quick, who had chosen to 'live in' again for Finals, was, 'Come to think of it,' oddly invisible. Still, our assessment of Jim was pretty consistent: he was very able, hard-working, perhaps too self-contained for his own good. Over Barnaby, we differed. The Ancient Historian saw a scholarship boy who'd failed to deliver, rightly forfeiting his bursary; the Mediaevalist and I suspected something was amiss – there was a rootlessness. I was charged with finding out what it was; preferably redeeming him.

Tyler was the one student I didn't feel able to discuss, much as I'd have liked to. He came in when the Dean and I were out together – there are only so many times you can refuse a pizza – and I had to pretend disinterest. It was unfortunate, really; I'm sure the Dean caught me looking at the rest of the American's gang, and what Tyler would make of me being there with the Dean I didn't like to think.

'Always surrounded by women,' the Dean observed waspishly, 'but he's one of those who never puts a foot wrong. It's very disappointing.'

I didn't have to ask what he meant – he was determined to tell me. 'So much of the Dean's role is routine. We compare notes, you know: it's all minor misdemeanours. We long for something egregious to add a bit of spice.'

'You can't be serious!'

'Why ever not? Wait 'til you do your turn: you'll be itching for someone meaty to take to task. The conceited or self-righteous are much the most satisfying. Look out for the likes of the Winston guy on those American schemes – Fulbright, Marshall and Rhodes: anyone told they're at the pinnacle is at risk of crashing down.'

I couldn't think what to say.

Tyler didn't mention the pizzeria when we overlapped in the Lodge a few days later and nor did I, though I was sure he'd seen me. Instead we talked about hiking gear. He was preparing to kit himself out specially – no lack of funds there, courtesy of Cecil Rhodes and his diamond mines – and wanted advice on what to buy. We began one of those ridiculous conversations that you're sure the other person can't be taking seriously, about boots and different types of waterproof. There was zero sign of sanctimony and not a whisper of self-importance; on the contrary, Tyler was delightfully self-deprecating. Eventually I remembered myself, picked up my post and turned to the Head Porter, who would have heard the whole exchange, joking that I was the last person to consult on matters sartorial, was I not? Cue cheerful banter with his staff about my struggles with the hood of my gown, which I had often accused of falling the wrong way. The porters – all men of course – had draped mine many a time. Thankfully Tyler took the hint and disappeared.

I left soon after, wondering how the preppy look would adapt to mud and rain.

As term drew to a close, I decided I'd been paranoid.

It came upon me one afternoon in Eighth Week when I cleared my desk of the term's dross.

My parents had given it to me for my twenty-first, when I was about to embark on my DPhil. I was fond of it: old but not properly antique, it was of the era before the educated classes – men, mostly of course – expected the size of their desk to reflect the scale of their responsibilities, plus the corners were nicely battered and the leather ink-stained, which gave it character. Mum had thought it an odd choice when I might have had a more feminine present, even a small piece of jewellery, but Dad had understood. Bidding together at the local auctioneers became an important part of the present, a sign of faith in the future.

Pulling out drawers and sorting notes from my colleagues, I revised some hasty judgements. The courtesies of Loxton and his ilk might not have been patronising. Yes, there was misogyny – a thought triggered by sight of a superfluous scrawl from the Ancient Historian, pointing out something I already knew, which went straight in the bin – but there was also respect. As for elitism, the details in the College 'bible' – and more importantly the students themselves – showed the place was more meritocratic than I'd feared, though there still weren't enough from state schools.

What mattered most, I thought, chucking rubbish at the

wastepaper basket, was that *I* hadn't got in on false pretences. The undergraduates liked being taught by me; I'd had my first referral from another college for tutoring – a tick there; there'd even been an anonymous note on a lectern on Valentine's Day, offering to buy me a drink, which I'd read aloud at the seminar to cause maximum laughter and maximum embarrassment – that merited a gold star. Plus I'd unearthed interesting material for my article on Ivy Williams, courtesy of some chance pointers from Jenny, and for my second set of lectures on women and social reform; research was going well – another tick.

Pictures flitted into my head and disappeared as fast as the paperwork. An image of Andy, kicking aside the abandoned post in his digs, came and went: loudly I tore in half a wodge of correspondence similarly overtaken by events – not needed!

Next in line were communications from the Dean. These sent me spinning back to an evening we'd spent at the Turf Tavern. Making our way back through the narrow alleyways, he'd lurched into me by mistake – at least so I'd thought at the time – and turned a steadying grab into a bit of a grope. Now I thought differently: as if one night entitled him to anything else! Besides, he had more of an eye for the students. Fun, but a bit of an ass and certainly predatory. Not bin-worthy yet, but dangerously near.

I leafed through the last of the cyclostyled sheets, assessing my role in the College. High Table was no longer an oral examination, nor the SCR an inspection, and I felt less like an interloper from the provinces. I'd convinced the College doctor that talks about contraception should be given to *all* the Freshers, not just the girls. Better still, I'd ventured a comment at Governing Body that wasn't rebuffed, though someone said that in this case I might not know the history. Any difficulties were rarely about being a woman; some were about being an outsider; most were to do with being new. I was holding my own.

Finally, all was done. I pulled a couple of cushions from the low chairs, lobbed them onto the window seat and sat watching the comings and goings with my legwarmers on and a rug tucked around me.

The best thing of all was the attendance at my lectures. High from the start, when Barnaby counted over fifty, it had peaked at nearly seventy; even Tyler had come along, despite it not being his subject, which was rather remarkable. And the Faculty had picked up that there was standing room only and rounds of applause: I'd been ribbed about commanding a bigger theatre next term. This was what the Warden wanted to hear.

It was seven o'clock. Figures began to drift past the lit windows below, ready for Hall, and there the American was, prompt as ever. I watched him come down the glow of the staircase diagonally across the quad, his long scholar's gown billowing, waving to someone I couldn't see, and tried to remember when I'd registered that those were his rooms.

Lifting my own robe off the hook, I set off down the stairs, cloaked in black, taking them at an even jog but slowing partway to adjust my hood. And it occurred to me then that Tyler, by contrast, had just done it in runs of two, which was important, if I could only remember why. When I tried it myself, my own gown breathed in and out with that same little pause after every other step, just like his.

Saturday

Suddenly the Reading Party was upon us.

My suitcase lay open by the chest of drawers, pressing for a decision about what clothes to take; even on routine days I'd get stuck, torn between not caring and admiration for people like Jenny, who knew instinctively what to wear. Nearer, the open door into my study allowed a glimpse of desk, where my papers waited to be tucked into my briefcase – a battered thing, with weathered leather and blackened buckles, to which I'd stayed loyal ever since my uncle passed it on. This, too, demanded attention. Eventually I got up and padded about in my dressing gown.

Loxton had advised walking boots or footwear with a good grip; he'd been particularly robust about it with the women. I'd collected my well-worn pair at Christmas, which meant suffering a large boot bag in my narrow cupboard for weeks. Now I wondered whether they'd get sufficient use to justify the trouble; wondered too how many of the students would have an equivalent – Eddie or Priyam, for instance, who were both from London, or Lyndsey, from that huge secondary school up north, who looked as if she was as hard up as I had been.

And would everybody *want* to walk? Loxton's photograph of Godfrey and his crew in hiking clothes, ready for a tramp, wouldn't have amused everyone. What if students didn't like the idea of scrambling on the coastline or failed to keep up? Pastoral care might mean sticking up for them.

Jim would be fine: wiry enough to be a walker, with the gait of a boy toughened in urban backstreets. Barnaby and Martin, too – they looked as if they liked the outdoor life. But Hugh, or Rupert? And what about the girls? Gloria wouldn't want to be dragooned and Chloe would also be spirited: they might put up a fight, like my suffragettes. Mei, surely, would not. Speculating inconclusively about who might need support, I wasted half my head start.

As for what to work on, Loxton had made clear that he and I could do as we wished: no need to confront texts like the students, so long as we set an example of quiet application. I'd decided to take the draft of my article and the cards for my lectures in Trinity term. If things went well, I'd knock my paper into shape and embellish my speaking notes. Now it occurred to me that it might be awkward to work while surrounded by students. Would Loxton know if I was unproductive? Would the Warden get to hear? What cover might I need?

Eventually I squeezed two books into my briefcase: a hefty biography of a minor eighteenth-century social reformer – useful 'secondary' source material, and a slim working-class memoir from the 1900s – a first-hand account published by a new feminist press. At the last minute, I picked up a new box of my favourite pencils: yellow and black, with a pink rubber set in a thin filigree of brass at the end. It had a pleasant rattle, like a box of spillikins, and its pristine state made me feel anything was possible.

What, I wondered, would Tyler take with him?

Under the fan vaulting of the Gatehouse, most of the talk was of what people had packed, particularly footwear and reading matter. And there of course was Tyler, with Priyam and Barnaby examining his pristine boots, which he'd tied together by their laces and was holding aloft like a set of scales, laughing that he should have bought the worn-in variety. Even as I arrived, he raised a foot to compare the treads on those loafers of his and, chuckling, clutched at Priyam to stop himself from tipping over. He was a nice shape, I noted – the limbs in good proportion, like his hands. That was really not helpful.

Behind him Mei ducked, and smiled that slow smile of hers that suggested she was grateful for something. She and Hugh were on their haunches trying to fix the zip on her small suitcase, which had caught on a white bra strap, all hooks. They were discussing packing routines. Hugh suggested people could be separated into two camps: those who filled a case to its limits, on the grounds that you never know what you might need, and those who always left scope to acquire new things on their journey. The size of the receptacle and the requirements of the trip were immaterial, he said – except, of course, if you were a scholar travelling from Hong Kong: that must have been a challenge.

Mei's face brightened as I joined them. 'Which sort of packer are you, Dr Addleshaw?' She looked at me from the flagstones, her head level with my knees. I put my belongings down and crouched at the right height to see the offending zip.

'Oh, always hopeful. That was my clothes shifting just then: not many; there's space in there still. Not much, mind – I didn't dare bring the bigger one, for fear of Dr Loxton's tape measure! How about you two?'

Hugh indicated a battered rucksack leaning against the limestone wall – long and narrow like its owner, its material faded and water-stained. 'I'm afraid I'm the opposite: not much spare in there,' he said. 'Try it!'

Leaning sideways to reach over, I pushed down on the

top. Almost no give: he was right that it was packed tight. Squeezed further, a point appeared under the waxed canvas near the base. 'Don't tell me, the bottom is all books?'

'I've been very restrained this time – only three. One I have to read again – that's the Herodotus, so *you* should approve; one I'd like to read afresh – that's the Plato, which gets better every time; and one that will be diverting if I flag – my trusty Loeb sampler, which I ought to know by heart now, but don't.'

Behind us came the sound of Gloria calling '*Hola!*' across the quadrangle. I stood up and turned to look. Chloe, standing next to her, started running, leaving Gloria alone and statuesque on the steps of Hall. Soon Chloe was halfway round the quad – Ho Chi Minh Square, as she and other College revolutionaries had dubbed it – and was waving wildly to Eddie on the other side. They lurched in parallel towards us, mirroring each other's steps – Chloe compact and ordinary despite the dungarees; Eddie rangy, eye-catchingly androgynous in his version. Gloria abandoned her pole position and made her own drama of joining the group. The noise of greetings ballooned briefly.

Loxton walked in from the street, deposited a case that looked as if it had come straight out of a wartime movie – like an oblong box, its sides dimpled from years of use, its surface spattered with the remnants of stickers – and handed me a set of car keys on a fob from a rental company, indicating the second of the Ford Transits lined up outside.

'Good morning! Everybody here?'

'Not yet,' I said. 'We're missing three, I think. Morning to you too.'

He disappeared into the Lodge, a remark about deliveries from the kitchen drifting over his shoulder as he went. He was wearing a thick, ribbed jumper, twill trousers and burgundy shoes, similar to the kind Jenny's father wore – polished, but free of that complicated tooling. Perhaps he'd left formality behind with his jacket and brogues.

As I looked around to check the numbers, Jim too came through the small open doorway in the massive wooden entrance gate, again partially blocking the light. He paused, seeming uncertain whom to join. Of course, he was the only one from his year.

I lifted a hand in greeting. 'Morning! I was forgetting you lived out. How's the Cowley Road?'

He started in my direction, but Barnaby was calling out to compare boots, so Jim clomped over to join him instead, shedding some caked mud as he retied his laces. He gave me an apologetic look, shoulders raised, palms out. Not a gesture I'd seen in him before; oddly good-humoured for someone normally so remote.

The counting reminded me of being a prefect, not that I'd lasted for long – far too rebellious in the sixth form. It certainly wasn't how I wanted to be seen by anyone now, even if the younger students were behaving like excited children milling in a playground. And yet Loxton had thrust the role upon me.

'Has anyone seen Martin?' I scanned the group, already missing that reassuring presence. I'd had a boyfriend like him after Andy; the solidity was all too comforting.

Gloria stopped what she was saying to Rupert, who had appeared from nowhere and was already near the centre of the melee as if they'd been his year all along, and looked round. 'He's coming by car, from home. I thought he told you but maybe not. He's such a turkey.'

Why had Loxton not mentioned this – or was I forgetting?

'Of course. Let's hope he's prompt. And Lyndsey – anyone seen her this morning?'

That figured: she'd be the absent-minded one. By the time she arrived we'd nearly finished loading the vans, some of the students were already seated and Loxton was back in the Lodge, negotiating with a steward about access to the cellar.

Lyndsey looked surprised at the fuss being made. 'Am I late? I was sure it was nine-thirty. Nine o'clock sounds so abrupt.' She dropped a small piece of luggage onto the pile by the back of the second vehicle, and balanced a satchel and another bag on top. 'Have you all been waiting?'

Gloria called out from inside: 'Well, yes ... anyway, it's twenty to!'

I was right: Lyndsey was known for poor timekeeping. She had that look about her, of someone whose thoughts faced inwards not out.

Hugh, at my side, swung her modest bag awkwardly over the metal step under the rear doors and followed it up with the rest of the luggage and a muddle of coats. He shoved them all into line behind the third row of seats, Gloria's large suitcase at the edge where it wasn't so much in the way, and then got in and held his thin hand out for Lyndsey.

'Here. Dr Loxton's preoccupied with his wine: they forgot to bring it up. Jump in and he may not notice – missing bottles are much more important than missing women.'

The two of them sat down behind Rupert, Chloe and Gloria, who had arranged themselves in the row of seats immediately behind mine – the girls on one side of the gang-way, where Chloe, pulling out a tin of tobacco and some Rizla papers, began rolling another fag; Rupert with space to himself on the other. Hugh checked something with Lyndsey and opened a window. My brothers had never been so polite, not even the elder one when smitten with Jenny.

'I'll need a map-reader,' I said.

I looked at the group still milling on the pavement by the front van. Tyler was nowhere near, but Jim was on the edge again, watching. 'Jim, I bet you're good with maps. Would you mind coming with us? I'd like company in the front to tell me where to go.'

He nodded, picked up his bag and walked over. 'Where is it?'

'On the seat, with Dr Loxton's directions.'

Loxton emerged from the Gatehouse accompanied by one of the porters with two wooden crates on a trolley, one considerably larger than the other. He stopped as he passed, head tilted, as if to ask whether I'd produced a full complement yet. Jesus!

But I only nodded. 'She's here. Some confusion or other.'

'Good, good. You've got Hugh, just in case? So we're all set?' He was watching the wine being loaded; maybe that would take the edge off his irritation.

'Think so. We're seven, so you should be six. Tyler might like to join you in the front, if that's okay.'

Loxton glanced at the group on the pavement.

Something compelled me to explain: 'You must remember him teasing about that American thing, at the briefing.'

'Ah – "seeing the sights". We've heard that one before. Beware of granting favours! Shall I lead?'

To begin with, it was a relief to have Loxton in front of me. The minibus wasn't hard to drive – it was similar to the van Dad and I had hired to move my things down from York – but I didn't know the way and was easily distracted. Jim was a good navigator but spare with words, which was helpful. Mostly we were silent.

When Loxton's steady pace and his fastidious changing of lanes became monotonous, Jim and I resumed our tentative forays into chat. This was such hard work that I stopped asking questions and talked about my own family, hoping to draw him in. Gradually he interposed the odd aside suggesting a frugal upbringing in Cardiff with no father in evidence; an allusion to a girl he knew – a friend of his sister – whom he saw when he went home.

We kept going like that for a couple of hours, until Somerset, where Loxton was in the habit of breaking the journey at a favourite lay-by – one of those long cul-de-sacs that offer the illusion of a country lane. We got there exactly when he said we would, Loxton indicating in such good time that I could hardly have missed it – no need for theatrical signals from his crew.

As we drew up behind them, Eddie hopped towards us on one sneakered foot, dangling a long scarlet sock in our direction, the other foot naked. He was sporting a cap, like they wear for American football, tilted over the face. It looked ridiculous but he clearly didn't think so – he almost pirouetted.

I opened my door and waited. Over by the other van Tyler and Barnaby watched together, arms raised to shade their eyes, sleeves dropping back to bare their wrists – Barnaby's still tanned, Tyler's with that honeyed hue.

'Did you see my traffic light?' Eddie stuck his hand deep in the sock and spread his fingers. The wool was ribbed, soft and still rather new-looking, with a thin grey band at the top. 'Rather fine, isn't it? If only I had my green ones,' he continued, 'I could give you the go-ahead too, but they're packed.'

He rubbed his bare foot against the other leg as he looked to the passenger side. 'How's our rally driver, Jim? She doing okay?'

Where did such people come from? He was insufferable! And because of the draw, they were going to be sharing!

Jim looked nonplussed at the comment, the freckles draining of colour. 'Why wouldn't she . . .'

Behind us, the van began decanting noisily. I chucked the keys onto the dashboard and put out a hand to muffle the clatter.

Jim tried again. 'On your tail all the way, mate. We'll beat you yet!'

Eddie toyed with the sock, throwing it between his hands, then hopped once more to maintain his balance. 'In your dreams, boyo,' he said.

Rupert arrived by the bonnet and studied Eddie's bare foot. It was slender, almost feminine, with very long toes. Eddie wiggled them coquettishly.

Chloe pushed Rupert and his shrug away. 'Dig the red sock!' she said and pulled it off Eddie's fingers, holding it swaying above her feet. 'It looks just my size. Lend them to me?' And she ran off up the slope, a flash of red at her side.

Jim watched as Eddie, still one-legged, hopped after. 'Dickhead,' he muttered, and thrust the map into the glove box.

We ate lunch amidst the birdsong, sitting in the sun on the grass verge – an irregular line of blobs against the greenery that was broken periodically when the students helped themselves to more food or stood to watch the gulls in the newly ploughed field.

I'd fleetingly imagined a picnic in wicker baskets laid out on tartan rugs, but Loxton's version, prepared by the kitchen staff, was more austere, consisting of pungent cheese and pickle sandwiches together with a choice of Scotch egg or chicken and ham pie. The savouries must have been familiar to the students. Tyler, who was funnier than I'd expected, said you could tell the day of the week by the chutney that surfaced in Hall at lunchtime, Saturday's having the sweet taste of slowly sautéed onion to welcome the weekend. He also claimed they'd invented the nickname 'Peggies' for the eggs, which had an unusually thick crust of home-made breadcrumbs. Gloria began to explain for my benefit, stopping abruptly when Loxton came over to refill our beakers. I never heard the conclusion.

Next to her Rupert lay back on the bank like a male

model – hands locked behind his head, elbows making a bow with his shoulders, velvet jacket gently puckering – discussing the smell of the great outdoors with no one in particular. When Loxton announced we should be making a move, he settled further into the long blades, ignoring the packing up that was going on around him.

Loxton looked at me. 'Might I have a word?'

He stepped a few paces away and stared down the empty tarmac. There was a pause while he dabbed at some loose chips with the toe of his shoes.

'It didn't occur to me to think of it,' he said, nodding towards the students. 'The men can sort themselves out, but I think the women . . .'

What was he talking about? My mind drifted about its mooring, considering the options; then the rope tightened. Ah, the men must have relieved themselves behind a succession of hedges, but the 'gentler sex' could not. Poor Loxton, embarrassed by normal bodily functions – how would he cope in a house full of women?

'Of course! Though we're quite capable of holding our bladders, you know – you have to be very good at it in College if you're in the wrong spot.' I thought of the older staircases, known as 'Hell', which were notorious for a deficit of female loos; those with new facilities were 'Heaven'. Maybe Loxton hadn't picked that up.

'A stop at the next service station?' I suggested.

Loxton looked vague.

I shouldn't have teased.

Jim had loosened up over lunch. We chatted our way happily through Devon, crossed the Tamar Bridge talking about the wonders of Victorian engineering, and continued as we drove over a new landscape of generous curves dotted with sheep. The meadows were now the colour of moss – brilliant green with a russet dusting – and the contours were like those in a basket of apples writ large, a jumble of rising and falling mounds.

He mentioned the laid slate walls interwoven with ivy and bramble, whose base disappeared into the moss as if into a drift of green. He'd repaired dry-stone walling on the Gower the previous summer, he said, to supplement his grant: it was heavy, windy work but satisfying; a good wall might stand for centuries. We contemplated this revelation companionably.

'You're in danger of losing him,' he said, as we pulled away from a roundabout, his tone suggesting that he too saw the possibilities.

Soon, Loxton's light blue van was far behind us. Ahead, tufts of gorse emerged from the hedgerows, occasionally dusted with vivid sulphurous yellow, and the trees thinned.

We drove across the bottom of the moor as instructed, taking in the scrubby patches that peppered the slopes – in the distance the gorse now like a dark spattering of sheep droppings; in the foreground the long, yellowing grass tufty and doughy, like the dunes on the coast at home; only very small trees. I wound the window down to sniff the air.

'Is this Bodmin?' Lyndsey called out from the back.

In the mirror I could see Gloria and Rupert glance out and then resume their flirtation in a conversation about Benazir Bhutto's farewell debate at the Oxford Union the previous week; Chloe, who was now next to the window, was dozing against the glass. Behind them Lyndsey sat forward, holding onto the back of the seat in front and craning past Hugh, all eagerness.

'Isn't it glorious? Haven't you always longed to see the moors here? If I were out there I'd run around with my arms aloft, like this, and I'd twirl and twirl . . .' And then she was off, hands wafting above her head, saying something obscure about du Maurier to a shaking of the head from Hugh. Impossible to hear the words above the chatter in-between.

We began our descent towards the coast. Another brief patch of moorland, more pastoral than before, and we went steeply into another town.

'Not far now,' Jim announced to the mirror as we left the buildings behind. 'And we're still ahead of Dr Loxton.'

The road followed the line of a small river, gradually descending to its level. Steep fields came down on one side; on the other was a low wall and beyond it the stream. Daffodils appeared on the slope – great drifts of them.

By now we were all looking out of the windows, taking in the sombre greys of the stone buildings lifted by white-washed houses with slate roofs. Mevagissey was not as I'd expected; too big for a village but small and tight-knit for a town. There were glimpses of boats at the ends of the side alleys as we drove through, but we didn't get the measure of the setting until we were above the bay and could look down to the harbour and across to the surrounding hills. Mevagissey had the air of a place created by tossing boulders into a valley and seeing where they settled: dwellings jammed against each other, streets irregular and narrow – everything lined up in a jumble to face the water, focused on fishing.

I slowed by an imposing Georgian building with a soaring flagpole: almost the kind of 'sight' that Tyler might have wanted to see.

'What do you bet that was once the harbourmaster's house?' I said to no one in particular, looking up at the confident granite façade with its three tiers of windows decreasing in height as they ascended – an orderly hierarchy neatly expressed in the scale of the slate lintels, softened by the white columns and architrave of the doorway and the dentils under the roof. It comfortably dominated the street.

'Hugh, didn't Dr Loxton say the harbourmaster built here before he bought the spit of land with the chapel?'

But Hugh had forgotten the details, beyond the fact of a seafaring career that had culminated in considerable wealth, and nobody else could recall what had been said.

We carried on up the hill, leaving behind the view of the bay. The bungalows gave way to pastureland as the road turned inland and the sea stretched out again in the distance, beyond the soft undulations of the clifftop.

Then, just as Jim touched my arm and pointed, Hugh called to me to 'stop driving like a mad woman' or we'd miss the turning.

It wasn't much more than a farm track – a raised strip of earth flecked with a gravel of sorts setting out across the turf. The surrounding ground would be a mess in wet weather; someone had paid, and people had toiled, to make it passable. Astonishing, what people had done to tame the landscape. I opened the window to listen for the sea and marvelled.

'I thought he said it was grand,' said Rupert, as we moved off towards the horizon.

'No, you *wanted* it to be grand!' The bench behind me shook as Gloria pummelled him, laughing.

There was clearly an attraction, or maybe they were already going out; both 'blessed', they would make what Mum called 'a handsome pair'. We hadn't allowed for lovers; was that what the Dean had been getting at?

Lyndsey piped up. 'You're missing a breathtaking view: look at that! Don't you want to be out there with the birds?'

We were nearing the high point on the far side of a short bay. Along with a gust of wind came the sound of gulls calling and a faint smell of seaweed. In front of us the track swooped back on itself and down into a bowl alongside a small ragged beach and then swept up the slope on the other side towards a brief ribbon of green above the pink-tinged grey of the rock face. Just before the ribbon narrowed there were a few pine trees to the rear and, on the near side, in the midst of the expanse of green, a large square house not unlike the one we'd just seen, surrounded by shrubs, standing proud of a smattering of smaller buildings, some whitewashed, some in the same pewter stone. At the extremity of the point, just beyond the last of the trees, was another white rectangle – a small chapel edged with grey quoins. Everywhere the woodwork had been painted a jaunty blue, the roof tiles were uniformly slate, the planting was shades of bottle green. Someone had chosen a harmonious palate, which blended the buildings seamlessly into the hues of landscape, sea and sky.

Carreck Loose – 'Grey Rock'. It was a fitting name.

I thought we knew what to expect, but this wasn't it: even Jim was straining forward at my side; the back of the van was a babble of exclamation.

For a start, the track had turned back into a drive – mossy down the middle, and definitely in need of attention at the sides, where grass encroached on the sparse gravel, but still suggestive of a certain grandeur, whatever Loxton had said. It swirled into a green-tinged turning circle edged with primroses and daffodils in front of a shallow portico where the house faced the sea, the circle clearly built at a time when carriages did nothing as mundane as to take the short route to the stables. That explained the side track we'd passed, I thought: it must lead to the buildings at the back.

Then there was the house itself – a thundering imposition on the landscape, whose scale, proportion and sheer nerve suggested a confidence we'd long lost. It completely dominated the grouping and more than held its own in the craggy landscape despite the majesty of the rock face below.

And the views! The outlook from the front rooms, facing south, was clearly going to be breathtaking. Even those at the side would have their bit of coastline.

I hadn't thought through the implications of arriving first:

we'd all assumed Loxton would do the honours. Now it struck me as inconvenient as well as unkind to have beaten him to it: we couldn't get in. Hugh wasn't there to ask – he'd set off across the grass in the direction of the tiny chapel, with Chloe and Gloria mucking about alongside him, Lyndsey somewhere behind. It was Jim who stood with me by the front door amidst the bags, uncertain of the form, his tough-boy glower suddenly at odds with the setting, while Rupert tilted a few flowerpots in case there was a spare key.

The three of us did a quick circuit outside the house, taking in the area of mown grass and the occasional massing of pompom palms that continued round to the north-west until the 'lawn' – more like a gently sloping meadow – petered out into shorter shrubbery. From there we could see through to a tennis court and the end of the low stone building we'd spotted from the track, which Jim soon established as the old stables and coach house. On the other side of the courtyard was the mirroring pair of cottages, painted white but empty, with the back route coming in between some old greenhouses at the rear. Rupert admired the way the arrangement framed the extension at the back of the house: it would all be very pleasing, he opined, if it weren't so weather-beaten. I disagreed, thought it pleasantly relaxed just as it was. And I liked the shaded aspect further round to the east, where there were pines and another patch of shrubbery – you got an enticing glimpse of the rocky outcrop with the chapel. But it was cold. Soon we were at the front door again.

Still no sign, not even of Martin. We tried the windows, but most were shuttered and, where not, the deep beds, sprouting bulbs between bare sculptural forms, made it impossible to see in. Even the modest conservatory at the end of the extension was unrevealing: really a large porch with a few pot plants and some ailing Lloyd Loom furniture. So we retreated to the terrace and sat contentedly with the others where the crazy paving caught the afternoon sun. A sense of collective own-ership began to develop, with ideas about walking the green ridge, of playing football where the slope levelled out, even of tennis by the outbuildings. Rupert said he would work in a front room – he'd imagine Edwardian house parties and taking tea on the lawn. Gloria was right: he was the one with the grand ideas.

Eventually Loxton's van moved serenely across the brow of the field on the skyline in front of us. It delved silently into the gulley and soon we heard the crunching of gravel.

When we got to the front of the house, Loxton's team had already disappeared inside, but Rupert wasn't to be hurried. He made us stop to enjoy the flagstoned hall, bisecting the house from front to back, which had a shabby splendour, and the scale of the mahogany stairs, with their square turn. I was more taken with the old portraits, their puckered canvas loose in elderly gilt frames – wanting to know who they were and which, if any, was the harbourmaster himself.

That was when Tyler appeared, collecting a bag or some-thing, catching the end of my speculations. What had I said? It mattered that it shouldn't be stupid.

But Tyler didn't seem to have noticed. 'Good paintings!' he said, glancing round. Then, indicating a three-quarters view of an elderly woman: 'She's nearly as bad as that woman in Hall. Just better dressed.'

Why hadn't I said something like that? 'You mean the washerwoman?' I asked. 'But she's *meant* to be ugly . . .'

'Sure thing,' he said.

Maybe the Dean was right. Too suave.

The three of us moved on past the open doors, through the corridor and . . . Wow, what a noise!

In the kitchen everyone was greeting each another, crowding round the Rayburn, pulling chairs back from a long oblong table, making squeaking noises on the olive lino, banging cupboard doors in search of the makings of tea, opening and closing drawers to find the teaspoons, talking hard. Loxton was a little terse with me, I suppose because he was smarting, and it turned out there'd been a spare key all along, not that he'd bothered to tell anyone – but our exchange was drowned out. Tyler and Jim began dragging the little table from the conservatory to fit lengthways across the end of the main one, so we had enough places, and Hugh was calling, 'Clear the way!' as he deposited extra chairs from the dining room. Within seconds, all fourteen of us could have sat at that PVC tablecloth, with its cheerful pink and orange daisies, had we chosen to do so. The excitement was palpable: an air of being demob happy in a different place with different people, waiting to be let loose; a sense of camaraderie and adventure, of being in it together, though we didn't yet know what that 'it' was; almost of being on holiday.

If Loxton was concerned about this moment – when he had to recap on the rules of engagement – he didn't let it show, though he was peevish about Martin being late, as if that was somehow my doing.

He passed the buck to me. 'Dr Addleshaw,' he said, 'will remind you where you are sleeping. I suggest you sort yourselves out upstairs and put on some extra layers. We'll reconvene in ten minutes for a quick walk before the light goes, whether or not Martin has deigned to join us, so you can get your bearings. After that we'll light one or two fires and decide who's sitting where, ready for a prompt start in the morning.'

So I whizzed through while Loxton looked on. If there'd been time to think, I wouldn't have done it; guys like Tyler would remember where they were going – no need to treat them like children. Besides, the Finalists clearly thought the allocation indicative only. Rupert, in the van, had engineered a switch with the courteous Hugh; there would be other such manoeuvres. And why not? Who cared?

Loxton and I stayed put in the kitchen, trying to maintain a conversation, as the students came and went. They were still essentially children, he opined, capable of endearing moments of abandon when collective enthusiasm took over – one saw it every year around Freshers' Week. Really? But surely it felt different, arriving this time? He said it was too early to tell, but perhaps there was a frisson that had not been there before – and he waved in the direction of the rest of the house and the sound of joshing, bags being shunted across the floor and feet running up and down wooden stairs. We listened as the noises drifted in from the hall and then started again from above, footsteps pattering over our heads in the extension and then disappearing back where they'd come from; it was a kind of detective work, guessing what was going on.

It was then that Loxton said he had a piece of social history for me and, leading me into the corridor, opened the pair of doors opposite the boot room. I'd taken them to be cupboards, but one door revealed a small loo, still with its sixties wallpaper and its pale yellow porcelain, and the other a narrow set of stairs – the servants' access. The sight made me think of holidays with my grandparents in the joined-together cottages they occupied as tenant farmers: routinely my brothers and I had been shooed outside to stop us clattering up one boxed-in run of stairs and down the other.

Now I took in the curl of the dry wooden treads, registering the mustiness of the air caught in the funnel – a complete contrast to the main staircase, so large and polished that it was like standing in a public building – and listening to the muffled sounds from above. Loxton followed me up and we had a quick reconnoitre of the annexe – the whole upper floor of the extension – which he said had been the housekeeper's domain in the days of having staff. Its exclusion from the arrangements surprised me: it would be warm enough, above the Rayburn – rather nice, in fact, like a little bachelor flat; surely Loxton would have found it cosy? He must believe being part of the collective required him to sleep in the main body of the house with everyone else, and that you might as well not join the party if you were going to opt for the annexe. Strange, really, given how private he was.

By the time we re-emerged in the kitchen, the babble elsewhere had subsided and the students had begun drifting down again. I carried my case quickly up to my bit of the attic – at the front of the house, with gabled windows overlooking the turn of the drive in one direction and the shrubby area in the other, the sea clearly visible beyond – and took the opportunity to check out the floor.

The girls were on the landing. Gloria, who'd won a room to herself, was protesting at Chloe's plan to migrate to it; Priyam, who was meant to be sharing with Chloe across the corridor, sounded as if she would be glad to lose her. Would I be expected to arbitrate?

I busied myself casing the rest of the joint. Put my head round the door to Eddie and Jim, but they'd abandoned their cramped quarters. Found Martin's tiny cubbyhole at the end of the corridor: door open, he'd see all the comings and goings. Discovered the bathrooms were doubly *ensuite*, with no access from the landing – typical of the Dean not to explain things properly.

There was no time to check whether everyone was okay on the first floor, let alone to sneak a look at their rooms – the students were gathering noisily for Loxton's quick constitutional, as he was rumoured to call his shorter walks. By the time I'd got downstairs and put my boots on, the last of them was going through the gate in the hedge and into the longer grass of the field beyond. Once again, he'd contrived to put me at a disadvantage: the front runners were nearing the end of the next field before I caught up the rear. Still, each group seemed oblivious to those behind – absorbed in conversation, navigating the slope of the pastureland and taking in the views. Maybe nobody noticed.

It was the most glorious setting. In one direction you could see beyond our spit to the coastline further east, with its succession of promontories merging in the distance into a dark and crumpled ribbon; in the other was our little beach and, further round, the long curve of the far bay. There the green pasture slid down into patches of gorse, bracken and bramble, whose deep greens and reddy browns merged imperceptibly into the olive of whatever clung to the top of the rocks. Between the two vistas stretched the long expanse of the sea, greener and more lustrous than the beige-grey of the sand, frothing and turning relentlessly as we watched, even at a distance reeking of seaweed.

I joined Rupert and Mei as they mounted a wooden style to cross one of those very dry-stone walls that Jim had talked about, its crevices sprouting ivy and brighter, fuller, glossy greens. Instead of following Mei down, Rupert clambered up to stand in the wind on a loose slither of slate.

He pointed at a distant patch of white and grey, almost indistinguishable from the heavy cloud hanging over the same promontory. 'That must be Mevagissey. We should have brought a map,' he shouted. 'Do you know where there's a map, Dr Addleshaw?'

Why would I? Loxton was the one who would know. I wondered whether they'd address me formally all week and if Tyler would do the same.

Rupert didn't wait for an answer. 'What we need is a map that shows the contours – and Martin to tell us how those rockscapes were formed.' He picked his way down and the three of us trudged on together, sharing our ignorance of geology.

We didn't go far. Loxton was concerned that we should get back while it was still light – at that time of year, he reminded us, it would be dark by six, and very cold. Too true: by the time we regained our long field, the square box of the house, the low bulk of the nearer buildings at the rear and the clump of pines beyond were all beginning to merge into the gloom and becoming indistinct; only the white cottages and the little chapel still stood out clearly. In the dusk, the gleam of the conservatory lights was like a beacon – with a dark blob, presumably Martin waiting to be let in. Gloria was right: he was indeed a turkey.

As we looked, she sped off ahead, running towards the back entrance and reappearing in the glow a few minutes later as a second silhouette, just distinguishable as a separate entity before the blobs merged – she may have been standing between us and him, or giving him a hug: it was hard to tell. By the time we all filed through the front door and jostled our way through to the kitchen, she was standing next to Martin in the archway leading to the conservatory, laughing at something he'd said about all the hellos, watching the scene. It might have been their house, with us come to visit, they looked so at home.

Loxton had volunteered to cook that evening, on the grounds that he was familiar with the place, while the rest of us got ready for the first proper day. He co-opted Eddie as his helper.

Knowing the ropes, he explained, wasn't about knowing the kitchen and its equipment but setting culinary expectations at the right level and ensuring that the opening evening was a success. I was relieved to be out of it: cooking the meal would have been a test too many. Besides, the Dean had told me that the inaugural meal followed a set pattern: Loxton cooked with one of the First Years and together they provided a nursery staple. So it wasn't so much that Loxton was letting me off the hook; more that he wanted to deliver a party piece.

The rest of us, meanwhile, wandered the ground floor to choose where to work.

Carreck Loose was a stolid building, well proportioned but with little by way of graceful decoration, and it had a masculine feel about it despite being an old family home. To the right as you came in the front door, facing south and east, where it looked towards the chapel, was what Loxton referred to as the 'morning room': small, with a couple of pieces of campaign furniture and a two-person sofa in vivid orange stripes – another of those sixties touches, now a little tired. That led discreetly to a study, an interconnecting space with no access from the hall; and beyond that, on the north-east corner, to a 'library', which had one of those tables with tooled leather, and buttoned chairs of the kind Rupert had described, except that these were in an advanced state of disrepair. To the left of the hall was a spacious drawing room facing south and west, with traditional chintz on the window seats and a massive suite in the same tatty state, awkwardly arranged to allow for a small grand piano, and beyond it the dining room, with window seats looking west and north, where a lot of empty space surrounded a once-glorious table that was clearly capable of seating still more people if the extra leaf were put in place.

Hugh said they mostly ignored the main entrance, using the back door and arriving via the corridor from the extension, where the turn of the stairs above cut off the light. That seemed to me symptomatic of what was so appealing – having the legacy of a rough kind of grandeur, without being constrained by it. For there was space for everyone, and more, but this great lump of a house wasn't the least forbidding. Nothing was new – and equally, nothing was properly antique. There were almost no ornaments and those few were clearly nothing special. Even the piano looked unprepossessing: no lacquer-like sheen here, but a lid soiled by watermarks and piled with sheet music and colour supplements that hid none of the damage. It was a house that had been buffeted by years of use and went on standing no matter what storms were flung at it, inside as well as out.

Some people chose to park their reading matter in the library. Perhaps it was simply that they were used to working in such spaces and, by force of habit, selected the environment that most nearly replicated it; maybe Hugh had sat there happily on his previous trip. In any event, there he was with Lyndsey, confidently clearing space for their own piles on the central table. As I walked through, Tyler came in and asked to join them – only a modest amount of reading, I noted – and then Loxton arrived with a hardback, notebook and pencil. So that wasn't for me; one option conveniently removed.

The morning room was less popular, having fewer suitable surfaces, but it had a large heater. Gloria and Chloe were there – Gloria draping the kind of cardigan coat that Jenny would have worn over the end of the old roll-top she'd angled for, Chloe bagging a campaign table and chair with her poncho, poking around in search of an ashtray. They seemed wedded to being together – who was protecting whom?

Most surprising of all was that somebody – Jim, I suspected – had earmarked the little study, presumably to work in solitude.

The occupants of the other side of the hall were equally spread out. Priyam, Rupert and Martin were preparing to sit at the big dining table, but the logic of that particular trio wasn't obvious. I'd half expected Priyam to be with Mei; as for Rupert and Martin, who didn't seem to like one another much, why park themselves together? Yet there the three of them were, grouped at the end nearest the hall, with a spectacular view across the garden and towards the sea.

77

In the drawing room Eddie had chosen the sofa and pulled up a footstool; Mei had placed her books neatly on an occasional table between the windows – odd, really, to have your back to the others and no view, but maybe she planned to avoid distraction; and Barnaby had pulled an armchair up to a games table – given the general air of tattiness, a surprisingly lovely piece of Georgian furniture with an inlaid chessboard. Others were gathering here to watch the lighting of the first fire, savouring the whiff of burning newsprint, waiting for the kindling to crackle.

As for me, I collected my briefcase and chose the dining room, opting impulsively to settle for a while amongst the fading waxed peonies of the window seat. Once my legs were braced – shoes off, feet against one of the cushions – I could sit comfortably under a rug with my knees drawn in and the Edwardian memoir on my thighs, the list of students as a marker. There I stayed, happily absorbed in my reading, barely noticing the cold and the condensation and the smell of damp cotton; ignoring the sounds of the students exploring talking and laughing; stopping to gaze vacantly into the blackness of the garden while pondering a thought; looking up and chatting briefly when anyone came to the door. It reminded me of childhood days sat perched in an alcove during that long-gone era when there was a real prospect of finishing a novel at a single sitting. How quickly you could slip back into that space where the world on the page took over from the world around you and everything stilled.

Supper, when it came, was a genial affair, although it was hard not to feel slightly on the fringe; Loxton knew the form and the students knew each other, whereas I was on the outside.

We ate in the kitchen – it seemed the Reading Party had all its meals there, bar the final night. You could see why: it was warm, with the Rayburn in the corner; squeezing in made it cosy; plus you could bask in the smell of sausages and Bisto gravy. Yet there was no rowdiness – we were too uncertain for that and we were only drinking cider – only some nice moments of spontaneity.

One came when Eddie planted two great baking tins of toad-in-the-hole in front of Loxton's place at the centre of the table, with a flourish and a joke about being only the 'sous chef': there was applause and friendly banter about who liked the crunchy corners and who preferred the moist bit in the middle – Tyler asked for the latter, saying he liked it 'succulent'. That prompted what I suspected would be one of many erudite, but not entirely serious, discussions of language, some of which must have been beyond him. Why was it 'toad-in-the-hole'? Why a toad? Was the hole literal – the bubble of Yorkshire pud; or figurative – a toad in a spot? And if figurative, what kind of spot was he in and why? Martin proved the most inventive, holding the room with a riff about Rat, Badger and Mole grappling with Toad, who of course was Martin himself, and all the while Loxton looked on, like the head of a family enjoying the young ones' amusement. I began to see the sense in having a first night like this, with a menu chosen for its potential to break the ice; could even see why Loxton should be dishing it all up from the middle of the group. Perhaps the Dean, who'd been so spiky, hadn't liked sharing the limelight.

The other notable moment came towards the end of the meal, when the scent of cloves and vanilla took over – we had baked apple with Birds Eye custard – and the table was a mess of scraped pudding bowls pushed to the side, rings of yellow where the blue-and-cream jugs had dripped, and detritus from the main course such as a forgotten serving spoon caked with batter. Very comfortable. Gloria, who'd been leaning over to chat, suddenly pulled back to listen to Tyler and interrupted with, 'Is that all?' before topping his story with one of her own. That sort of thing was normal at home, and certainly in the house Andy and I had shared in York, but rare at High Table – and I'd missed it. It was a good way to end the meal, with the students cracking up and Loxton sharing the joke, smiling as he picked up his pipe and found the little sachet of tobacco that he always carried with him, acting the paterfamilias as if he'd had years of experience. I chuckled too – how could I not?

By the time the laughter subsided, several people were carrying the dirty plates away. There was no dishwasher – not that we were expecting any mod cons – and more than enough of us were trying to help, given the small area for circulation. But actually it was fun standing with crockery in one hand and cutlery in the other, waiting for space to clear around the kitchen sink, joking about the boys suddenly finding they had other things to do. It would have been too much to impose a washing-up rota, though I half expected Loxton to produce a schedule. Or perhaps that was another job he planned to spring on me: taking the men to task. The Dean had warned it would be like him to do so.

Instead, Loxton put his mark on the evening in another way, by assuming the party would continue the tradition of playing board games after supper – chess, Scrabble, backgammon and the like – while he listened to his organ music and smoked his pipe, just as the Dean had predicted. So that's what we did: we played games amidst a reedy booming from an ancient stereo. We all moved to the drawing room, pulling the two folding card tables from their place beside the big cabinet from which the various boards emerged; clearing the long, low footstool between the armchairs; hijacking the little inlaid table, which Barnaby had earmarked for his own, so we could use it too. Looking up once we were underway, distracted by the sudden quiet and Loxton rising to turn the album and tend to the fire, it was easy to imagine the Reading Party of old – rather Spartan, rather uncommunicative – losing itself of an evening through serious concentration on a set of squares. With women in the mix the dynamic was surely different. There was chat between the groups, teasing and quipping – almost a flirtation – but any idea of doing this repeatedly, as some kind of week-long championship, was scotched by talk of all the other amusements that might make better use of a large house. Only a few seemed to be taking the competition seriously – Chloe triumphant when Martin was gammoned; Hugh delightfully taken aback, but chivalrous, when his studious game with Mei came abruptly to an end in his own checkmate. Cue jokes from Tyler about having a female Bobby Fisher in our midst, which amused me at least.

Loxton and I chatted briefly about the undertone of competitiveness, after I found him sitting at the empty table in the kitchen with the beginnings of a shopping list. That he should already be thinking of what we needed was more of a surprise to me than his doing supper; the sudden picture of the tedium – and loneliness – of bachelor life made me think of my uncle, alone in his fussy little flat, surrounded by newsprint. Did Loxton cook for himself, in his place in Park Town, or did someone come in to do such things for him? Perhaps that was why he was such a regular in Hall: it might satisfy a more complex need for nourishment. Either way, he looked frail on his own, methodically planning ahead while the messy business of real life happened elsewhere. Another thing that might have been comic if it hadn't been a little sad.

He accepted my offer to make him a cup of Nescafé and, as I pottered about learning where things were, we talked a bit about how people were settling in. He was disappointed that Martin hadn't arrived in time for the walk, which of course had been too short, but that could be remedied tomorrow; he had noted the closeness of Gloria and Chloe, which threatened to set them apart – one didn't get that with the men, he claimed, even those who had been at school together, which those two had not; Jim had indeed chosen the study but was in there on his own – we should watch that, as people shouldn't work in isolation; and so on. Was there anything I wanted to report?

I joked that on my floor, as the Dean had foretold, there'd already been a fuss about the bathrooms and a change in the sleeping arrangements. It turned out much the same had happened below. Tyler, who was now sharing with Rupert, had suggested they be gallant and swap with Mei and Lyndsey so the girls got the view from the front of the house. Loxton thought this most appropriate. I was amused that Rupert's own switch, presumably to avoid being at the rear, had misfired. And it was a relief to know that Tyler would not, now, be underneath me as I padded about. Would it have bothered me if Loxton had been directly below? Possibly, but not in the same way.

Curiously, Loxton didn't comment on my miscalculation about the loos. Perhaps he was more generous than I thought.

I said goodnight to the students in the hall and set off up that sturdy panelled staircase, passing the door to the housekeeper's empty suite – shut to avoid draughts – and then crossing the landing on the first floor, wondering what to say if anyone was not fully dressed. It was almost disappointing to get past Tyler and Rupert scot-free.

Once in the servants' stairs to the attic – as narrow and dark as the 'cupboard' outside the kitchen – I paused a moment. I could hear the talk in *their* room, which meant either of them, if they were listening out, would hear *me* making my way up that second resonant funnel, only a thin screen of lath and plaster and a few layers of wallpaper away. And though you couldn't hear precisely what was being said, we'd all get attuned to these things and there'd soon be little privacy. So I didn't linger.

All the doors on the landing were closed apart from my own, which was ajar. Anyone could have peered in and seen my suitcase lying wide open – my simple cotton under-wear, which had caused the Dean to mock, tossed in like an afterthought, in full view. It was too long since I'd bought anything lacy; by now I should have kitted myself out in something special, like Jenny, whose silky knicker drawer always seemed to reflect the state of her relationships, bur-geoning as she went from this lover to that, so that it was a kaleidoscope of fancy pairings; whereas I was always mixing simple bras and pants, and could never be bothered to match the colours. It would be a shame to be discovered in any of my lazy offerings: almost better to be braless and brazen.

I began unpacking my clothes – another jumper, jeans, a cord skirt and that pinafore dress with the enormous pockets – stashing them in the gloomy recesses of the small Victorian wardrobe with my sole change of shoes. There was little else to sort. A novel went onto the bedside table. My briefcase and the walking boots were downstairs. Other than that there was just my towel and my washbag, the latter as much of a giveaway as the rest of my luggage: a messy assortment of toiletries mixed with a few items of make-up, mostly from Boots. I stared at them blankly, trying to remember why I didn't have a separate bag for 'doing your face', as Mum called it, but nothing much was ever done to mine, and Jenny's tiny Mary Quant set, an expensive present even for her, was almost unused.

There was a moment's loneliness. Whom would I talk to when all this was over, with no Casanova in sight, unless you counted the Dean? And while I was here? Not Loxton, for sure. I almost envied the students who were doubling up, who could end the day chatting companionably to their roommates. If Jenny had been there she would have been giggling about something or other: Hugh's asexual gangliness, Martin's innuendo, Lyndsey and her notions. We would have laughed about me getting ahead in the van, analysed the insouciant snobbery in Eddie's little spat with Jim, discussed the moments when my confidence faltered at everything again being new.

Above all, Jenny would have teased about sex. We'd have played the game that had amused us as schoolgirls and had kept us sane through our undergraduate years when presented with a choice of male talent: 'If you had to do it with one of them, which one would you choose?' When we first played in our teens, it was a matter of who we could imagine snogging; later we progressed to who we might screw. The game was never about being seduced – we always had the initiative and there was no question that the chosen bloke was bloody lucky to be under consideration at all. If none of them took our fancy, we pictured them naked except for their socks. It always made us smile.

Hypothetical, of course, given that they were students, but Barnaby was good looking – or maybe I'd choose Tyler, although it was hard to say why, when he was the opposite of rugged. Jenny would have gone for Rupert straight away.

Sunday

Light, streaming through the dormer windows, roused me early – a reminder to close the curtains. So for a second day running there was time to spare, to lie in bed looking and listening. What a treat.

It was what you'd call a pretty room, with old-fashioned sprigged wallpaper dotted about with prints in walnut frames, an oval mirror over the diminutive grate reflecting a glimpse of the sky; to my left a small chest of drawers and a dressing table; to my right a small wardrobe and the door. But what really interested me were the sounds. Nothing as yet from my own floor, which was hardly surprising, but something must have carried up the stairs or through the flues to wake me – a creak as somebody tiptoed around, or a door banging in a draught, perhaps. Looking out, I saw Loxton with a tall figure – probably Hugh; Rupert was too languid, surely, to be up at this hour; Tyler I would have recognised – striding along the track near the crest of the hill. True to form, Loxton was taking an early walk.

I decided to stake my claim on the bathroom. Gloria would probably dawdle: if anyone had an air of entitlement, she did; all those years of boarding school, yet it wouldn't occur to her that anybody else might also need the loo. The other girls would be using it too, unless they mucked in with Martin, Eddie and Jim. So there could be four of us wanting it at the same time.

Overnight the room had acquired signs of the other users. There were already two towels – a luxurious creamy one, bath-size (presumably Gloria), and a skimpy bottle-green one with gold edging (which might be Priyam, whose clothes often had touches of filigree), plus a mucky cotton washbag in a psychedelic print (which would be Chloe). The surprise was a zip-up leather box, on the floor beneath the sink, spewing bits of shaving kit (Martin muscling in on the girls?) and far too many toothbrushes (who else?).

I didn't dally. Once done – remembering how exposed I'd been on New Year's Day, returning 'the morning after' in full view of anyone who cared to see – I removed all signs of my presence. No point encouraging gossip.

Carreck Loose was waking up. On our floor, there was intermittent chat and water was running again. From downstairs, there were sounds of other people: the odd voice calling – one that might have been Tyler; footsteps scampering; doors opening and closing. Time to brave them all; find out the breakfast routine.

The walkers beat me to the kitchen and it proved to be Hugh who'd accompanied Loxton. It seemed he wasn't the kind of student who rose late, looked dishevelled and grunted a greeting; no, he'd been to church, though it wasn't the right one, and now he was rueing the mud on his trousers and cleaning his shoes. As if God would have cared!

Loxton was formal, rhetorical. 'Good morning, Dr Addleshaw. Did you sleep? Hugh, here, says he was woken. He's not sure which was worse – having a bad dream or it being six o'clock.'

I said something innocuous about sunlight banishing anxieties and set about making coffee. Loxton wouldn't be used to seeing women who'd just got out of bed. It was important to put him at ease, or the mixed event might be doomed.

Unlike the previous evening, the table wasn't laid. Instead, cutlery, and the blue-and-cream crockery Loxton called 'Cornishware', had been put out in piles, along with boxes of cereal and anything that you might want to spread on a slice of toast. Comfortable self-service.

'Brown or white, Dr Addleshaw?' Hugh asked, as his own slices popped up tanned from the machine, smelling of Hovis.

'No, keep them – I'm fine, thanks. I'll help myself later.'

Loxton had *The Times* on his knee, neatly folded to quarter the back page, and was doing the crossword. 'We're always a day behind, at breakfast: no deliveries,' he explained, flapping the paper for emphasis. 'As for the crossword, we have a rule: no peeking and no one else fills it in, but you're all welcome to help.' And he resumed work. He was incredibly quick, pausing occasionally to sip his tea as he considered a clue and then putting his mug down to write in small, tidy capitals, much easier to read than his script. The upper half of the puzzle was already filled in.

He read out a clue – 'Sixteen across: "Kidnapped man? Rocket engineer we hear." Nine letters' – and gave three of them.

Why hadn't the Dean warned me when he mentioned Loxton's work on codes? I was no good at crosswords – my uncle was always ribbing me about it when he came to stay – so this might be embarrassing. At least Hugh was swift with the answer.

'Good.' There was silence while Loxton filled in two of the down clues single-handed. By this time, some of the others had joined us.

'Twenty-one across: "Meant mischievous Matilda, perhaps, and what she did,"' Loxton called out, again without looking up, before adding, 'Dr Addleshaw, perhaps?'

I looked at him crossly, convinced he'd done it on purpose, relieved that Tyler wasn't down to see me stuck. A chair scraped the floor as Eddie settled next to Martin with a not-so-mumbled greeting; the rest of them watched me expectantly. Thankfully Lyndsey, her pale face colouring with enthusiasm, piped up with the answer before the gap became embarrassing. I don't think she was making a point, or even trying to be helpful – mostly, she seemed blithely untouched by the stuff of other peoples' lives. Her complete lack of artifice on this, as on everything else – looking as if she might not know what clothes she'd put on, making absolutely no attempt to charm – was almost comforting. What did Loxton make of that, I wondered – an 'English rose' who failed to do what was expected of the breed? Or was he just impressed by her brain?

By the time the rest had arrived, it seemed we were all focused on Loxton's dratted puzzle. I suppose it acted as a kind of decoy, removing the need for anyone to have a proper conversation, though of course some of us did, and certainly it introduced an element of shared endeavour, even though we didn't all contribute. You could say nothing, occupying yourself with the kettle or the toaster, and nobody noticed; or you could 'chat amongst yourselves', as Tyler was doing with Priyam about some legal issue that interested them both, and ignore the crossword altogether. But you were always aware of it, there in the background like a big piece of furniture, getting in the way.

As for having women there, would it have been so different when it was just men? Probably not. Martin's cry of 'Watch out, women about!' was only a joke. It wasn't as if anyone was making a thing of it, arriving for breakfast dressed like a dolly bird. Only Gloria oozed sexuality, and she was in jeans – she didn't even have to try.

'Last one – well, it's two words,' Loxton announced, and read out a conundrum that made no sense to me but clearly did to Rupert, who got both parts immediately. Loxton checked his watch and noted something in the margin.

'Twenty-two minutes: we'll have to do better than that.' But he said it less with regret than with anticipation of the challenge. The crossword would feature every morning whether I liked it or not; an integral part of domestic routine.

It was also clear that, for Loxton, completing the puzzle marked the end of the period before work. If he could have gone straight to his desk, with the world temporarily tidied, I'm sure he would have done so; a table to clear and crockery to wash were obstacles between him and the most important thing. At home he wouldn't have to worry about such trifles – but then of course there'd be the lonely business of working on his clues and sorting himself out solo. The thought put a slightly different complexion on the tersely determined way in which he used the game to gather company about him. Perhaps that was part of the reason for his attachment to the Reading Party: it gave him companionship – a substitute for family life; it was probably the closest he got to intimacy.

But the students would be different. If *they* weren't minded to move to their desks on the dot of nine, I'd have to do my duty and chase. Hugh should be okay – there was a rumour that he'd brought an alarm clock – and Jim was probably strict in his disciplines. Hard to imagine the same of Rupert or Eddie, who looked the type to amuse themselves as long as they could manage – and Barnaby and Martin were surely too genial to be timekeepers. As for Tyler, I couldn't decide. It was as if the extra couple of years – or being a foreigner – made him inscrutable. He'd be a hard worker, when he chose to settle, but then he didn't defer, so he might not take orders: that combination could go either way.

Easier to speculate about the women. Priyam probably worked to the clock: she would be matter of fact about rhythms. Mei might fear letting herself go – the Dean suggested her discipline neared the pathological. We already had a steer on Lyndsey – she might drift into gear mid-morning, or get up to see in the dawn and then fade in mid-afternoon: that could be difficult. And if Chloe lived up to her reputation, she would be unruly – active when it was dark and quiet; tired and crotchety in the day. As for Gloria, whatever her patterns, I would hesitate to tell her what to do or when.

It wasn't going to be straightforward.

And yet there they all were, rising without a challenge, calling to whoever was holding things up to 'get a move on'. No one demurred or said they needed to do this or that before they settled at their desks. How did Loxton do it? It was a little miracle!

That first day I found it difficult to get started, which was embarrassing, given that I was meant to set an example. There were so many distractions: wondering how the historians were getting on, what exactly Tyler was reading, whether Eddie would come to the village when he was meant to. Or maybe I just happened to have an 'off' day. Whatever the case, it was unnerving not to be able to settle, and I didn't want the Warden as well as Loxton on my back.

Around eleven I gave up and turned my attention to leaving without disturbing the other three, who were still heads down, seemingly absorbed. I'd chosen my spot so as not to encroach, but inadvertently it suggested the position of invigilator. Would they chat as soon as I left?

In fact, they barely noticed me, whereas Eddie made a show of huffing from his sofa as I entered, shut his book and chucked it onto the shamble of belongings that constituted his 'desk'.

All was quiet as we walked through the hall. I felt again uncomfortably like a prefect, although nothing was amiss and Eddie wasn't being hauled in front of anyone, least of all by me.

'Promised I'd help with the dogsbodying!' I whispered.

There were carriers in what must have been the old scullery – a dark and icy space next to the servants' stairs, lit by a small window above a large china sink. It looked like a wartime recycling centre – pickling jars lining the shelves, paper bags hanging from pegs, milk bottle tops here, string there; everything carefully stored. Loxton would have a field day, being of the era and a fusspot to boot.

Eddie scribbled at the kitchen table as I checked the pantry shelves. Just as well – Gloria may have volunteered to cook with Rupert, but their list was remarkably vague; if we'd relied on that, there'd have been hardly any supper at all. He'd bragged that he'd never peeled a potato: probably true, I thought, banging about – there were plenty who hadn't. And she was so casual. If you offered to help, you should do it properly; having *asked* to come, you should pull your weight.

Of course we couldn't find what they wanted, on a Sunday. The village 'shop' was a small operation serving as post office, newsagent and emergency store. It still had its domestic curtains, together with velour wall lamps; was as much a relic of times past as our pink and black-tiled bathroom – almost quaint.

Eddie and I squeezed through to a tiny second room, which had a few shelves of groceries, a large freezer and some scraps of fruit and veg.

'This is unreal!' he exclaimed. His granny specs looked out of place in that setting: perfect spheres conjuring John Lennon where Lennon didn't belong.

'Never mind,' I said, trying to remember if I'd seen Tyler in glasses. 'They can improvise – it's not a competition. Anyway, there's nowhere else today.'

Eddie having shopped, it was Mei and I who got lunch ready. This division of labour now bothered me, though it had been my suggestion; there should have been at least *one* man on his feet. But Mei didn't seem to mind. She arrived in the kitchen unprompted as we thumped our booty down on the table; said nothing when Eddie, his part 'done', disappeared with a cavalier 'I'll get back to work, then'; and began, unasked, to put things away.

When the boys and I were children, I realised, Mum must have faced a similar conundrum. One of us would always have been wriggling out of the task we'd been allotted, were it not for her vigilance and her sense of fair play. Somehow she contrived always to know what we planned to do before we actually did it. When we reached for the door she'd call out, 'Remember to bring me the such and such!' as if we'd only momentarily forgotten. Then, when the job was done, she'd tell us to 'run along, and don't get into mischief', like little Peter Rabbits who needed permission to leave. She kept the upper hand even where we'd hoped to best her – and, remarkably, on quite a few things it was gender-neutral.

This was the knack that I had to acquire, or some modern and adult equivalent of it, if the jobs were going to be shared fairly. Meanwhile, Mei and I set to.

'I haven't got used to the cold,' she confided, stooping to pick up a lettuce leaf, her light twinset gaping as she bent over. Underneath was a thin fringe of lace with a satin bow suggesting a vest such as I'd worn as a child; she was virtually flat-chested – the peep of bra would be padding.

'Remember you arrived in a heatwave,' I said, sounding horribly like Loxton. 'Last summer wasn't typical. You'll catch cold in a top like that.'

I went off to find a proper jumper. The polo neck I brought down was voluminous on her tiny frame – as outsize as my boyfriends' jumpers had been on me – but she kept it on, saying she liked the way I always looked relaxed. It had been difficult, she said, learning what to wear and how to shop, despite the prepping at an international school. She didn't want to ask the family she lodged with in the holidays, and she'd tried exploring during term, but the other student on the Hong Kong programme was male; she might ask for Priyam's help, but hadn't done so yet. There was so much work to do, to deserve the opportunity she'd been given, and there'd been so little time ...

So her scholarship was even more of a burden than Tyler's! What a fearful thing, to be so alone and so determined.

By one o'clock we'd laid out a traditional 'ploughman's lunch', as I told Mei, explaining that we would eat it as if we were down the pub with our friends, reading the Sunday papers, talking politics, arguing about what to do next. Goodness knows what she thought of the messiness of it when they all tipped up – people chatting over each another, the cheeseboard getting stuck down the table, no one paying attention. It was a bit of a free-for-all.

Rupert began talking again about the Oxford Union debate, but it seemed only he and Gloria had seen it. It was only when they spelt out the details that the others began to pay attention. Jim was quick to say that he hated even the idea of the place. Barnaby thought it was puerile lining up Paul Gambaccini, who'd always been good on the John Peel show, against an old soak like Auberon Waugh. But Martin was amused by the motion Ms Bhutto had chosen, that 'This House Likes Dominating Women'. We should have it again, he said: he and Rupe could lead the two sides.

I didn't warm to the Union either, but this sounded fun, so the two of us won Loxton round – he was always worrying about the clock – and debate it we did. For simplicity, we split the table down the middle: the far end, led by Rupert, with Eddie and Gloria embellishing the *double entendres*, arguing for; the near end, with Martin backed loudly by Chloe and Tyler, arguing against; words like 'virago' and 'dominatrix' featuring heavily. I was pleased: there was meant to be larking and now there was. But I worried about Mei. What was an innocent Chinese girl, parachuted in from Hong Kong, meant to make of such horseplay?

After lunch we set off for a proper walk to enjoy the sun. It was Loxton's idea, building on the enthusiasm of the day before.

Perhaps we should have been clearer in our guidance about what to bring. Only half the group had what Loxton considered proper walking gear. Interestingly, Gloria's boots were well broken in, like my own; the rest of the women were dismayingly ill-shod for the occasion. As for the men, even Hugh, who knew the conditions, was still in the heavy lace-ups he'd been cleaning earlier in the day: perhaps he was one of those impoverished Catholic aristocrats whose richer relations underwrote the cost of a monastic school. Loxton's glance flickered over the down-at-heel cowboy boots (Lyndsey), the velvet loons (Eddie) and the long coats (Rupert and Chloe) as he checked we had everyone with us, but he didn't comment – and of course there was nothing to be said now we were there, other than to hope it stayed dry. Still, on impulse I suggested we raid the battered wellies and parkas that lined the boot room, and that held me up.

I'd hoped to walk with Tyler, whom I'd still barely talked to – something about not wanting to be conspicuous – but as the fourteen of us started off down the drive I got caught with Hugh and Lyndsey. Easy to feel thwarted. They were in the middle of a discussion about the library and how the harbourmaster might have used it: all very earnest. Now Lyndsey, who had been walking head down, negotiating minor puddles, had stopped to stare at Hugh, astonished at a reply.

'But would you *want* to have all the books in one place?' she asked, as we moved onto the grass.

Hugh didn't seem to understand the problem. 'If they were

my books, yes, why not, and especially if they were important.' He carried on, as if there could be no other logic, all
the while fiddling with the collar of his donkey jacket – a
ridiculously bulky object on him – in the effort to keep the
wind off. 'I mean, it would be a bit odd to go all over the
house whenever you wanted a reference. Besides, he'd have
treated it as his study.'

'What about the little room, where Jim is?'

'Well, we're *calling* that the study, but we don't *know* how
the house was used, do we? That's one of the first things you
learn in philosophy: the difference between what is *perceived*
and what actually *is*.'

I stepped in to pre-empt a disquisition on appearance and
reality – it seemed even more incongruous in the middle of a
sunny hillside – and turned to gesture in the direction of the
house, still just visible above the slope behind us. 'We should
put this in its social context: a society organised around men.
Probably the morning room – where Gloria and Chloe are
sitting – was where the man of the house received visitors,
with the study used rather as we would use an office, for him
to do business. That would leave the library as his private
space where people didn't intrude. Let's ask Dr Loxton what
the family knows.' And I waved him over.

'Some pad!' Lyndsey sounded almost aggrieved. She raised
her voice against the blow from the sea. 'Imagine having
three rooms, all devoted to you. I'd never had my own before
Oxford – my dad kept loads of stuff in mine at home.' She
paused, then carried on, 'But it sounds so compartmentalised.
Don't you like the unexpected? I like looking up and seeing
things I didn't know were there – not having it orderly all
the time.'

Loxton arrived. He did indeed know more. 'I think he was
an "orderly" man, Lyndsey,' he said, with a little puff from
the effort of catching us up. 'You may like to imagine him as

a swashbuckling adventurer, running boats from Falmouth to the East Indies, making the family fortune, but actually he was an official – ran the Packet Service, carrying mail across the empire. And only a tolerable administrator could have handled the paperwork for a top fishing harbour, as he did when he returned to Mevagissey. Dr Addleshaw could tell you that.'

He didn't wait for confirmation. 'Carreck Loose, built when he retired, merely reflected his status. He'd had an important public role; people would have pestered him. Even coming out here, to such an isolated spot, he'd have been surrounded by children, servants, visitors. I imagine he saw it as a retreat, but things were still expected of you. That, surely, would be the reason for all those rooms.'

Really, Loxton could be quite the social historian.

We moved off down again, bracing ourselves against the gradient, pondering the kind of man the harbourmaster might have been. Tyler had joined the conversation, I noticed; he was now on Hugh's far side.

'If you had a study, Lyndsey, what sort of space would it be?' I asked, thinking momentarily of my uncle who said his own domestic cubbyhole made him feel like 'a Cambridge man', despite not having been there.

'Of my own, you mean? Cool! But would I want a "study"?' She was doing her considering thing again, swiping tufts of grass with those incongruous cowboy boots. 'I might like a space that was mine, but not one that was just books, though of course there'd be lots of them around. I'd have to have, you know, bits of fabric, postcards, "found" things, and paints and brushes too. A space where I could do anything, really.' And she trailed off, clearly musing – visualising something and trying to work out what it was. 'Like a junk shop, but full of my own stuff – a treasure trove of me.'

'What about you, Tyler?' I asked.

'Sure, I'd have one. But perhaps not a treasure trove: that would be distracting. Besides, if people came in I might want to keep something in reserve.'

I'd have probed on what he meant, but Hugh got in first, asking about my set in College and whether it was any different from the men's.

'I don't think so. We all have a room that's a combination of all three,' I said. 'Morning room, study and library rolled into one. It's where you lot come for tutorials, it's where I work and yes, it's where I keep my books.'

'So they haven't made any allowances?'

'Why should they, Hugh? My needs are no different,' I said.

'But women like sewing and things – you know, domestic stuff. I assumed they'd give you a special place.'

'Hugh!'

Tyler stepped in. 'And what about privacy?' he asked.

'Good question,' I began, wondering why he asked it. 'It's a challenge: people visit all the time. Even when I'm alone, it can be hard to have it as the backdrop for my own thoughts – images and bits of conversation from the times when it's busy tend to float back in.'

'That's just what I meant.' Hugh seemed oblivious. He was nodding just above my field of vision, his chin dipping gently in and out of my frame of the clifftop, the sea and the green, just when I wanted to finish the line of thought with Tyler. 'The harbourmaster had a space to receive people and a space where he was left alone. He got Jim's room too, because it was in the middle – a link between the two worlds.' He turned to face us, wind blowing his hair across his face, stumbling backwards over little hillocks of yellowed grass as he walked. 'Not bad – I mean, you could really get on with things.'

It struck me then, watching the gulls and listened to the waves, savouring the tangy smell and the buffeting of the wind, that this exchange nicely proved the point: the personal was *always* political. It was men who expected studies and places for billiards, and women who were amazed to get their 'room of one's own'. Hugh was not only inept; he had completely misunderstood. If anything, *he* was the one who should be reading Virginia Woolf, not Lyndsey. Better still, he could read Kate Millett or Germaine Greer. And so could Loxton.

Tyler, of course, would have read them already, or the American equivalent – someone like Betty Friedan; he would know exactly what I meant. It was there in his face, in that hint of amusement.

As they deposited their gear in the boot room, I asked what the students were reading. Almost without exception, the books were written by men. Precisely! But it wasn't the moment to make a thing of it: everyone was primed to pick up where they'd left off; it wasn't fair to distract them.

There was a brief transitional period as we settled around the kitchen table in our socks, enjoying the warmth from the stove, the bumper pack of chocolate digestives and our mugs of builders' tea. It continued in the hall, with people disappearing to the loo or to change muddy clothes, which led to a fair bit of calling out and joshing. But as soon as we returned to our posts, quiet descended again.

I had to admire Loxton for the way he marshalled us. He hadn't asked anyone to do anything; he certainly hadn't instructed. Yet, without our noticing, he'd again got us up from our chairs and down the corridor – and then, magically, we were back reading! It really was a mystery.

Tyler had said it was a bit like that in Loxton's tutorials. He was nicely modest about it. Apparently Loxton rarely pronounced on the topic he set, preferring to prompt his students to greater clarity. The way Tyler put it, it was as if Loxton perceived your more interesting thoughts before you knew you had them and then did you the honour of taking them seriously. If you had genuinely struggled to write something useful, that marshalling of your argument could be extraordinarily enlightening. But if someone had just knocked their essay together, it was excruciating. Not in a vindictive way, designed to make them feel bad, just mercilessly dispassionate, exposing the emptiness of what they had said.

Tyler likened it to an autopsy: the words had died and the students and Loxton were engaged in the forensic task of establishing what might have been wrong with them. You weren't meant to take it personally, although of course it was hard not to. It was completely different from university teaching in the States.

Looking up at the window, it occurred to me that I too had been marshalled by Loxton; I certainly hadn't been marshaller. I'd trailed at the rear of the group leaving the kitchen, enjoying that second patch of conversation with Tyler when I was meant to be more like a shepherd, rounding up the stray sheep.

The trouble was, it was so *easy* to be beguiled into thinking, feeling, behaving like the students, and so *hard* to do the don bit with conviction. I almost resented the effort required to jump another hurdle. And yet, this was what joining the ranks of the dons was about. There was now a 'them', represented by the bowed heads in front of me, and an 'us', which was me at the end of the table, or Loxton at his, and I had to remember that I'd switched sides. I wasn't meant to enjoy the students' company too much.

As for the analogy of a postmortem, I was just glad Loxton wouldn't be 'peer-reviewing' *my* paper. As currently drafted, it would never get through.

Needless to say, it was Loxton who got the cooks underway: he was the one who came to the door when Rupert was needed in the kitchen and, when we all sat down to eat, it was he who gave Gloria credit for volunteering them both as our first pair of cooks. I felt a little marginalised, but I didn't know how to right the balance; neither Loxton's equal nor one of the students, I was awkwardly in-between.

As we gathered around the table I got sandwiched – I'm not sure how it happened – between Rupert and Tyler, who were comparing culinary skills, Tyler bending forward so he wasn't chatting rudely across me. The banter continued once we were seated, a bit too cosily – I was very conscious of his thigh alongside mine, unavoidably pressing; the square jaw and the wavy locks disarmingly near to the soft of my cheek and the peach of my hair. It was soon clear that the cooks had little experience in the kitchen. Rupert even bragged about it, saying that at home, his mum produced TV dinners; living out, a succession of girlfriends and housemates had cooked for whoever was around, roping him in to chop the odd vegetable because he was good company, not because he knew what to do with them once chopped. No humility there, then.

'I'm particularly good at carrots,' he said, taking a steaming oval serving bowl from Gloria, who'd been pulling dishes from the base of the Rayburn. He indicated with his chin the mound of orange coins, their outer rings lighter than their middles, glistening where a knob of butter had melted: 'I bet you've never even thought about the difference between having them sliced, diced or cut into neat little strips. Well, just wait and see – there's more to it than you might think. Ever made a carrot flower?'

Tyler and I shook our heads and watched as the splash of colour and the smell of something caramelising was sent further down the table. Then Rupert was back at my side, gesticulating over my head with his tea towel.

'You should read a few recipe books! No need to cook; just know the names. There's one here, *The Cookery Year*, with all the translations. We're having them "*braisée au beurre*" tonight, not to be confused with "*carottes glacées*".'

On my other side, Tyler was passing serving spoons to his neighbour. 'Rupert's very particular,' he said, leaning into me, although we were already very close, talking just loud enough to be heard by the others. 'Everything's orthogonal. He lines his toothbrush up with the toothpaste and then his razor with his shaving cream, and he lines them up again – just so – if you muck them about.'

Rupert grinned, running his fingers through his hair as if determined to enjoy the pleasure while it lasted; already it receded gently on either side of his forehead – he'd look like my father in no time. 'Standards, man! You and Lyndsey may not have any, but Mei and I are fastidious.'

He called across the table to Mei and asked if hers was the dainty washbag in their bathroom, so orderly inside. A couple of people stopped talking; Mei looked taken aback.

'Have you been peeking into other people's belongings, Rupert?' I asked, wondering if I'd have to take this up with him and still distracted by the closeness of the chairs. 'That's not fair. Besides, you're meant to be using the loo across the corridor.'

'Oh, but that's such a drag! Anyway, why ever not? The bag's sitting there; she hasn't taken it away. Very revealing – very chaste. Lyndsey's was equally disappointing – hardly a washbag at all: no unguents, none of those little pots of coloured stuff that Gloria has, whereas Tyler's has things I've never seen before, which must come from the US. Perhaps someone sends them over.'

It was nonchalant showing off – like the speedboat we'd seen on our walk, flashing across the bay without regard for the wake – as well as a gross invasion of privacy. And he didn't let up: 'Is it your girl, Tyler, or does your mommy do parcels from home? Hey, have some of my sprouts: they're crossed at the bottom – that's how we do them here.'

Rupert, too, was insufferable. His parents were probably no

grander than mine, but you'd never know it. At least Eddie was properly posh.

Tyler ignored both question and jibe, and carried on teasing about Rupert's habits. Their room faced two ways: over the garden and over the courtyard. Who did I think had the bed with the best view? Rupert, of course, on the grounds that Tyler, having sacrificed a place at the front of the house for the sake of gallantry, clearly wasn't fussed. He was a demanding roommate and you had to fight your corner: Tyler was becoming messier by the minute, in retaliation. He was quite funny about it.

By this time Gloria was passing plates again and Rupert interrupted afresh to explain what we were eating. I forget exactly what it was meant to be – he had a complicated French name for a layering of potato and cheese, vaguely reminiscent of a side dish served on High Table, which Martin called 'veggie hot pot to you and me'. It seemed to have shrivelled in the cooking, which was oddly comforting.

Tyler too looked as if he was, again, trying not to smile. We tackled the crunch on the top – more of the Red Leicester, burnt bitter and almost black – and he and I began swapping notes on what we'd brought to work on. He was halfway through a book on systems of justice by a fellow American, which he said was a good bridge between political philosophy and what he'd do later – law in some guise. He was interesting about it; made it not sound dry. I talked about my article and Ivy Williams's battles with what seemed, with hindsight, the ludicrously retrograde legal profession of the time, about which he asked some good questions. He would have been in Loxton's category of 'a pleasure to teach' – anyone my age would have had to work hard to stay ahead of him – but it wasn't easy to have a proper conversation. First there was too much crossfire; then noisy applause as Gloria made a show of serving her pudding. After that, it would have been too obvious to continue; our end of the table moved into discussion of the relative merits of pastry and crumble and the moment was gone.

There was outcry when someone asked who was playing whom at chess. Whoever it was – Hugh, probably – was quickly shouted down. Board games were too 'tame' – more exciting diversion was called for.

Ideas were batted around with an increasing undertow of double entendre. Martin, who had lots of layers on under his fisherman's smock, suggested strip poker; Chloe, who wore fewer, launched volubly into the trap. There was a loud argument about the objectification of women, which quickly embraced both the provision of condoms in the College loos (in the men's only) and the outrage of Miss World in the Royal Albert Hall (hosted, to compound the offence, by old crooners like Sacha Distel and Andy Williams). Martin continued with a maddening stance that was clearly not serious; Chloe, full of *Spare Rib*-style fury, tried to enlist me – and then, just as swiftly, refused to engage further. I was two-faced, she said, qualified support a betrayal. Even to discuss the matter with him was to accept his terms of reference, you shouldn't give in to sexism, and so on.

It was a relief she didn't move onto the absence of female historians, on which she'd already taken me to task. She'd accused me of being a 'faint-hearted feminist', like the journalist who'd coined the phrase. No need to tell her I read Jill Tweedie religiously – Chloe already had it in for me. And now, likewise, best to let the matter rest.

Loxton may have thought things were getting out of hand, but he didn't say so. Somehow he contrived matters so that instead of drifting off to play blind man's buff and grope at our companions, as Martin had suggested, we stayed in the warmth of the kitchen and turned to paper games. Possibly the unexpected appearance of a couple of bottles of claret did the trick. I think Tyler had a hand in that – he certainly helped open the crate. Whatever the case, the rebellion fizzled out. And maybe staying put was the right thing to do; if we'd decamped so early in the proceedings, the spell might break just when it was beginning to take effect.

It was Barnaby, not Loxton, who suggested the dictionary game. He said he used to play it with his cousins in the holidays, which was revealing – I'd assumed he went home to his parents, who were posted abroad. Anyway, Jim said there was a big Cassell's in the study but someone should clarify the rules, and Hugh, ever decent, 'reminded everyone' about identifying the one correct definition amidst the fake ones. We were all set.

I, too, had played as a child, but playing with strangers is much more revealing. You don't know who will be good at lying or dissimulation – or, for that matter, who can ape the language of a lexicographer. I expected Hugh to be good at it, classicists being better versed than most in declensions and the like – and he was, but his definitions were predictable. Martin was better, because his were both plausible and slightly risqué. Lyndsey was better still, conjuring obscure meanings that were both convincing and haphazardly preposterous, but she was no good at reading them out, having nothing of the performer about her. Gloria, by contrast, was a brilliant mimic. You might have to wait a minute or two, as she wouldn't say anything until she'd memorised the words, but then she'd deliver as if at an audition, adopting all manner of regional accents – Cockney, Yorkshire, Somerset: she knew them all – for comic effect. And she did all of this deadpan, however much the rest of us cracked up, until she relaxed out of the part. She was so good, it was almost worrying – if she took it into her head to deceive us, we would all be 'had'.

After that it was hard to know how to carry on. The group

by the conservatory switched to consequences. Barnaby started fiddling with one of the candles, letting loose a pool of hot wax that drifted dangerously across the table. Loxton took the opportunity to collar someone to help with the washing-up. Meanwhile our end of the table split into separate conversations, and Tyler and I could talk more comfortably, chairs turned inwards, arms draped over their backs.

He said he found these word games very English, though what he considered 'foreign' – our use of language or our sense of humour – I wasn't sure. He clearly loved the accents and it was that – me exaggerating my Norfolk burr – that led us to the more personal. It turned out he was brought up in San Francisco, though his parents were often elsewhere on business, so they were utterly different from mine. He said he nearly didn't take up the scholarship, not because it was irksome – and there was another smile there – but because it meant postponing his legal training until he was twenty-five. In fact, he was glad that he had. He could see more of Europe, which he'd largely missed in his gap year, and reassess the favoured track of Harvard, Oxford, back to Harvard for law school and then on to one of the big East Coast firms. He still thought he might reject family tradition – do the doctorate he'd mentioned here or in the States and then look for a teaching post. He had a small window – diminishing by the day – in which to decide.

There was a pause while he fiddled with a knobble of the burnt cheese, spinning it round with his fingertips. Then he reverted to our conversation in the Christmas vac, probing about my opting for academia. So I told him how, at the beginning of my third year when the 'milk round' started and we were being wooed by potential employers, I'd been unable to imagine anything other than doing a doctorate. Although it might seem an odd thing for a tutor to confide, I talked about the men in my family being into science and the assumption that women were in support roles; that apart from my uncle, who as a journalist was the odd one out, no one had a feel for the humanities; how encouraging he'd always been about my successes – getting the bursary for school, doing so well in my degree, being offered another full grant, seeing my book in print. I even mentioned how kindly my uncle had listened when I phoned after the letters from Oxford arrived. I'd been astonished – and terrified – at the notion that you were allowed to climb the ranks until you were nearly seventy, and he'd reassured me about living up to it all. All that just spilled out, as if no-go areas didn't exist.

Tyler said he admired my determination to do my own thing; he was in danger of having decisions taken for him. He even said something about radicalism, I suppose based on the bits of oral history in my monograph, or on what I'd said in those lectures. I thought that was overdoing it – people like Studs Terkel, a hero of mine whom he claimed to have read, had started long before me – but I was flattered. It was disconcerting to enjoy talking so much; he might be clever and handsome, but he was a student, after all, and I was not.

Still we carried on, discussing the difference between being temperamentally radical (which I liked to think I was – though people are always confusing feminism with radicalism) and finding that timing had landed you in the vanguard (which had definitely happened to me). He said he had his own internal debate. He felt he might be progressive as a thinker in academia; he wasn't sure you could do the same as a practitioner in one of those big law firms, and he might not like a smaller one – that was why the decision was difficult. I said I didn't know him – or them – well enough to comment, which was probably a good thing, considering how long we'd been talking. Gloria had her head lowered to her neighbour and was whispering again. She'd been watching. What had she heard?

*

Tyler's reference to radicalism came back into my mind later on, climbing my way carefully up the servants' stairs to the safety of my little attic, and merged with ideas about Loxton and his preference for the status quo.

He was a bit like those bourgeois politicians of the 1840s, making little accommodations with the masses in the attempt to stave off revolution. That night, with his wine and his willingness to play a different game, he'd bought the students off successfully, without them even registering. But in future he might not adjust fast enough and then they could rise up against him – as I'd tried to do with my teachers in '68, organising a protest about a rule we found offensive from the safety of the school assembly hall.

If that were to happen at Carreck Loose, with Loxton and the students at loggerheads, would I be expected to mediate? And if not, on which side of the barricades should I be?

Monday

You couldn't hear the sea from my bedroom – well, you couldn't exactly *hear* it from any part of the house; it was just that bit too far away and of course we had the windows shut because of the cold – but the air was different.

Oxford had been dank when we left – musty, like an old floorcloth abandoned in a cellar. Sometimes, waking in College, I would walk the few clammy steps to my window seat and open the curtains, just to watch the early morning in the front quad. The mist often seemed to collect there as if poured from above, and the lights above the staircase entrances would look strangely spectral, like drops of brightness seeping into dirty water. The damp oozed everywhere and hung there; you were steeped in it.

Whereas Carreck Loose was absolutely icy. It made you think about the drudgery required of the servants when the harbourmaster had the house built: carting wood and coal about and laying fires in the early morning, carrying jugs of hot water up the stairs to fill the washbowls. But at least the cold was a clean, dry cold; brisk, bracing, almost stinging – you could do battle with it.

On went the rusty bar heater. I got back into bed and listened to the sporadic crackle as the filaments gradually turned the colour of smoked salmon and the room lost its edge. Would it have been better under a duvet, like that huge thing of the Dean's? Possibly, but I liked the weight of the three blankets – tightly woven, coarse and almost sticky, as if the natural oils of the wool had yet to be washed out – and the quilt. Nothing had come adrift; whoever made the beds before we arrived knew how to do a 'hospital corner' and it was still intact.

As the scout on my staircase told the story, when the first female students arrived in College, he and his colleagues – still mostly male – had said they should drop this part of their duties. Their logic? That the women knew how to make beds and would naturally make their own, and if the scouts weren't going to do it for them. then why do it for the men? According to him there was quite a tussle: the Student Liaison Committee got involved and there were discussions about whether the charges on battels, for board at the College, should drop to reflect the change in service. He didn't see anything offensive – on the contrary, I think he was proud of taking a stance. And in a way it *was* progressive: why should the students have such things done for them? Why should anyone? He was absolutely right on that score. It was the assumption that the girls would, even *should*, know how to make a bed that got me. Of course they should, but why did it take their arrival to say the same about boys?

None of my colleagues had mentioned the saga: they probably didn't dare. But someone like Tyler would have seen and enjoyed the humour in the situation: he'd have recognised a tradition that had passed its day.

Mum must have shown me how to make a bed – no one else changed the sheets when we were small. Would she have told me the tricks from her nursing days or would I have picked them up from seeing it done so many times? Either way, to her credit – for she was no feminist and hated me banging on about these things – on that point too my brothers got no special treatment. But perhaps we weren't typical.

It was hard to imagine Gloria being taught at home – they'd have had a housekeeper in England, just like Carreck Loose until a few years back, and then staff in Peru and all those other places they passed through; at best, she'd have picked it up at boarding school.

The attics included some extraordinary sleeping contraptions, worthy of proper scrutiny. Mine had a traditional metal frame, but not brass. The black ironwork at the head and the feet was dull, rusty and flaking; it was a bit like lying between a pair of old gates. I thought of all the maids, endlessly airing the mattresses or tucking in the sheets, whose workaday hands had banged into the hard metal, scraping their knuckles and ripping their cuticles, year in and year out. Only a man could have designed a detail so unkind. All it needed was a curved edge.

Someone should write a social history of the bed.

Martin was on the landing, by the door to the stairs, when I surfaced.

'Your things have gone,' I said. 'Have you been ousted?' His washbag, with its whiff of Old Spice, had disappeared.

'No one ousts me,' he said. 'I've defected to the men's side, to keep the peace between Eddie and Jim. Anyway, Gloria takes an age – likes to bask. Blokes with beards are swift.'

As if on cue, Eddie crossed the floor in the bedroom beyond, miming horror at being caught with only a towel round his middle like an actor playing someone camp. He was a bit long in the body, the area of the abdominals almost concave. Not one to pass muster with Jenny, socks or no socks!

Martin turned back from the spectacle, unmoved. 'I'm planning an egg. Dr Loxton doesn't seem to do eggs, but I'm an egg man myself. Must be all those chickens at home.'

We clattered down our little cavity, our hands gathering dust from the walls and the stair treads – me again pitying the poor maids, who'd warranted no handrail – and stepped out onto the landing.

'Ah, Tyler. I'm sure you're an egg-eater. Sunny side up?' Tyler nodded – he looked as if he'd only just dressed: the eyes childlike; the soft hair rumpled; his chin slightly raw from shaving – and gave again that almost hidden smile.

'Whereas Rupert here,' and Martin clapped him rather too forcefully on the back, 'claims to prefer thin toast and that very fine marmalade. Isn't that so, Rupe?'

Rupert said something about having had enough of fatty cooked breakfasts. The four of us carried on down the main stairs, discussing the pros and cons of 'having the works'.

In the kitchen, Jim was cracking a couple of eggs into a cast-iron dish that was warming on the stove. 'Want to add any?'

It was amusing to watch. Martin and Jim were clearly used to sorting themselves out, whereas Rupert hung about, leaning against one bit of furniture and then another, as if waiting for things to happen – probably for food to appear.

Tyler was handing out tumblers he'd part-filled from a carton of fruit juice. He was considerate, like Hugh; you couldn't fault him on that. It was almost annoying. I wanted him to loosen up, to stop being so polite.

'Orange, Sarah?' he asked, and seeing Rupert look up, added, 'Hey, we're allowed to call you that, aren't we?' And he carried on pouring and handing round.

'Of course,' I said to his back, now unsettled, as he stretched across the table. Then I added, 'But I'd be careful about calling Dr Loxton "Dennis". Best not to presume.'

'Yeah, but he doesn't mind. He suggested I call him that at the end of our first tutorial.' He waved a glass in the opposite direction. 'Hugh, you call him Dennis don't you?'

Over the other side of the table, Hugh nodded. 'But I don't think Chloe does.'

That seemed unlikely, but Tyler didn't see it that way. 'He's more formal with women, then,' he said. 'Swell.'

He turned back to me. 'So what do your students call you?'

I was still thinking about Loxton and his odd inconsistencies and for a moment forgot what Tyler had asked. As it happens, I couldn't recall discussing names with any of the students – only debating it with Jenny.

'We call her Sarah.' Jim, oven-cloth in hand, was on his haunches checking the dial on the Rayburn. 'She suggested it.'

'Did I really?' I had no picture of the occasion.

'Yeah. You said in your family "Dr Addleshaw" was assumed to mean one of your brothers. You were pretty cross about it.'

'They call you other things too, of course,' said Martin. 'What was it Barny said? The "thinking man's crumpet", like that woman on television. Quite a compliment, really.'

I wasn't sure about this. The Dean had called Joan Bakewell 'the Bakewell Tart', and then wound me up with a claim that I was 'Histotty' to some of my colleagues, which was even worse – not least as he was capable of doing the coining. The ensuring spat – I'd remonstrated; he'd said I had no sense of humour – had been definitive.

But perhaps 'crumpet' wasn't such a bad nickname to have amongst students, especially from one as likeable as Barnaby. It could have been worse.

'Lay off. You'll embarrass her,' said Jim, 'and him.' He was almost protective.

'Never,' said Martin, and he gave me another of his winks. 'Sarah's above embarrassment – she's far too worldly. Anyway, Barny needs embarrassing.'

'Are they embarrassing you, Sarah?' Tyler asked, passing me tea.

'Not a bit,' I teased back. 'Besides, Barnaby's a catch. It's the blue Guernsey: he's got that rugged sailor look.'

After that little exchange – why say that to Tyler, of all people? – it was a relief to escape to my reading.

Loxton wanted the two of us to move around – it was his way of policing. The act of carrying my things to the drawing room set me pondering again how the house used to function, looking for clues. That door, for instance: it was a normal one, whereas the ones to the study were made to look like a continuation of the wall. Why? After the evening meal, had the women of the house always withdrawn to sit with their needlework and their sketches, leaving the men to talk over cigars and port? Perhaps the family hadn't bothered with such formalities – would there have been much entertaining in such an out-of-the-way location? And what about the servants – when had they been allowed to retire? It was a puzzle, like the harbourmaster himself. I wanted to work it all out.

Back in the present, Eddie had swapped the sofa for an armchair and had his legs draped over the side, a new colour of sock clearly visible. He looked languid yet absorbed, his face oddly childlike despite the stubble. Amazingly, he was still – though stillness might be another act, a ploy he was trying out for size.

Mei was at her little table, surrounded by neat notes. She used an ordinary pencil like mine, except that she stuck one of those awful plastic figures on the end, and kept a piece of paper for the shavings, carefully creased so the lead collected in the middle, whereas I spilled and smudged everywhere. Such precision!

Barnaby, my supposed admirer, couldn't settle. First it was the games table, which can't have been quite level and had him crouching underneath to find the fault; then it was the pile of books, which were endlessly shuffled and then thumped to the floor. Perhaps I should have recommended one of the women after all; at least they were diligent.

What was Tyler's quip about historians and their reading habits? Something about being like the lawyers – always skimming. Doing moral or political theory, as he was now, he said you got reading lists of only three or four articles, but soon learnt it was a good day when you got through a dozen pages. That was endearing. It was that same modesty; he didn't make a thing of being brainy.

I settled into a cushioning of chintz and suddenly it was mid-morning, Loxton collecting shoppers, Barnaby helping with the coffee. Good to see Loxton allowing it – perverse of him to like bracing walks but rule against stretching your legs, and Barnaby did seem to work better after that, though he was always fiddling with something: worrying at his scalp, scratching a shin, or stroking the back of that bronzed neck. I wanted to catch his hands, pin them down and say, 'Stop that!' as Dad had done with me when my skin flared. But although Barnaby joshed with the women, he didn't invite touching. Odd, for a guy so straightforwardly good-looking: you'd have thought he'd be used to intimacy.

When later we all trooped into the kitchen for lunch, Eddie was making fun of Loxton's shopping habits with Mei silently looking on. Apparently, they'd been to both Mevagissey greengrocers, Loxton having a favoured supplier but needing to check the competition. According to Eddie, he was a demanding customer – fruit and veg often described as 'disappointing', like an unsatisfactory student – and would itemise deficiencies for the purpose of instruction in what 'good' looked like. Mei now knew how to distinguish a bad apple from a good one, and would be screening all produce for the duration.

Funny though the story was, it seemed pretty far-fetched – Loxton was much too polite – but Eddie was less concerned with the truth than with making us laugh. He ignored Mei's protests about exaggeration – brave of her, I thought – and carried on with his mimicry until he had several of us clutching our middles, urging him to stop; even Tyler, who could look a bit polished, rather too dignified, was chuckling away. When Loxton came back, Eddie made no concession to his arrival and delivered his punchline with such aplomb that Loxton could hardly get crusty – in fact he remained remarkably good-humoured throughout the meal, telling the odd anecdote about past Reading Parties and entertaining us in his own reserved way. Easy to see why Tyler thought of him as the quintessential 'English gentleman'.

It may have been a function of it being the second proper day, or maybe it was getting used to the presence of women: anyway, Loxton had palpably relaxed. Perhaps, now that we'd got the hang of what Carreck Loose had to offer, he felt he could leave us to it. The tinge of hysteria from our first evening had segued into more sustainable low-level banter – Loxton and I often included in it. Suddenly everyone was proposing things we might all do and Loxton wasn't objecting.

That afternoon it was surprisingly still outside – pines almost motionless, plants upright, blue sky – and Rupert asked about the tennis court, which looked as if it needed to be used. A dull ochre mould was creeping in from the edge where it was too close to the shrubs, and the lines were fading into the asphalt, which had bleached to pale grey – Jenny's parents would have been appalled.

Loxton said it was a long time since anyone had played on the Reading Party and he couldn't remember whether the racquets were kept in the house or the outhouses, but he didn't say "no", so Rupert and Gloria set off to track them down while the rest of us cleared the table. They came back when we were finishing coffee, having located a 'sports room' in the old stables. Apparently there was lots of ancient kit – wooden racquets with catgut strings, a rounders set with four markers, even croquet – and the adjoining horsebox was stacked with bicycles. They were loud with the possibilities.

Eventually Gloria sat down, still looking hot, charged even – her skin luminous, almost glistening. Abruptly, she changed the subject. 'And this place is full of cupboards and wardrobes. How many did we find upstairs, Rupe? Everyone seems to have one.'

'God knows. Somebody liked buying those ugly Victorian things; there's nothing new. Dr Loxton has a vast one, the kind with a bank of drawers in the middle and a shelf where the valet could lay things out. Not that we peered in *there*.'

I should hope not, I thought, glancing for Loxton's reaction: how cheeky can you be? And what else had they been up to?

Lyndsey leant into the table, jiggling like an excited child: 'I know just what you mean! So roomy you feel they might expand, like the Tardis, or take you elsewhere, like the one that goes to Narnia.' She looked around. 'D'you remember that book, *The Lion, the Witch and the Wardrobe*? I read that so many times. I'd definitely have been Lucy. Weren't they playing sardines or something?'

Gloria seemed to snap back into attention. '*Voilà*! We could play sardines, or murder in the dark!' She turned to Loxton, her face alight. 'This is the perfect place. After supper one day? Our last night, p'rhaps. Fab!'

Pushing the boundaries again, just as I would have done. You had to admire her nerve. If she could get that past him, it would be quite a change from chess.

*

Rupert went back to retrieve the racquets, taking Lyndsey and Priyam to check the state of the bicycles, while Loxton mapped out another walk for those interested in seeing the village on foot. His plan was to start out on the drive with the cyclists and then cross the fields to the coastal path. I meant to join the walkers, but Rupert had roped half the men in to play doubles – funny how they stuck to type and went into a huddle centred on sport; even Tyler did it – and Gloria wanted support, so I switched to tennis.

It was a good court. Full size, facing the right way and, although the surface was ropey, the tarmac was still sound; only once did a ball land on a pimple where something was growing through, or maybe the raised edge of a crack, and veer off in an odd direction. The setting was stunning. Someone had thought to put a park bench – silvery wood, simple shape – dead centre on the coach-house side of the court, where you got the wildness of the view and yet might be in shelter if you were lucky with the wind, and there was another protected spot near the larger shrubs where the lawn sloped upwards to a rockery of sorts, which would be good for sitting on the grass in the summer.

By the time I wandered over, they were well underway, a creditable rally audible before it was visible. They may have been a little embarrassed about another woman being left out – Barnaby immediately offered his racquet – but they were already absorbed in the game, so I waved it off, sat on the bench and acted as umpire, rather than muscle in on the court as I'd have done if we'd all been students. At Jenny's house when we were just into our teens, the two of us would happily be 'ballboys', though I was stroppy about the phrase. But I wasn't about to fetch and carry now; besides, it's easy to pick up your own balls, playing doubles. However, Gloria seemed happy enough to make a thing of running across the court, bosom heaving, and there was a lot of teasing going on. So much for the sisterhood.

Rupert and Tyler had paired against Barnaby and Martin, which turned out to be a good combination: they were pretty evenly matched. Tyler, who had such a supple body despite not being really tall, had that knack of looking graceful at the start of his serve and then, as he turned, giving a devastating thwack; Martin wasn't remotely elegant – far too chunky – but he was very strong, good at Björn Borg-style ground strokes. Rupert and Barnaby weren't a patch on them. In fact, altogether, Rupert's form wasn't as good as he seemed to think – his backhand was lousy – but he did make the odd unexpected shot. If he'd been more consistent, he could have played a strategic game.

It was too cold to sit still for long, even on a sunny day, so I was shifting around, rubbing my hands. Perhaps they noticed. Soon enough, Tyler and Barnaby offered to drop out and I thought, Why not? So Gloria and I swapped with them for the remainder – and we did okay. I saved most of Rupert's balls and Gloria made Martin work hard. He was a good opponent: cracked jokes the whole time and stopped Rupert from getting too serious. Still, it was just as well we played creditably, as we had quite an audience, with the walkers also watching towards the end. Tyler was very gracious about our performance on the way back and said something about me being 'nimble' in my use of the court. There was nothing suggestive, though he must have noticed me, too, bouncing around, getting hot and bothered, but somehow the very absence of comment left something hanging. It was Martin who joked that 'the girls' had put him off his stroke. He said we'd been 'quite a spectacle'. Rather cheeky of him, really.

In a place that size you easily lose people. We gathered vaguely for tea, prepared by Loxton with Priyam and Lyndsey, who were spilling over with stories about the bike ride. In the mess of the kitchen no one spotted that we were actually two down, or if they did they didn't say. Probably, like me, they assumed the others were around somewhere; after all, nobody was counting. It was only as it got closer to 4.30 that I caught Loxton checking the register on his hands.

Eventually he asked outright, 'We're missing Chloe and Eddie. Did anybody see them get back?'

Priyam thought they'd peeled away as she and Lyndsey rode through Mevagissey; Lyndsey said it was later – they were there when she stopped to look down to the harbour.

'Oh, they'll turn up,' said Gloria, shunting crockery nearer the sink. 'Chloe's never far behind.'

Loxton, Gloria and I were still in the kitchen – Loxton fretting about possible accidents; Gloria reassuring – when we heard the clicking of bicycle chains and saw Eddie waving a gloved hand through the glass.

'They're back,' I said superfluously, looking at my watch: nearly twenty to.

'What did I tell you!' Gloria said, without looking up.

And as Eddie and Chloe came through the door, she set off down the corridor. It seemed wrong to join the others – I was meant to be his sidekick, after all – so I stayed put.

'Hiya!' Eddie glanced round the table, now clear of everything but the teapot, a pair of mugs and the dark crumbs that were the end of the fruit cake. 'Don't we get any? We're not that late.'

Chloe came up behind and edged him to one side so she could see. 'Sorry about the time.' She flapped her poncho to let the cool air in. 'We miscalculated.'

'Indeed you did,' said Loxton. He might have been her father, preparing to tick her off.

Chloe seemed oblivious. 'We stopped to look at that place – the one Sarah thought was the harbourmaster's old house,' she said, as if it was *my* fault. She took her poncho towards the boot room, arm raised to the height of the hooks.

'Just a minute,' said Loxton in a manner that brought her back to stand next to Eddie, who was sitting at the table, checking the pot for tea.

Loxton leant over and moved the mugs out of reach. There was an awkward silence until he'd had eye contact with both of them. Then he was swift, which Dad had comprehensively failed to be when my brothers or I had misbehaved.

'I had hoped to make it clear,' he said, checking eyes again. 'The Reading Party is a collective activity. We may read on our own, but we do so as part of the group. The same goes for activities after lunch: it is a shared endeavour.'

Eddie fiddled with the tea strainer; Chloe rocked the neighbouring chair on its hind legs. I didn't move, remembering dread of my own.

Loxton carried on. 'I am not interested in how late you are or why and nor is Dr Addleshaw. We expect each of you back in time to start promptly, along with everyone else, afternoon as well as morning, unless a different time has been agreed. In future, you will pay attention, please.'

He was fingering the lid of the teapot. I wondered if he'd ever smashed anything, as I could do in a strop, but he left it where it was.

'Now, if you'll permit me, I would like to get on with my work.' And he set off down the corridor, his feet slapping the flagstones.

Eddie reached for the clean mugs. 'Oh Christ, a dressing-down!' he said, pouring tepid tea. 'Heavvvvvy! I haven't had one of those since Westminster. We used to get them from the housemasters. The polite ones are always the worst, don't you think, Sarah? Much easier if they lose their rag.'

Chloe took a swig, made a face and poured the remainder down the sink. She opened her mouth to say something, looked at me and shut it again. How had I achieved that?

'That's enough of divide and rule, Eddie,' I said quietly.

121

'Now you'd better both get back, or I might have to lose my rag too. On this occasion, I'll clear up or you'll be even later. Next time I won't.' And I watched, amazed at this new tone of voice emerging unasked from within, as they did just as they were told.

That little scene might have put a pall on the end of our afternoon, but in the drawing room it hardly registered. Eddie was now sitting upright up in his armchair, Mei was chewing the rubber troll topping her pencil, Barnaby was lost in the books on his little table. Nothing was said.

I sat down and tried to get back into the groove.

The article I was working on embroidered a subsidiary theme from my doctorate, about women campaigning for social justice. My plan was to submit by the end of the vac, to free my mind for my main area of research. It was only my third academic paper and I was still learning the craft; it wasn't the cinch I'd hoped it would be.

Having loosely mapped out my case in a handwritten draft and ploughed through my source material before typing it up, I was now trying to home in on the key line of argument and weave in the evidence without losing the balance of the whole. You could see how hard this was from the annotations I'd been joking about with Tyler; bubbles of handwriting and curling arrows indicating where material was to be inserted far outweighed the crossings-out in the main text. I wished I'd brought my little Olivetti and could retire to a place where it wouldn't disturb, such as the suite above the extension, to type out a clean copy. The frustration – and the anxiety about the deadline – was getting to me.

It felt like the rising panic that he'd alluded to in talking about a short dissertation he'd written back home before he got the hang of things. That afternoon at Carreck Loose, staring at the loops and deletions that had made Tyler laugh so, thinking of Loxton and all the little tests I'd failed, the worry bug got me. Probably caught it from the others: there was always someone going white about Finals or fretting about their grant running out – a febrile mood under the surface, just as Loxton had said. Anyway, briefly I lost my own nerve, wondering if I could pull the thing off – not just the article, but the whole enterprise – and what else I was equipped for if not. Made my stomach juices churn as I speculated about what happened if you failed your probation, and where you went if you lacked the 'rat-like cunning' to be a journalist, like my uncle, or the itch to make money, like Jenny's stockbroker dad. What were women meant to do if we didn't want to be secretaries? Teach schoolkids? Marry?

Thankfully the wobble didn't last long. In the end I got up to stoke the fire, poking a split in a log to get a hold, pulling it aside to make space in the glowing charcoal and selecting a new wedge from the basket. The wood was crusted with liverwort, which left olive streaks and a pungent aroma on my hands and jeans. Something about the action and the smells that lingered once I'd returned to my seat restored me to my senses. I put my article aside, picked the bottle-green memoir up again and found a comfortable place in my armchair, watching the tiny flames reflected in the old windowpanes and listening to the spitting as the logs caught and the mild thud as they settled in the grate. The panic went almost as swiftly as it had come, with the light going outside and the sparkle of the fire taking over. After all, a moment's doubt was nothing in the wider scheme of things. It didn't matter whether I'd solved the Ivy Williams problem that afternoon; I was much clearer on the timeline and I'd satisfy the Warden in due course. Meanwhile, nothing could beat being in this place with its mix of quiet companionship and rowdy fun, working out what you thought about your subject, your companions – life, even. What greater privilege could there be? The Reading Party was a preposterous institution, really – very hard to justify – but also wonderful. Why had I assumed this kind of thing wasn't for me?

The historians had decided to cook together – not that I knew that or noticed when Barnaby left. But looking into the kitchen after a trip to the loo, there they were, standing by the worktop amidst the smell of baked potato, swapping stories about their sisters. I offered to help, but Jim said they were doing fine: two historians was enough for the moment – perhaps a hand later with laying the table? It was almost disappointing.

When I returned, they still didn't need me. They'd progressed to their taste in music – Martin had brought a few albums, but his leanings were more mainstream than Jim's and he didn't share Barnaby's fondness for Lou Reed's deadpan – and they only wanted to know if we could move to the drawing room afterwards, where they could sit and listen. Banished, I went briefly back to my papers. The fire was fine, though the basket of logs wouldn't last through supper. It was Eddie who kept feeding them in; he probably had central heating at home.

The others must have been hungry. By the time I remembered to go back to it, the kitchen was full and the only place left was at the end of the table, next to Barnaby.

'I can't sit at the head with you, like a Big Cheese,' I whispered over the patter of water on metal as he drained the vegetables. 'I haven't done a thing!' But Barnaby was adamant, muttering elusively about 'figurative help'.

After he and Jim had doled out the spuds and the rest of us had chosen our fillings, Barnaby picked up the conversation. He was enjoying the week, he said. It was easy to concentrate and good to get to know people like Jim from the other years, but he still didn't understand why he was there. Priyam, sitting on my other side, said her parents too had wanted to know what selection meant. I punctured a potato skin raised like a blister and did my best to reassure, wondering if Tyler – only a couple of chairs away – was going to join in, and then asked what they'd felt about the invitation.

Barnaby expanded on what he'd told me before: that most students knew about the Reading Party – it was something of a legend in College – but that he'd had mixed feelings, both chuffed and apprehensive.

'We were surprised you agreed to host it,' he said. 'Dr Loxton's a bit of a dry old stick.'

'I could hardly turn it down,' I said.

Priyam, too, had been bemused to be invited. She hadn't asked to come, she said, because there were lawyers who were cleverer than she and she hadn't wanted to be turned down. Besides, she'd had enough of asking for things when she left school: too many years of checking what her City bursary covered and enduring snide references to 'people from Paki corner shops' when she did anything extra curricular. Her teachers – and of course her parents, who weren't even *from* Pakistan – had drilled in that academic merit was the route to success. But she still felt she was at Oxford on false pretences; was always the Indian from the East End waiting to be found out. Events like the Reading Party were usually for other people.

Barnaby and I were shocked at this, though we'd both, in our own ways, felt second-class citizens at school: he sent over by the army; me bussed in from a rural chemist's. For a while the three of us talked about racism – not the overt type seen at the Notting Hill riots or when the Sikh teenager from Southall had been killed the previous year, but the insidious sort that people endured day by day. Eventually this led us back to more general questions of privilege and the lack of it; being accepted or not; knowing your worth.

'As to false pretences, Priyam, that's nonsense,' I said,

thinking of the Dean disparaging her diligence. 'You got plaudits from everyone. No one doubts your ability, any more than they do Barnaby's. Maybe it's more a question of how cleverness is used? There are so many different ways of being clever, aren't there, not all of them interesting – especially the male kind. Besides, cleverness isn't the only thing that counts.' And I touched on Loxton's criteria – would the individual benefit and would they enhance the experience for the group – relieved that Tyler was no longer listening in.

'It's so nice when people are reassuring!' she said.

All the same, she looked unconvinced. We talked for a while about what she called the 'looming wall' of Finals. It wasn't so much the danger of being unprepared, though she said she'd twice had a nightmare about starting the summer term knowing she hadn't begun her revision, with no possibility of catching up. Instead Priyam was worried about insomnia, saying she was prone to bouts of it when she was working hard and her head was fizzing. What would she do if it hit her at the wrong moment?

We shared a few war stories – I talked about my eczema, which still occasionally flared; Barnaby muttered again, this time about the mix of fear and gloom which could lead to a tightening in his chest – and eventually she promised to revisit the College doctor, so she had a remedy to hand.

'As for you, Barnaby, I didn't know you got panic attacks,' I said, reminded of a conversation with my dad about a man who hyperventilated. 'So many people do.'

Priyam too was solicitous. 'But you always look as if you could absorb anything, like a cushion,' she said. She clearly hadn't seen him scratching.

Barnaby seemed surprised and perhaps a little touched by this, though he brushed it off with a comment about having too many dinners in Hall, saying the worry lines were merely under cover.

'That's not what I meant,' Priyam said, leaning across me to give his stomach a poke, 'and you know it isn't. I meant I'd never have thought of you being anxious, or having Fifth Week blues.'

She looked around the table, which was loud with the crossfire of so many conversations. 'Some people are always having essay crises. You're like Tyler – you always look calm.'

'Well, that's the irony, isn't it?' Barnaby replied. 'Swans paddling and all that – though I don't suppose *he* paddles at all.' He didn't say anything further and that effectively shut the conversation down, which was a shame – I'd have loved to know how the other students viewed Tyler. It wasn't until Barnaby had dished up the pudding that I was able to raise the subject again, but then it was to ask whether he'd had any attacks since I'd been teaching him.

He smiled at that and said no, he hadn't. On the contrary, our tutorials had restored his confidence in having something interesting to contribute. And he picked up on an incident he'd touched on before that involved another tutor, not at the College, whose comprehensive lack of response to his contributions had, he said, made him dry up inside. This was a man who placed his watch on the floor next to a glass of water at the beginning of every tutorial and, on the one occasion when Barnaby had felt they were making progress, had shoed him out on the dot of the hour, even though it meant their discussion was left hanging. Instead of being angry, Barnaby had found it crushing. That was when he began having that ghastly sense of his rib cage seizing up, as if a metal belt were tightening, though thankfully it didn't last.

'I'll remember never to take my watch off!' I said, leaning into him as if he were a brother in need of moral support. It was completely different from Tyler's leaning: uncomplicated and affectionate rather than conspiratorial.

'But that's just it,' he said. 'You never look at the time, though we've often run over.'

'Have we?' I asked, straightening up and trying to recall. The sessions with Barnaby were always enjoyable – right from that very first tute. He too was fascinated by oral accounts; the way they made history come alive. Possibly that's what made me think of him for the Reading Party: the support was almost mutual. I didn't say that, of course; just mentioned an essay of his that had been particularly stimulating.

'But it's often such a struggle,' he said, as if it was obvious what he was referring to.

'Is it?' I asked. 'Which bit, exactly?'

'Oh, you know. The whole thing.'

A sign of the change in temperature came over coffee. Barnaby had gone to sort out the stereo; suddenly the students' music was on. It was the new Fleetwood Mac album, *Rumours*, and it throbbed away at the other end of the hall, infecting the mood as we cleared up, turning it lush and provocative. There was a brief discussion of what we might do: no one was up for anything as demure as board or paper games – they wanted action. For some reason – I forget why – charades was voted down in favour of an unknown game that Hugh said was a Reading Party staple: two strangers, sitting on a train – in this case the sofa – had each to insert a word or phrase into the conversation without the other party identifying it as incongruous. Perhaps charades was too tame, or they wanted novelty. Anyway, railway carriages it was.

It was soon obvious that this could take a cerebral form, if you made the mistake of choosing an erudite expression (Tyler's 'habeas corpus' for instance, but then he had the excuse of going first). Equally, it could become ribald. When Martin, with 'call a spade a spade', and I, with 'cucumber', ended up talking about digging allotments and whether he'd planted his seeds yet, our audience collapsed into laughter. We were 'a hit' and it was wonderful – and of course Tyler learnt the trick immediately.

Some of the students were a revelation. Priyam proved so resilient under questioning that I found myself speculating about grillings at home and what part that might play in making her a good lawyer, while Jim slipped into singsong patter – gliding up and down, rolling his 'r's and generally sending up his Welsh roots – in a way that was totally unexpected. Even Mei relaxed her controls, dissolving into such giggles that she slid off her cushion and onto the swirls of the carpet, flapping one arm to stop the teasing and holding her side with the other. When Gloria said to 'leave the girl alone, you can see she's about to wee her knickers', Mei did disappear for a bit, presumably to the loo. I hoped she wasn't upset – it wasn't exactly a kind remark. But perhaps Tyler and I shouldn't *both* have reproached: that was my job, not his.

Others might say that we were all just 'letting our hair down' and that there was no need to read much into it, but I'd got out of the habit of messing around in a group, not having any old friends to hand. I soaked up the affection like a dry sponge, enjoying the inconsequential warmth in the kitchen when we piled our dirty coffee cups in the sink, bumping into each other and laughing as we moved away. There was Jim, relieving Mei of a handful of mugs, giving a quick smile as if they might share a secret, though so far as I knew there wasn't one; and Martin, curling his head round Gloria's neck to check her expression as she stood next to him, in the manner of someone allowed to share her space – which apparently he had done the previous year, with Chloe and others, in a house in Jericho near the canal. Even Tyler – who'd occasionally been reserved at the start, as grads sometimes are amongst younger students – seemed remarkably comfortable, chatting to Lyndsey, drying-up cloth in hand. She did one of those quick whirls of hers that set her hair flying and I wondered if she was capable of flirting. Either way, he looked charmed.

Soon the sweet tones of the Eagles and *Hotel California* drew the students back to the drawing room. I asked Loxton about support for anyone feeling the pressure. He was surprisingly helpful, talking about the ubiquity of anxiety and the different ways in which it was expressed. He filled me in on the counselling service, which I didn't know about, but it was clear he thought the most important thing we could do, as tutors, was to foster a sense in the students of the value of their contributions, whatever they were, provided they knuckled down and invested the necessary time. It was a more liberal approach than I expected, particularly when he acknowledged the rewards of music, drama and the endless societies, though he still saw these as 'ancillary pursuits', not the main focus. Nobody could study productively all the time, he said, so diversion was welcome – even necessary – but academic work remained at the core.

That's why he had been firm, he continued, about Chloe and Eddie. If you signed up for the Reading Party there was an unspoken contract: in return for the privilege of participation, you played by the rules of the game. They weren't many, but they were non-negotiable. We had to respond at the first transgression.

He was rattled when I asked if it had to be so black and white. He said it was the principle of the thing: the individual shouldn't undermine the experience for the group. Time out cleared the head, but the reading hours must be respected. Whether someone was five or fifty minutes late was immaterial – any lateness broke the spell. You had to put down a marker.

This still seemed a little harsh – it had hints of the tutor who had quashed Barnaby. 'But they were only minutes behind, Dennis,' I said. And then, thinking of the conversation about housemasters and rebukes, added, 'Anyway, they got the message.'

'I wouldn't be too sure,' he said. 'In my experience – and remember I too have done my stint as Dean – there are some who always chafe at restriction. Their impatience may or may not infect others. Either way there's a risk. *They* may need protecting from themselves and the *others* may need protecting from them.'

'Well, Gloria seems to be tiring of Chloe without any help from us,' I said.

'Perhaps. Gloria is altogether more conventional, don't you think?' And Loxton gave me an enquiring look.

We sat silently for a minute or two. Gloria's behaviour was straightforward enough, but she had a volatile streak that didn't seem a natural fit. I tried to put this into words, but they didn't come out as intended.

Loxton diagnosed the cause immediately, just as Tyler had predicted with his autopsy analogy. 'Ah, the appeal of a strong woman. But there's a difference between wanting your own way and being a rebel, is there not?'

He looked at me carefully. 'If I may venture a personal remark, I suspect you have been known to exhibit a bit of both.'

Tuesday

My novel of the moment was a new feminist classic – a well-thumbed paperback from the States that was circulating like Samizdat literature because it hadn't yet been published here. Rashly, the next morning I stretched for it immediately. Even that minor disturbance to the soft blur of my bedding was enough: the weightlessness – the luxurious feeling of being suspended, without edges – disappeared, just like that. Gone.

In fact, I didn't read but allowed myself to doze. For what seemed ages I lay staring at the wallpaper, clocking the way the pattern repeated, although whoever had hung it hadn't done well with the lining-up. I stared too at the wide boards of the floor with their uneven edges falling into dark cracks; they probably hadn't been waxed for years but someone had rubbed them long ago. I heard, but didn't really listen to, the sounds in the house – the lifting of a door latch, the padding of feet – and wondered if the early occupants of my attic had ever had the luxury of listening to others rising before them, aside from when they were ill.

As the dozing trickled into wakefulness, I began mapping out the day and what might realistically be achieved. There was also the question of the desk. Idly, I pondered my options. So much depended on whether the students started moving too. After days of resisting the gravitational pull towards Tyler, it was tempting to give in to it, but who knew where he would be ...

That notion was the killer, banishing that delicious lull. Within seconds I felt self-conscious, as if the mere thought of him was taboo. Worse still was the fear that I'd been found out: even tracing back to the beginning, I wasn't sure what Gloria could have picked up, but she'd found something to dislike. What was it?

I'd been aware of his presence, yes. He was a participant in all College activities, as if he didn't want to miss out on the traditions, but he was so tall and distinctive that anyone would notice him. It's true that I was forever spotting him going into Hall, running up and down his stairs or walking slowly round the gardens, but that was no different from Eddie. I'd registered he usually he had a companion, though it was rarely the same person, and that he didn't seem to have a girlfriend, though there were plenty of girls around – but I noticed such things about many of the students I knew – and we'd known each other since that very first collision.

As for running into each other in the Lodge, collecting our post; that happened with plenty of people. He had regular letters from home and abroad – those blue airmail envelopes with their striped corners appeared as dependably as any normal ones that I received – and standing there, flicking through, vaguely chatting, was unavoidable. We'd never say anything much – it was surprising what you overheard in the Lodge; people forgot that *anyone* might be listening in, porters included – and certainly we'd shared no more than I did with anyone else. It was just pleasantries.

Other than that, the collision itself and the walk with the bicycle, there was nothing. So the only thing that might seem out of the ordinary, given that I didn't teach him and we didn't share a staircase, was that indefinable ease, the thing that had turned those inconsequential chats into little pin-pricks of pleasure dotted across the year.

But how had she latched on to that?

Perhaps it was something to do with our second evening, when Tyler and I had sat and talked so long – another pinprick treat. Gloria had seemed put out, like Mum was at Christmas when two of our guests turned out to have a shared past. So that was one possibility.

And there'd been that business of Mei rushing off to the loo, and the way Tyler and I had joined forces in suggesting Gloria make amends. That had been another.

Well, she'd got her own back. She'd asked if Tyler was taking a social history paper. I'd explained that no, that wasn't an option with PPE. 'But I thought . . .' she'd begun, and left an awkward gap. Stupidly, I'd filled it with the business of the collision, then stopped for fear of 'protesting too much'.

She hadn't said anything, but I'd felt her disapproval. It was that boarding-school mentality again: she drew such hard lines around things – teachers and pupils, male and female, them and us. No wonder she was suspicious.

If so, I thought, swinging my legs out of bed, to hell with it. Gloria got away with lots of things – why shouldn't I, on something so minor? Since when was mere talking 'off limits'?

It was only later, as I paused on our own landing, that I thought through again and twigged. Of course! It had been *Gloria* with the parcel in the Lodge, flashing by with the long hair, when Tyler embarrassed me with talk of my book. And if it had been *Tyler* on the stairs outside my room – which would account for me recognising his footsteps later on – his visiting wouldn't have made sense to Gloria, standing below, unless I'd been teaching him.

But why would Tyler have come to see *me*?

When I arrived downstairs, mind made up about where to park myself for the day, Priyam was in the pantry checking for stores while Hugh read out a recipe from his seat at the kitchen table.

'I thought you thought domesticity was for women,' I teased.

'Well, men can repent their sins,' Hugh replied. 'Actually, I like cooking.'

'Never! And what are you making?' I asked, expecting to hear of some minor contribution to the evening meal. But it turned out that Priyam and Hugh were planning to bake together. A Johnnie and Fanny Cradock in the making, then, ready to perform.

'Hot cross buns before Good Friday? You renegade!' I teased.

'I know, three weeks ahead! But it's wet and they're easy to make and we thought it would be fun,' he said, and got up with the *All Colour Cook Book* in hand and walked around the table. 'That's all right, isn't it?' he asked, slipping a postcard from the dresser into the groove of the spine.

'Fine by me. But you, a Catholic! I bet you didn't have them early at Ampleforth.'

'You'd be surprised. Of course some of the monks said such liberties destroyed the point. Lyndsey's like that: she says if she believed, she'd have to be a Catholic, because they do it properly. High Church wouldn't be enough. But I think any church is better than no church. Anyway, Priyam's a Muslim.'

'Don't blame it on me!' Priyam called out. 'I'm not responsible for your transgressions!'

By then the kitchen was filling up and we could have a vote on the teatime menu. It was won by the irreligious contingent – hot cross buns it was to be.

Rupert had been flicking through the back of the cookery book, where there was a section on matching drink with food. Already we'd learnt that you didn't have to have beer with curry, you could have 'a low-tannin wine with generous fruit', whatever that meant. Now he turned his attention to the buns.

'Much more intriguing is you *knowing* how to bake, Hugh,' he said 'Or *owning* to knowing how to bake.'

'And why not! Butcher, baker, candlestick maker. It's a perfectly proper skill.'

'Not in my home it isn't; not for blokes. Anyway, why pick baking? Why not some other thing?'

This was interesting: another squabble in the making and Rupert again in the thick of it. Hugh looked at him as if deciding whether or not to answer seriously, but it was Martin who retaliated with, 'Well, it's better than arsing around with half-baked views on wine!'

The vigour seemed to take Hugh by surprise. In fact the whole episode prompted another shift in my picture of the individuals and the group. Hugh might make pat assumptions about having a study and the like, but he wasn't really a male chauvinist, whereas Martin liked to pretend he was and Rupert was genuinely well on the way. And the unexpected alliances and enmities between the students were disconcerting. People who appeared to have little in common would turn out to be remarkably at ease, and spikiness would emerge where it was least expected. It was awkward, not being one of their number. That's why it was comforting having Tyler there: he was in a similar position, being that bit older than the rest. You could see it in his face, sometimes, if you caught him watching – that look of remoteness. He too was neither completely in nor out.

After that we moved on. Mei took it upon herself to gather orders for the shops, and Loxton, arriving with the paper, to do – of course – his crossword, announced that he would accompany her, which freed me up for the morning. There was a discussion about how we might spend the afternoon if it continued to drizzle, Loxton being fussed about people getting wet. Priyam and Hugh offered to cook supper too – and why *not* curry, since Rupert had mentioned it. If they could find what she needed, she would teach Hugh to make a proper masala, and they could get underway while they finished the buns. Martin suggested an outing to the pub after supper, if we ended up being in all day. He looked to me rather than Loxton for confirmation that that would be okay, which was interesting. The Dean had cautioned – he'd harped on Martin's capacity for booze – but it all seemed fairly benign to me.

And so it continued as we settled for the morning session. Loxton braved the rain to check supplies in the wood store; the students went back to their desks, with minimal changing of places; and I went to collect my pile of papers from the grand piano. How curious, I thought, flicking the edges: the first two evenings they'd gone back with me to the attic, whereas this time I'd left them out overnight, where anyone might leaf through. How trusting of me, with nosy parkers like Rupert around; how relaxed I must feel.

Tyler was already at his post in the library – he was turning out to be scrupulous in his habits, almost at the expense of joining in – but he barely acknowledged me: a mere lifting of the fingers from their place on his book. My rhetorical 'Mind if I join you?' was addressed more to Hugh and Lyndsey, who smiled as they resumed their seats.

There was a subtle change from my last visit, hard to identify. I scanned the table and chairs, wondering whether Loxton had spread himself out differently from me, and then realised it was the light: the room was brighter, the door into the study now wide open.

I tiptoed over and paused inside, remembering the discussion about the three linked spaces and puzzling why such a small one warranted such a big window – something to do with the elevation, perhaps. Jim was already at the desk, with that view of the pines. The other door was ajar, muffled talking from beyond.

'Would you like this closed again?' I asked softly, enjoying the warmth of a patch of sunlight.

'No, it's okay, thanks,' he said, raising his head.

I pointed at the other door. 'That one?'

He gestured with his hands to suggest open but not too open. So Carreck Loose was doing Jim good; he was thawing. We shared a smile.

'How's it going?'

'Fine, I think. I'm doing well with Collingwood, though it's not *my* idea of history.' There wasn't much scope to lower his voice, but it dropped a fraction. 'This place is better than I expected. You were right – not snobby at all, really.'

'Cool beans.'

His voice dropped further. 'Eddie's a bit of an arsehole – he's got loads of those socks, pink ones too – but you get used to him.'

'That's a relief too. So he's not spoiling it for you?'

He shook his head and reverted to a normal whisper. 'Anyway, I've got this, which I like – on my own, but not completely.'

I nodded. 'I'm on my travels. I'll be working in there next!' And I doffed my head to the morning room, where the talking was turning to laughter, barely suppressed.

He grinned – the first proper grin I'd had from him privately – and I walked through.

Chloe and Gloria had been joined by Eddie, who was struggling to do a yoga tree on the sofa, his sneakers gaping abandoned on the floor, sky-blue socks prominently on display. You had to smile – the peacenik wobbling on one leg, arms tilting from the horizontal like a spaced-out scarecrow – but Loxton's injunctions had been clear, so I tapped the glass of my watch, grimacing in sympathy.

'Freak me out!' Chloe shot forth. 'Not you too? You were meant to be on our side!'

She huffed theatrically as she took up her William James. Unlikely she'd find much to enjoy in a nineteenth-century psychologist, but at least she was making a gesture.

Eddie unfolded his legs. 'Okay, okay. We know. Just a little high now we're on our own again.' He sat down on his cushion and retrieved the books that had fallen to the floor.

Gloria started flicking pages to find her place. She pressed on the gutter and pulled that peacock concoction she wore around her, feigning concentration.

I moved into the cold air of the hall, pulled the door to, paused and listened. Was there still silence? Apparently so.

With Loxton in the drawing room, there was no need to include it in my rounds, so I crossed to the dining room. Rupert, Priyam and Martin were in near identical poses to those of our first day. How constant we were, how set in our patterns! If you caught any of us from behind, you would recognise the postures; we were all indomitably ourselves, even doing nothing.

Patrol over, I returned to my place, quickly becoming oblivious of the students – even of Tyler, though of course I knew he was there, chewing his cheeks as he read, sending that little ripple down his jaw.

In no time at all, it seemed, Loxton tiptoed across the carpet to speak to me. He and Mei were off to shop – anything else we needed? I thought of the mild Mei stuck on her own with Loxton and wondered whether to go too, but two tutors to one quiet eighteen-year-old might also have overwhelmed. Hugh may have had a similar thought or been fussed about his cinnamon and mixed peel; anyway, he offered to join them and – oddly – Loxton agreed.

Probably Loxton recognised a youthful, unpolished version of himself: clever, kind, but a little gauche. And Hugh would like being needed – he had that air of suffering a deficit of friendship. But Loxton was gruff and Hugh wasn't – and it was

140

hard to imagine he ever would be, because, baker or not, he'd marry and have children in good time. Loxton, by contrast, would have suffered a slow and lonely accretion of gruffness, unnoticed until it was too late.

I needn't have worried about Mei. When we assembled in the kitchen it was clear the shopping trip had been a success, though they'd struggled to find yoghurt or any of Priyam's spices. Maybe no one ate curry in Cornwall.

The table looked immaculate, which Loxton credited to Mei, and we had a new salad – chicory and chopped segments of orange – which he said reflected Hugh's culinary expertise, causing much speculation about the standard of cuisine we might expect that evening. We made a few appreciative noises as we tucked in – lunch was now a mere pause in the rhythm of the day, not to be fussed over excessively – and everybody was easy, good-humoured.

It was when we'd moved on to fruit, perhaps lulled by the benevolent mood, the sight of sunlight glinting on the sea and the hedgerows, and the sound of Priyam kneading Hugh's dough, that the students revived the plan for a trip to the pub. It gathered momentum gradually, through discreet discussion of venues and routes – some favouring a trip to the harbour, which meant wheels, while others preferred the village, which could be managed on foot. I doubt Loxton even noticed: he was reading the paper, two students leaning over the newsprint alongside him. Still, when the coastal path was suggested, he raised his head to say it was out of the question. If we went at all, we would have to be sensible; it would be dark, after all.

Rain having given way to a gusty day and the grass having dried off, we decided to play football while Hugh and Priyam waited for the dough to rise again. Roughly half of us piled into the narrow conservatory which, as the boot room over-flowed, was functioning as a second back door and a further repository for our outdoor clothes. The rest of us lingered in the spice-scented warmth just inside the door from the kitchen on the pretext of waiting for space to change our shoes. And then we too were outside, jogging down the slope that led to the first field, trying simultaneously to button our clothes and avoid the longer tussocks, enjoying the sharpness of the air and the freedom to stretch and shout.

Chloe and Martin opted to be goalies, operating between brightly coloured scarves. I've no idea whose side the rest were on: it didn't seem to matter. Soon we were all running across the tufty, springy grass like children, stumbling and picking ourselves up, yelling at each other, trying to be heard against the wind. At some point the bakers took themselves off to see to their buns – Rupert lobbing the ball at Hugh's back as he departed – and the two teams coalesced afresh. At another, I realised there'd been a swap, for Chloe was in amongst us at our end of the notional pitch, aggressively tackling me and the more adroit Jim, her ruby Dr Martens flashing in and out between our legs, laces flying, getting her own back – and yes, there was Barnaby in her place between the markers, still in his Guernsey, still looking like a younger version of Alan Bates, who'd been my heartthrob since I saw *The Go-Between*, thumping his gloved hands together and running on the spot to keep warm. Eddie played referee, whistling through his fingers because he couldn't hack it with a blade of grass.

Perhaps that was when I registered that Loxton was neither with the bakers nor with us, and that Tyler wasn't there either. Of course Loxton wasn't the type to sprint anywhere, let alone scramble around a makeshift pitch – he was far too precise and interior a person. But as a youth? Maybe cross-country running, when he might have turned the exercise into a test of navigational skills. As for Tyler, I wanted to see how he dealt with something closer to a contact sport – how physical he might be. He'd have played basketball at home – you could imagine him leaping to shoot. But here, mucking around on a slope with a ball you couldn't hold, how would Mr Suave do?

And then, at the very moment of thinking of them, there they were – two little figures, so far away they were almost colourless, moving smoothly across the slope of the meadows in the distance, the descent to the sea a few hundred yards to their left, the world inland to the right.

When we arrived back in the cinnamon-filled kitchen – hot, breathless and pink-cheeked – to flump down on the chairs, there was no one hovering about as a reminder of why we were all there. Instead the exercise, the cold air, the fooling around and the grappling of laughing bodies made a combustible mix of excitement that a flash of rebellion would easily ignite. By the time the buns were on the table to absorb the adrenaline and calm us with their stodginess, the vague idea of an outing after supper had become a coherent plan to drive to the village and play darts over a round or two of beer.

Loxton and Tyler returned just too late to hear what was afoot, but in time to appreciate the bakers' achievement. The ribbons of paste crossed the surface as they should; the glaze was suitably sticky; the raisins hadn't burnt. Yes, the dough was a bit brittle around the edges and certainly it was a curious colour, but it tasted good. And what a contented feeling it was, to sit after strenuous activity having a second helping and savouring hot tea, surrounded by people you liked, planning an escapade! Even that dignified pair looked as if they might be loosening up, wiping butter from their fingers.

All those buns did us good.

Loxton had told the students that seven hours' reading was plenty. Of course he assumed they were *good* hours, but the wonder of it was that at Carreck Loose those two stints – the four hours in the morning and the three after tea – so often *were* productive. You ate, played and slept well; then you had the work you'd brought and nothing else, so you got on with it. If by chance you failed to get absorbed immediately, some quality of the place would gradually envelop you.

That 'something' was hard to define. The house was so still, so lacking in visual clutter or noise other than the wind bashing outside and the odd creak within, that you could forget it completely – and, being unfamiliar, there were no reminders of tasks undone or memories of important moments to distract you. Even the views, long and spare – no houses or people to be seen – were restful. We could sit together comfortably, the house and the people in it a mere backdrop.

That day it was Lyndsey who came to find me when I failed to turn up for supper – standing beside me, as Loxton had, until I flinched at the sudden awareness of her.

They'd been betting, she said, on how long it would take me to realise they'd all disappeared: Tyler and Mei had suggested the longest time. I was taken aback, disconcerted, then confessed that blocking things out had never been a problem. Stuck between brothers who were always rampaging, you learnt to ignore them. Lyndsey said that, as the only one, she was more used to being on her own, but she too could create an invisible bubble when she was working. Everyone said that I'd been like that wherever I sat, just like Loxton.

That also took me off guard. I didn't like the idea of being discussed – or of being identified with my co-host.

Lyndsey said she preferred her faculty library to the College equivalent, where there was too much activity, and she liked to sit with people who didn't know each other, as there was none of that intrusive passing of messages, but nothing was a patch on Carreck Loose. With that, at least, I agreed.

*

In the kitchen a general rowdiness was taking over.

Perhaps because it was day three, there was another bout of testing of the boundaries. The idea of the trip to the pub surfaced again in the heat of the curry and the zing of the ginger, and failed to be dampened by dollops of Priyam's cucumber *raita*. Probably the modest amount of beer that Hugh had got past Loxton loosened tongues and created an appetite for more – adventure included. The plan was now to take the vans to the end of the drive and then, because most of us hadn't actually walked that day, to do the rest on foot. I didn't hear the proposal being put to Loxton, who was halfway down the other side of the table, but I caught the conversation that followed, alerted by the insistent questioning. Gloria could sound quite like Chloe.

'So there's no objection, then? No reason why we shouldn't go?'

Loxton's expression changed to one I'd seen before when he thought a line of argument rather cheap, a rhetorical cliché; something about the mouth conveyed a tinge of dismay. It was a look I'd also seen on the Warden's face, in Governing Body, when he didn't like what a colleague had said – some were left floundering; others were goaded into aggressive repetition.

'We haven't had an outing of that kind before,' Loxton said, sucking his pipe: three little intakes that allowed him to focus on the bowl and whether the tobacco was drawing properly, a delaying tactic that was also now familiar. He would be considering whether the absence of a precedent was material, whether the proposition could be examined on its merits.

By now, it felt as if all thirteen of us were waiting, hushed, to hear the outcome.

Chloe, who must have drunk more than her share of the beer, could take it no longer. 'But that doesn't mean we shouldn't go, does it? I mean, we don't always have to do the things that people have done before.' She scanned the row of faces opposite her, stopped at mine and spurted out: 'It's not sacrosanct.'

'Of course not,' I said, before there was time to think about it. 'Traditions rarely are.'

Besides, what did Loxton imagine might happen? That they'd abscond? It was like the stories of dons who thought 'infants' would ensue the minute male and female students were allowed to cohabit. 'Think of the consequences!' one faction had reportedly said, horrified. It was laughable – we had to stick up for ourselves.

Gloria had just helped herself to another piece of Cheddar. She sat with her head down, moving crumbs round her plate with the point of her fork, not saying anything. Opposite her, Rupert was smiling. I wondered if they were playing footsie under the table, leaving the rest of us to fight her corner. It was the sort of scene the Dean had conjured up.

Martin was quick to pile in. 'We don't have to drive, if that's the problem.' He looked round the table, as if he, too, was calculating support. 'We could walk the whole way, there and back. It would make up for playing football.'

Loxton was still fiddling with his pipe, head tilted down, the brain computing. He didn't fill the gap.

Next to me Jim tilted back in his chair, watching. On his far side Priyam too observed, unexpectedly mute. Tyler, sitting beyond her, turned back to his plate and cored his apple, balancing the pieces carefully, silent. That was frustrating, when he might have chipped in: did he never risk anything? Perhaps the Rhodes Scholars really were goody two shoes.

Eddie leant across Gloria to grab the cheeseboard. 'Sounds cool.' He cut a hunk and passed it on around the table. 'A jaunt, together. There must be torches somewhere.'

'Or a moon. It's not a full moon, but there's a moon out there; I saw it earlier, sitting on its side.' Lyndsey leapt up to pull back the curtain — she could have been a child of seven or eight. 'There! We can "dance by the light of the moon".'

Loxton put his tamper down by his plate and turned to me. 'Sarah?'

Typical! It must have been the third time that I'd been asked to pronounce, to give the decisive view, so he didn't have to. And why drop the 'Dr This' and 'Dr That' in front of the students now, as if he and I were suddenly allies?

'I don't see why not,' I said. 'Martin can introduce us to the local beers. Let's take it to the max.'

Loxton snuffed his pipe with a brisk prod. He stood up, pushing his chair back so sharply that it jerked against the stickiness of the linoleum. There was a grimace as he looked down behind him; then he carried on.

'So be it. I dare say the kitty can stretch to another round. All hands to the deck here and then we'll go. I've no problem with firsts — for that matter, we've never had home-made buns before — but I don't want any stragglers on the way there or coming back.' He glanced about to check the students had got his meaning and tapped the table with the ball of his pipe. 'Chop-chop. Who's washing up?'

It took a while to find the torches. By the time Barnaby and Priyam came back, triumphant — Barnaby holding a search-light aloft while Priyam dangled a couple of pocket torches by their cords — we'd just finished putting things away. There was a moment when everyone was waiting for everyone else; and then a scramble as we all headed for our coats and made for the door at the same time, as if to stop anyone changing their mind.

Outside, the air was almost balmy, moist with dew rather than cold and frosty. It had been another complete change, starting wet, then gusty, now still. Good weather for an evening stroll.

We set off in a genial gaggle, a single mass of people chatting together, enjoying the unexpected outing. By the time we'd got beyond the drive, the mass had shifted into two groups, both thumping awkwardly on the tarmac in the way you do going down a hill at slightly too brisk a pace. When the road levelled, the group in front spread out until they straddled it. Someone near the centre linked arms and leant forward, calling to the others to do likewise – Tyler, which was a surprise. A few more paces and they were all at it, forming an uneven line that stretched from one tall hedge to the other. There was a bit of skipping until they were walking in unison; laughter as the shortest struggled to maintain her stride.

Loxton and I hung back as the rest of our group copied the first and bounced on ahead of us. Then at the front there was a shout of 'Car!', the arms unfurled and we all stepped to the side to let a lone vehicle through. After that, we stayed in twos and threes – small bobbing clumps of darkness amidst the slaty hues.

The pub was in the centre of the village, a few doors from the shop I'd visited with Eddie, the light from its frosted windows draining colour from any uncurtained windows elsewhere. In the smoke-filled public bar, chosen because of our boots, we were a large and conspicuous group standing around debating where to sit. The space by the dartboard was already taken, and we were lucky that two elderly men moved along unprompted so we could have a pair of tables to ourselves.

Loxton and I sorted the orders with the help of Martin, who was suitably knowledgeable about the Cornish ales, and Hugh, who ferried glasses to the corner our group had adopted. As the two of us leant against the bar chatting, relegated to onlooker status, I wondered when Loxton might last have been in such a setting – it was hardly his natural milieu.

But he told me that he and a colleague who lived near him had met in their local for a gin and tonic every Thursday for years. He was typically exact about it, calculating that, as they normally had a couple each, he would have drunk roughly 2,600 measures since they began. What kind of brain chooses to make such a calculation? It was on a par with his ability to cite intriguing facts about a given date, also on display that evening. Apparently the fifteenth, the Ides of March, wasn't only the day of Julius Caesar's stabbing but also of George Washington's great speech against the Newburgh conspirators and of Germany's invasion of Czechoslovakia. How did he remember such things? I certainly couldn't compete, even on my own territory, but then I'd never have been sent by the intelligence services to Bletchley Park. That required a singular mind.

It was a relief when Hugh came back and I could sit with the rest of our gang.

After that it can't have been much more than half an hour before the publican called for last orders, but in the absence of the sobering influence of darts, part of our group contrived to down a couple of double whiskies apiece, relegating the beer to the status of chaser, and became pretty merry.

I should have paid more attention, or listened harder to the Dean: both, probably. I'd allowed myself to get distracted, enjoying another conversation.

The main culprits seemed to be Martin, who had introduced them to what he called the local 'boilermaker', and Rupert, who ignored a glance from Loxton and airily funded another round just before drinking-up time. Whatever the case, it was Chloe who helped herself to unfinished tumblers and ended up the worst cut, with Eddie close behind. She sat at an angle on the edge of the plastic banquette, deep in garrulous talk with him, periodically making large gestures that threatened to thwack anyone who was rash enough to get in their way, while Gloria and Rupert bent closer together at the end of the bench, the other side of Tyler and me. When we all stood up it was Chloe who misjudged her footing, landing in a mess on the floor with a raucous 'Oops-a-daisy!' that must have been heard by everyone, and it was Martin rather than Eddie who helped her to her feet. Rupert continued to the door, holding it open for Gloria as if nothing was happening, least of all anything to do with him. It was left to Mei and Jim – together again! – to help Loxton and me pile the empties back on the bar.

At such moments the difference in age – five years or so – seemed like a chasm rather than a matter of degree: it was aeons since I'd last set out to get smashed in that way, although in my time I'd done it too. But I still didn't pay much attention. It was only a few drinks – nothing exceptional – and we'd all enjoyed ourselves.

We set off back up the road, joking about hobgoblins and whether our fingers would fall off in the cold, and soon enough we'd all spread out and my mind was elsewhere.

Tyler and I were somewhere in the middle of the group, trailing the front runners and ahead of the rump. We'd picked up the conversation we'd begun in the pub about the business of 'growing up' – more lighthearted than any we'd had before, on a par with the flirty one by Magdalen Bridge – and had started joshing more personally, about whether he was the archetypal only child and me the classic middle one. There was a lovely moment when he paused to look at me and I did the same to him, swinging round mid-step and fired up with the repartee, ready to launch another rejoinder. It was a bit like Gloria and Rupert in the car, just before she pretended to pummel him.

That was when I registered we were probably out of sight, alone for the very first time. What difference that might have made I'm not sure: it's one thing to suggest you take responsibilities too seriously, as we had when walking back from Magdalen; quite another to do anything about it. I barely knew him – what was I thinking of?

We weren't given a chance to find out. Suddenly Martin came puffing up behind us in the darkness, coatless, to say that Chloe had puked into the hedgerow and couldn't get up.

Of course we did exactly what was expected of us – we could hardly do otherwise. Tyler volunteered to run the rest of the way up the hill for help, disappearing up the slope into the blackness until the sound of him was lost amidst the breeze and the hedgerows, and I went back down again with Martin, the little torch splaying light feebly ahead, to check how bad Chloe was. The moment had gone.

When we reached her, Chloe was slumped with her lower back against the steep bank where hedge merged into grass and ivy, legs braced against the camber of the tarmac, head lolling forward towards her knees. Eddie, meanwhile, was crouched unstably on the far side of her, pale in the darkness, shivering as he groaned that they would get a real bollocking now. Beyond that, there was just the smell of damp earth and crushed greenery.

Poor girl. I squatted down on the near side, lifted the great-coat back onto Chloe's shoulders, tucked the strands of hair away from her cheeks and checked her forehead: still clammy. When Eddie resumed his lamentations, Martin told him to 'shut the fuck up' – the priority was fetching transport and blankets. Chloe would be fine.

That of course was true. We'd all been there before, had too much to drink and then recovered our stomachs and our dignity – it really wasn't an issue. In fact, in other circumstances it might have seemed funny, a predictable rite of passage. But somehow making a joke of it wouldn't do in Cornwall. With Loxton around we had to have a fuss. Uncharitably, I reflected that you could be all for interesting women – my research was full of them – but find this sort of thing a nuisance with men like him to witness it.

After what seemed an age – it was horribly cold and we were going numb – we heard the shuddering of the van and then saw its lights appearing around the bend of the lane. Loxton parked just beyond us, came out with his silly first-aid box, swapped a few terse words with me and waited grimly by the back door as we got Chloe to her feet, slumped against Eddie but with Martin taking the bulk of her weight. It was only a few steps to the rear of the van, but they were awkward and the boys' muttered instructions all too loud in the emptiness. Then it was Tyler's turn, now inside, to help Chloe onto the rear bank of seats. Nobly, he sat between her and the window, where he was a buffer as she flopped sideways. The rest of us climbed in behind. Loxton took us lurching down in search of the next turning, reversed into it and then drove us jerkily back up the hill, changing gears at every opportunity.

Inside the van you couldn't get away from what had happened. Chloe had straightened up in her seat, turning away from Tyler to lean on me instead. She was awkwardly positioned, a heavy press of body giving off heat and moisture, her lank hair a little too close to my face, a rancid smell lingering somewhere. Tyler and I exchanged rueful glances and concentrated on keeping her upright; Martin and Eddie were atypically mute; Loxton too was silent, hunched over the wheel. Chloe, needless to say, was not. By the time we got back to the house, she was properly vocal – cross rather than embarrassed. 'Shit, I hate whisky,' she complained.

We parked by the front door and Loxton waited in the driving seat while we got her to her feet, Eddie and Martin backing out of the van in case she crumpled forwards, while I followed with Tyler, keeping the coat in place. Chloe allowed them to help her down the step and across the short crunch

of gravel but then pushed them away in the hall with an irritated, 'Fuck off, will you?' Pausing next to me at the bottom
of the stairs, one hand on the big wooden ball at the end of the
handrail, she gripped my arm and the two of us started slowly
up to the first floor. At the half landing we stopped to look
up at Gloria, emerging from the room that Rupert shared.
There was an exasperated, 'Oh God, what's she done now?'
and then Gloria came down to take over from me, arms out,
like a mother handed a tiresome child.

Upstairs, their bit of the attic was a tip, even after three days.
Clothes were strewn across the floor on Chloe's side: used
underwear was chucked against the wall; a box of Tampax
blared its colours. Gloria's was little better: a satin dressing
gown, spoiled with creases, lay underneath some jumpers; a
drawstring bag spewed its contents. An air of abandon, which
might have been glorious but actually was sordid, seemed to
infect every corner. The mess was disproportionate, the smell
of smoke stale.

We set Chloe down on her bed and then Gloria moved
around, tossing a couple of pillows in her direction, tugging
the covers where they trailed on the floor, issuing instructions
in weary parental mode, while I stood back, a dirty ashtray in
my hand. Chloe was monosyllabic, like a resentful teenager.
She sat on the edge of the mattress, waiting for help in lifting
her poncho over her head and then discarded it, inside out, in
the direction of the piles.

'Where are my fags?' she asked.

'With luck, downstairs, where they are meant to be and
where this is going,' I answered, raising the offending ashtray.
Still, I offered to make her a sweet tea, as Jenny had once done
for me in our schooldays. There was no reply.

On my return, Chloe was leaning against the pillows in
a large white t-shirt with a black-and-red picture of Che
Guevara, her face washed – still sallow, a few strands of hair

sticking to her skin – watching Gloria close the little curtains. I put the mug down, picked up the damp flannel and stood by the door.

'There's no need to hang about,' Chloe said dismissively, shifting her legs under the covers and patting the surface beside them. 'Gloria's seen me be sick before.'

Gloria looked at me, her face expressionless, her voice flat, much as I supposed she might have looked at the matron at school. 'It's the whisky: it disagrees with her.' She bent down to pick up a tangle of garnet lace and chucked it towards the laundry bag, talking into the floor as she went. 'Maybe Rupert shouldn't have got that second round, but she could have said no.'

She straightened up, turning towards her friend, still brusque, unsympathetic. 'It's boring, Chloe. We were having fun.'

Embarrassed, I asked if there was anything else they needed. Gloria's 'No thanks' was almost automatic; Chloe barely turned her head. They were back on some habitual track of their own and I was the hapless neighbour, unwittingly intruding. Pulling the door to I heard the metal bedsprings crunch and then Gloria saying, 'I don't want to sit there. You wear me out.'

Back in the kitchen, Tyler had disappeared. I should not have hoped otherwise.

There was a brief discussion amongst the remaining students about whether anything needed to be done, but it seemed Chloe had a reputation for excess and the students were just as interested in whether a storm was brewing outside. No one mentioned the tots of whisky and Rupert wasn't there to apologise; instead they spoke dispassionately of Chloe's escapades, as if it wasn't that cool to get drunk, and poked fun at Eddie for his theatrics on retreating to bed. There was none of that banding together to protect people's privacy that I would have expected; more a need to be blasé, to take it in your stride. Had we been like that at York, when people got plastered? Impossible to remember.

When they'd drifted off and the two of us were left alone, Loxton took me to task – first for my comment about 'taking it to the max', which I suppose was fair enough, and then for allowing the second round of whisky to be ordered, which I thought completely unjustified, given that he'd been there too. Then he switched tack to minor ailments triggering major ones, which I knew to be rare; Dad was always saying how robust the body is. We had a polite little scrap about the line between sensible precaution and hypochondria – I'm not sure he knew how to have a proper row, least of all with a woman; he was all taut expression and icy understatement – until he conceded that he might be overreacting, which I suppose was decent of him.

In the circumstances he was remarkably forgiving of Chloe, despite the indelicacy of anyone being sick. Where I was annoyed that a woman should let the side down, he saw student experimentation applied to the smaller vessel. It was akin to the matter of the bike ride, he suggested, sounding parental again – there were always students who needed to defy. If you'd lived with them as long as he had – and so far he saw no reason to think the women were any different from the men – there was no point being disappointed or even surprised; it was what you came to expect. But it was unfortunate that it had happened in front of other people. He was minded to apologise to the publican on behalf of the College. Meanwhile, women's bodies being what they were, we should be careful. If I had any concerns about Chloe, he was happy to call the doctor – the number was right there, on the pinboard.

I thought an apology excessive, even from him. It was a pub after all – people got drunk all the time. As for getting medical help, his concern seemed to me misdirected. If you were going to worry about anything, surely it should be the emotional dynamics – the mixture of mutual dependence and tension between Chloe and Gloria; the way Rupert had egged the drinking on; Martin's mix of passivity and aggression; Eddie's uncertain contribution. Hadn't the Dean mentioned something about Chloe, north London intellectuals and a broken home? But after Loxton had heard me out, he said he preferred not to speculate – it was none of our business – and again he closed the subject down.

That was my cue to say goodnight. There was no ratting about the smoking, as I couldn't see the point, and by the time I got back to my room, thoughts of Gloria's exasperation had given way to my own. Besides, you couldn't ignore the wind. The sound of it in the chimney was like the sound of a kettle as it starts to whistle, except that the screech didn't mount and there was no relief. It was relentless; it drowned everything out.

I stood by the side window, looking out to see how bad it was, reflecting. Opportunities to talk, unobserved, were so rare. Tyler was probably standing in the same way in his own room, watching the same palms do their demented bending and shaking in the moonlight, listening to the same wind thrash about outside with its low rumbles, its sudden bursts and its eerie moments of silence, as if it were trapped in a vast cosmic flue of its own. A shame such moments could not be shared.

Wednesday

A house like Carreck Loose was rarely completely silent, even after a storm. There was a constant backdrop of small noises, which carried a long way, though, perversely, you would have had to holler from the bottom of the stairs to be heard at the top.

Take the mornings, when people began moving around. If there was an early riser on our floor, you'd hear the latch being opened on the door at the top of our stairs, then the clatter as it banged shut, then the echoey thud-thud, as whoever it was ran down the wooden steps in the enclosed space, and then you'd hear another clatter as they came out onto the landing on the first floor and the latch of that door banged in its turn. If you listened hard, you might even hear them on the main stairs as they carried on down to the ground floor – there was a spot where the tread creaked as you turned the corner in a way that for some reason carried right up to our floor. Or there'd be silence and you'd wonder whether they'd switched to the back stairs via the housekeeper's lair – the quicker way to the kitchen – in which case it was as if they'd gone into a void, because almost nothing from the annexe reached our floor. And meantime, unless it was very early, there'd be all the other noises: a door being opened and banging shut, a loo chain being pulled, a bath being run, people talking, someone calling somebody else.

What you couldn't hear was what anyone was saying. You could tell when your neighbours began talking and you might hear murmuring from below, but you couldn't distinguish the words. What you *could* tell was who was on the landing. It was a matter of recognising the timbre of the voice. Even Mei was identifiable when she popped up, ostensibly to speak to Priyam – though she did everything so quietly you couldn't be sure if she'd gone in to see Jim or disappeared downstairs again. Tyler hadn't been up to our floor yet – at least not when I was there.

That morning someone decided to solve the problem of how to be heard from the kitchen. Martin and I were chatting on the landing when we heard the din. Even with the stair door closed we could hear it coming up from below.

'Must have dropped something!' he said, grinning and adjusting his dressing gown so it left less of a gap at the throat. Martin had abundant chest hair, but the early-morning chill made no concessions to vanity. 'And again!'

'It sounds like one of those metal trays, but not much like the tray being dropped.'

'No, listen!' Priyam came out of her bedroom to puzzle with us. She opened the door to the stairs, leaning in, trying to hear better.

The din came again, and then was suddenly louder as the door at the bottom opened and light steps ran up.

'Did you hear that?' Lyndsey asked, once she'd caught her breath. 'We're trying out the pans.'

She looked at us fiercely, as if we should know what she was talking about and be focused already on her guessing game. 'Could you tell the difference, the high sounds and the low? The lower sounds are the saucepans. The boys know why.'

It turned out that Eddie, of all people, was experimenting with cooking pans as a substitute for a gong. The idea was to have two sounds – one in the morning, before the eggs went on and one for afternoon tea – so everyone turned up in time. This was a pretext to try out several pot sizes, even though Hugh said the physics made that unnecessary. A small frying pan turned out to be the highest; it might sound better with a wooden spoon.

'Good thing we're on this floor and not below,' I said. 'What an atrocious noise.'

'But that's the point. You're not meant to like it; it's meant to get you up,' Lyndsey said, still fierce.

Priyam was amused: 'So why are you, of all people, devising that?'

Martin didn't wait for the answer: 'Quite. And who said I want to get out of bed? I like my bed. I particularly like my bed when someone wants me to leave it . . .' – he paused for effect, putting his arm round Lyndsey and trying to pull her in – '. . . or join me in it!'

She paid no attention, as if immune, and resisted the hug, leaning away. Hard to imagine how anyone would get close to her. Reassuring, I thought, remembering her twirling by the sink; the women I'd seen with Tyler were completely different – glamorous and self-aware. She wouldn't be his type.

Downstairs the din began once more. If Eddie was trying to send Loxton up, he'd got him wrong – Dennis would have been more subtle.

'Is this really in the spirit of the Reading Party?' I asked. 'I'm not sure about being dragooned, even for breakfast.'

'Seems pretty typical to me – there's plenty of other dragooning round here.' Chloe emerged, rubbing her eyes, grinding a loose spec of kohl into the lid. 'What the fuck is that noise?'

Martin turned round. 'Ooooh. There speaks someone who had too many whiskies!'

'Don't give me aggro,' Chloe began, but Martin was giving her a squeeze, so the rest of the sentence came out like expiration. 'I've had enough already, not least from her.'

That's a bit rich, I thought.

Martin did a show of rocking back, surprised. 'From Sarah? Surely not! Let me guess: we haven't been smoking upstairs, have we . . .?'

Lyndsey chose that moment to start again on the sounds that might carry to our floor. She seemed to have no antennae at all.

Chloe talked right over her. 'Give us a break, you dolt. Sarah's the fuzz, not you – or Martin. I've enough of a head already.'

'Why not tell them we don't like being woken by the contents of the kitchen sink,' I said to Lyndsey.

'Particularly those of us with hangovers,' Martin added. 'The hangovers and their mates vote for a more mellifluous sound.'

I fetched some of Loxton's Alka-Seltzer, but Chloe rebuffed all offers of help. No scope for pastoral care: she'd clearly been there many times before. It puzzled me. Usually students don't go on getting drunk for nothing. I'd had my own patch of boorishness in my first year, angry at the smallness of my parents' lives, trying to compensate with my peers. A miserable period, looking back – I was lucky that Jenny and others had got me back on track. If the Dean was right about Chloe's family, she might actually miss those structures; Loxton could even be a kind of father figure, someone whose affection she needed to test.

Eddie's experiment with the cooking pans dominated conversation over breakfast. Perhaps it was less alarm call than decoy, like the crossword, but this time to provide cover for the whisky-drinking team. Whatever the case, talking about gongs – where we'd seen them, how they worked and why they were considered infra dig – allowed us to avoid discussion of the previous evening. Rupert breezed in, playing a tinny drum roll on the base of a frying pan with his knuckles as he walked by and then repeating the gesture on Gloria's shoulders; Chloe stood by the Rayburn, examining the accumulation of black sediment inside another of the pans, and then turned instead to make herself a piece of toast; Eddie told a long yarn about a gong in his aunt's house, which was a bit far-fetched; Martin juggled with the abandoned wooden spoons. In fact, those who'd been most involved in the drinking and its aftermath kept off the subject. A few of the others asked how Chloe felt – no one asked about Eddie – but she batted them away dismissively.

Even Tyler was rebuked. When Loxton pointed out that it was 'our American' who'd sprinted nobly up the hill, Chloe said, 'Quite right too. Penalty for hobnobbing with you lot,' and gestured at the two of us.

I spent a few minutes pondering the logic of that one. I didn't dare to look at Tyler, least of all with Loxton by my side.

There was no more talk of escaping the house; instead, the chat was about how people were getting on with their reading. It was as if they were all trying to prove that their minds were where they were meant to be, or that one act of subversion was enough. So, to his credit, Loxton chose not to issue another crisp reprimand. And he was perfectly pleasant with me. It was as if we'd never 'had words' at all.

Soon enough the ritual of the crossword took over and the pockets of conversation meandered in other directions. Martin and Lyndsey had agreed to keep each other company in the kitchen and were discussing the evening meal: he could only do stews, he said, but that was a larger repertoire than Lyndsey's; we weren't to expect anything much. Barnaby was talking about the wind, which had brought more dead wood down from the pines and would have washed driftwood high up the beaches – could we have a bonfire on that patch of blackened ground beyond the cold frames? Priyam was asking if anyone had seen her glasses, which she'd mysteriously lost; there was chat about a book of Tyler's that he'd mislaid; someone else had run out of fags. And on it went.

That was part of the pleasure of the Reading Party, I realised, thinking back to the previous afternoon – the tight structure had benefits beyond the hours of quiet. Once you had got the hang of it, it absolved you of responsibility for most daily decisions. The reward wasn't just the pleasing rhythm of work and play, it was also the holiday from the minor choices of daily life.

So after breakfast there was no point in debate about whether or not to work that day: you went back to your books, 'period', as Tyler liked to say. Similarly, there was no need to discuss what or when to eat: meals were provided and the gong now announced when they were ready. Even the strictures on luggage had helped – no one fussed about what they wore because they had so little with them and were so keen to keep warm. We could focus on the important things – like what to do during 'time out'.

Also, it being midweek, we were getting into our stride. We'd done our bit of pushing at the edges of the structure to establish boundaries, discovering which were flexible. We'd got each other's measure, which changed the balance of power. The gap between Loxton, who had always known the score, and the rest of us, who hadn't, was narrowing. Even Tyler was easier to read.

Playfully we argued the toss between the ideas for the afternoon. The consensus was that having a bonfire would be the most fun, now we were in the flow. What would the Dean have made of that? Were we still being too tame, or getting suitably frisky?

*

Having skirted round the subject of the morning after the night before, we settled contentedly back into our pattern. There on our tables were our books, just as we'd left them; there were our chairs and sofas, waiting for us; and there were our companions, their foibles increasingly familiar.

In the library, the obvious quirk was Hugh tapping the table. Mostly he tucked his hands away, bringing them out only to turn a page or pick up his pen and then stuffing them deep in his pockets: it was as if he found it a distraction, the fingers trilling unasked but insistent.

Lyndsey was soundless but had an extraordinary presence, her Pre-Raphaelite tresses regularly raised over those bony wrists and flicked away, only to sink back like a shroud.

Tyler, by contrast, was a dark figure at the opposite end of the table, the face beneath the curls in shadow unless he tilted towards the window. There was something curiously sensual about the way he took his chin in his left hand: his thumb would rest beneath the jaw line; his forefinger would stroke his upper lip, which was fuller than you'd expect; his other fingers would curve round to fan out across the bottom half of his face and occasionally slide below his mouth, caressing the skin in the patch where the stubble was sparse, or settle into the little nook below. I could have spent hours watching him, if I hadn't been absorbed in my work.

Having stripped away some of the biographical detail in my paper, I'd simplified the chronology and clarified the strands of Ivy's battles with the authorities in education and the law. Now I was tracing them through the sheaves in coloured-pencil marginalia, trying to assess their relative importance. I was nervous of excising hastily: there might be unintended consequences.

It reminded me of my grandmother's pruning of the roses on her garden wall, which dominated our childhood visits in the autumn half-term. First she'd trim the new shoots and snip off the dead wood, so she could see better; then she'd identify the stems that were too close; but before she did anything to them, she'd check for old branches that needed to go. She'd consider how removal might change the shape of the whole and then she'd lop decisively at the base. There was always a nerve-wracking moment when the offender was taken out, bringing all its subsidiaries with it. Then we'd stand back, surrounded by clippings, and assess the result.

The boys never stuck around long enough to see the whole process, but its purpose had sunk in with me. Perhaps Granny even explained it, as she fiddled with her raffia and her ties, to shut up my chatter. Or Grandad, coming over with rosehip syrup and tea.

In any event, looking afresh at my draft I found too much about arranging free legal advice for the poor, which is what Ivy Williams originally intended to do (and how I'd come across her), and not enough on what later she had actually done – namely, win for women the right to receive degrees and to practise as barristers, just like men.

Once seen, the rest was obvious. I knew where to lop!

Perhaps my excitement got the better of me: all of a sudden the three of them were watching. Lyndsey had tilted her head, causing the hair to shift; Hugh had stopped mid-page turn, his hand poised alongside the print; Tyler's chair had returned to the floor with a thump.

'Did I say something?' I asked without thinking. 'What did I do just then?'

I glanced at Tyler, but he was in the gloom, his expression unreadable. Lyndsey, next to him, sat up from her slumped position.

'You came out of your bubble and clapped,' she whispered.

'What do you mean, clapped?'

Hugh pressed his page down to stop it flapping. 'Like this,' he said, and he clapped his hands as a child would: two excited

164

little pats with his palms that made the leather buttons on his sleeves wiggle on their threads.

A memory flashed of me wearing a hand-knit over a dress I got on my fourth birthday, clapping Granny's efforts as a huge frond of rose landed on the grass and then stamping on it in my stumpy wellingtons.

'Did I really?' I said. 'Goodness!'

Now Tyler was watching. I could feel it, though I couldn't see it. 'Perhaps you solved a problem,' he said. 'Was it important?'

'Do you know, I think I did.' I gestured to the marks about the competing threads – Ivy aspiring to help the poor, taking her degrees, becoming the first woman 'called to the Bar', being the first to teach law at an English university – and lifted my hands wide with pleasure. 'And yes, it is important. I'm writing about someone wonderfully daring – a pioneering don at one of the women's colleges, whom I've been discussing with Dennis – and I've just sussed how to tell her story.'

'Eureka!' said Lyndsey, looking a little manic, as if the excitement – the relief, even – were hers.

'You've something in common, then,' said Tyler, as if he was testing the idea, thinking it through.

Was he flattering me again? But it was still an interesting notion: historians need to get on the inside; it's no good being just an observer.

'Actually,' I said hurriedly, 'she was way ahead – born nearly a hundred years ago. I noticed that this week, when I was looking again at the dates. A September anniversary. That'll make it easier to get people interested.'

'There you are!' said Lyndsey, squeaking again.

There was a noise from the study, where the historians had been trying a new arrangement, working with their books in their laps – Barnaby sitting in the armchair in the recesses and Jim using the desk as a prop for a single elbow rather than a surface for both. Now they were standing in the doorway, one behind the other.

'Why the fuss?' asked Jim. But the roughness would only be awkwardness. Barnaby must have known that too; he put an arm over Jim's shoulder, leaning forward, listening in.

'Sarah's made another breakthrough in the paper she's writing – and a missing bit of the jigsaw makes it a dead cert for publication,' said Hugh. 'She gave herself a clap' – and he paused – 'without registering.'

The historians grinned, knowingly.

To make amends for all the disruption, I set off early to sort the coffee, hoping to recover my poise alone in the kitchen, but Tyler said there would be too many things to carry. We stood at the sink together, surrounded by stainless steel and the smell of Fairy Liquid – me filling the kettle while he balanced mugs on the ridges of the draining board – and chatted about those wonderful moments when things suddenly come right. He joked about people who made a habit of exclaiming out loud and we laughed at the memory of me chuckling about Loxton's handwriting in the Lodge. He said he'd had only one eureka moment during his time at Oxford, to do with an issue in epistemology with which he had struggled and which, without warning, he had suddenly understood. He had written that essay in a blaze of clarity and then wondered if he was going mad – 'crazy', he called it. The relief when Loxton grunted approval, after utter silence as Tyler read aloud, had been extraordinary.

I watched the coffee granules melt, hoping he might continue, but instead he gave me one of his quick looks and, almost as quickly, went off in search of a tray, creating a sudden draught of cold air.

We'd been very close by the taps, again nearly touching; there was a vacuum after he moved, as if he'd taken the warmth with him.

That put paid to my morning. Two sorts of embarrassment – maybe even two sorts of eureka – and I couldn't work out which was worse: that moment of professional unguardedness or realising quite how much I fancied him.

Just as well it was my turn to chaperone the shoppers.

By now we'd almost given up on my idea of splitting shopping from cooking – conceived in ignorance of how Carreck Loose worked. I stood Eddie down and, instead, took Lyndsey and Martin, who'd petitioned for a break from swotting. The three of us bumped our way uncomfortably to Mevagissey in Martin's little car – which looked fetching but had next to no padding under the cracked leather – armed with the local ordnance survey map and copious instructions from Loxton. I posted a letter to her parents for Priyam and did the boring shop at the Co-op; they disappeared down one of the narrow side streets, so Martin could distract Lyndsey by showing her the mechanics of Cornish fishing. He was still in his canvas smock, appropriately enough.

They came back laughing, with the pasties but without receipts – that was going to complicate Loxton's accounts! You didn't get paperwork with 'the real thing', Martin said. The way he told it, half of them came from a cottage in one of the cobbled streets leading up from the harbour, with a sign propped inside the window saying 'Pasties Sold Here' and a grumpy woman serving, which sounded much like the place in my parents' village where Cromer crabs were dressed in the back kitchen. The rest came from the shop Loxton recommended, which was more like mass production. We could all decide which were the best.

I wasn't sure I believed him, but it was a good story, so we agreed to hold a blind tasting. Back at the house we popped the pasties in the Rayburn, knocked up a quick salad and called everyone in to eat. When they were all assembled, tantalised by the smell from the oven, Lyndsey cut the puffy pasties in two – she made a bit of a hash of it – and Martin sent the plates down the table with instructions to have a half of both versions. Of course, we were soon in a complete muddle: the halves looked much the same; the plates underneath them were identical; no one could remember which was which. Loxton, who said he knew a thing or two about tastings from buying wine for the College, quibbled about the conditions – he too might have been pulling our legs – and we enjoyed ourselves eating with our hands and arguing about flavours and which taste was best. The consensus was that 'the old bag pasty' had marginally the edge – meatier, but a tad dry, while what Tyler dubbed 'the Loxton special' was shorter on filling but had a better crust. However, Barnaby was sure we'd been hoodwinked and suggested the pasties had all came from the same place – which one being immaterial. He was familiar with such pranks, he said; the only thing in Mart's favour was that Lyndsey would have said if he'd been making it all up.

Either way, Lyndsey had calmed down – and she'd eaten properly, for once – while the rest of us had had a lot of fun. If Loxton had been with them, I reflected afterwards, they'd never even have discovered the place on the harbour, if it really existed: they'd have been quick-marched off to his favoured shop and that would have been it. Loxton liked his trips to be purposeful, a matter of getting sensibly from A to B. It was the same with his walks: he didn't do wandering off to see what might be there. In fact, come to think of it, he didn't meander anywhere on foot, any more than he did in his head. But despite that you couldn't call him a control freak. If he was with you, he fussed about the shopkeepers, but if he *wasn't*, you could buy from anyone – and provided everything got crossed off his list, he didn't mind what else appeared. Such a man of contradictions! I still wasn't sure I'd got his measure.

Even funnier was the language he used. He called it 'the shopping detail'. Where would he have picked up such military slang, given that he hadn't been on active service in the war? Couldn't we just 'go shopping'? But no, the whole concept was imbued with that 'Boy's Own' feeling of adventure, as if doing the trip was something out of the ordinary for which you had to plan, like a ground campaign, to minimise the unforeseen. Out came the route maps and the comments about 'mustering' here or there – and while there was nothing wrong with preparing the ground, this too was a little ridiculous when we were shopping every day. It reminded me of my uncle's sometimes comical habits, which we'd been forbidden from making fun of. That was the sadness for bachelors of Loxton's vintage: their irrational fixations – buy the pasties here, only play board games, stop at this little layby not that – got more and more entrenched. If Loxton had only had a family – a pair of rowdy boys and a tomboy of a daughter, say – such fads would have been teased out of him.

Barnaby got his way about the bonfire. We built it after lunch once we'd inspected the remnants of an old construction betrayed by an ugly splot of darkness beyond the greenhouses. Blackened soil and grey ash, an acrid mix where it was still damp, defaced the turf; at the extremities the grass crept inwards, curling over the offence and a few charcoal-edged logs suggested what might have been. A row of tree stumps, lined up against the cold frames, waited to be arranged in a curve at a sensible distance. People must have sat around that spot before, staring into the flames – it was a tradition calling out to be revived.

Before we'd even begun gathering wood, Barnaby and Martin had reassembled the circle and were discussing how much heat was needed to bake a potato, forgetting we didn't have any. Thoughts of eating by the fire would have stayed entirely hypothetical had it not been for the marshmallows I'd bought. The prospect of those little bags of rubberiness got me lots of brownie points. All we needed was a fire that would keep going into the evening; then, if the embers were still alight, we could toast them on sticks.

The problem was the dearth of raw material. There was some dead wood on the ground by the pines, not so much branches as gnarled excrescences that might have fallen under the own misshapen weight even without the wind. But mostly that area provided pickings we could only use as kindling: curling spindles of still-pliable twig, topped with a green pipe cleaner; curved sheddings of bark, like rusting cheese graters; and endless tight little cones, too small to collect one by one but big enough to be caught together in the wooden rake.

The real mass of the bonfire had to come from elsewhere. Tyler, Priyam and I explored the outhouses, the two of them deferring noisily to my supposed foraging instincts and swapping stories about where they'd gone as children to escape the city. In the stables we found rotten timber from what might have been an old shed, which Loxton agreed we could use; and there were neat piles of garden waste in the corridor between the greenhouses – trimmings from the shrubs and the area of hedge and so on. Still, we all had to work hard to assemble a good structure. Some of the students went down to the little beach in search of driftwood, returning with a few sizeable pieces washed naked and smooth by the sea. They'd looked for what would have been lying around for a while, they said, finding it mostly at the extremities, under the cliff edges. Anything recently thrown up was too waterlogged and heavy with sand to carry, let alone to burn.

By the time everyone had returned and added their contribution, the pile was nearly too high to see over the top. Eddie didn't believe we would get it to catch, given that some of the wood was damp, and there was a brief debate about using firelighters to give it a kick-start, but the purists won. Jim took Barnaby to collect newspaper and matches from the house and, on their return, the two men crumpled the sheets into loose balls and stuffed them into gaps at the base of the edifice. Then Mei lit the tapers, working with Barnaby from opposite sides, her face almost as studious as when she was at her books. It took several goes to get it to catch in enough places and then, all of a sudden, she was springing back from the crackle and smoke, colliding with Jim and, not so briefly, being held.

Moments like that, which might suggest a burgeoning relationship, made you wonder what was going on behind the scenes; whether you were reading things correctly. After all, Tyler and I had collided and that wasn't necessarily significant.

The thought of Jim and Mei being drawn together made sense; you could imagine them slipping naturally into each other's lives. Not so with the other apparent pairings, which were more of a puzzle.

Rupert and Gloria's behaviour was often an irritant – he'd play her until she seemed more interested in him than in anything else that was going on – but mostly it washed over. I now assumed they'd once had a fling and were reviving the relationship. Then there'd be a moment when Martin and Gloria sparked again with disarming familiarity and I'd think, I've got it the wrong way round! As to how Chloe fitted in – that was anyone's guess.

With Hugh and Lyndsey, who seemed mostly to enjoy each other's company, it was hard to tell whether it went beyond being 'just friends'. If you eavesdropped – and some-times you couldn't help it – you might think they aspired to a kind of rarefied spiritual relationship, with Hugh pursu-ing platonic love or some Catholic equivalent and Lyndsey exploring a romantic notion of her own, all very intense. The Dean hadn't said anything about this – he was pretty dismissive of people he saw as Loxton's pets – and there was never a gesture to suggest it was physical, but then you might just have missed it.

So, as we stood about the bonfire, I watched. Rupert and Gloria were larking again, playing tag behind the backs of those standing on the far side of the fire. Lyndsey and Hugh were in different groups – Lyndsey's trio standing chatting way back from the heat, Hugh poking between pieces of wood to let the air in, flicking stray twigs back towards the flames, discussing the shape of the mound with someone else. Jim and Mei were standing near but not together, talking to other people. I might be imagining things.

When Loxton next came over I alluded to possible two-somes. He conceded he'd noticed but didn't contribute any thoughts of his own; instead he repeated his mantra about not probing into people's private lives. What they got up to outside the reading hours was their own business – always had been and was still so now – and our role was to keep out of it. As if to make his point, he did a quick circuit and retired to the house. I stayed outside for a while, determined not to cave in, but in the end I too went back to the kitchen and the job of making afternoon tea.

Loxton's firmness felt like another ticking-off, a reminder that we were there to set an example of application, not to connive at the distractions.

Tilting back in my chair, foot on the crossbar of the table for safety, sheaves of A4 in my hands, I began to ponder the politics of publication. Should I go for the kind of journal that was now mainstream, like the *Journal of Social History*, where my argument might gain acceptance as a nod towards fashionable trends? Or try somewhere more radical, a feminist publication, say, which might make up for what it lacked in academic kudos by placing me amongst friends?

The issue wasn't just about this particular article – it went far wider. Mine wasn't the kind of history in which Oxford generally traded. Social history might have broad acceptance, but oral history and the poorly documented history of the illiterate was another matter. And Carreck Loose was a reminder that it was indeed the history of *ordinary* people that interested me, the people whose stories hadn't been considered worth recording and who had lacked the means to record them themselves, whose descendants the oral historians were now busy taping in factories and fields, to the dismay of the academic traditionalists. I wanted to know about the very people who had made houses like this possible – skivvying away at scrubbing flagstones, polishing woodwork, carrying water up and down stairs – whose world was shaping us even as we conducted our Reading Party.

Where were the studies of the masses, I wondered, whose labours had allowed the harbourmasters of the day to prosper and whom the likes of Ivy Williams had later aspired to help? Where was the history of the family, rich and poor? Why wasn't there a journal of women's history? Why no female professor in my field?

I stared at the bookcases on either side of the end window, vaguely aware of the burgundy of one row of leather bindings and the blue-blackness of the rest. Tyler had been right to talk of trying to pioneer: I wanted my work – this article – to get noticed. But had it been right to give up York or the radical universities I might have moved to, to argue from inside the fold? Must I now choose the orthodox route again? And how did it help to be in remotest Cornwall, indulging in a quintessentially Oxbridge experience and seeking an accommodation with a symbol of the *ancien régime*?

After Lyndsey had been gone for a while, I took a break to check how she and Martin were getting on with supper: they were such an unlikely pairing. There was loud chatter and an excitable whoop or two from the extension. The two of them were trying to stop parsnips and carrots from rolling off the work surface. Lyndsey, responsible for the whoops, seemed to be in charge of the chopping, while Martin ribbed about her ignorance of livestock.

He threw a question at me: 'Ah: Sarah! What cut would you use in a beef stew?'

I said something about relying on the butcher to advise.

This amused him. 'And you a Norfolk girl! Try living amongst our cows for a few years!' He explained about the cut he'd insisted on. But, he said, that was the sum of his knowledge. He never helped his mother – the kitchen was her territory. Anyway, theirs were dairy herds.

Lyndsey picked up an onion. 'We were trying to remember which of them to put in,' she said, circling the knife in the direction of the other vegetables.

'Watch out!' Martin sprang out of the way of the blade. 'Hopeless! As bad as Rupert – only good at chopping things – but at least he has proper respect for knives.'

'You can talk!' she said. 'You were the one who wanted that thing with an "m".'

She indicated a large brown mixing bowl, covered with a large plate. 'Would you smell that?' she asked me. 'See if we've missed anything. He says it needs at least an hour, so we're behind.'

I took off the lid and made approving sounds while trying to identify the herbs they'd used. There were a lot of grey flecks of uncertain origin, but then that might be me. Jenny, who was good at marinades, always joked that I was the world's worst cook. Even *she* thought a woman should be able to provide.

'Perhaps a bit of garlic salt?' In my experience, this could transform a dish, turning failure into success.

I laid the table as they clattered about behind me at the

worktop, gossiping about the houses they'd lived in. It turned out that Martin's mates in Jericho spent a lot of time sitting around talking and their music was always on loud, whereas Lyndsey had chosen to go back to living in, even though it was expensive, because she hadn't liked the endless chat or the 'multicoloured food' her housemates favoured and preferred to eat quietly in Hall. Then I left them to it.

When eventually they were ready to feed us, their stew proved tasty enough. The students allowed Lyndsey her share of the credit. Martin didn't seem to mind; he was easy about everything.

Loxton and I had ended up sitting in pole position as joint heads of the table, able to survey the scene like parents watching over a very large family, occasionally catching each other's eye. He looked rather happy in the role, whereas I was reminded of our disagreement the night before and the way families gloss these things over. And there were only two days to go before we returned to the routine of College life! I wondered what happened to these Reading Party friendships and whether everyone settled back to their old patterns or found a way of fitting the new mates in. It would be a shame if they lost touch but perhaps that was the way of things – especially for someone like Tyler, who'd go back to the States if he didn't stay for a DPhil.

Priyam, sitting next to me, must have registered the pondering. 'You've gone very quiet, Dr Addleshaw,' she said – she was the only one who had stuck to formality. 'My mother always says, when I go silent, that something must be the matter; she prefers it when we talk too much.'

There was no obvious response to this. *I* was meant to be looking after *them*.

'Is it going as you hoped, now it's mixed?' she asked.

'Well, I'm not sure I had any expectations,' I said, 'and of course I've nothing to compare it with, so it's hard to say.'

'But you always look so at home! That's one of the things we admire: the way you carry things off as if they were nothing.' She paused a minute, which was just as well – I was still trying to take her comment in. 'Dr Loxton seems to think it's going okay. He says it's more relaxed than it used to be.'

'Ah, but does he think we're working as hard?' I asked.

'He didn't say we weren't. I think we must be, don't you? I mean, no one's slacking. I'm ploughing through my Roman law. Even Chloe said she'd got on well today.'

'And what about the play bit of "work hard, play hard"?' I asked.

'Oh, I think it's cool. It's been so serious this term, with everyone panicking about how much revision they've got to do. But here we're having some really good times.'

She gave me that look again, as if trying to decide how much to say. Then she blurted out, 'We're going to sit around the bonfire. Will you come too?'

How had Priyam read my mood? How did anyone read the mood of more than a dozen people? Somehow you sensed that parlour games were *not* what was required that evening. The group hadn't recovered its desire for performance; it was still in reflective mode – subdued, questioning, uncertain.

Martin, excused from washing-up duties because he'd cooked, readied to go in search of sticks for the marshmallows as we'd planned. Muffled in long scarves, torches in hand, we made our way past the glasshouses to the garden shed, where we rummaged in near darkness for something suitable, much as Tyler, Priyam and I had done earlier in the light. It was extremely cold and, as we moved the sacking that blocked the way to the back, we discussed the possibility that a firelit evening wasn't such a good idea, that we would all freeze or poke each other, that it was all a bit infantile. But we'd promised, so we stuck to it, returning with implements for everyone. I had smooth canes about four feet long, most of them already grey from exposure to the elements and split at the base where they'd been pushed into the earth, the few that were still in their pristine golden state easier to see in the gloom; Martin had some longer, bendy shoots of hazel, burgundy coloured, lightly freckled, slightly rough to the touch.

By the time we rejoined them, there were several people by the bonfire – three or four seated on the stumps, the rest moving around, one of them writing in the air with a cigarette as sparkler. The fire had got to that stage where, its initial bulk having been consumed, most of the remainder had sunk into a dense mass of embers, sizzling quietly and only occasionally spitting. Barnaby was trying to lift a portion back into the centre with a pitchfork; having shifted it, he looked around for what to do with the fork, then speared the ground with the two prongs and left its handle rearing up behind the seated group like a thin figure listening in. Priyam, on her piece of log, began pushing marshmallows onto the canes – one open bag in her lap, the other leaning up against the bark by her feet. Ever neat, she was carefully alternating pink and white so she ended up with equal quantities of each. Behind us we could hear Rupert and Gloria cavorting about as they manhandled the wooden bench from the tennis court across the moist clumps of grass; by the time we turned to look, they were on the seat, laughing.

Eventually we were all gathered. Even Loxton came and squatted awkwardly next to Priyam, chatting, though he didn't stay long, which made me wonder briefly if I too was meant to leave them to it.

We toasted the marshmallows, savouring their vanilla-rich sickliness. Barnaby and I lost a couple in the too-hot heat and then burnt our tongues on the melting sugar when they first hung glutinously from the tips of our sticks. After that Jim and I chatted happily about nothing much – me leaning on a rake, he on the pitchfork, each of us occasionally stretching out to reach the fallen charcoal and kick it into the fire. Later still, Tyler and I exchanged thoughts on the quality of the wood we'd gathered earlier, stringing out a mundane subject until neither of us could find anything more to say about it. Instead we stood contentedly in the near darkness away from the flames, watching, trying not to bump into each other – not quite succeeding. That was dangerous, of course; already it felt illicit, a slide towards something that shouldn't be there. It was not the same as the original – accidental – collision.

We were interrupted by a spat between Hugh and Lyndsey. Unlike Gloria, it seemed Lyndsey didn't like being chased; when Hugh slipped on a twig, she retreated and sat on a tree stump, arms around her knees, skirt – as ever – trailing, unmoved. There was a glimpse of Chloe, alone on the bench, similarly huddled forward, smoking her roll-ups. Somewhere Eddie was puffing at his Gauloises Bleu: even at a distance you could smell their dark aroma, a whiff of the intellectual in a workman's café. Tyler joked about his own experiments with smoking, the exaggeration making me laugh enough to lose my balance again, although I probably didn't have to. Our hands grazed each other in the blackness and suddenly, out of nowhere, came the briefest hidden exploration, a teetering on the contours of the fingers so slight that no one else could have noticed it, but enough to be unmistakable. Still I didn't go in.

Who knows who rolled the joint? Presumably Chloe. Eventually I got a waft of skunky weed and saw it being passed around – and to my surprise it was Lyndsey who was taking a drag; fey little Lyndsey, who normally had her head in the poets and her childhood reading, who had wanted the window open in the van and whom I'd never seen with a fag in her hand.

Why did that have to happen? It was too obvious to ignore.

I shifted a fraction, and maybe Tyler did too. Either way, there was a cooling in the air between us, another of those tiny gaps. I carried on talking, fists back in my pockets, wondering what to do. The ban on smoking upstairs was understandable – it probably kept dope out of the house. But dope elsewhere? Loxton couldn't mean to extend the rule where it was bound to be broken. Had I been one of the students, I'd have had a few drags. Such mellow moments almost called for it.

When the joint threatened to get too close, however, I lost my nerve, made a stupid remark about becoming publicly complicit, which made Tyler say, 'Phooey – you worry too much!', and pulled away properly – just as Priyam emerged from the gloom where I thought it had been empty. I could feel Tyler looking after me as I set off for the house. Genuinely annoyed or merely amused? It was too dark to tell.

Priyam may have seen us or caught the end of the conversation, but if so she didn't comment; just walked back with me on the pretext that she needed the loo, chatting away as if nothing had happened. Standing by the fridge, milk bottle in one hand, door handle in the other, I asked her to keep an eye out for Mei, who might not be used to such adventures. She looked straight back at me. 'It'll be fine,' she said. 'Don't worry. We're just hanging out.'

Loxton must already have gone up. On the one occasion when, possibly, I was meant to check in with him, there was nobody about and the house was silent. I lingered a few minutes, collecting this and that – vaguely hoping that Tyler might follow, so I got the chance to explain – until the empty spaces began to unnerve me. It was okay going past the wasted privacy of the annexe, which somehow never spooked me; the heebie-jeebies came when I was walking up the second flight of stairs in the stillness, imagining myself stuck in the middle between latches that wouldn't lift, slowly desiccating in the dark of an abandoned building, and had to stop myself from pounding noisily to the top. Back in my lonely attic, lying in my freezing bed – socks on, knees pulled up under my nightie – I got quietly crosser and crosser, asking myself why I'd made such a fuss, wanting someone to blame.

It was that line that I hadn't wanted to recognise, the line that separated the students from the dons. Had I left the bonfire earlier, like Loxton, there would have been nothing to see and the question of what to do about it wouldn't have arisen. Instead it was horribly clear that you couldn't be on both sides of the barricades at the same time; there was no escaping the need to choose.

Still, by the time I switched off the light I'd found my solution. I wasn't going to be one of those creepy lecturers who let it all hang out with their students, pretending they weren't an authority figure when of course they were – the Dean strayed dangerously close, with his spiky hairdo and his clingy jeans. No, the students and I were in different camps, and it was best not to pretend otherwise. But I didn't have to be craven. Dope was no big deal; Tyler was right. And the proper response to silly diktats had always been reform. In fact, a College happily in the vanguard in one area should avoid petty battles in others. So if Loxton complained about the spliffs, I would say it was beneath us; the students should smoke what they liked outside.

As for the more important things that might be off limits, which Priyam might or might not have registered, I barely dared to go there; that wonderful slide into the depths was too frightening to think about. It could not – would not – happen.

Thursday

After all that agonising, it was odd to find the following day starting as normal. The only unusual bit was the plan about the beach.

The landing was fast becoming the hub of our floor – a place of conversations and glimpsed views of private space. We joked when we passed or stopped to talk. We left doors open, stood on thresholds watching, wandered in on each other. And if the students hesitated where I was concerned, it was pretty minimal.

That morning, for instance. My door was ajar; soon there was a gentle knock.

'Are you decent, Dr Addleshaw?' Priyam spoke just loud enough for me to hear.

'Just about. It's fine – only my shoes to go. Come in.'

She pushed the door wide, let it swing back and then sat on the little chair that looked so pert with its high back screening the wallpaper and its embroidered cushion catching the sunshine.

I glanced away from the buckle on my platforms, wondering if she was about to embarrass me. 'All well?'

She nodded. 'Groovy. Just wanted you to know.'

'Well, that's good of you. Was it a late one?'

She nodded again but didn't expand – nothing about Tyler or anyone else – so that can't have been why she was visiting.

But there was no time to ask how she was getting on, as Martin was sticking his head round the open door.

'Big room, Sarah,' he said, bounding cheerily across the floorboards and into the recess of the gable window. 'How come yours is so big?' There was a tease about preferential treatment and the lucky dip.

'Has she told you the plan?' He gestured at Priyam.

'No way! It's your plan, not mine. Anyhow, Dr Addleshaw may not approve.'

Martin ignored the last bit. 'Well, I'm game. Can't leave Barny to brave it alone.'

He turned back to me. 'We thought we'd go to the beach – the long bay, not the short one – get everyone to scramble down that track. We could play ball games, smell the sea. Some of us might even go in.'

'Fine by me,' I said, liking the picture, wondering what the limits of decorum might be. I was a good swimmer, used to the North Sea; if I'd had my costume, I would have joined in. 'Which bit were you seeking approval for?'

'Oh, I don't know. You never can tell – sometimes he fusses, sometimes he doesn't.'

'Quite. Well, better check that he's okay with it. He'll want the balls kept dry. And it'll be icy: you're not serious about going in?'

But Martin said he was and claimed to have checked the bay out with Hugh. It was easily deep enough for a game, he said; a great U-shape where the clifftop dipped, with boulders at the rear and a curving expanse of sand, so any balls should be fine. He only stopped his gesturing as he opened the door to the staircase to let us go first.

'What do you think?' he called out behind me, above the clatter of our footwear on the wooden treads. 'Rounders or Frisbee?'

I should have chosen the American game, but I was

concentrating on Priyam's head as she spiralled in front of me: if you went down too fast, you risked banging against the dusty walls, which of course we did all the time; the servants would have done the same.

'Either. Beat you at both!' I said, and held open the door with its diagonal bracing. We used the back stairs for the rest of the way, so we could surprise the early risers by emerging from the 'cupboard'.

In fact, only four people were up – thankfully not Tyler – and none of them paid much attention. Still, being ahead made it easier to assess the mood of the day. So much was revealing.

Take Rupert, for instance. He rose earlier than I'd expected and was much quieter at breakfast – almost emollient before his wisecracking revved into action. Unlikely he reserved his spikiness for later in the day; probably it just took him time to get underway. Besides, there was the distraction of the papers: he liked to read them over his cereal and was always grumbling at being a day out with the news. So long as he had that to occupy him, he would focus his barbs on politicians, union leaders – anyone he thought was an ass, which was pretty much everyone in public life – rather than us. It was when that was done that you had to watch out. He was a bit like the Dean, really.

And there he was, true to type, although this time he was reading out scores from the Centenary Test, which was on a knife-edge down in Melbourne, or had been when they went to press. Of course that set him off again: a huge house but no TV or radio; it was ridiculous to have to sit in an icy van just to find out what was happening in the big wide world – but if he could have the keys, he might go and do just that, get the results.

Jim too seemed to be a morning person, though that didn't

make him any more forthcoming: the silent type, as the Dean had said, but more interesting than that implied. He was always in the kitchen before me and, having introduced porridge to the menu, had created a role that eased his prickly path into the group. There'd be discussion about how many he was cooking for, debate about the merits of salt versus sugar, teasing about the consistency of the gloop. It was never he who started the talking, but he was part of it, the focus even, in a roundabout way.

That day he was at his post again, defending his oats from the charge of going bobbly, and it was Mei who stuck up for hot breakfasts and asked for another spoonful. I thought of the scene by the bonfire and tried to remember the details: Mei was normally too shy to intervene.

Meanwhile, Loxton was sitting in the conservatory, scarf on, crossword, as ever, on his knee. He gave me a little wave. If anything had been amiss, surely he'd have risen to claim my attention? But when he did enquire how the evening had gone, once we were by ourselves, he exhibited none of his forensic curiosity. He didn't even wait for a reply.

'Usually a bottle of spirits, or some other drug, appears on such occasions. I won't even ask if it did last night. Generally I find it is best not to know, which is why I absent myself. If I'm not there, there's no need for any decisions. But it's harder for the younger tutors. At your age you can't win. "To fuss or not to fuss" is almost an existential question!'

And, as if he didn't want to embarrass me further, he refrained from asking how I would answer it. Instead, he set off towards the corridor as if it was just like any other day.

This was positively avuncular, although it would have been more helpful earlier on. Loxton began to grow on me.

After breakfast, I took my papers to the morning room to complete my circuit of the house.

It was a reassuring surprise. For a start, Chloe had removed herself or been banished; Gloria was still at the roll-top, wrapped in that cardigan of hers; Eddie, on his sofa, was motionless; and it was Rupert in the campaign chair, legs stretched before him, crossed at the ankle. The dynamics had changed; it was a model of silent application.

I sat down at the only remaining place – the little side table between the windows, where you could check the goings-on, should you need to, in the mirror above your head – and parked my wodge of papers. There was no chat and barely a shifting of positions as I spread my notes in a great arc beside my chair.

Remarkable how quickly you could sink back into the same mental space. I reread my paper, checking the logic of the croppings and reorderings of the previous morning, and felt reassured. It was now coherent and compelling – I could even imagine applause at the end, if I turned it into a lecture, when the argument was so satisfyingly brought together. As for the question of where it should be published, the answer seemed suddenly obvious: it should go where it would make waves. And so what if people were taken aback! Since when had I fussed about that? Now wasn't the time to be feeble.

It wasn't until Loxton's shoes appeared in my line of vision that I registered the time. An interruption – damn!

In the kitchen there was Mei, patiently waiting to do her turn with the shopping, and to my surprise there was Jim, offering to give us a hand. The transparency of the gesture was sweet: the dour Jim was indeed warming to the gentle Mei – a lovely thought. Did it matter if he took a short break? Surely not. He was too dogged by half – deserved a bit of fun. I would defend him if Loxton complained.

In the little town we wandered down the tiny high street, chatting inconsequentially over the crying of the gulls – an awful sound, like cats wailing – as we bumped our way along the narrow pavement. I looked at Loxton's list. Tyler had added the things he and Chloe needed; then there was a gap, followed by 'Chocolate?', the 'C' billowing in his cursive script. How had he guessed? Or was he thinking of the others? Either way, it was propitious: there in front of me was the confectioner's with its yellow-filmed window display revelling in the trappings of Easter – the colourful tiers of egg boxes, the fluffy chicks with their orange legs strutting around the straw beneath, a nest of pale blue mounds and a garden gnome peeking out from behind the clumps of fake daffodils. I paused to look, wondering whether the kitty might run to some chocolate extravagance, wanting to give Jim and Mei some space.

'Do you mind if I nip in here?' I asked. 'You could do the bakers and have a wander while I finish off?'

Jim seemed uncertain, shifting the empty basket from one hand to the other. It was Mei who murmured about seeing the harbour. She was more single-minded than you might think, not really bland at all.

When I returned to the car park they were just ahead of me, each holding a handle of the shopping bag suspended between them, each with a loaf under the outer arm. Jim said they'd been doing some research of their own. There was a clear view to the warehouses from the harbourmaster's house – he would have seen everything that went on along the quayside as the boats unloaded. They could picture him at the window with his telescope, watching. It made it easier to understand his hold over the little town.

Hadn't Jim said something about a girlfriend back home? That would complicate things. The details had gone from my mind, but it didn't stop a flush of concern for him and Mei, both so lacking in guile.

*

It was a jolt, coming back to Carreck Loose after the sounds and smells of Mevagissey. You might expect a house with that many people in it to be rowdy, but it was still and silent, as if it were empty. For all we knew the students had decamped to the little beach, creeping out without Loxton noticing – or he might have taken it into his head to change the routine and whisk them off on a morning walk. But no: bowed heads were visible through the dining room window as we opened the back door. So we kept our voices low and unpacked the bags. Job done, Mei and Jim returned to their books, Jim charged with sending Eddie to give me a hand.

And in Eddie came, stretching his arms wide and then standing by the table with them locked behind his head, assessing the task but doing nothing.

When he saw the paper bags of sweet-shop gaudiness, he sprang out of his trance. 'Hey, Easter eggs! Don't you just lurve things that are bad for you?' He tipped out the Creme Eggs, one hand hovering as they rolled wonkily across the table, the other scrunching abandoned paper. 'My absolute fave! How did you guess?'

Typical. If they were for anyone, it wasn't him.

'Don't be such a solipsist.' I said. 'We didn't – you just got lucky. But if they're such a favourite, you can decide when we get to eat them.'

Eddie was all for pleasure now not pleasure later, so we agreed to have the eggs with coffee, instead of at teatime. That decided, he set to and together we assembled the lunchtime spread, chatting all the while about Restoration comedy, which he liked and which he'd be doing before Prelims. I asked if he'd come across a friend of mine who was researching the female playwrights of the era, but no, he hadn't heard of her or of them – he hadn't thought there were any. What about Aphra Behn? Oh, was that a woman? He hadn't realised. At school they'd done Vanbrugh, and he'd seen Congreve too, but they were later, weren't they?

187

I was shocked. Here he was, studying English literature, and he hadn't read the first woman reputedly to earn her living as a writer? Nope, he was afraid he hadn't, but he promised to order her up from the stacks when we got back. What about female actors, and the significance of having the King's mistress on stage? Yep, he knew about that, but he hadn't been looking at it from my perspective. This wasn't about being a historian or gender politics, I said, and anyway he shouldn't presume. How could anyone understand a comedy of manners, devoid of its social context? You'd miss half the jokes. Oh, he said, he just liked the bawdiness: it was so explicit, so liberating. Fun to act. He'd been Lord Foppington in *The Relapse* in the sixth form, which had been a hoot.

The glibness was oddly undermining, as if someone more worldly had shown me up as an obsessive. And he was still at it, gaily saying he'd never been taken to task before.

After that we moved on to the business of acting. It was easy to see why he was spending so much time with the University and College drama societies – even why he liked farce: he had a facility for mimicry and almost total recall of large chunks of what he was reading.

'But how *do* you remember it all?' I asked.

'Oh that! That's the easy bit. My father always says the brain's elastic – the more you make it remember, the greater its capacity.' Eddie finished what he was chopping and pushed the pile to the edge of the board. 'He found that out doing medicine. Once you learnt the trick of memorising all that anatomy, remembering more just wasn't an issue. So he learnt poetry too. He can still recite screeds of it.'

'And the difficult part?'

'Inhabiting the character. Definitely. It's much harder getting inside a personality, suppressing your own and finding theirs. That's why I like farce – the characters aren't complex, so it's easy to do.'

As soon as he said it, it was obvious that the flamboyant Eddie might find invisibility a challenge. At least he'd admitted it – not what you'd expect. Perhaps not so insufferable after all.

'What about directing?' I asked.

'What about it?'

'Have you ever considered directing instead of acting?'

But before he could answer, the others began to troop in. That was one of the frustrations of the Reading Party: somebody was always interrupting an interesting conversation. Still, even broken ones – like the tantalising snatches with Tyler – were better than nothing, and you had to remember you were in credit overall.

Besides, the conviviality was wonderful, the interruptions almost worth it. By that stage, our fifth day together, lunch had become a noisy affair. Loxton no longer dominated and even Jim was vocal. People were always getting up and down: they knew where things were, would disappear into the larder to retrieve the mustard or go to the fridge when the butter was getting low, leaning across the table as they came back to deposit what was missing, loudly pulling their chairs back into place, tapping a shoulder two places down, calling out if that didn't work, pulling a face if anyone hushed them down. Even the two big Easter eggs were started without so much as a by your leave. It was like the gatherings we'd had in my last house in York, when we cooked brunch on Sundays for a rabble of friends, except that in Cornwall there was the exhilaration of new relationships, all jumbled in together – nothing was stale.

The chocolate and the weather helped. That day it was glorious. The kitchen, which drained of colour when mist or cloud lowered over the promontory, was bright with the contrast of blue sky, green meadow and grey stone wall outside, and the glitter of red, blue and gold foil within. The door into the conservatory was open, so we could feel the warmth and smell the geraniums. Even the sea looked enticing, meeting the sky in a sharp line, as if two pieces of clear blue film had been laid alongside, one merely paler than the other. It demanded a visit.

Martin and Barnaby were now standing by the wicker chairs, matt curves of crazy-paving chocolate in their hands, considering.

'What's the verdict?' I asked, holding the tray of coffees, waiting for them to choose.

'Oh, a definite yes. We have to go. Much more fun than playing up here.' Martin returned a scrunch of green foil to the tray and turned to Barnaby. 'You agree, don't you, Barny?'

'Yeah, the beach it is. And rounders.'

Ah. So we wouldn't have Tyler perfecting our technique at Frisbee.

'Actually, I meant the flavours,' I said. 'Which do you prefer, easy-going Galaxy or Bourneville sophistication?'

'Not bothered, so long as it's chocolatey.' As if to make his point, Martin polished off his last snap of shell and smacked his lips.

'And going in? Are you still thinking of going in?'

Barnaby nodded. 'Of course. Why not?'

Behind us, Loxton came up with his pipe, puffing. He was a milk-chocolate man here, I'd noticed – on holiday from the SCR fare. Tyler liked it dark.

'Do I gather you have yet to change your minds?'

'You do.'

'And Sarah's encouraging you?'

'She hasn't said no.'

'I can't pretend surprise.' He paused and then seemed to change his mind. 'Well, that would be another first. We've had games, but we've never had swimmers.' A further puff of the pipe. 'How many of you are being rash?'

'Rash? Who said anything about rash?' Martin puffed his chest and beat it with both hands. 'We're hardened. We've got the boat on the water before most people wake up – or at least we used to, until you all made us work so hard.' He raised his arms, now expansive in his patch of sun. 'Me. Barny. P'rhaps Jim.'

'I was forgetting. Always admire a chap who rows. And a Blue, too! Or is that Barnaby?'

Before either could answer, I stepped in. 'Hang on a minute! The women row too – we're just as hardy. It was the women, not the men, who were Head of the River last year – ask Gloria.'

Loxton was punctilious. 'I stand corrected. Sarah always picks me up when her sex is being maligned. Either way, men or women, you must take towels. And coats.' He looked at the southerly horizon. 'Yes, you must take coats too. No one's to catch a chill on my watch.'

Then, in his infuriating way, he turned to me just as Martin had suggested a master might turn to the house matron. 'You'll see that they have enough coats, won't you?'

The others were bound to be watching, Tyler among them. 'I'm sure they can look after their kit without help from me,' I said, pleased even as I realised how it had come out.

'Good one!' said Martin. 'You can count on Sarah to give as good as she gets.'

He was such an ally.

I picked up a discarded Creme Egg, which threatened to ooze fake yolk on the sill in the wake of a sticky gloop of opaque egg white, and turned back to the kitchen, saying to nobody in particular. 'All done? All ready?'

It took us a while to get down to the shore. There was the walk across the fields, with their pretty wild flowers, to get to the soft undulations around the cliffs; then the trudge on the slopes until we reached the bulge above the main bay; then the clamber down the tiny path that trickled between the gorse bushes and boulders, negotiating protruding shards of slate and sudden lumps of stone and worrying about spraining our ankles. At the very end you were almost forced to do it on the run, with a leap and a crunch onto the flat of untouched beach.

As it happened, our timing was perfect. The tide was out, the sea looking still in the distance but slopping gently to and fro against the boulders by the rock face, and swelling and ebbing near the centre of the bay. A great expanse of sand – more like a very fine shingle really; grey, uneven and elongated, being slate-based – lay between the water and the bowl of the cliff, at such a shallow gradient that it was kept in a state of glistening wetness several yards deep as the water threw itself up the beach and dragged back to the depths. Further back was a shorter, moon-shaped stretch where the sand was out of the water's reach, soft and dry, and here we dumped our things and the wooden bat.

Loxton must have played rounders there before: he took off with Barnaby to set out the bases with the towels, the posts proving hard to see, and paced the lozenge so it sat comfortably within the shape of the bay and the balls wouldn't be batted into the sea – three of the bases on the dry area, the other on the edge of the damp portion. By the time they'd walked back, the rest of us had formed into two teams where we stood so, as it happened, Priyam was the only woman on my side while Loxton found himself with more women than men. Serve him right! In other respects we were evenly matched. My team was the taller, at least on the male side – Hugh outstripping them all, Rupert and then Tyler coming close behind, Eddie and Martin still well above me. Loxton, on the other hand, had Gloria, who was sporty; the other girls, all potentially 'nimble'; and Barnaby and Jim, who would fight.

It was a rowdy game from the start. The scale of the bay, the buffeting of the wind, the difficulty of running on such a surface, all encouraged yelling and ungainliness – and of course it was a release, too, after the hours of quiet and sitting still. Approaching the first base, the one nearest the water, you had to make a quick calculation, if need be leaping aside to miss the froth. If you passed that hurdle, it seemed impossible to get round the course without stumbling elsewhere: turning the second and third corners, the dry sand gave way and sent you scrambling for balance; even on the straight a stray step might sink in, leaving you lurching wildly. No wonder, at the end of the circuit, we were each triumphant: it was a feat to stay upright.

So there was no surprise in the unleashing of wildness – it was a glorious feeling to have the wind tingling against our faces, a stickiness growing on our hair, the build-up of heat under our coats and then the shock when, the top layer being thrown off, the cold belted through. Who wouldn't have let rip at such a moment? But we did it in different ways. Curiously, Priyam and Mei, both normally so polite, were amongst the most raucous – Priyam screaming support as our team careered round the mounds of towelling, mittened hands cupped around her mouth; Mei jumping up and down as her side reached the end of the circuit. Tyler hollered as loudly as the rest of them and batted well too; it was good to see him flushed, panting and grinning with pleasure when he thumped back into the sand beside me, sending out a mini spray of his own. Even Loxton did his bit of shouting, though you couldn't say that he 'ran'. It was Hugh who looked ill at ease, a matchstick man almost lost in the shimmering distance when he was part way round the course, arms and legs splaying at awkward angles when he returned to base – he might have been made of balsa wood.

After the first innings Loxton produced two bottles of

lemon barley from the knapsack where he kept his emergency supplies – he was infuriating, the way he treated us like children – and we stood in the shadow of the rock, a clutch of pink faces tilting back to the sky as we swigged, wiping the neck with his handkerchief but sniffing loudly when our noses ran. And then Martin was chasing Gloria, and Gloria was grabbing Rupert's velvet jacket where it flared at the hip, trying to evade pursuit, while the rest of us – onlookers only – tried not to be pulled to the ground.

Midway through the second innings it became obvious that Loxton's side would win. Except that, whatever he claimed, it wasn't his *team* that was doing well; it was his *women*. At that point tribal emotion broke out: Priyam and I were supporting our sisters, the men were in similar collusion and the cohesion of the two teams was rent from within. Gloria was the last to bat and she hit the ball way down the beach as I had tried to do, sending Eddie racing to retrieve it. While he swirled around, looking frantically about him, Gloria rushed round the course, floundering a bit at the second base and then regaining her stride. By the time he'd found the ball, she'd skirted the froth and was coasting back to the final post like an athlete confident of reaching the finishing line, arms raised, exultant.

And then the unexpected happened. Instead of slowing down, Gloria picked up speed, turning into a wide arc behind the base. As she came back and levelled with the rest of us, running inside the strip where the ground was firm, she began to pull off her sweater – tugging until it was half over her head and she nearly lost her footing. When it cleared she tossed it amongst the deposits of seaweed and carried on, unbuttoning her shirt, fumbling and slowing further. Then she stopped, bent over and we could just make out the unlacing of boots beneath the wildness of her hair. She chucked them too up the beach, in the direction of some boulders, yanked off her trousers and threw them aside along with something too small to identify – presumably her socks. And as she did it she was yelling, 'Come on, Martin. You said you would.'

With a quick look at Rupert, who was standing as if transfixed, Martin began running out to the water, pulling off his jumper as he went and stuffing it under his arm, calling to Barnaby in turn, and then pausing, head down into the wind, to fiddle with the top of his trousers. When Barnaby made to follow, Jim started rugby-tackling him to the ground in a heap of boisterous male show – and then they too scrambled to their feet and headed off.

Before any of them got halfway to her, Gloria, a large dot in the distance, had stripped to a dark bra and knickers. She was too far away for us to see where she dropped her shirt – it looked as if she just held out her arm and let go where she stood – and I wondered if the bra would come off too in a gesture of women's liberation, and what Loxton would do about *that*, but no. Perhaps the abandonment was more a personal than a political statement – whatever the Dean said, Gloria wasn't one for the language of female oppression. Then she was running across the patch of wet sand in her underwear, ploughing through the froth, shrieking with the shock of cold, shrieking too at the men behind her, heaving her body through the water until she was in to her thighs, shrieking again as a wave hit her and she struggled to maintain her balance, and then momentarily silent before she lifted her arms, dipped and plunged. Within seconds she was jumping in the water, yelling in shock and exhilaration, facing the men as they ran in behind her, their arms held parallel with the sea. Then she turned again towards the ocean as they too ploughed into the water, and the four of them powered away from the beach with a few strokes of the crawl.

It happened so fast that the rest of them, silenced with

admiration for the folly and the glory of it, had barely resumed talking before the four bathers were on their feet again and stumbling through the water, Gloria briefly turning round to run on the spot as the others caught up, the little group then jogging back towards us in loose formation, tiny figures bobbing against the murky silver and beige-grey backdrop of sea and sand. As they crossed the dark meander of seaweed in the distance, they drew level and, barely slowing their pace, lined up with Gloria off-centre, arms locked across each other's shoulders, just as Tyler's group had done on the descent to the pub. We could just see them briefly looking down, slowing to match their pace, before they carried on towards us, trotting in unison. When they neared we could see the grinning, the shared congratulation, the euphoria.

Where was Tyler? This should have been me, not Gloria.

Then she broke away, waved and started running again, ahead of the other three, and I spotted him joshing with Rupert, man to man, oblivious.

'The towels! Where are the towels?' Mei rushed to and fro, darting between us, almost desperate.

I glanced at the piles around us, trying to remember what we'd done with them and where Loxton was, my mind momentarily blank. Danger of hypothermia! And what would he think of all this nakedness?

Lyndsey shouted something into the wind and began an awkward sprint up the bay, bending at the first and second bases to pick up the small heaps of colour and then at the third base handing them over to Mei, who'd made straight for the final marker. It would have been faster the other way round – Lyndsey really wasn't a sportswoman and she was hampered by her skirt, whereas Mei's neat clothes followed the hard curves of a gymnast's body, all toned muscle – but that was how it happened. So the two of them only caught up with the swimmers after rejoining the group.

By then Gloria had Martin's heavy coat draped around her shoulders and was trying with her spare hand to grab her jumper, held at the other end by Rupert, who picked that moment to yank it just out of reach, taunting. Her hair had turned to the dark brown of the earth and was dripping at the ends as it swayed to and fro, leaving stray strands clinging to a cleavage that bulged from the wet nylon; her skin, which had been stunned into blotchy redness around the tops of her thighs, was beginning to acquire a purple hue. Perhaps the tug of war ceased to amuse her, or she was suddenly aware of near naked-ness; whatever the case, she turned sharply away, shrouding herself in the towel that Mei held up to screen her, and, muffled by wrapping, called out to Chloe to get the rest of her clothes.

Meanwhile the three men stood shivering a few paces away, nostrils flaring, arms clasped across their chests, talking so fast they could hardly be understood, waiting to cover up while Eddie joked around with Loxton's tea towels. Barnaby, suddenly chatty as he tried to convey how cold the water had been, stood with his legs braced and picked at his pants, unleashing a pocket of water, which ran in rivulets down to his ankles, curving its way past muscle and hair. Jim, self-conscious again in white Y-fronts that had gone loose and heavy with wet, barely lifted his head as he took a towel, but then grinned sheepishly once he had it firmly tied it round his middle. Martin, louder in something red with a white elastic waistband, tossed his to Barnaby and then reached out again.

Normally Martin was good with his thank yous, but he too failed to acknowledge Mei. Instead he stood motionless, his outstretched arm still laden, watching as Gloria pulled his coat back onto her shoulders and bent to brush sand off her feet, steadying herself with her hand on Rupert's arm. Seconds later Martin was turning back to Barnaby and Jim, muttering about laying down his robe but losing the prey, and then vigorously rubbing his chest.

To break the awkwardness that followed – something about the abundant bare flesh, Loxton studiously busying with his thermos and handing round tea, or the fact that Chloe still hadn't moved in response to this unscheduled 'happening' – I called out to Tyler and we set off down the beach to collect the clothes. Somebody had to do it; besides, even ignoring him could seem obvious. Most of it was easy – Jim and Barnaby had left their things in a single pile and Martin's were spread over a small area, but Gloria's belongings were strewn around and it took a minute to track down her footwear, beyond the biggest of the boulders. The two of us stood together in the blow, arms laden, scanning the sand and the line of seaweed as the light began to dim, discussing whether socks really mattered. Then I saw the last one lying waterlogged at the back of a stray crest of slate, a tiny pool forming around it, halfway down the slope to the sea.

'There it is,' I said, glancing over the rock at the rest of the group.

Tyler balanced the pile of belongings on the sand and went off empty-handed to get it, waiting for the lick at the end of the wave to peter out and recede before he risked the short dash. He came back squeezing out water and flapping it flat. Smiling, he presented it to me, dangled between the thumb and forefinger.

'One sock, not red and much inferior to Eddie's!' he said.

I reached out – we were standing next to each other, both facing into the wind – and wobbled slightly. And there he was, raising his arm to steady me just as he had before, even though he hadn't needed to.

'I thought *you'd* be the one to go in,' he said.

'She beat me to it,' I replied. 'So annoying!'

'You could have gone too,' he said.

'That's not what I meant. It's just that it's so frustrating – all these things I'm not supposed to do.'

'Who says?'

I didn't answer.

He stopped to look me full in the face. 'I'd have joined you. Should have stripped off myself. It was just bad timing – a split-second thing – missing the moment.' Then he rested his arm lightly across my shoulders – a curving glow of warmth.

Was Gloria watching? Had the others spotted us? I was torn between wanting his arm there and urgently wanting it not to be.

'You know, I'll remember this,' he said, lifting the hand to gesture vaguely and then pulling me properly into the shape of him, so that my cheek brushed the ribbing of his jumper and my hair nestled like a carroty beard under the nook of his chin. It was another of those wonderful pinpricks of pleasure, but he didn't say whether he meant the view, the group reassembling in the distance, the Reading Party as a whole, or even the pair of us standing together, and it was over in a second, so it was hard to guess the significance.

Briefly, an image sped by of Andy and me on the beach at Holkham in the days when we were still captivated by each other's company. We'd stood together in much the same way, spray from the surf stinging our faces, and then he'd turned to kiss me – a long, sensual kiss that began with the taste of salt and lingered as our hair flicked around us. Only the yapping of the family dog at our feet had brought the clinch to an end.

Too long since there's been any romance, I thought; people like Jim and Mei had no idea how lucky they were. And then I remembered Gloria's eyes and Loxton's fussing, and before I knew it I'd said, 'We should go – they'll start looking,' and pulled away.

'Phooey,' he replied – it was that word again. 'They've got other things on their minds.'

But he too stepped aside, the warmth went and we walked

back across the sand, heads bent and with 15 feet between us, as if we'd had a tiff, which I suppose in a way we had.

Our troupe arrived at the house with less than five minutes to go before library conditions resumed. The climb up the cliff had been arduous and perhaps we'd dawdled a bit on the home stretch – certainly the fourteen of us were more spread out than usual, the swimmers in their damp clothes straggling at the rear with their groupies. Loxton was clearly rattled and there was a hint of that vengeful hypochondria in his repeated fussing about the danger of chills, an old-womanish edge even greater than before, perhaps because he was embarrassed by all that flesh or once again at odds with me. He was brusque in the kitchen about the resumption of celebratory chat, packing the swimmers off for hot baths and a change of clothes, overruling Priyam – with whom he was normally so gentle – as she put mugs on the table. The two of us would do another tea round, he decreed; everyone else should do whatever they needed to do and then settle back at their desks.

On impulse, I suggested we might simply push everything back half an hour, which would give the bathers time to recover and the rest of us time to draw breath. Loxton seemed surprised, annoyed even, at the intervention. We had a tart exchange that might even have got heated had it not been for the presence of others. In fact, he only conceded the point when some of them voiced their support – notably Tyler, actually, who was to cook with Chloe and said they'd welcome a few minutes to plan. By then Loxton's tetchiness was looking ungracious – and although we all tried, with the ceremony of tea and the cake Mei and Jim had chosen, we seemed to have forfeited the normal convivial slide into the late afternoon. There was no lounging around as a group; everything was fragmented and abrupt.

Back in the morning room, the mood had changed from the peaceful start to the day. Eddie decamped for the appeal of a larger sofa, which left me stuck with Rupert, who looked tense. Gloria appeared, bringing with her a waft of pine bath suds, her hair freshly damp – brazen again. Then Rupert switched to Eddie's place, which meant a third change. Plus there was a tautness in the air, what you might call 'an atmosphere', which made it even harder to concentrate.

The descent into evening didn't help. The windowpanes became shiny black mirrors, amplifying the slightest movement. Gloria and Rupert were unnaturally still until a flurry of something or other – secret messages I suppose. Distracted by the reflections, I got up and closed the curtains, flinching as each set of wooden rings scraped the length of the rods, ready to say sorry, except that neither of them raised their heads.

The tiniest noises became infuriating. Being linguists, they each had a dictionary and, periodically, something to look up. I hadn't noticed the pattern in the morning; that afternoon, it was as if they did nothing but search for words. Every time I was conscious of the pages turning and the slide of a finger down the leaf; could almost *hear* the gap while the definition was digested; was distracted equally by the sound of a jotting and the absence of note-taking; noticed again as the dictionary was pushed away or put down. I kept straining to work out what was going on. Was it more passing of messages? Who knows.

When I wasn't focused on the mood and the sounds, clips from the drama on the beach replayed themselves in my head: the enviable moment of Gloria's abandonment, running in a curve like a footballer after a goal; the bleakness of Martin's barbed reference to Sir Walter Raleigh; Jim's look of embarrassment and pride as he shivered in his Y-fronts, his skin so pale it was almost grey; Mei rushing around with the towels.

I kept seeing, too, Tyler's body poised, elongated, arm stretched aloft in that extraordinary freeze before it snapped down in the act of bowling; the yelling of my side, during our innings, after he flung the bat into the sand in front of me and sprinted away, when I, watching the way he ran, forgot it was my turn; the moment we all realised that Gloria was going to go in, when everyone turned to watch and I caught his reaction – that impulse to join them which I had felt too. Most insistent of all was that arm on my shoulder, rocking me in oh-so-briefly. What had that meant, why say 'Phooey' again, and, above all, what was I *doing*, gliding towards waters into which you shouldn't go?

Round and round the spool went, wasting the reading hours.

Within minutes of the gong, Gloria, Rupert and I were milling in the hall with everybody else, waiting for the temporary logjam in the corridor to subside. It reminded me of College before dinner. For a period there was always a crowd of students waiting to go into Hall, trying to be heard above each another, wanting to sit with their mates. You half expected to see Loxton, like one of the stewards, counting us through.

Did we get through the meal faster than usual? It certainly seemed so. For the first time there was proper political argument, a ferocious, rapid-fire discussion about unionism, unofficial strikes and the absence of *The Times* the previous week, which then moved on to the Grunwick dispute, sweatshops and the right to union recognition. Probably we were all a bit 'tired and emotional', still drunk on the events of the afternoon, or maybe it was Chloe's chilli con carne, which suffered from an overdose of paprika – there was a surfeit of something. It wasn't clear to me how the row started, but Rupert certainly goaded it once it got underway: there he was down the other end of the table raising this issue and that, as if he'd been charged with involving them all, and then lobbing in remarks that seemed calculated to provoke. He riled Priyam by referring to the 'strikers in saris', which she said was demeaning, unworthy even of hack journalists. But that was predictable enough. The surprise was when the reaction came from Barnaby – normally so steady, phlegmatic and unrufflable. Suddenly he leant forward.

'Stop playing bloody games, Rupert. All this point-scoring, as if it's just a matter of good or bad argument, all form and no content, loftily seen from above. It's not. And you're not some great arbitrator in the sky. You have to take a position, like everyone else. Yes to picketing or no?' He was compelling; I was proud of him.

Jim, who'd been fiddling with the cuff of his jumper, tensed visibly, waiting.

Tyler, sitting between the two of them, pushed his chair back to give them space.

'Perhaps I don't have a position,' said Rupert slowly, scoring the peel of an orange into neat quadrants and stripping them off, so the tang of the zest mixed with the honeyed smell of molten wax.

Jim pushed his plate away. 'That's a luxury some people can't afford – and I don't mean only those who walked out, the women on twenty-five pounds a week. Inflation's always hurt the poor most of all – Sarah could tell you that. Anyway it's not true, is it, about not having a position? Barny's right. Of course you have one. Everybody does.'

There was no time to work out when I'd said anything about inflation and the poor: Rupert was again underway. 'I don't see why. One doesn't have to have a position on everything. Ask Tyler – he's great at avoiding them.'

But Jim ignored him. 'In the real world you do – people have to decide whose side they're on. We've got whole towns out of work in Wales. Going on the dole isn't what you do in the holidays, not if you're a miner. This isn't about smarty-pants disputation – which Tyler *doesn't* do, by the way. It's about making ends meet and it's no joke.'

Rupert pulled at the pith on the last quarter and flicked it towards the pile at the base of the candlestick. 'I never said it was.'

'But you behave as if you think it is. Look at you with your fucking orange, airily above the fray.' Jim leant over the table and plucked the piece of fruit from Rupert's hand, where he'd been holding it between his fingertips, knife at the ready to peel away the pith. 'You should try it for real. There are people back home for whom it's not a matter of neat dissection, making the perfect cut and tidying the skin. They need the bread, Rupert. You may not, but they do.'

'Who said anything about money? I never mentioned the subject. If you'd stop being so chippy ...'

'Don't you dare judge me.' Jim was suddenly incandescent.

Rupert froze, blade upwards. The room fell silent. Mei's head had lowered, as if shrinking from the raised voices; Loxton's was alert like a bird that has heard the wrong sound.

My mind flipped to my conversations with Jim, in our tutorials and in the van. Something had suggested an austerity of experience, even downright poverty, though he'd never seemed 'chippy' to me. But he'd always had that boy-of-the-backstreets look about him; easy to imagine him in a Cardiff brawl. Could he lose it completely? Would he lose it now?

Within seconds I was on my feet and leaning across the table: 'Whoooah!'

I took the knife from Rupert and the orange from Jim. 'Stop it, both of you. You're as bad as each other and you're not to ruin our evening.'

I pushed the naked fruit to Gloria. 'Here. Pass it on, would you?'

Jim was still white, his lips drained of colour. He swiped his arm across the bit of table in front of him, sending a spoon clanging into a jug. 'I don't want any of his bloody orange.'

'You don't have to have any.' Gloria said. She finished separating the segments of orange and held the plate in front of Rupert. He shook his head.

'No. Pass it on, Rupe.'

There was a moment's hesitation. Then he took the plate and held it out to Jim. 'Peace offering. No offence meant.'

Jim ignored him.

Tyler handed the plate on down the table.

'Come on, Jim,' Martin sucked at his piece of orange and, mouth full of flesh, continued. 'He's just being a jerk – they get a bit up themselves in the Manchester suburbs.' And off he went on some madcap story about a trip he'd made to see Man United at Old Trafford, liberally laced with innuendo and the accompanying winks – Martin was always winking. It was just enough to cool things down.

Soon pudding arrived to defuse any residual tension. Tyler had made pecan pie, a feat I'd like to have watched but had completely missed. Now he circled the table with Chloe to show off his handiwork, face beaming.

'No shitty behaviour,' she said, putting the dish down and jabbing in Jim and Rupert's direction with a spatula, 'or you won't get any of Tyler's dinner-party special.'

She started working out how to cut it into enough portions, pausing to consult with her knife at different angles. 'Oh shucks! Isn't that what you Yankees say? I'll just divide into sixteen: whoever's nicest to me can share the last two.'

As we picked up our spoons Tyler lobbed in something about 'Yankee' not being the right expression, given the composition of the Federal Army in the Civil War. 'Now here's something on which I *do* have an opinion. Want to know what it is?'

He may have meant to divert, but most people weren't listening and Eddie, who clearly *had* heard, was waving both arms in a theatrical 'No!' Even I preferred to focus on Tyler's pudding and the clotted cream – respite from the drama. A misjudgement then, but a minor one and hardly his fault; the visceral nature of our industrial relations might have seemed as impenetrable as that business with the chocolates in the SCR. A bit of an egghead, then, but I found myself wanting to ruffle his hair.

Gradually conversation shifted to the choice of the evening game, with murder in the dark or sardines still the strongest contenders. Somewhere along the way, sardines emerged the winner. Perhaps a game with both aggressor and victim would have been too close to the mark for the students, Jim and Rupert still too unpredictable. And I was relieved too. I wasn't sure what would be worse – to have to 'kill' Loxton, or be 'killed' by him. It was hard enough maintaining any authority as it was – no need for additional complications.

But Loxton declared himself *hors de combat*. Watching him settling down to read by the stove as if voices had never been raised, I wondered whether there had been such rows before – rows about religion or politics that threatened to get personal. He'd made no mention of them when we touched on the areas to watch – it had all been about keeping to the rhythm of study. The same was true of the evening entertainment – he'd said nothing much about what the students got up to or what he was prepared to countenance, just implied it was all very tame. In fact, come to think of it, there'd been no intimation at all of the day-to-day ups and downs, the ceaseless ebb and flow of the week, the possible need to intervene. It was as if emotions didn't exist.

Nearly two days since we'd last checked in with each other and I had no idea whether he thought matters were getting out of hand or happily easing from our tentative start. What, not to put too fine a point on it, did Loxton think about any-thing? Rupert might claim to have no view on this or that; the trouble with Loxton was that you knew he had a view but you didn't know what it was. He was as bad as Tyler.

As to what Loxton *felt*, that was anyone's guess. It was that habit of secrecy again. No wonder he was on his own; nobody could live with that.

Sardines in a house that size and with that many people would take ages — that much was clear before we could even begin.

Hugh and I went to turn the bulk of the lights off: my idea, to make it more fun. 'Trust you to be racy,' he said. We started at the top and came speedily down — he doing one side of the hall, me doing the other. I was amused to see the state of some of the bedrooms. Tyler's room was orderly but comfortable on his side — smart clothes slung casually over the chair, a peep of white boxers just visible — whereas Rupert's side mixed fussy folding with laziness of the kind that made Mum say, 'Don't expect me to tidy up after you!' Loxton appeared a bit anal: personal paraphernalia marched across his bedside table, all the relationships orthogonal.

What would anyone make of my space, with its carefree disregard for cupboards and drawers, were they to hide there? I should have tidied as we passed by.

By the time we got back to the kitchen they were on the last track of the Elton John album, the washing-up was done, and too many helpers were fussing around with damp towels finishing the drying. Martin explained the rules to Tyler, who said he'd never played, not having any siblings, which seemed rather sad, and there was brief discussion of how many we needed to count to for the hider to get about. Meanwhile Eddie produced a pack of cards and assembled a single suit: whoever drew the ace had to start. Loxton agreed to hold the fan and police the counting, and we gathered at the end of the kitchen table to take our pick. It was Priyam who was sent off. She would hide easily, we agreed, and the countdown was brisk.

'Ninety-nine, a hundred!' And with comic levels of squealing and jostling we were let loose.

You'd be surprised how unnerving it can be in the dark, with so many people disappearing goodness knows where and you wondering what they're up to: I was relieved to hear the giveaway sniggers. There, in one of the bathrooms on the first floor, were Priyam and Tyler, crouched in the white of the tub, a third figure on the lid of the loo, two more by the sink, everyone trying not to laugh, because then the others would too. We waited briefly for the rest of the party to join us, making more and more noise with each arrival. Eddie was the last to find us, just after Rupert. They were pretty bad tempered, given that it was just a game, but then those two seemed to get under each other's skin.

By the second round we'd got the hang of things and began winding each other up. On the ground floor people were feeling their way around, rattling the curtain rods as they checked the window seats, making a drama of peering behind the larger pieces of furniture. There were lots of outstretched hands and ill-suppressed giggles, as if we were combining hide and seek with blind man's buff. I did my own bits of mock feeling-up, but failed to chance upon anyone interesting; as for myself, only once did I think a touch might be him – when a hand slid onto my waist from behind, making me spin round – but the shape in the darkness was too bulky and the groping too theatrical: it was only Martin.

Mei's hiding place was a bit odd: she must have forgotten how large the rest of us were. By the time I found them all, the door to Martin's cubbyhole would hardly open. How galling to be the last to arrive when they were on my own floor!

Back we all went to the kitchen. Loxton gave me no time to think – started the counting straight away, as if purposefully making it difficult. I set off up the back stairs – no point choosing the ground floor when the best place had already been taken. Without thinking, on reaching the landing I started up the little flight to my own comfort zone, and then changed my mind and came down again. We'd just been there – go somewhere else. Then hesitation. Where to go? We'd already done a bathroom, so that was out. I ran through the space occupied by the girls – too open; then through Tyler and Rupert's – didn't feel right. I thought about the housekeeper's suite, but they would hear my footsteps from the kitchen. Across to the other room at the front, forgetting that that was Loxton's. Round to the bathroom door. Damn, locked from the other side! I could hear people coming up the stairs. A quick glance. No way out: the door opened onto the hall. Behind the door? No: the white glare of papers on a bureau – we couldn't disturb his papers. Between the bed and the wardrobe? A nightstand with enamel box and photo frames: they'd get knocked, the pills would spill and the silver would dent. Beyond it on the floor? Perhaps.

Steps! I had to act. Scramble oh-so-fast onto the bed. Lift the blanket. Lie crossways. Face the ceiling. Pull blanket over. Shut eyes.

Why did I shut my eyes?

Blink. Honeycomb weave, fuzzing. Satin edging, tickling. Smell of wool, overpowering, like being buried in sheep – ugghhh.

Whoever pushed at the door didn't look hard enough. The steps went elsewhere.

A different panic. Shoes still on: stupid! On Loxton's bed, of all places! And they'd all pile in. He'd be horrified.

Space needed – wriggle along. Pillows toppling – push them back.

Tyler was the first to find me. Why did it have to be Tyler?

'Nice one,' he was saying. 'Nice' what? Nice to hide in that room? Nice to be in a bed? Nice to find me alone?

I could hear him slipping off his shoes, those American loafers that no one else wore. Why did his shoes have to come off so fast?

He was clambering on, making the mattress dip, the bed rock. This was too much – what if someone came in?

No air. Raise the blanket. Breathe deep. Stay calm. Pretend.

That supple body next to me – all wrong. Clothed from top to toe. Contact in stupid places. Conversation impossible.

Somebody at the door. Stiffen; clench.

Footsteps; prodding.

'Found you!' Hugh: he would be spindly.

Mattress tipping. Blanket sliding. Springs complaining.

Whispers: Priyam and Mei. Both small.

A sagging and a rolling into him – the give of muscle, that smell of almond.

Scuffling at the door. A voice saying, 'Trust *her* to choose *his* room!' A return guffaw: Gloria with Martin, someone else behind. Who was the someone else?

'Underneath, underneath! We have to crawl under the bed.' Lyndsey.

More scuffling. Giggles. Breathing.

Tyler's body, scorching; pillows flopping, cool.

Legs passing my head, sidling down the bed.

'Any space? I'm not lying next to Rupert.' Jim, gruff.

Blanket lifted: better.

More dipping and rocking; shoving too.

Creaks. Whispers. A spring pinging. Laughter. 'Shhhhhh!'

'Will it hold?' Was that me?

'Sure thing.'

'Got enough room?' Inane question.

'I'm good. You?'

'Smothered by pillows!' Not quite true.

Gradually the rest of them arrived, Eddie – now cheery again – keeping tally.

And then, pandemonium when Chloe found us and pulled the blanket off. 'Fuck a duck!' she said, and started tickling. In seconds, everyone was squirming and squealing; the bed felt like a bucking horse.

All too short a wait for them to calm down and get up.

Tyler whispered, 'All over!'

I gave a return squeeze of his arm, which I hadn't been aware of holding. Then we eased our bodies apart.

The students returned to the kitchen and dawdled there, exhausted by the excitement. As soon as I could, I slipped out. Loxton was right – it was better not to get involved, easier not to be pulled in both directions. Another case of learning lessons the hard way.

If he'd still been around, I'd have apologised for invading his bedroom, but he'd disappeared. Instead there was a fuzz of light at the base of his door, which was now firmly shut. I nearly knocked but couldn't imagine poking my head inside, chit-chatting about the things in his room, and Loxton certainly wouldn't want to be discovered in his pyjamas. Probably he wore a dressing gown too, paisley-patterned with piping round the collar, like my uncle's. I didn't care to find out.

Back in my attic I leant against the wood of the door to hear the silence, staring at the private space that, judging from the rucks in a rug now lying skew-whiff, must have been trampled through. The skin on my cheeks went tight where a few light tears – of frustration, dismay, I know not what – had trickled down. I must have undressed eventually, but it didn't register. There was just a blankness tempered by an occasional blur of anxiety about Loxton or a flash of something much worse, connected with Tyler – his comment 'I'm good', which might have been heard; that hand on his arm, which might have been seen – and what you did or didn't do. It took me an age to get to sleep, listening to the to-ing and fro-ing in the hall and on the stairs – hushed whisperings and suppressed giggles continued well into the night – wondering in whose direction the steps were going. Why it should have bothered me so much, I don't know; there were always students creeping around my staircase in College, muffling their voices until they thought they were out of earshot. It wasn't as if it was a surprise.

Friday

There are days when you want to wake early and days when you don't. That day, it would have been good to be in a rush, to have no time to think. No such luck. Before I'd even opened my eyes, I was wondering about puffiness – whether the tears would show. Before I'd moved even a fraction, I was replaying every second of the scene in Loxton's room.

After a while I braced myself for cold, reached for the curtains above my head and pulled them aside. The bright blue of a clear sky made no difference. Round and round I went on the same track, one minute elated, the next collapsing into gloom.

Leaning on the cold porcelain of the sink as water rinsed away the toothpaste, I stared at the person in the mirror, the rash of freckles, the unkempt hair. Sitting on the loo, confronted by proud boobs, taut thighs and small knees, I pondered the shape before me. Where had she come from, this woman? Where was this body dragging me?

Back in bed with my paperback, I tried to wean myself off the loop of film. It didn't work. In fact, these clips were almost worse than before, more incriminating than the scenes in the lane, by the bonfire and on the beach. The new ones were of 'ordinary' things – like our exchange about the portraits in the hall, the grin he gave when he served up his pudding, the spark when I teased about the mess in his room – and all had assumed extraordinary potency. They went right the way back, every pinprick of pleasure remorselessly exposed, past the walk from Magdalen Bridge and the meetings in the Lodge to the fateful collision before the start of the first term. At what point had the crucial shift taken place or had there always been something? How did you extract yourself when you were so drawn? He was out of bounds.

Perhaps it was just as well that Priyam came to the door, though it was a surprise, two days running; usually she was with Mei, who liked our floor.

'Are you up, Dr Addleshaw?' No more than a fractional pause. 'May I ask you something?'

Ah, that was why she'd visited the day before.

'Of course. Come right in.'

She appeared in her Viyella nightdress, looking small.

I thought of myself, dishevelled. 'Don't look too hard, I'm only half dressed.'

'Me too. Gloria's bagged the bath again.'

'And? Is everything okay?

She didn't reply.

'Would you like to talk about it?'

She sat on the edge of the bed, making the springs ping as Loxton's had the night before, and then, with a 'May I?', swivelled round on the shiny quilt to lean against the clothes draped over the frame at the foot. She didn't look comfortable, so I passed the spare pillows and watched as she created a better support, bent her knees and tucked her nightdress under those delicate toes. She had most of the light behind her, so it was hard to see, but under her dark skin she looked wan.

It turned out that Priyam had slept badly too, fretting about her mother's birthday, which fell the following day. The problem may have been Finals, but she didn't mention that so neither did I; instead she talked about family and letting people down. Gradually it all spilled out. Everybody would be there – cousins, second cousins, distant uncles and aunts. Her mother hadn't complained and her father never expressed a view on such things, but they'd done so much – how could she have been so selfish? She piled it on further, saying it was all very well for her sister, who looked out for herself, had boyfriends, went her own way. Priyam preferred to maintain common ground, observe the traditions. She'd made a mistake: she should never have come. She should have gone back as normal and studied at home, like everyone else.

I shifted at my end of the bed and the silky top layer started to slip. 'Here,' I said, pulling it back from the floor. 'Put your legs underneath. They'll be warmer.'

So she slid the quilt from underneath her, lifted it up and reassembled it around her, her legs now stretching down by the side of mine but running in the opposite direction. If it weren't for the rest of the bedding, our shins would have touched.

Maybe that bit of companionship turned her thoughts, because she began talking about her reading and why the week had been special. It seemed she'd ploughed her way through a volume of tort and had only fifty pages to go. That was more than she'd hoped for, but that wasn't the only reason why Carreck Loose had been important. It was all that we'd shared together, students and dons alike: the conversations and the walks, the games and doing the crossword; even the washing-up had been fun with the stereo at full tilt in the background.

'Surely your parents will understand,' I suggested, thinking of my own. 'They'll be pleased for you, and proud.'

She sat silent for a few moments, picking at a loose thread in the stitching of the eiderdown. Then suddenly she dipped her head and her shoulders curled forward as she disintegrated into tears. It was all too much, she said into her lap. Everybody wanted something from her – family, friends, tutors – and there weren't enough bits to go round. Sometimes she felt as if she was getting smaller and smaller, now a mere slip of a thing who might disappear through a crack in the floorboard like the one in her room in College that gaped as you walked towards the window. Even here there'd been moments when she felt herself shrinking. They were all so clever and witty, they knew about so many things. She was like Mei – she knew about her subject, because she'd worked hard, but she didn't know how to do the other stuff. Whereas Rupert and Eddie, even Lyndsey, in her oddball way . . .

'Oh, I wouldn't worry about Rupert,' I said. 'He's a show-off and he likes to discomfort – he does it with everyone. And I'm sure Eddie and Lyndsey have their own troubles. Besides, women are always comparing, especially with men. It's a lousy habit. We should do things our own way.'

I handed her my clean but crumpled hankie and we talked about feeling as if you were on the outside and how far that might be part of the human condition, or at least the female condition – and though, for much of the time, it wasn't clear to me whether she was still talking about her peers or whether the conversation was really about her family or the pressure of work, it seemed to be helping.

Eventually we got back to the birthday and a plan emerged. She would make contact again, so her parents knew she'd been thinking of them. No point in finding a phone box and reversing charges – her mother wouldn't chat in the shop. A telegram – those frightening blue-and-white envelopes with the Post Office crest – suggested bad news from abroad, so that was no good. But a card could happily be read out. She could use one of the shots of the harbour that I'd picked up in Mevagissey and point out the harbourmaster's original house, grandly standing watch; if we posted it that morning it would arrive the next day. Besides, we'd be back in Oxford the following afternoon: if she was quick she could get the fast train and be home by suppertime. I would track down her scout and sort out anything to be left behind.

Problem solved, at least in the short term, we stayed there companionably for a few more minutes, propped against our pillows, sharing chat about ambitions, families and the demands they make. After she'd gone I realised that for the best part of an hour I hadn't thought about Tyler at all.

The rest of them were nearly done by the time we arrived for breakfast, the table a mess, the crossword all but complete. Hugh – ever domesticated – was at the sink with a pinny on; Mei by his side with a tea towel, passing crockery to Jim to put away.

At the far end Chloe stood holding forth about some scheme in the making, involving hidden treasure, while Lyndsey sat with a dictionary of quotations, scribbling clues onto folds of paper piled by her plate. Eddie, across the table, was turning one of the cereal packets on its corners, tapping absently. Tyler, too, appeared to be gazing at nothing in particular; he certainly didn't look at me.

Somewhere in the middle Gloria and Rupert were in a huddle over the remnants of an earlier paper, discussing why we'd got involved in Concorde if landing rights were going to be such a problem. At the near end, screened from the rest by a box of Weetabix, were Martin and Barnaby, reading aloud about a competition.

They were all so absorbed that Priyam and I got away with an absent-minded exchange of greetings. No one seemed to notice us cutting it fine. There was a vague shifting of chairs to let us through, but no questions, let alone any jokes about sardines – they must have exhausted the subject. Loxton said nothing at all.

We snuck past the washers-up and sat down in the gap opposite the newsreaders, pulling bowls and spoons towards us. Tyler was uncomfortably near, but there was no alternative: I would have to pretend.

Chloe raised her voice again to flag that this would be no ordinary treasure hunt, which made Lyndsey protest that she was just having fun with some quotations – she couldn't have been more like the Dean's parody. But for once, Chloe's need for attention had an upside – it gave us a kind of cover.

'Haven't we had this conversation before?' Barnaby looked around the faces as he lifted a teapot.

Chloe spun round between the end of the table and the step down into the conservatory and then wobbled back, bumping into the chairs as she passed. What was she up to, I wondered. She would have had no truck with ballet as a child – hard to imagine her in a tutu. It was Lyndsey who talked of whirling like the gulls, who would shut her eyes on a walk so she could sway with the elements.

'Yup,' Chloe said, steadying herself with a hand on the cross bar of Rupert's chair. 'And if we can have hot cross buns and Easter eggs ahead of time, why can't she have an Easter hunt? Besides, nearly all the clues are done, aren't they Lyndsey?'

If there was an edge of mockery, Lyndsey didn't pick it up. She smiled as she scanned a few more pages. 'Two to go. Here's a good quote.' She lifted the book up for Chloe to see, indicating something down the bottom of the page with her index finger. I knew that finger from the day in the library: it usually had ink on it, and a little compression with a ridge on the side from gripping her fountain pen. Tyler's hands had always been clean, the skin above the knuckles dusted with that fairish hair, the nails shapely and almost flat. Attractive hands, undeniably male.

Eddie made a lunge for the dictionary, prompting Lyndsey to lift it out of reach. Chloe grasped it and spun again, in my direction, trailing a thin wisp of smoke. If she weren't careful, she would slip, or drop the cigarette.

'Spoilsport,' Eddie said.

'Oh, get lost! I'm just helping Lyndsey. You're the one who's trying to look.'

'But you're such fun when you're cross!' He grabbed again at the book and then checked himself as Loxton stood up.

'Well, you can't have it.' Chloe dropped onto the soles of her feet again. 'Anyway, you're meant to be helping with the shopping list. Is it done, Dennis?' And she bent across the table, giggling into his face as she plucked the piece of paper away. The gesture had such a familiar edge, she might have been winding up her dad.

I waited for Loxton to remonstrate, but he seemed remarkably relaxed. All things considered, he was surprisingly tolerant of certain kinds of exuberance. Maybe invading his bed wasn't such a heinous offence.

Eddie shrugged theatrically and pushed his chair away. 'In that case, if there is no further need for my services, I'm off to do my duty in the drawing room.' He turned to me. 'Where have you got to on your rounds, Sarah? Will I be free to misbehave?'

'Not in one of those yogi poses!'

Across the table Tyler joined the chuckles – that rumble of his, turning at the back of his throat, causing me to look at him. A confident smile beamed my way but took in several others. Perhaps that, too, wouldn't be so awkward after all.

Until that moment I hadn't thought about where to sit that day. But, taking things off the table, it struck me that a large surface would be preferable to spreading myself across the floor. The library was out – it would be too distracting – so that meant the dining room.

In fact, it was the same group of us at that huge expanse of polish: Martin, Priyam and Rupert – who had returned from the morning room, it wasn't clear why – and me. We were even in the same places. Remarkable, the way people stuck to a spot – they might have been in one of the University libraries. But something had put me on a more relaxed footing with the students; I was no longer the invigilator. Martin looked up and winked as I came in; Rupert, who never made way for anyone, silently shifted a pile of books; Priyam said, 'You're back!' and then covered her mouth with her hand.

I spread my papers generously, so they drifted down the table rather than fencing me off at the end, and picked up the index cards for my lectures. This time, perversely, concentration was a doddle. It was as easy to slip into the right mental landscape as it was to slip back into that comfortable chair. At some point Priyam must have left to join Eddie and Loxton on the final trip into town, but I was oblivious. At odd moments I noticed the clock ticking in the hall – had it always ticked? – but not as an irritation. I raced on, immersed in the lilt of my eight linked arguments, until Martin suddenly appeared by my side with a cup of Nescafé.

'You forgot again,' he whispered.

Christ, the tea round!

'What about the others?' I whispered back, thinking of all the workers deprived of their morning cuppa.

But Martin and Gloria had done them all.

For a few minutes my mind flitted around, wondering whether Gloria had made it up with him and what made us call it a tea break when most people drank coffee or needed a fag. I teetered on the edge of daydreaming – did Tyler take his with or without sugar; how would he hold a cigarette? – but was pulled back by a change in the light and a shifting of bodies; outside, a hawk hovered over the slope leading to the bay. After that, oblivion again until my stomach told me it was time to eat.

*

In the kitchen there was an air of things drawing to a close. The table was laid with mementoes of earlier meals bulked out with chunks of pork pie. Somebody had pureed leftover vegetables – would that really have been Loxton? It could hardly be anyone else – instead of serving up our favourite variety of Campbell's condensed soup. Even the big fruit bowl looked less abundant than usual.

We sat down after the usual crescendo of bitty talk as people caught up with each other. By the Rayburn Loxton ladled his soup, with Lyndsey carefully sending the bowls on their journey down the table. At the far end of the kitchen units, one of the boys cut bread into teetering piles of thick slabs that diminished rapidly as the breadboard lurched from hand to hand.

Was it rowdier than usual? It certainly felt so. Speculation began at my end of the table about what Loxton would be serving up that evening – Priyam trying to keep it a surprise while Eddie provoked ('What can you make with onion, milk, a lot of potato and a few scraps of fish?'). Down the other end they were discussing Lyndsey's treasure hunt, which was devoid of gold, as she'd forgotten to add chocolate to the shopping list, and which might not be a hunt at all because she hadn't got round to hiding the clues. Somewhere near the middle elderly hands reached over the heads and set down two litre bottles of the cider we'd spurned at the pub.

'What's this?' Martin examined the label ostentatiously. He turned to Loxton. 'Are you going soft on us? It's eight per cent – just think what disasters might befall us!'

From the other side of the table, Tyler caught my eye – something beneath the surface glistening. Immediately I knew things were all right. It was a wonderful feeling.

Loxton produced one of his little smiles, not as tight as it used to be – had it really changed, or had I misremembered? – and said something about doing a rough calculation and finding we were in credit. He was prepared to relax the rules, he said, looking at me, although I'd had nothing to do with it, so long as we kept to a glass each and walked it off afterwards. There was a murmur of approval and the sound of tumblers being pushed forwards while Martin poured.

Emboldened by the general bonhomie, I stood up and raised my own, catching a whiff of bruised apple as the air moved. 'To Dennis, Keeper of the Kitty!'

Almost instantly, everyone was on their feet, sending chairs rocking but just failing to topple. There was a clinking of thick glass – 'To Dennis' – and then more scraping on that infernal sticky lino as we all sat down again.

I should have known Loxton would need to return the courtesy. Briefly his tumbler touched the table; then he rose and held it aloft again. 'To Sarah, fomenter of fun and, if I may say so, most fetching of Fellows!'

They must all have joined in – it was very noisy. I wasn't sure which pleased me more: Loxton's teasing endorsement or Tyler cheering with the rest of them.

When the banter had subsided, Lyndsey disappeared into the conservatory to retrieve the pile of quotations. At some point it had been decided that, instead of waiting for a trail of paper clues to be set up outside, they would be read out in sequence over coffee, leaving time for a last proper walk. So we sat on in the kitchen with our mugs of Nescafé, chatting over the debris of the meal, waiting for Lyndsey to hand out the pieces of paper. Now it was she who did little pirouettes as she went round the table, hair flaring out with each spin like a small girl dancing between guests on a special occasion – putting napkins on laps or doling out Christmas crackers, say. If she'd whispered in someone's ear and then sped on, giggling, I wouldn't have been surprised, but she didn't. Even so, she might have been half her age.

Chloe may have been piqued that Lyndsey had reclaimed the game. In any event, she now looked sullen, refusing to engage. Lyndsey carried on twirling regardless, her long thin arm rising and falling as she completed her circuit. After that, it took no time at all for the rest of us to blunder our way through her quotations, trying to work out where the clues were meant to lead to. It was all a bit chaotic, for nobody paid attention to the notional sequencing, but it caused great hilarity. As expected, Rupert was omnivorous in the references he picked up, but Hugh was the best at recognising the sources. Even that success wasn't enough to win Lyndsey over – Rupert got one of those remote smiles, but Hugh got nothing, no prize at all. There was awkwardness between them now, and yet they'd seemed so comfortable at the start of the week; it was hard to fathom.

Still, as we set off on our walk they were vaguely together – Lyndsey tripping along the crust of the farm track as Hugh trudged dutifully through the sodden bit. In fact there were a number of now familiar allegiances: Martin and Rupert, with Gloria between them; Eddie and Chloe just behind; Jim and Mei with Barnaby; Priyam, Tyler, Loxton and I at the rear. No one dawdled because there wasn't time; instead we maintained the kind of pace of which Loxton approved.

Tyler sent a few inconsequential words in my direction as we started out – enough to make me wonder what on earth I'd been worrying about, as he clearly wasn't embarrassed – and then began leaning sideways to talk to me behind the backs of the other two. It didn't really work. As the four of us got into a comfortable rhythm we gradually drifted into pairs, with Loxton and Priyam walking slightly ahead, chatting companionably as they so often did, while Tyler and I kept pace in their wake, trying to avoid the wild daffs. It was just enough of a gap to allow a semi-private conversation – not that we said anything revealing. I mentioned switching from

my article on Ivy Williams to my lectures on women's suf-
frage; Tyler said he'd finished the John Rawls treatise; and we
had a happy exchange about the pattern of our mornings – so
innocuous, easy and free of intensity that I'm sure we would
happily have chatted for the rest of the walk. But we lost
each other at a gate between the fields, when the challenge
of negotiating a wet patch caused the various groupings to
merge. Suddenly an expanse of glutinous mud, pockmarked
by absent cattle, lay between us.

When we all started off again I found myself next to
Barnaby, with whom – apart from that evening over supper –
there'd always been a respectful distance, perhaps because I'd
been tutoring him. For a few minutes the switch was unwel-
come, but Barnaby seemed on the point of opening up. Tyler
could wait, I thought, suddenly certain. If you totted them
up, we'd had several long talks and, at the very least, there
was Gloria's jibe about hobnobbing to take into account; it
might look suspicious if we disappeared again into a space of
our own.

So Barnaby and I navigated the narrow coastal path companionably, talking in little bursts, first one and then the other
walking ahead, and gradually something unlocked. There he
was, on our last day, revealing his love of using his hands,
whether it was gripping an oar, furling a sail or planing a piece
of wood. And the surprise of it was all the greater because he
admitted that this was probably more important to him than
what he was currently doing. As he put it, he'd been climbing
the mountain because it was there and everyone expected him
to; he'd now realised that while the views might be marvellous at the summit, he didn't have to go up if he didn't want
to – climbing didn't have to be his thing.

How did we get to such a place in such a short time, I
wondered, when we reached the end of the outward lap,
comfortably apart from the rest of the gang. This, too, was a

conversation we'd never have had in Oxford, one that took its cue from the days of doing ordinary things together. Without that intimacy we could never have sat so happily chatting on the clifftop, watching the birds lifting in the slipstreams and the waves thrashing through the fallen rock, listening to the wheeling and the pounding, enjoying the taste of sticky salty air on our faces. We saw a cormorant flap idly across the surf, dip down and resurface some distance away, and tried to distinguish the harsh trilling of the terns from the sounds of other wildlife. Only the shouts from the rest of our group caused us to set off again.

By the time we got back to the house, it was clear that Barnaby had had some kind of crisis that year without me or my colleagues being properly aware of it. Giving up rowing had been a trigger, he said. He'd missed being taken out of himself at the start of each day, the peace of the river, the uncomplicated friendships, and his mind had slackened with his body, leaving him listless. But mostly it was down to feeling at odds with a cerebral existence. And perversely, as he described it, our tutorials and the Reading Party had helped him find a way out of that inertia, of feeling terribly tired and dull. First there was the contrast of the few aspects of History that he enjoyed and the many parts he did not, and then he'd had some sort of epiphany sharing with Hugh, who was so patently cut out to be an academic. And realising that he did *not* want to be a schoolteacher or go into the professions had relieved the pressure; meant he was less terrified of flunking. After all, Finals weren't everything; they wouldn't define who he was. Too many people had presumed to tell him what he should do with his life. If he'd known how to listen to the voice inside, he'd have realised that he should make things – boats, probably. He would become a craftsman, pass something on, if he could find someone prepared to teach him. That would be enough.

It was a privilege to be there just when his picture became clear.

By contrast, I reflected, there really was *nothing* else I would rather be doing. If anything was happiness, it had to be this! What could be nicer than to be stuck in some wild place in the middle of nowhere with interesting work and a bunch of people whom I liked and who seemed to like me. Although there was only a day to go, it felt, in some extraordinary way, as if there were still time for everything.

Except there wasn't time: back at the house we were up against the clock. So I offered to do a tea round. Loxton raised an eyebrow at my addition of biscuits – probably thought eating at our desks was a bit like getting drunk in the pub, beyond the pale – but didn't object.

Everywhere, the students were a picture of silent application. Even Tyler seemed oblivious as I reached over with his mug, the weight of my braless breasts gently swinging under my jumper.

Back in the dining room I stood next to my lecture cards – rearranged into eight new piles, the division and sequencing even more clear.

'Mind if I move up?' I asked no one in particular.

We stayed like that, tight in our new square formation, until Priyam left to help Loxton with the cooking. Then we shifted slightly so the balance was preserved.

Loxton had decreed that our final supper should be held in the dining room to mark the occasion, just as the Dean said he would. Our lot got a dispensation to stop work early so we could get the room ready in time, but we were so absorbed that it took Priyam's reappearance from the kitchen, in a fluster about agreeing place settings, to remind us to wind down. Shortly after the clock in the hall cranked out the hour, we moved our things to the window seats and turned our minds to the table. There was ample space in the room for fourteen chairs and Rupert was adamant. What was the point of an elegant table, he asked, if it was never fully extended. Actually, why have a house like this at all if you were going to leave it so tatty? The idea that you might not want grandeur or have the necessary resources didn't seem to enter his head.

So we fiddled around until we worked out the mechanism to unlock the extra leaf. And, to be fair, the table did look rather splendid when it was stretched to a single thickness all the way through, even though it sagged in the middle. But then we disagreed on how to lay it. Priyam sided with Rupert, arguing that Loxton would be pleased if we made it look special, while Martin and I balked at turning our final evening into an elegant dinner from a TV costume drama. We had a funny argument about *The Pallisers*, which Martin had clearly loathed, though for different reasons from me. In the end, amidst jokes about who might be Lady Glencora (Gloria was thought the most appropriate, particularly if Rupert was Plantagenet Palliser) and which role better suited Martin (the admiring Burgo Fitzgerald or the handsome Phineas Finn), we compromised. Priyam returned the two large candelabra to the sideboard, but was allowed to use the silver cutlery stored there; she even got to lay side plates.

I'm not sure if it was the right decision. I liked our messy evenings in the kitchen with dirty crockery piling up on the worktop behind us and the cooks fussing around – sometimes in control, sometimes not – in the general melee. That had a friendliness about it in keeping with the aura of the place, whereas the dining room, returned to its original use, made me uneasy. We were transporting the formalities of High Table to Cornwall, just when we'd managed to shake them off.

Oddly, the rest of the students didn't seem to mind; it was like so many of the rules of the Reading Party – they just *were*, and nobody questioned them. When someone rang the gong – with a drum roll for extra effect – and they all piled in, nobody paid much attention beyond a few more teases about the Pallisers. It was as if they'd come to accept the glitter of Hall in the evening and barely noticed its reintroduction here. Tyler probably liked it – the preppy jacket had gone on again. Even Mei, pausing over the cutlery, was learning about hallmarks. She listened attentively as Rupert, diagonally across the table, explained about Sheffield plate, resting her shoulder all the while against Jim, who was sitting next to her, ostensibly so she could hear. And Jim, who normally might have taken the opportunity to make a political point, appeared happy to let things be.

Besides, maybe the grandeur was warranted. Loxton, with help unspecified from Mei and Priyam, had quietly produced a humdinger of a meal. It was again emphatically his show. We had a starter, a formality we weren't used to; then – it being Friday – a fish pie so large that it was produced in two separate dishes; followed by a curious upside-down pudding, made with apples and pastry, which perhaps hadn't entirely worked, and cheese. Most importantly, we had an awful lot to drink.

Loxton had told me that the Wine Committee reviewed more than 2,000 wines a year. It was a perquisite normally reserved for Emeritus Fellows, but he had argued, without irony, that tastes changed and that the younger Fellows should be represented or the College might end up with bottles that it didn't want to drink. At first I thought he was having me on, but soon I realised that this was a serious matter. There was the lucrative conference trade to think of; the quality of the cellar was a consideration. Besides, wine could be a good investment. Occasionally Governing Body would be informed that we'd replenished our stores in dramatic fashion, the sale of a few cases of a superlative vintage funding the acquisition of many more of a lesser one.

And that was the justification for his biggest treat of the evening, which arrived after the main course when we were already fairly merry. Priyam and Mei came tinkling from the hall, carrying trays of small receptacles – mostly glasses, but there were delicate coffee cups and a few egg cups too – and set three down before each of us as neatly as their varying shapes and sizes allowed. Then Loxton made his entrance – putting his head round the door almost coquettishly to check we were ready – and advanced to the table with a tray of three bottles also gently clinking. Mercifully, those sitting at his end of the table ducked so that he could set it down safely.

And then he explained. Perhaps we'd had 'pudding wine' at Christmas or on some special occasion, but the sweeter wines could also be exceptionally good with cheese. So he had brought a sample of three vineyards from the College cellar: a 1949 Chateau Climens, because he liked to match Sauternes with a strong blue cheese, though perhaps not as ripe as this piece of Roquefort would now be; a 1948 Taylor Port, for those who preferred to try the clothbound Cheshire, with a box of dates and a jar of his own quince jelly; and a German Auslese, the Kiedricher Gräfenberg from 1959, with which the tarte Tatin should be perfect, for those of us who preferred dessert. It was almost as if he needed us to share his discovery of the finer things in life – as, perhaps, he'd done himself with his predecessor Godfrey on one of their trips to the Lakes. So he showed us how different a viscous liquid could be. It wasn't just a matter of colour and depth, but of how they each poured and clung to the side of the glass. Typically, he stressed that it was an imperfect test as we couldn't compare like with like, not having the best receptacles – and besides we were drinking rather than tasting the wine – but at least we would get the idea. It was important to sample the best.

And, though some of us may have resisted the idea of possessing, let alone consuming, anything quite so valuable as those bottles must have been, it was hard not to be drawn in with the first sip – treacly, like nectar. So we sat on after we'd pushed aside our pudding bowls, trying the crumbly cheese with and without the quince and the dried fruit, comparing what was left of the wine, toasting the dead Godfrey, without whom there would never have been a Reading Party. I began talking to Tyler, whom I'd managed to ignore like a treat that had to be savoured at the end of the meal, and we swapped attempts at describing the scents and the tastes. There was a gloriously mellow feeling inside, matched without by the warmth of all those bodies, the softness of the shapes and colours in the low light, and the gentle rise and fall of the conversations.

I didn't notice Hugh leaving the table, only the sound of something being moved next door. Turning to look, with a view straight through to the piano, I saw that the lid had been propped open and, in the triangle below, caught Hugh's lanky frame bending to lift the fallboard and then sitting down at the stool. Still there was a moment of perplexity, wondering what he was doing.

The fact that no one had said he could play made it remarkable enough; that he played so well – as it seemed to me – made it a double surprise. The various conversations around the table didn't all stop immediately, but they soon wound down. By the end of the piece several of the students had quietly left for the drawing room, while others were leaning forward on the table to stare silently into the bowls of their glasses, or sitting sideways on their chairs to listen more comfortably against the hard wooden backs and arms. Tyler, next to me, was lost – deep in the same space.

Under cover of the clapping, the rest of us moved through. Someone – probably Martin – began re-stoking the fire; someone else – Mei or Jim, perhaps both – went off to make coffee. Eddie and Chloe cavorted about, bringing additional soft chairs from the morning room with a loud 'Mind your heads!' as they passed them over, and soon all fourteen of us had found a place in which to settle. All the while Hugh was riffling through the piles of sheet music, looking, he said, for a collection of Mendelssohn's *Songs Without Words* that had been there last time, occasionally lobbing in a suggestion when he found another piece he was happy to play. There was no false modesty: it was a matter-of-fact discussion of what people would like to hear. Nor was there even a tinge of showing off. Rather, he was like Loxton with his wine – he took for granted that others would enjoy the experience, so he shared what was his. Having chosen, he settled back on his stool and, without waiting for quiet, began playing again.

The first piece sounded vaguely familiar – one of Chopin's easier 'nocturnes', he explained. What came next – one of the Mendelssohns – was completely new to me. Naturally the mood on our last evening together made it very special.

I'd found a spot in the corner near the hall door and was sitting with Barnaby, who was sketching the curves and angles splaying out in front of us, with Mei sitting next to Hugh as his page-turner (another surprise), round to the busyness on our side of the mantelpiece. Jim was in front of me on the sofa, Lyndsey with her feet tucked up on alongside, Gloria on the floor with an arm draped on the upholstery; Martin was in the armchair next to her, occasionally tickling her with his foot; Rupert sat in his crushed velvet diagonally opposite by the fire, glass in hand, looking ever more like a Plantagenet in the making. Loxton and his pipe were in the curve of the piano, with Priyam next to him, his hand once advancing to pat hers as if she were a favourite godchild; Tyler was at a comfortable distance again, jacket off and feet on the footstool, but we could share a glance if we dared; Eddie and Chloe were a minor distraction by my side. Glasses, mugs, shoes and bits of clothing were dotted about. It was untidy, companionable, peaceful, and if you closed your eyes, it seemed as though the music was billowing with the heat that drifted from the fire, being lifted ceiling-wards and variously rippling, rushing and cascading down again.

How long did Hugh play? There were several 'songs' and most of us were there for all of them, though Chloe and Eddie didn't last long. I particularly liked the one he played first, 'Duetto', which for me perfectly evoked the lingering sadness of the end of our time together. Perhaps nothing could cap that. Anyway, after the last of them Hugh got up, did a mock bow amidst the clapping and then stepped across to the coffee table to help himself to an After Eight, as if his astonishing performance had been nothing. Standing in the midst of the outstretched legs, looking for a place to sit, that habitual air of loneliness crept back into his face like a blush – one minute not there, the next his expression was suffused with it. Lyndsey drew her feet in and patted a space where he could sit down, but even as I leant forward she moved further away. The pity of it made my thank you even warmer. Hugh was so multitalented, so generous, and yet somehow he remained always on the fringe – a 'square' straining for acceptance. Jim, next to him, ill at ease in so many ways, had a more compelling, physical presence.

I left soon after that, not wanting to spoil the serenity with the game of cards that Martin proposed, least of all with ghastly pictures of the Wombles emblazoned on the backs. But – Sod's Law – instead of silence there was the sound of laughter and running feet bouncing from the kitchen into the corridor and then the hall. It stopped as I entered with my tray of empty glasses – Rupert and Gloria, frolicking again. What a shame, I thought, turning on the tap. They might feel obliged to help. In fact, for a few minutes they did make a nod in that direction, working together at the drying-up rack, but it didn't last. Soon Rupert had got hold of both damp tea towels and was taunting Gloria just as he had on the beach, but with more success. In no time they'd clattered up the back stairs, so I carried on with the job by myself, alternately staring into the blackness beyond the window and focusing on the mirror in the glass.

I could tell it was Tyler as soon as the figure appeared in the reflection: the height, the gait, the sound of the shoes now all too familiar. Thankfully I'd turned from the sink to sort the silver into a pair of baize-lined cutlery drawers placed on the kitchen table. He walked down its far side to put the bottles he was carrying into the box we kept in the conservatory, and I heard them clanking softly, one, two, three, four, five: he must have been carrying three under one arm and two in the other hand. Then the loafers squeaked their way back and paused by the chair at the end.

Perhaps he was undecided.

'Sounds like a lot of bottles,' I said. Stupid, the things one comes out with.

He didn't reply, but the loafers changed direction. They kept getting closer until they stopped next to my slipper socks. Still I hadn't looked up: my world was that grouping of feet in a patch of olive linoleum with fake tessellation, the tapering wooden chair legs with their black-rubber bungs, the stray crumbs and the little puddle of water, and above it all the edge of the table and the vestigial whiff of silver polish.

Tyler's hands swung into sight alongside mine over the pile of cutlery and hung there for a moment, waiting, the pads of his fingers upturned, the side of those flat thumbnails just catching the light.

'Hey, let me help.'

And for a few seconds we continued the sorting together, forks onto forks, knives onto knives, until the knuckles bumped, both of us holding dessert spoons, tidying into the same pile. He must have let go first – or was it me? – and then, as those stupid spoons clanged into each other, I sensed that pivoting again, the heat of him shifting.

My mind swung to the blind above the worktop, which wasn't down; the undrawn curtains in the dining room, with that oblique view; the waft of air from the corridor, which meant the door was open; and the conservatory – there was so much glass! Any of them could be anywhere looking in, or eavesdropping nearby. We wouldn't know.

It didn't stop me turning, lifting my arms, leaning into him as he bent his head.

I won't even try to describe what followed except to say that that captivating, luscious kiss – that curling, roaming, lingering of tongues – was both something and nothing much at all. Like most significant things – like all the little collisions, even – it's largely a matter of interpretation.

After that there was a silence, not empty but full.

A soft voice said, 'That wasn't meant to happen,' and I realised it was mine.

'Sure,' he replied. 'But it did.'

For a while we continued there, motion suspended. I could feel his breath on the side of my neck, where the hair had slipped, leaving the skin naked. Eventually one of us must have moved fractionally away, or possibly we both did at the same time – it's very hard to say.

Saturday

The day of our departure I slept through to the gong and, having failed to pack the night before, found myself doubly short of time. Unlikely that anyone else had been sensible, except perhaps Loxton, but then I too was meant to be setting an example. On occasion, it was easy to forget.

I did my packing quickly, glad to focus on the practical. Placed my horrid vinyl suitcase squarely in the middle of the bed, lined the base with the mistakes that could go straight back in my cupboard, chucked in the rest of my clothes, closed the top and pressed. The metal zip wouldn't zip. Why was everything harder at the end than at the beginning?

My briefcase took a little longer. Looking at the typescript of my article, with the loud renumbering of pages and the looping swirls to rearrange text, I began reading afresh instead of checking for missing pages. Then there were the books; the Virago paperback must still be downstairs. The cards with my lecture notes – were they all there? I leafed through, trying not to rearrange. Was that a good result? It felt solid enough. Besides, the benefits of the week weren't to be measured in pages written or turned: that would be a travesty. No wonder the Warden had spoken of incommensurability.

It was no time for dawdling. Within minutes I was in and out of the bathroom, back in the same clothes bar the blouse, through with using my fingers as hairdryer, done with my stick of mascara. Finished – or, as Gloria would say, 'Terminada!'

Priyam's neat luggage and Martin's disorderly pile were ready for evacuation when I emerged from my room, their voices just audible from the stairwell as they arrived at the floor below. Through one open door, Chloe and Gloria were talking crabbily as they shifted the disarray from their beds to their bags; across the landing, Jim and Eddie were flapping a sheet to see how loudly it would crack, making a noise not unlike the wind on the night of the storm, but friendly enough. From somewhere came a vague smell of bacon. Of course – full cooked breakfast to send us on our way.

Downstairs, Rupert was at the Rayburn taking orders for eggs. He had a system going: the rashers, tomatoes and field mushrooms were already grilled and were sweating away in the low oven; on the hotplates he had a couple of frying pans, and two of simmering water, one shallower than the other. It was the first time I'd seen him actually cooking.

'Boiled, scrambled or fried?' he asked as I walked past. 'Or poached if you want to be foxy. Actually, I'm rather good at poaching.'

'Goodness, what a choice!' I said, lightly, assessing. 'And I thought you hated eggs. What do you exact in return for poaching?'

'Oh, I don't know. Indulgence of some foible I suppose. A "get out of gaol free" card.' Rupert, too, was remarkably cheery.

'That sounds dangerous. I'll stick to boiled.'

He didn't rise to the bait. Even in a good mood, Rupert was curiously humourless; he poked fun at others but he didn't like being the butt of jokes.

'How many?'

'Oh, two I think, if there are enough.'

Priyam, emerging from the larder with the tail ends of

several jams and an egg box in her arms, called out, 'There's plenty. Here.' She handed over the eggs and started setting down the jars. 'Who's having toast?'

'Is anyone *making* toast?' I asked, addressing the room at large, pleased to find it just as normal.

'I'll do it.' Hugh got up from the table and headed for the machine by the bread bin. None of us could be fiddled with the wire mesh you could use on the hotplate.

Martin, grappling with bacon rind, was asking what there was to do before we set off.

'Pack, tidy, clean? I'm not sure. Ask Dennis: he's probably got it all written down. You won't be off the hook.'

'Any idea where he is?'

'Isn't he up?' I asked, amused.

Tyler came in, bringing jackets from the boot room. 'He's outside. We've been checking the vans.'

Amazing how easy it was to behave as if nothing had happened. He looked just as he always did.

'What's there to check?' Rupert could be so dismissive, it was almost rude.

'You're a fine one to ask!' said Priyam. 'I don't know how you got a reputation for tidiness: we're always clearing up after you. Look!' And she gathered a pile of eggshells and took them to the bin.

'If it's important, I remember.'

'Yeah. Dream on.' Martin clearly wasn't convinced.

Chloe's voice was coming down the back stairs: 'Can't you smell? It reeks of vinegar down there. Don't tell me: now Rupe's doing his party trick.' The latch rattled as she emerged from the door of 'the cupboard', still talking; Gloria right behind her, ribbing back, defending.

I waited for scrutiny, interrogation, but there was none: she was much more interested in Rupert and his eggs; even Martin's offer of bacon was completely ignored.

237

Eventually we were all seated. It felt different from our normal breakfasts and I don't think that was just me. Now the students were talking about what they'd been reading instead of preparing to do it. Curiously, we'd spoken very little about that side of things before. But suddenly they were reviewing the week and comparing notes on what they'd got through. It would have been nice to know the historians' verdicts, but Barnaby's account was lost amidst an outpouring from Lyndsey, which fizzed and sputtered like an experiment in one of her children's books, and Jim was sharing his views with Mei and Tyler and couldn't be overheard. I was always missing key bits of conversation.

Eddie – fearless Eddie – asked Loxton what he'd achieved. Loxton claimed to think I had the edge on him; I seemed to have finished a paper, whereas he had only gathered his thoughts. He was rather envious of such productivity, he said. It would be nice to call it a triumph of quantity over quality, but he feared it was one of youth over advancing age. We should all take note. The absence of a sting in the tail so took me aback that I didn't know what to say.

Tyler's verdict also escaped me, which was even more frustrating; it was almost as if people chose to clear the table precisely when you didn't want them to.

Somebody suggested meeting after Finals, and there was a brief spurt of discussion around the washing-up bowl of how and where that might be done – and whether Loxton and I should be included – but timetables were too different. It was never going to work. By the time the damp tea towels were piled up for the cleaner, the conversation had moved on. Hugh offered Jim the lease on his house – everyone else would be leaving; Chloe was planning a thrash when she cleared out of hers – if they were nice to her, they were all invited; Martin and Barnaby planned to travel together – anyone who fancied a bit of sailing . . . There was a breezy confidence that they'd all run into each other. It occurred to me that Loxton and I were the only people certain to remain in Oxford: willy-nilly, the two of us would be left behind. That was sobering.

Loxton did of course have a checklist, if only in his head, which he proceeded to relay to us. Beds to be stripped and turned back to air – no scouts here. Rooms to be tidied, 'desks' to be cleared, bags to be left with boots and jackets in the hall. When that was done we would tackle the remaining tasks in pairs. Some of us were allocated the main part of the house, refilling the wood baskets, re-laying the fires, checking downstairs for stray books and making sure the upper floors were empty; others, in the kitchen, would be on final washing-up duty, clearing the fridge and the larder, and taking charge of the packed lunch. He estimated an hour and a half.

Where did he pick all that up? Mum would have been impressed.

We did the first part to the sound of Dylan's new album *Desire*, at full volume on the stereo; it was a bit chaotic, with a lot of calling out between the rooms, and bumpings on the landings and the stairs. By the time we got to 'Joey', the people who liked that trailing ballad were singing along; the chorus to 'Sara' had us all wailing in tandem – Tyler too, though it would be nice to think *some* parts of the lyrics meant more to him. Around the time Priyam and I went off to inspect, we'd switched to *Hotel California* again, and that had the two of us warbling. It was all very good-humoured, almost another game.

The rooms looked forlorn as we scooted through the relative peace upstairs – blankets rolled back, wardrobes and drawers gaping, towel rails bare. The spaces revealed little, denuded of personal paraphernalia, except that some people were more considerate of the cleaner than others: Loxton was notably chivalrous, wastepaper basket placed by a pile of folded sheets, curtains tucked neatly into their hold-backs. In one room a heater had been left on; in another we retrieved a hand towel – nothing worse.

The surprise came when we glanced into the annexe over the extension: there were signs of illicit smoking in the tiny sitting area and the bedding was undeniably rumpled in the sparsity beyond. Priyam didn't comment, beyond a reference to the game of sardines; she just picked the stale fag ends out of the pot plant and went off to dispose of the evidence. It was me who stood in that curious space alone and unconvinced; several of us might have looked in – I'd done so myself – but no one had hidden there. No, this was what the Dean had been getting at: it was a bed, after all – and yes, there was a lock on the door. Had it been Eddie and Chloe sneaking off the night before? And if not them, because surely they had other leanings, could it have been Lyndsey and Hugh, or Jim and Mei? Neither seemed likely, not at this stage. But Gloria and Rupert – that figured, and they'd run up the back stairs. Had they been bonking away while Tyler and I were in the kitchen below? Were they still at it when we went chastely to our beds?

Whatever the case, it was too much for me. Within seconds, I'd thrown the blankets and pillows to the floor and was tugging furiously at starched sheets that had lost their sharp creases and were far too loose at the corners for comfort. Whoever it was, they had had it too easy.

When we were done, a drum roll on the gong called us to the drawing room for a reward of tea and the remains of all the packets of biscuits before the regulation group photo, which was to be taken outside the front door. The kitchen contingent was running slightly behind, so the rest of us had a last chance to lounge about and crack jokes. As the others reappeared from their duties we made space for them – Jim

240

discreetly gesturing to Mei to join him on the arm of his chair. There was something about the manner of that pair that had made them untouchable – nobody had teased or done anything that might make them uncomfortable, and they didn't do it now – but, before I could pinpoint what it was, Loxton too was coming in from the hall, the front door open behind him, letting in a drift of cool air and bright-ness to revive us before the Reading Party was recorded for posterity.

We posed on the steps – one of the harbourmaster's grander gestures – for various versions of that same shot, because several of us had cameras. To begin with it reminded me of the compositions my family took at Christmas, assembled relatives standing neatly as a group, splaying out from the focal point, tall people at the back, the rest arranged broadly in order of height, leaning in and out so that everyone's face would be visible – all vaguely formal. That didn't last long. Perhaps all the tidying up created a need for abandon. In any event, somebody in my row started tickling the trio of girls in the front who of course completely lost control, and then the rest of us collapsed into giggles. I blamed it on Martin: he never missed a trick. After that we pretty well gave up. A few smaller groups were taken – Tyler asked Loxton and me to pose together on our own, which was testing but not as bad as I expected – but the sun had gone in and I, for one, had run out of film.

And then there was no avoiding it: bar the washing of the mugs and the packing of the vans, we were ready. Martin and Eddie contrived to miss that bit, setting off in his little car, waved off by a bunch of us. I hadn't cottoned on to their plans. It turned out Eddie was staying the night because he wanted to see a theatre on a cliff edge further west and had somehow inveigled himself into Martin's arrangements. The group felt strangely denuded without them. Martin should have been there, telling jokes and flirting, and we missed Eddie's fond insensitivity. The Party was unravelling just as we got the hang of it.

How was it decided who would travel with whom? It just seemed to happen. Suddenly Priyam was nabbing the seat next to Loxton, Gloria and her crew piling in behind them, Hugh dutifully passing up their bags. My lot turned out to be Jim and Mei in the last row of seats, Tyler and Lyndsey completing the foursome in the back, Barnaby next to me with the map. I would rather not have had Tyler, let alone immediately behind me, but the historians insisted; besides, it wouldn't do to make a fuss. At least he wasn't visible in the mirror – that might have affected my driving.

We agreed to rendezvous with the others at a service station near the halfway mark; failing that we would meet up at College – or not, as the case might be. Loxton handed over the packed lunches and off we went, craning round to wave and then settling back for the journey.

Barnaby and I chatted for a while but he didn't revive our long conversation on the walk, even the less private part, and anyway, given that it was raining, my focus was on the road. Eventually he twisted round in his seat to join the chatter in the back. Periodically, I vaguely listened in; mostly I barely noticed what they were saying and left them to it, glad there were no additional demands.

Then Lyndsey began singing along to a tape of Joan Baez. She sang atmospherically rather than well, but it didn't matter – it was nice having her voice waft into the front of the van. Next to her Tyler began chatting with Jim about Pete Seeger and the American protest song, but they soon stopped. When it got to 'We Shall Overcome' Jim began to sing too – a wonderful rounded sound that encouraged the rest of us to join in. After that we all sang along until when we got to 'Where Have All the Flowers Gone', which he did on his own. I couldn't see his face without turning round, but I could see the top half of Mei's head and, during a brief patch of straight road, watched her looking at him with a kind of wonder, as if astonished that he was letting her in.

Loxton wasn't at the service station when we filled up with petrol, but we sat in the canteen all the same, drifting into a bout of reminiscence over our hot drinks, sharing out the sandwiches. Tyler said Cornwall wasn't what he'd expected from the tales of all the little rituals, which had had a touch of the Boy Scouts about them – very British – and they all agreed that Hugh's portrait had been more ascetic than the reality, provided you forgot about the cold. Nobody put this down to the individuals; the consensus was that it was the result of going mixed.

As for co-residence generally, they said it had been all to the good – or perhaps it was mostly Barnaby and Jim doing the talking as we squidged about on those plastic-cushioned chairs that stick no matter what you are wearing. The five 'male' colleges were all happier places mixed than single, they said; life was less earnest, more fun, with women around. If anything, the pressure now was to enjoy yourself as much as everyone else – a new sort of conspicuous consumption.

That was when Tyler chipped in, wiping chutney from his lip with a paper napkin and leaning over the red Formica tabletop. 'You know,' he said, as if he had to reassure me, 'it doesn't stop us working. Ask anyone who's done the single-sex thing – wondering how to get laid is far more distracting!'

Whatever he meant, I was amazed he could say it with a straight face. Of course he didn't have to; we were all laughing with him, other heads were turning. It was a great moment.

Barnaby was really funny about it too. 'There's only so much looking in the mirror that a man can do,' he said, pretending to preen at his reflection, 'before venturing out in front of the women.' According to him, the whole thing had been one big fuss about nothing: you had to go with the flow – people had grown up since the sixties, the zeitgeist had changed. Take the condom machines that Chloe was so cross about. Everyone assumed they would always be running out, but whenever it came to servicing them, College turned out not to be a hotbed of sex at all. It was the dons who did the letching, not the students. Barnaby thought the Dean had almost been disappointed; all those misdemeanours he'd hoped to police . . .

I nearly spilt my tea. It wasn't the only story I'd heard about 'the Man', as they called him, but this one had a different edge, changed the picture somehow. But then why shouldn't the students have twigged? They'd known the Dean longer than me – if there *was* anything predatory, they'd have picked that up long ago; Gloria would have revelled in it.

I caught Mei looking puzzled, as if she hadn't got the joke, and Jim telling her not to worry. Tyler too was staring at me, his expression watchful, the cheeks working away.

'You know him, Sarah,' he said. 'Tell us what he's really like.'

Why did he ask? Surely there'd been zero to see in the pizzeria: two colleagues eating together; nothing odd about that.

'I couldn't possibly comment!' I threw back. 'Ratting on a colleague? How unfair of you!'

Amazingly, I got away with it. They moved on to the comprehensive thrashing of the men at rounders and the fact that Gloria had been the first to swim. Soon enough, it was time to leave.

Back in the van, Barnaby stuck *Blue* into the cassette player. It seemed an odd choice and Lyndsey, who couldn't soar like Joni Mitchell, got in the way of Mitchell's purity. After 'Carey' her own efforts petered out. Quiet conversation took its place and rapidly thinned. Perhaps it was too con-templative an album – or we were all exhausted. Next to me Barnaby stopped talking altogether and began to doze, his hands resting in the gutter of the map. Glancing round, I saw that Lyndsey had started to read. Tyler was staring out of the window, inscrutable again: was he puzzling about the Dean? Behind them Jim and Mei seemed, again, to be in a bubble of their own. Sometimes there was the steady murmur of their muted chat; sometimes they were silent, Mei resting her head in the little cave between Jim's chin and his shoulder, where the freckles clustered the way mine did. They must have been sitting differently from before; although I could glimpse them in the rear mirror, the picture cut off below the collarbone.

By the time we got back to the ring road, Barnaby had roused himself and was helping me navigate, intermittently chipping into the conversation in the back, where the others were talking quietly as a group again. As we picked our way through traffic and crowds just like the ones of the weekend before, the students turned to the business of pushing off home. The conversation soon faltered; somehow the return to Oxford was oppressive. They were almost mute as I pulled up outside the College and we began emptying the van, apologising as they banged into each other passing to and fro, their previous ease unexpectedly drained.

It was only when the bags were all deposited in the Gate-house and the six of us reassembled next to them that we managed to heave ourselves briefly into jollity again. Mei piped up to say that she hadn't expected such friendship from anyone, let alone me. She would always treasure it, more even than the honour of attending. Then the rest started pitching in with their own summings-up. After that, I could only wish them well in my turn. One of the porters emerged from the

Lodge to see about the crates of empty bottles; a Canadian postgraduate arrived to ask Tyler how it had gone; we were all poised to move on.

Through some fluke of timing, at that very moment Loxton and his van drew up. In seconds our two groups had merged into one, the disorderly mass of bags and people so dominating the entrance that it was hard for anyone else to get past. I could tell Loxton was uncomfortable – the locked knees and the fingers turning in the small of his back gave him away – and, just as the whole palaver threatened to start over again, he did his usual. He put up a hand and said briskly into the sudden silence that no goodbyes, and most certainly no thank yous, were needed to either of us; if anything the thanks should be ours. He and I would be in touch – and here the hand hovered briefly above my arm – with a date for the reunion and we hoped that everyone would come. Then he disappeared. If it sounded a little curt, they all knew that wasn't how it was intended.

The students began talking again. I picked my way through to the front quad and the calm of the great square of lawn – so trim compared with Cornish ruggedness that it looked fake – ready to move on myself.

Priyam detached herself from the rear of the group. 'Just wanted to show you this, which was waiting for me . . . ' she said, and she held out an envelope, neatly inscribed and neatly opened. She was about the only person who used the Lodge paperknife.

Inside was a notelet from her mother that could almost have been scripted to put her mind at rest, telling her that Dadi and Dada had arrived safely, that everyone had asked how she was doing, and how proud her father had been to explain where she was. There was even a postscript saying that they looked forward to seeing her, but that she wasn't to rush: her studies took priority.

'Well, isn't that a relief!' I said, putting the card away carefully and handing it back. 'So you can take your time; no need to race to the station.'

She nodded and gave a little wave to Lyndsey, who was approaching with her tiny suitcase and her satchel in one hand, her bulging tote bag in the other, a final book precariously balanced on top. It wasn't clear to me which of us she was after, or how she would manage the dozen paces between us without dropping something.

But Priyam knew somehow. She said she was off to check on the Indian elections – in the Lodge they were talking about a rout, the end of Indira Ghandi and the Congress Party; her family would be agog.

I turned my attention to Lyndsey, who might need a hand – but no, she just wanted to say something, whatever Loxton had proscribed.

'It really isn't necessary,' I said, watching as she retrieved the paperback and stuffed it under her arm, the picture of a bluestocking. In the background the group in the Gatehouse was dwindling, the pile of bags diminished. Tyler would be leaving soon.

'But I might not have got to go at all, and it did sort of encapsulate the Oxford experience – a miniature version of all this,' Lyndsey said, gesturing vaguely at the creamy buildings streaked with grey, the expanse of blue sky above our heads, the mass of people still in the Lodge.

She burbled on awkwardly, as much at risk of overflowing as her holdall. 'You know, the reading and the games; the conversations and the people; it being such a wonderful place and ...' – there was an intake of breath here that caused the book to slip again – '... the sheer exhilaration of it all.' She stopped short as I leant forward to save her reading matter, and tucked the volume back herself.

'Goodness, that was eloquent.' I said, wishing Loxton had

been there to appreciate the evocation, wondering how to get away. 'Well, it was a first for me too and I won't forget it either. But thank you for the thank you.'

Behind her another pair of figures had left the group; Barnaby was waving at someone, possibly me – he was off to catch up with the boat race, which it seemed we'd won, in a plastic boat of all things. Tyler too was suddenly halfway to his staircase, the Canadian guy at his side, yet again the moment lost.

'We should move,' I said, indicating my things. 'Time to go.' And off I went, alone.

Easter

After all the activity of Cornwall, College seemed unnaturally quiet. There was no High Table and the Fellows' Dining Room, like the SCR, was nearly empty, a source chiefly of refreshments and newspapers for the dons who 'lived in' and any creatures of habit amongst those who 'lived out'. As for the students, the majority had gone home for Easter. The few who contrived to remain were mostly students from abroad, perhaps short of other offers, or postgraduates, whose patterns were unchanged.

The Dean was predictably catty about the atmosphere as we settled into his favourite corner in the pub, ready to discuss the mess the government was in and, when we'd reached the usual impasse on Callaghan and the Social Contract, how our weeks had gone.

He ridiculed the academically minded 'scurrying into their burrows' in the vac, saying the best of both species – dons and students alike – cleared off into the real world as soon as they could, as he was about to do. I assumed he meant the little house in the backstreets, his bolthole from the eavesdropping of people like Gloria. But no, he was off to London to hobnob with Keith Joseph and his cronies. Did I know that Joseph was a Fellow of All Souls?

Unsurprisingly, my take was different. Why disparage people just because they were working, I asked, reaching for my glass and pointedly distinguishing academic from political, let alone commercial research. As for them 'scurrying', perhaps they dived for cover because they saw *him*, I said, flicking in his direction with a beer mat; they were afraid of that acid tongue about to be unleashed at their expense.

The exchange reminded me of that moment in January when, wrapped in his duvet, we'd had that spat about working women. This was no more amusing; fundamentally we had different world views. But he'd stopped chasing, which was a relief. Perhaps he was the kind who lost interest once he'd had his prey.

He was equally catty about the Reading Party, dismissing it as 'Loxton's little marketplace of ideas' and indulging in viperish portraits of the sort of people who 'crowded under the awning of that little bazaar', I suppose because he was jealous. The fact that he hadn't been to Carreck Loose for ages, and didn't know the students as well as he claimed, didn't stop him opining about it or them; as you'd expect, given his belief in free enterprise, he floated opinions on everything, just to see how they fared.

Even worse, he embroidered the analogy, suggesting you could find out almost everything you needed to know about people by considering their economic activity. It didn't matter whether trading was fast or slow; the way people participated, their behaviour as consumer or producer, revealed all, right down to 'the trade in *amours*'.

I thought this a horrid notion and a frightening view of the world, reducing us all to bit parts in some mercantile drama. Even our brief bedroom tumbling was more than a mere transaction – there was certainly no credit or debit balance on either side. When he threatened to develop the analogy further and started quizzing me about what we'd all got up to in Cornwall, I had to ask him to quit it. Pique brought out the worst in him – it was a hideous way to behave.

Still, the comments stayed with me, rankling, as his easy mocking so often did. I could dismiss his picture of people 'lingering on' in College – after all, I was constantly being invited out – but felt self-conscious about what time I did spend there during the day. It was something about the thought that Tyler might be there too, equally solitary, open to interruption but uninterrupted. And yet students had to be left to their revision, even when you felt like asking how they were. Priyam's parents were right: finals had absolute priority and nothing should interfere. The ethics of seeing him didn't even come into it.

I tried not to glance towards Tyler's rooms, where the lights were intermittently on, and stopped sitting in my window seat. But all too often it was like Basil Fawlty saying 'Don't mention the war': the more I determined not to think about Tyler, the more I found that I did. Ridiculous, really – as bad as a schoolgirl.

I considered writing a note, but couldn't decide what to say or how to get it to him. I had no reason to visit his staircase, was wary of the pigeonhole. Even the scrunched-up drafts made me feel exposed: what if my scout noticed when he tipped out the bin?

At one wild moment, I imagined us passing messages on pieces of A4 held to our windows, but of course that was a nonsense: everyone would see.

Then suddenly, on the Wednesday, I received a note from him. A tiny envelope in amongst the others, a small sheet folded twice, one line of his loping script, no names.

'Have gone into purdah,' it read. 'Bear with me.'

I sent one back immediately. 'Understood,' it said. 'Work well.'

That made it easier. I tucked the slip of paper from him into my purse, where I could easily look at it, and busied myself with my own work, typing up a clean copy of my article and checking the references and bibliography. Like taking medicine, you loathed it but you knew it was good for you.

When I couldn't face another day of tapping at my little typewriter, I picked up the thread of my lectures on the women who'd fought for our right to vote and worked longhand. Surprising to find how far my thinking had progressed in a mere week away – something about understanding better how to keep people interested without resorting to glibness, which I must have picked up from Loxton or the chats with Barnaby and Jim. This was more creative than dealing with footnotes, and the softness of my pencil was welcome after the jabber of the machine.

Oddly, it was a chance meeting with Loxton outside the SCR a couple of days later that made me feel better about the Dean and his comments. I was on my way in, having forgotten about lunch – my thoughts still with the notes on which I'd be working. Loxton was on his way out, his coat already buttoned. Even in the vac he was more punctual than me.

He paused at the junction between the stairs and the passageway linking the quadrangles, standing in the gentle scallop in the paving where centuries of people turning had worn the stone down.

'Ah, Sarah.' Even in greeting he barely raised his voice. 'Good afternoon. Did you see my note?'

My mind lurched to the pile of admin relegated to the floor by my desk: not for me the pleasures of being up to date with committee meetings and other bureaucracy. But there was surely nothing there; it must be something waiting in the Lodge.

'No, I don't think so. Tell me. What did I forget?'

As soon as that slipped out, I was cross with myself. Already we'd reverted to type, young and old, with Loxton taking the lead. And why be so defensive? Why was I always worrying about that trial period, as if the tiniest slip would disqualify me, sending me home? At most, I was one day behind with the mail.

My foot edged to the bottom stair, poised for a quick get away, but Loxton wasn't moving. 'Forgotten? Not at all, not at all. It's just that we should exchange views before I report back to the Warden. And the Dean will be interested, as you can imagine – particularly this year.'

I thought of our all-too-prompt drink in the pub and decided not to mention it. It had been hard to be circumspect in the face of all that probing.

'Does he join us for the debrief?' I asked.

Loxton looked shocked. 'The Dean? Oh no, I don't think so. Do you? No, that wouldn't help at all. He does quite enough interfering as it is. Far too ready with his views.'

He pulled on his gloves and patted the front of his coat in the wake of this sudden indiscretion.

'Let me know about the time, won't you?' he asked, and set off towards the gardens, leaving me stunned. It had taken me so long to see it, yet that was exactly what the Dean did: he sprayed opinion like a tomcat marking out territory.

After lunch I popped into the Lodge. There was the envelope from Loxton lying in my pigeonhole along with the afternoon post and some inter-college correspondence. The contents were brief and to the point – a little formal, given that we'd just spent a week in each other's company, but courteous. He hoped the vacation had begun profitably; he would like to share thoughts on the Reading Party before we forgot the details; would Monday suit, for afternoon tea?

I wrote my reply at the counter, inserting a friendly response at the foot of Loxton's page, then initialling and dating it. Returned the note to its envelope, changed the name of the addressee and popped the envelope into the cavern above his name. He might not appreciate the lack of ceremony, but the message was warm.

Three days later we met promptly at 4 p.m. It was the first time I'd visited him in his set, which was on a staircase in the back quad; a tranquil spot with a pretty view of greenery. The layout of the elements in his study wasn't unlike my own – a central grouping of chairs under the eye of a desk – but in other respects there was no comparison. The scale was altogether more generous and his furniture was uniformly antique and polished to a sheen, whereas mine was a hodgepodge of old and new, none of which warranted such attentions. And Loxton was ready for me, which I never was for my guests. The coffee table was laid with a crisp square of white damask, some intertwining of initials at the centre, rosebuds round the edge. On it sat a pretty sprigged tea service – roses again, he was obsessed with roses – with an elegant teapot, a dainty jug of milk, two shallow cups cradled by their saucers, and three side plates, the top one arranged with four neat slices of fruit cake. The porcelain was so delicate that, as the cups curved gently upwards, it became almost translucent, the fluting thinning until it met the fine line of gold that softened the rim.

The last time I'd seen anything so exquisite was during my interviews, when I'd been invited to 'take tea' with the Warden; the array of fine china had been even more intimidating than his questions.

I made some polite remark and Loxton explained that he'd acquired the tea set years ago, in the days when you were given such things. Later, he'd brought it into College because it would get more use; important to share treasures and show how things should be done. Still, he didn't use it in tutorials; only when students or colleagues chose to visit.

He busied himself in an alcove behind the wall of books. I looked around the room, spotting those same travelling photo frames on his desk – sadly facing away from me – and listened to him tipping water into a sink, spooning loose tea leaves from a tin, filling the pot from a kettle. Then he was back, explaining about Earl Grey and the little curls of bergamot, offering a thin slice of lemon as an alternative to a drop of milk. He sat down in the one chair that directly faced the windows, tucking an embroidered cushion – another flower – into the small of his back and began to serve. There was a glimpse of how it might feel to be a student, faced with such elaborate ceremony: unnerving, but also – if you were in the right mood – faintly comic.

Could the same be said of Loxton, I pondered. Not quite – and besides it would be unfair, even unkind: he was far more complex and far more rewarding than that. By comparison the Warden's manner seemed two-dimensional, all theatre and show. Perhaps you needed a bit of bombast to chair Governing Body, to get important decisions made. Bombast wasn't in Loxton's lexicon.

Tea poured and pleasantries exchanged, Loxton began his investigation, asking what I'd made of the Reading Party overall.

This was so open-ended that it wasn't obvious where to start, so I quoted Lyndsey's eulogy and said it struck me as apt; it was surprising what a difference a week in Cornwall could make.

He nodded and handed me my plate, soon followed by the offer of cake. The atmosphere had been a little more 'excitable' than before, if he might say so, but the women had been pretty conscientious when it came to work. It was exactly as experience in College had led him to expect.

'So we were a good influence?'

'Absolutely.'

He lifted the teapot – no chinking of the lid here – and poured again to an invisible waterline. Never before had I seen so little tea in a cup.

We chatted for a while about individual students and what an interesting age it was, on the cusp of adulthood, until we'd covered them all – Tyler included – without him saying anything that put me on the spot. But then I remarked that some good friendships had been made. I was thinking of Jim and Barnaby and how well they had got on, but he must have read it differently. He said to beware: students come and students go and it was best to avoid getting close.

This was uncomfortable: did he mean close in the normal way, on which there could surely be no cause for concern, or had he sensed – or worse, seen, heard or been told – something else? Perhaps he was dispensing general advice? Whatever the case, it would be awful if he thought ill of me.

But Loxton changed the subject before I'd worked out how to respond. He moved on to desks.

Desks? I struggled to adjust. Desks? We'd all found somewhere to work; I'd moved around as instructed. What could be the problem?

Loxton shifted his cushion. That wasn't what he meant: it was *the way* some people had done their reading.

Ooooph, I thought, taking a second piece of cake and retrieving a loose cherry. You wouldn't mention a trivial thing like posture if you had professional impropriety on your mind. And what did it matter how people sat, so long as the students delivered the goods? On that, however, Loxton was clearly of a different opinion: the way you worked affected what was going on inside. Lying on a sofa couldn't be as productive as sitting at a table, and – worse – was somehow discourteous when women were present. Lucky, I mused, that none of the women had chosen to sprawl. What would have happened then? It was like his fixation with punctuality, the mindset that a walk that didn't start on time couldn't be a good walk. It wasn't amenable to rational argument – so silly, in fact, that it was rather endearing. But I didn't say that; just joked a little manically that I at least had sat in an upright chair throughout.

Faced with my teasing, Loxton took the opportunity to recharge the kettle. When he returned, he leant forward. Now it was he who was smiling.

'A few things were a little unexpected.'

Bracing myself for the unspeakable – the pub or the beach scenes, the traffic on the stairs, the goings-on in the house-keeper's suite; anything, so long as it wasn't Tyler – I moved back in my chair.

'The game of sardines, for instance.'

Only that? I felt almost hysterical at the prospect of another reprieve.

'Ah, now that was entirely my fault, Dennis, as you must have realised. An unforgivable invasion of privacy – so embar-rassing. I hope you found my note the next day.'

'I did, on both counts. Actually, I thought it all rather amusing and so did the Warden. It might be wise to prepare for some ribbing on that account.'

He gave me a look I'd sometimes seen him use in Cornwall, as if a child had taken him too seriously. 'It's not about the hiding place, Sarah. It's just that sardines is one thing, murder in the dark quite another. So next time . . .' – next time? – '. . . there's no question: I will go to bed before it starts.'

Was *he* now teasing *me*? Perhaps he didn't think ill of me after all. What a welling of relief, like opening a sluice gate!

I made space for my cup and saucer on the tray, gently placing them back where they belonged, thinking now might be the time to leave. But Loxton wasn't done.

'I thought you might like to see something,' he said, ges-turing towards a section of shelving.

'You've got me there, Dennis,' I said, looking at the pha-lanx of books that marched round three sides of the room from floor to ceiling. 'You'll have to explain.'

'Naturally,' he replied. 'Let me get it down.' And he rolled a set of mahogany library steps across the rug and, with a click, locked the brass wheels. He had to stand on the platform at the top, holding onto the finial, to reach the shelf he wanted. Gently he eased out a floppy volume bound in waxed linen with a handwritten label.

'Godfrey's journal.' He took out his pocket handkerchief and gave the edges a wipe. 'It's got a little dusty. Here.' He held it towards me. 'Not a personal diary; more a record of his working life. I thought the element of social history might appeal. He began the Reading Parties soon after Ivy Williams was admitted to the Bar, though his focus is more parochial. Don't expect any big insights, but it might give you colour.'

I took the volume – cool to the touch, the cloth faintly ribbed – and flicked quickly through the yellowing pages, 240 in all. The journal was written in blue ink in a measured, loping script. Periodically, footnotes using roman numerals had been inserted in red and green ink. At the back there was a detailed index, in black apart from the same colourful cross-referencing.

'What an extraordinary document!'

'There are maps, too, if you are interested – they're represented by the green numbers. He was a geographer, good at cartography. Did I tell you?'

'I don't believe you did.'

'Well, some other time we can look at those too. He drew them himself.'

'And they show . . .?' I was still turning the pages. There were no maps here.

'The walks they did, terrain that interested him, the places where he found flowers. He drew pictures too. His botanical drawings were exquisite.'

'Do you have those as well?'

'A few. He gave most of them to the College. There's a group of four in the Warden's Lodgings, but they're just of things from the garden here, nothing special. I have a few of the orchids, which were his favourites. They're at home.'

He went to the window. 'In the early days, I had rooms over there, on Staircase Nine. Godfrey was on the floor above. I could hear when he came back from the labs – the walking about before he settled into his chair. He always stopped at six o'clock, when the steps would go over to the cupboard where he kept his sherry. If he thought I was around, he would come down with the bottle or invite me up to join him.'

He paused, and I wondered what he was remembering. Then he carried on. 'That's how I got to know him.'

I went to have a look, but the light was fading. 'May I borrow it one day? It would be good to look at it properly.'

Loxton began pulling at the curtains.

'I could promise to wear these,' I teased, pulling a bag of white cotton gloves from my pocket, dangling them in front of him rather as Eddie and Tyler had dangled the socks. 'Always carry a pair with me; you never know what you may discover.'

'Ah! A true professional. They should be obligatory in Duke Humfrey, don't you think? Manuscripts shouldn't be pawed, even in a library.' He smiled appreciatively, feeling through the plastic. 'But yes, that's what I intended. You'll let me have it back, won't you?'

'Of course. I'll be very careful.'

It was perfectly true, those gloves had talismanic status. My history teacher gave me a pair when I did well in my O levels. They were a seal of approval worn not to look at old manuscripts, which were in short supply at my school, but to encourage the belief that you might succeed – even that Oxbridge was a possibility, not that I followed that through. I became superstitious, laying them at the top of the desk whenever we had exams. Now there was a pair with me as a matter of course; one of the few clean things you could be sure to find amongst the rubbish cluttering my handbag. Whenever I went into the Bodleian to look at a truly ancient tome, which any of us could do for the pure pleasure of watching the unlocking and feeling the vellum, I'd whip them out in preference to using what the librarians provided. It tickled me to have the tools of my trade always at the ready: a female Sherlock Holmes, poised to sleuth.

Nevertheless, Godfrey's journal sat in a pile of books on the floor by my desk for a couple of days before I looked at it again. I'd slipped it into one of the acid-free boxes we were trialling in the Faculty, which made it hard to miss, but didn't want to be distracted. It was enough to grapple with Loxton. Why tackle his mentor too? What if their friendship featured, if this was Loxton's discreet way of telling me something about the nature of the relationship? It would be so easy to say the wrong thing.

When I did get round to starting the journal – on a wet afternoon after delivering my article to the post office, when I felt I deserved a break – it proved far too restrained for emotional revelations. In fact it was rather touching in a reserved, masculine way.

The record began in 1924, with the plan to take a group of students on a walking holiday in the Lake District, and finished abruptly in 1957. A few bits of ephemera were tipped in – an extract from the Governing Body minutes authorising the project; the occasional thank-you letter from a student – but otherwise it seemed to be as originally planned.

The report of each trip began on a fresh page and continued over several sheets: first a list – not unlike the College 'bible' – of who attended, their school, their subject and matriculation date, any bursaries and, clearly added later, the degree they received; then a narrative account, day by day, of the walks they did, the discussions they'd had and a few other observations, mostly of a topographical nature; and lastly a note of the mileage walked, the time taken, any injuries and the remedies prescribed, and a table of flora and fauna seen on the way. Then there were a few blank pages. Lastly, working back from the other end of the volume, came the immaculate index.

From a glance this made clear that Loxton had attended the Reading Party from his arrival as an Exhibitioner just before the war, when Godfrey must have been at least forty. The early lists showed that they'd overlapped for a decade or so, Loxton displacing another don as sidekick part way through, presumably when he himself graduated to Junior Fellow. Assuming the entries stopped when Godfrey retired, and that Loxton had then taken over, he'd had been going on the Reading Party for about thirty years.

Tyler would have been intrigued by all that, I thought, remembering our speculations about their relationship when we had ventured into the Carreck Loose chapel. Unfortunate digression: it stopped me reading on, although seconds before I would happily have done so.

When Jenny came to stay, I didn't tell her about the journal and we barely touched upon the Reading Party, except to share thoughts on Ivy Williams.

It was partly that we were rarely on our own. She was looking up old friends, so most of the time we were with someone in publishing, who lived with her boyfriend near the boutiques in what Jenny still called 'Little Trendy Street'. Not for Jenny a guest room in College with a bath at the foot of a draughty set of stairs, or a trip to her own *alma mater,* if she could stay by her favourite haunts.

The four of us spent an uproarious evening cooking chicken in a terracotta 'brick' that our hosts said was all the rage, and eating and talking over far too many bottles of wine. Eventually we worked out that I'd met the two of them years before at Jenny's twenty-first, when she wore one of those Annabelinda dresses in the Liberty-print Tana Lawn that she used to rave about – dusky pink tones, with plum ribbon on the smocking; a parental present whose extravagance had shocked us all.

I joined them again on the Saturday for a curious evening with a guy they'd all known. Jenny had 'had a thing' with him in her second year, mostly – she'd said at the time – because he was very good looking and even more promising in bed. Several years on, he struck me as less than promising. He was still doing his DPhil, still sharing the same house, and his new housemates drifted in and out as we talked in the damp basement kitchen, helping themselves to whatever booze and food was on offer (not a great deal), without even saying 'hello'. Later, in search of the loo, I walked in on them by mistake and was taken back to evenings at York after I'd begun to get bored with Andy. He and his mates would sit listening to equally spaced-out tracks from *Tubular Bells* or *Dark Side of the Moon*, passing a joint as they moved between cushion, ashtray and stereo – the business of getting high, as it seemed to me, an excuse for neither doing nor saying much, let alone getting on with any work, though Andy swore the dope made things clearer. I couldn't imagine Tyler saying that, even in the era he'd joked about by the bonfire.

It wasn't until Sunday that Jenny and I got proper time together. We did a tour of the College, which she barely knew, and of my own rooms, which of course she wanted to see. She was gratifyingly appreciative: although the buildings were older than those she'd lived in, they were much less institutional, she said – none of those long corridors with their pipes and parquet flooring, none of the hospital smell you got in the women's colleges. I told her she'd have to come as my guest at High Table in term time – there was institution enough there – but she said that wasn't what she meant. She'd lived in red-brick Victoriana, designed by an architect of civic buildings – asylums or prisons probably, or no, perhaps it was war memorials – rather than for the love of God. Here, the atmosphere was more contemplative, though her gardens had the edge even if they weren't pristine. As for my set, she wouldn't stop teasing me about it. My name above the door, like the other Fellows; the paraphernalia of a don littering my desk; my gown hanging ready for formal Hall.

Still, she said, as we banged around fixing our trademark gin and tonics in my miniscule kitchen, there was something odd about this life of cerebral industry. The place might be mixed, but the rooms were still monastic. Didn't I mind having so little space? This was smaller than her flat and at least she had a proper double, even if there was barely room to walk around it. Wasn't that a problem? It would be hard to seduce anyone in a bed the size of mine.

This had of course crossed my mind on several occasions – the College had provided one of those four-foot things, perhaps tactfully hedging their bets – but I wouldn't concede the point. After all, hadn't she done well enough in three-footers with the likes of the guy from the night before?

'Oh God!' she cried out. 'Wasn't he awful! What on earth did I see in him?'

'Big balls, I think. Or big something.'

'Uugghh. Still, you know what I mean: it was all very well as an undergraduate, but now?'

I made a limp remark about moving out sooner or later – to rent or buy one of those tiny workmen's houses, whatever was affordable, which might not be much on an academic salary – but for the moment it wasn't an issue.

'Oh come on, don't be so literal! I know it's cosy – they were clever to have squeezed it all in – but you can hardly have a romp. Anyway, that's not what I meant. A bloke would be screwing around – you're entitled to a bit of fun.'

And so within the space of a few minutes we were back in the old territory, talking about the men in our lives. She ripped through the things she'd been up to and then abruptly changed tack.

'You promised to point out the guy you got off with . . .'

I blanched. Surely I hadn't said?

'You know. The one you slept with after the party. On New Year's Eve.'

She made me pull out the prospectus so she could take a look. 'But he's a dish,' she said. 'Why give him up?'

I said she'd forgotten: *she* was the one who played the field; *I* never had. The thing with the Dean had been fun, but I'd gone off him and anyway it wasn't wise.

Jenny wasn't having any of it. There was nothing wrong with being wined and dined, or a bit of lighthearted sex. It did a girl good. Feminists had a lot to answer for, with all their stridency: you didn't have to *like* your admirers and there was no need to feel *guilty*.

'That wasn't what I meant,' I said.

'Well, what did you mean?' she asked.

I made another of my stupid remarks – about the College being such a closed society and everyone knowing everything. She said that was pathetic – who cared if there were rumours? I hadn't done anything wrong. A young and attractive woman – what did they expect?

'It would have got complicated, what with working together,' I said lamely.

'Just as well you've gone off him then,' she whacked back. 'Not ideal, bonking a colleague, but it's not as if he was from the Faculty – still worse, a student. You don't want to be compromised.'

That put paid to my confessions. No mention of my

friendship with the married historian, about which she was liable to get the wrong end of the stick, and not even a hint about Tyler, which had somehow gone beyond sharing.

It wasn't a great moment in our relationship. I'd never concealed that way before; seemed to have missed the opportunity to unload and, having missed it, couldn't get it back.

And even as we chatted – propped against my crushed-velvet cushions at either end of the window seat, our knees bent and our feet touching – it got worse. A group of students walked through the Gatehouse and turned into the front quad: Tyler and his Canadian friend, with a couple of girls I didn't recognise. So much for purdah!

I listened grimly as Jenny talked about how relaxed it seemed with the women as at home as the men; so unlike the feel of her own college, where visiting men were so conspicuous and there was such a hideous level of gossip about who was seeing whom. The boys must relish having the girls on tap, she said; their chances of scoring transformed. As for the girls, they must be having a ball, she continued, waving vaguely in the direction of the students as they disappeared up the stairs – fancying their tutors, trying their peers out for size (as it were), doing just enough work to get by. No wonder I'd envied them.

Had I? I asked myself. And when had I told her?

Thankfully she moved on, or it might all have unravelled. She wanted to talk of her latest conquest, who was taking her on holiday in the summer – our plans for the Greek Islands would have to make way. She'd be back in time for my birthday, so we could still celebrate together. Just think – twenty-seven!

Then, coming back from a trip to my little loo, she exclaimed. 'You never told me about that don – the one on your Reading Party!' She settled back on the cushions, ready for disclosure. 'Did you hold your own with him? And what were the students like? I suppose they were all getting stoned and bed-hopping. Are they still going to get Firsts?'

How funny that talking about Loxton counted as a relief! But as I described how my view of him had changed, I knew I could never explain what had been so wonderful about that week. The photos were back from the chemist, and I had the floor plan and the map, but all stayed in my desk. I knew that if Jenny had found herself in Carreck Loose, she'd have been in the sniping camp. Not in the way Chloe was, resisting authority; more like Gloria, generally impatient. In the off-duty hours she'd have poked fun and kept us amused, but the stints in library conditions would have made her groan. Loxton would have called her 'not quite Reading Party material'.

As for Tyler and the things that had made Cornwall so special? Well, Jenny would never have understood.

So I restricted myself to jokes about the regime and how it was received. Even that meant digging a bigger hole – soon she'd be labelling me a bluestocking.

'It all sounds very bookish,' she said finally, as we stood to gather her things.

Yes, I thought: in a way, that was the point. At least she didn't call it 'elitist', as Andy would have done – he'd have been scathing.

Left to my own devices again, I continued my new rhythm, based on the Cornish routine. In the morning there was work at my desk, starting earlier than we had on the Reading Party but taking a similar break in the middle to make a cup of tea. At lunchtime there'd be a trip out, usually to have a bite to eat with a Faculty colleague, which might be followed with a walk to Port Meadow or round the Botanic Gardens or the University Parks. After that there was another chunk of work before supper, usually out, or an evening with friends to see a film or go to a pub. On rare occasions it was back to my desk to work into the small hours, but mostly not. I stayed out too late for that.

Certain things would bring it all back to me, like the smell of hot cross buns by the baker's one afternoon, or the evening when the Mediaevalist's wife served up a pecan pie. And I made the mistake of buying the Dylan album, blaring out my namesake 'Sara' until I realised I was behaving like a teenager. Even the sight of the box with Godfrey's journal would send me back to Carreck Loose. It would be awkward if my suspicions about homosexuality were confirmed; easier to mull the idea that Loxton had been traipsing around on the Reading Party since before I was born.

Then early one afternoon there was Tyler in the covered market, buying something on the far side of my favourite stall – the green-and-white-trimmed 'purveyors of fruit and vegetables'.

'I assumed you'd gone away,' I lied, paying for my apples, waiting for him to finish his purchase so as not to be rude. He was holding some daffs wrapped in a furl of paper still dripping with water: white with a trumpet of apricot. What man buys flowers unless for a woman? Who was she?

Tyler picked up his pannier, rearranging things so the daffodils slid down behind a wodge of foolscap paper, and gave a wave to the stallholder, whom he seemed to know.

'Nope,' he said. 'Been here all the time. You?'

How frustrating, I thought, before catching up with the question.

'Me? Mostly here. I'll be off to Norfolk at the weekend, but that'll be it. You can get a lot done with nobody around.'

Tyler nodded, patting the pannier. He fiddled with the change he'd put in the pocket of his jacket. It was the same tweedy affair he'd had with him in Cornwall, surprisingly soft to the touch; he'd worn it at dinner on our final evening, sitting next to me.

I'd probably interrupted him – perhaps he was with one of the women I'd seen in the quad and didn't like to say – but concern for his work still got the better of me.

'Are those notes safe from the daffs? It would be too bad if they got wet.'

Tyler smiled as he bent down to adjust his belongings; he must have remembered the scene. When we were together in the library, Lyndsey had knocked over her posy of wild flowers, and because Hugh too used a fountain pen, it had made a mess of his jottings.

We were getting in the way of the queue, so I stepped aside, ready to move on. Really, the whole thing was too embarrassing.

'Are you busy?' he asked, straightening up again.

'Well, I've been tidying that paper I was working on. Footnotes, bibliography, you know the sort of thing.'

'No, I meant ... are you doing anything right now?' He waved his arm at nothing I could see. 'Hey, maybe we could have a coffee. If we're allowed?'

'Allowed?' This was annoying. I'd battled so long and hard with the concept. His use of the word took away the relief of him making the first step, which could otherwise have been held against me.

'Oh, you know, staff fraternising with students and all that,' he said. His Yankee poise slipped and he seemed faintly uncomfortable. 'Like when I came to say "hi" but didn't leave a message, or sending you that note, which had to be so brief – you're all so careful about what is and isn't "done".'

This was even more annoying. I didn't mind the brevity of the note, but why couldn't he have visited again, or told me he had? And in all my considering I hadn't considered it put like that – as if it was merely a matter of British restraint. But what came out, as if 'allowed' didn't merit any thought, was, 'Oh, I don't see why not.' Followed, as soon as we moved away from the stall, by, 'Anyway, no one's around to see us.'

Big mistake: that wasn't the thing to say. Tyler might have done the asking, but my response made me complicit. We made our way down the side street, neither walking together nor separate, his bicycle wheeling awkwardly between us, and we couldn't fill the gap in conversation. A near miss with a lamppost got us underway again but then our chat was banal. It would have been better to say 'no'. The whole thing was more than uncomfortable – it was fundamentally wrong.

And yet I didn't backtrack.

The café he'd suggested was popular with tourists – more a 'town' than a 'gown' place – because it was quaint and you were expected to have home-made cake, which was beyond most student budgets. I'd been there before, with a group of colleagues from the Faculty. We'd sat tucked away at a pine table between a pair of pews, where you could squeeze extra people amongst the patchwork cushions if they chanced to turn up. But now it was busy and Tyler and I had to take a little table in the middle – the pub kind with a cast-iron base, a round marble top and a pair of matching chairs – which was clearly meant for two and made us very visible. As we walked through, it was hard not to check who else was there, and every time the bell above the door tinkled through the hubbub, you wondered who the new arrivals were. Tyler didn't seem bothered, but for me the conversation was conducted at two levels. The first was an awkward exchange with somebody I was a little too pleased to see, and the second an internal debate about what to say if we were spotted.

I would have given a lot, at that moment, for quieter colouring. People say they envy hair like mine, but I often feel like a Belisha beacon.

At least choosing from the menu gave us something to talk about. When we'd exhausted the relative merits of the various cakes on offer, we talked about a café in the market that displayed nothing in the window at all; then about the fruit and veg man, who'd been friendly when Tyler was finding his way around. After that, there threatened to be another lull. The ease of Cornwall had completely disappeared.

I asked if he'd seen any of the other students. It was a poor choice of question – he said he assumed they'd all gone home or back to their digs. Anyway, this wasn't the time to drop by – everyone was frantic, revising. Had I seen anyone? This was equally unfortunate: he was forgetting it wasn't the same. No, I replied, it was surprising how little I bumped into the students in the vac; perhaps a tutor's day ran to a different clock. Ouch.

We started again after our order arrived. He asked about my work and I asked how he was getting on with his, and for twenty minutes or so, it can't have been much more, we managed a conversation about things that genuinely interested us – me about Ivy Williams and the way her story linked to the rest of my research, the timeline as a whole; Tyler about moral philosophy, which was as close as he could get to doing jurisprudence. We swapped plates, so he got to taste a Victoria sandwich despite his claim that he didn't like pips. As the cream and raspberry oozed, I made a joke about the change from our Carreck Loose teas and he laughed.

For a few glorious moments, we had it back. I have no idea what I said – something else about Cornwall and the fun we had had – but the look he gave me was lovely.

Then our waitress began to clear a neighbouring table and, panicking at the possibility of a further influx of customers, I asked for the bill. We paid – I made sure we went Dutch – and then got into a tangle, first about who should pull the table out of whose way and then about who should open the door, so by the time we were once again standing by his bike neither of us could say anything sensible. There must have been goodbyes – I really don't remember, other than giving him a rough olive russet so he could try out my favourite apple. Then, although the logical thing would have been to accompany him halfway back to College, we set off in opposite directions.

In fact, I did a huge circuit. Traipsed south through the noise and tat of Cornmarket and kept going down St Aldate's until Christ Church and the vastness of Tom Quad, which always looked empty even when it wasn't, and which you couldn't cross quickly without running, which of course you never were. Went past the Picture Gallery, through the great stone arch and then down the narrow walk by Merton, which led to their playing fields and the water meadows beyond. Stopped to sit on one of those wooden benches, grainy and green-tinged, where you could watch the geese pecking about and looking self-important, or follow the lines of the gnarled roots of the trees pushing up through the grass, and wished that he was there to lean on. It was almost as bad as sitting by the lake on campus at York at the wrong time of year, with only the greylags for company, staring at that feature-less fountain and smelling that fishing-net smell, save that in Oxford you might at least continue down a real river, where the colourful barges and the swish of the rowers suggested life carrying on as normal, leading elsewhere. But even that respite, and then the grace of Magdalen and the deer, failed to restore me.

All the while I needled away at the obstacles, trying again to find a way out. To hell with it, I wanted to say to all the objections, what was the problem with having a cup of tea?

Except of course that it wasn't just a cup of tea. If it had been, it wouldn't have been so hard to resist. It irritated me afresh that men had ignored such scruples for years – why shouldn't women do the same? But Jenny had been right to caution. There was a line – or a succession of lines, marking increasing levels of incrimination – that women just couldn't afford to cross. Whether men crossed them was immaterial. It was a matter of realpolitik – the penalty for male and female transgressions wasn't the same. To put it bluntly, for a woman an affair with a student – even one you weren't teaching – was taboo of a different order, more than unwise, a risk it wasn't worth taking. And I'd been culpable from the beginning: minor flattery about my book and I'd succumbed. If I hadn't laughed about Loxton's script, inviting flirtation, we might never have had that early conversation; even the collision had had an element of coquetry – I'd known as I bent for my papers that my t-shirt would gape.

When I got back to the Gatehouse, dusk was approaching. Usually this seemed an entrancing time – the grass in the front quad calmer, no longer its brilliant green; the sky a deep blue, almost indigo; the creamy glow from occupied rooms warming patches of stonework; artificial light pooling gold by the staircases. Now it seemed to snub me, as if saying, 'Still here? Still debating?'

I went home for the bank holiday, hoping for sunny diversion.

But it turned out the boys might not be coming. That put a pall on the start of the weekend, as if a sea fret had descended. Then too many of my parents' friends were invited over, making me feel like an exhibit. And when I did get Mum and Dad to myself, it was unsatisfactory. Mum asked if there was anyone 'special' – even wove in a reference to the Dean – which meant I remonstrated and she got upset. Then Dad said, 'You could try to be less combative,' which spoilt our long walk together.

My elder brother did turn up in the end. He drove down for Easter Sunday, producing a sweetheart for the first time – one of the lab technicians – which meant we were on best behaviour. I was pleased for him, but still a little disappointed. She was nice enough, but very much a traditional wife in the making – when one of the few female scientists came up in conversation, she said she couldn't do what 'women like her' did, 'risking their happiness for their careers'. Of course Mum thought she was charming; even Dad was rather taken.

My younger brother was on duty at Barts, so he missed the chance to voice an opinion. Not that he'd have shared my view: from what I'd gathered he was carrying on much as he'd done at medical school – getting drunk and sleeping around, treating the nurses badly. When I suggested he might reform, he complained that he 'didn't phone home to be lectured'. Out came the same old line about feminists taking things too seriously – it might have been that awful postmortem with the Dean on New Year's Day – and again no way to respond without compounding the 'error'.

Upstairs in my room, pondering the criticisms, only the view was consoling – the dark of the reed beds familiar and beautiful in the moonlight. But standing there made me think about Tyler again. It was too much like watching by the window at Carreck Loose, with the palms swaying, wondering if he was doing the same on the floor below.

I was back in Oxford by the middle of April. Checking my reading pile for height, there – still! – was the box with Godfrey's journal. It annoyed me to have it glowering, vying for attention with tomes related to my research. I tried tucking it away in a less visible stack – a trick that occasionally worked – but it wouldn't leave me alone. Besides, Loxton would expect it back before long.

In my penultimate week of freedom, it got the better of me. I'd returned from a late lunch to find a message from the Dean chalked on the piece of slate by my door for all to see, saying he couldn't make *King Kong* that evening, as if it had been me who'd suggested that ridiculous film. Anyway, that gave me the opportunity. When it got dark I drew the curtains, turned the bar heater on and settled down in a chair with a lager to read the journal properly.

Once you got the hang of it, deciphering Godfrey's script wasn't much of an obstacle – it was much easier than Loxton's – and reading his jottings didn't take that long. Some bits I skimmed, like the horticultural detail and the topographical references. Much more interesting were the glimpses of social history, as Loxton had suggested. Even then a significant number of boys came from grammar schools in the north of England, as the 'bible' showed they still did. And it seemed the men went from one male environment to another without the 'fairer sex' – Godfrey really did use that language – intruding. Until, that is, the references to Loxton.

According to one of the few personal remarks in the entire volume, in 1949, when Loxton must have become some kind of postgraduate, he was in danger of letting the side down. It wasn't immediately obvious why: perhaps Godfrey didn't like to document the offence, or the mere allusion was enough of a reminder. In any event, it wasn't until the final page for that year that I found the explanation. Loxton was 'moony' and the person he was moony about was a woman called Rose.

A woman! That complicated things. Godfrey was jealous!

On I read, wondering if Rose was a friend of the family or a more recent acquaintance and, if so, how Loxton had met her. There was no reference to her the second time Loxton accompanied Godfrey, so it began to seem that she was an aberration. But then she was back again in 1951, mentioned because her letters pursued them to the Lakes. After that, both she and Loxton disappeared from the narrative until a reference to their being 'betrothed' in 1953.

I stared and then flicked the pages faster: they had bit parts as 'Dr and Mrs Loxton' in an entry for the following year, when Rose suggested she and Dennis host the reunion – an offer that Godfrey must have refused, because it took place in College as usual.

Two years later a new name arrived as Godfrey's sidekick on the trip, alongside a caustic remark about how fast the married Fellows shed their responsibilities. Another few pages – by now I was barely skimming – the journal stopped.

Loxton married!

Had I said it aloud? Suddenly there was bile at the back of my throat, a reflux strong enough to make me swallow hard and reach for my glass. This small but momentous piece of information upended everything. Married? Loxton?

I stared down at the front of the volume, trying to take it in. So he wasn't what he appeared to be: not even a bachelor.

But Loxton courting? Loxton as part of a couple? Loxton in love? This was too big a stretch. It was a completely different picture of the man, just when I thought he'd come into focus.

Besides if he'd been married then, as the journal said, why was he *not* married now? Godfrey wouldn't have been wrong on a matter like marriage and, if he had been, Loxton would surely have pointed it out. If anything, Loxton must have assumed his marital status was common knowledge.

Suddenly, things were explained that hadn't made sense before. The tea service, for example. Of course – it would have been a wedding present! Rose probably chose it and they would have used it 'for best' when they had visitors. If she were no longer at home, it probably *would* get more use in College. No wonder Loxton had brought it in.

But then, if Rose were alive, why wouldn't *she* have things like the china and the inlaid tray? So what had happened? Were they separated, divorced, or – not to put too fine a point on it – was she dead? And what about children? Would Loxton turn out to be a father too?

The facts, at least, could be established by asking a straight question of a colleague – the Mediaevalist, say. Or the Dean, though on reflection he'd been grossly selective in his briefings. You couldn't trust someone who gave you all that stuff about the intelligence services and nothing about this; it was almost as if he'd set out to mislead me.

But my error of judgement was much more problematic – how could I have been so obtuse?

I rolled up my sleeve, feeling for the troublesome spot, checking for itches. On reflection, *nobody* had misinformed me about Loxton. In fact, no one had actually said whether he was married or not – the subject had never come up, even when Tyler and I were in the chapel at Carreck Loose, sharing what we knew about Godfrey. No, it was me who had leapt to conclusions unaided – that single men of a certain age would be bachelors, probably homosexual like my uncle. The urge to be enlightened had spawned its own prejudice.

I rubbed harder at my elbow where the skin was prone to crack and flicked the pages again, relief that I hadn't made a fool of myself with Tyler vying with the urge to find a let-out. Such a simple piece of information – why had nobody taken the trouble to fill me in?

All those examples of being wrong-footed by the College, usually over some procedural matter that no one had thought to explain. The Warden had said Loxton was hard to read, but he could so easily have given me a clue. As for the Dean, who'd affected to be my ally, posing as mentor but being nothing like – that was really unkind. He'd been a lousy lover too, every move a calculation. What had I seen in him?

The problem was, I was just as culpable. Had I revealed more than the essentials about my private life? I had not. I'd kept even the Warden's wife at a distance, and she'd been too polite to probe. It was a clear case of double standards: I was in no position to criticise.

I went in search of an aspirin from the little cupboard above the loo, and swilled it down from the tumbler. It tasted unpleasant, but that might have been the residue of toothpaste. Either way it meant another grimace.

Back in my chair, the full train of thought crept up on me. This was worse than any ordinary misjudgement; I'd tripped myself up as a historian.

How often had we been lectured, as undergraduates, to leave prejudice behind, to look for what our sources told us rather than what we expected them to say, to try – like scientists – to *disprove* hypotheses before adopting them as working theory? But in relation to Loxton there had been no testing at all, just wild guesses and extrapolations, one error of interpretation piled upon another. These were elementary mistakes. Had a student of mine made them, I would have been merciless. Like Loxton, in fact – forensic in the dissection. I had no conceivable excuse.

I picked the journal up and put it back in its box on the pile of books, turned off the heater and the lights, walked through to the other room and sat down heavily on the bed. Jenny was right: it was small, ill-sprung and uncomfortable. And why submit to a monastic existence if your academic credentials were shoddy? What was the point of any of it?

'You owe me a drink,' I said to the Dean when he accosted me a few days later outside the pub, just before the start of term.

'I do? Why's that? For blowing you out?'

'That too. But no, for not telling me he was married.'

He put on the expression he wore when he wanted to provoke – one eyebrow raised, the eye stalking. 'Now let me see. Which of your many potential beaux might we be talking about here?'

'Oh for God's sake. Loxton of course. Who else would I mean? Why didn't you tell me he was married?'

'He's not married. At least, he isn't now.'

'Don't be such a pedant. *Been* married. Why not tell me?'

The Dean lifted his shoulders – they were already too broad for any man's good – in a complacent shrug, and pushed through the swing doors into a blast of heat, noise and smoke. Had this, too, been a way of paying me back?

'Because Dennis is private. Because men don't like pity. Maybe . . .' he said, dipping his head to whisper in my ear, '. . . because sometimes you're too clever by half and I wondered how long it would take you to work it out.' He lifted up again to look for a gap in the crowd. 'I don't know. Does it matter?'

'Yes it does.'

'Why?'

For a moment I wondered whether it was worth explaining. Tyler would never have played tricks of that sort, nor would anyone else with an ounce of generosity. 'Because it was mean, that's why. And it made me think meanly of him.'

'Ah. Well, I'm sure we didn't mean to be mean.' He reached the bar and turned to me, shouting over a neighbouring shoulder, 'What'll you have?'

'Vodka and orange. And then you can tell me what happened; why you said "pity".'

But he didn't give up. 'What happened? I thought *you* were going to tell *me*. We're all agog to know how Dennis enticed you into his bed.'

'Oh for Christ's sake!'

'I'm afraid the joke's gone all round Governing Body; his standing has improved considerably.'

On it went. It was like fencing – one sally after another, all for show. I'd been a sucker for it, thinking him bracingly clever and his opinions so ridiculously extreme that they could be ignored, especially when he made you laugh so much. But then Andy had made me laugh too, and that hadn't been a good thing; twice Andy and I had ended up in bed together after I'd resolved to stop seeing him. Besides, on occasions like this, when it actually mattered, the Dean really wore me down. Unfortunately, that was the price of finding anything out.

And of course he did know what had happened to Mrs Loxton, though it took an evening's drinking to winkle it out of him.

'You've gone very quiet,' he said, after he'd finished.

Actually, there were no possible words. Instead, I got up and went to the loo, where I sat in the darkness – couldn't bear to switch on the light – until I'd recovered.

'Are you okay?' he asked on my return, all innocence.

'What do you think?' I replied, leaning over to gather my things. 'It's a desperate story. And that time when you mentioned Bletchley Park and losing people and I thought you meant in the war – that was just as misleading as letting me think he was a bachelor. You could so easily have told me.'

'You never asked and I just did.'

If we'd been anywhere else, I'd have yelled at him. Instead, what came out was more like a hiss. 'You can be a real arsehole, you know. It's bad enough to hear such things – I'm *upset* – without them being used in a cretinous game. And you might have told me before I made a fool of myself, rather than after.'

'But you haven't,' he said, draining his glass. 'It's all in your head. One of several things that nobody knows . . .' – and he tapped his nose like a pantomime villain scaring his audience – '. . . except me.'

Trinity

The Gatehouse got busy again when the students returned. They streamed past the Lodge, ignoring the new notices on the board, but the area was a hubbub all the same – everyone chatting, calling out to their mates; bags left against the wall while post was collected; people, possessions and noise spewing into the front quad.

Martin was delightfully friendly as I skirted the throng on a last trip out before term intervened. He waved Loxton's cyclostyled sheet in my face, teasing about the reunion and which of us might have done the accounts – clearly he didn't expect it to be me.

I asked about Eddie's visit.

He laughed loud enough to make people turn their heads. 'Our resident thesp! Amazing what he gets away with! Had me drive him all the way to Land's End and back, to see the Minack Theatre, before he buggered off. But he was very entertaining.'

'How?' I asked.

'Oh, you know, Eddie being Eddie. Mum was very taken with the cap and the baseball shoes; she'd never seen anything like it.' And he described their evening together, Eddie bragging about his childhood in Ladbroke Grove while the mother prepared supper. Apparently, when Martin's dad returned with muddy wellingtons, Eddie had taken him for a farmhand rounding up cows. The father, who had 2,000 acres and was one of Cornwall's larger milk producers, had not been amused. Being a country girl myself, I sympathised.

There was a skittering on the stone flags behind us, as recognisable as the wispy 'Hello!' that followed, and Lyndsey flitted into view between the other figures, the waist of her skirt slipping as she stretched to tug Martin's lapel.

'How many pasties did you eat?' she quizzed. 'And were they as good as ours?'

Nice that she remembered the outing. He'd been kind to her.

She registered me. 'Oh, Sarah, just the person. Tyler's got lots of photos, but they're not the right kind. Will you bring yours next week? I've begun a poem – an epic in heroic couplets – but I need reminding.'

She was swaying in that peculiar way of hers. Was that why she was so willowy, because she was never still? She looked even thinner now, but less manic about the eyes; still sustained by the ideas in her head, but cheerful, even elated.

Rupert breezed in with a casual greeting and, before I could ask about the pictures or Tyler, took over with a question of his own. He really was the limit, I thought, as I gave the crushed velvet a pat back, but it was hard not to admire the single-mindedness; he was on the make, whereas Eddie was only out to get what he wanted.

The three of us exchanged a few words and then I made to go, only to bump into my favourite colleague – the Mediaevalist, the man who'd had me to his house for lunches and parties – who had been away for the break. He gave me a tweedy hug and then stood back, appraising.

'You're very popular all of a sudden,' he said. 'It's that sodding trip of Loxton's, the jaunt to Cornwall. I shall have to have words! If I weren't such a tolerant man, I might start to feel jealous – we were hoping to keep you to ourselves . . .'

*

The accounts had of course been done by Loxton and revealed a minor surplus, which wasn't worth sharing. He suggested – this prompted another of our exchanges of notes, which were now akin to a running joke between us – that it be spent it on something edible that we could all consume together: buns rather than the standard College biscuits; cake, even. I thought a cake sounded better – it would be more of a treat.

That gave me the idea of a surprise of my own, as an affectionate gesture and a kind of memento. So I set about finding that old haunt of Jenny's from the days when she still enjoyed reading.

Tyler caught me outside the Gatehouse, examining my Clarendon Guide. Three weeks since we'd met in the marketplace and yet, after a couple of minutes' chat, there might have been no gap at all. Resentment disappeared; everything was suddenly fine. It was such a relief.

He teased that looking in guidebooks was what *he* was meant to do. 'I thought you were a native,' he continued, holding my tote bag open for me. 'You're supposed to know where everything is.'

'Ah, but I'm not, am I?' I said, putting the book back. 'And I don't know – you're a year ahead of me here.'

He laughed at that. We seemed to be back to our old ease, though we were standing in full view of everyone.

It crossed my mind that he might like to see the bookshop, but he got in before me. 'Do you remember Lyndsey?' he asked.

'Tell me,' I replied.

'You can't have forgotten! That saga of tramping around mapless, just to see where she ended up and what she found there ...'

I laughed in turn. Lyndsey's notions! She'd kept us all amused. 'And?'

'Hey, it's kind of funny. I mean, it would be great to be like that, but it wouldn't work for me. Or for you, I suppose; you're so different from her.'

That wasn't expected, nor was it what the Dean had said. My stomach clenched, weeks of tension gushing back. 'Meaning?' I asked.

'Only that you like to know where you're going and what you're doing it for,' he said. 'As I do.'

This sounded curiously like a reprimand. A little impertinent, too. I mean, he was still a student, and we were surrounded by people who would wonder what we had to talk about and why we were standing so close.

'Well, that's very observant,' I said tartly, drawing back, spoiling things. 'And how did you work that one out?'

The blondish head shot back; he looked at me straight, no room for deflection. 'In Cornwall. Watching and listening,' he said. 'It's not a criticism, Sarah – I am in awe.'

I felt myself thawing.

'Well, you're much the same,' I said, placatory. 'Always head down.'

'Ah, but I'm doing Finals,' he said. 'You've already made it. You've chosen your path.'

That decided it – sympathy took over. 'And right now,' I said, 'I'm going to leave you be, so no one can say I got in the way of your success!'

There was a smile from him, a softening about the eyes: surprise and maybe gratitude.

How long does purdah last, I wondered, as I went indoors.

Later that week, feeling a good deal happier, I cycled in the warm afternoon sun over Magdalen Bridge, past the spot where Tyler and I had started our walk back to College, and on down the Iffley Road. Just where it should be, there the shop was.

I'd forgotten how extraordinary it looked; going in felt like going on some kind of trip. Behind the psychedelic paintwork of the fascia and the chaotic tumble of the window display was one of those glorious warrens designed to maximise shelf space – except that, instead of the drab units and library-like quiet of a normal second-hand bookshop, every surface seemed to be painted a different colour and there was unrestrained chatting and munching. It was as if someone had bought a job lot of the lurid paints of the *Sergeant Pepper* years and determined to use as many as possible, adding great swirls of contrasting colour for good measure when they were done. Even the little paper stickers on the shelving were garish, with vivid purple felt-tip marking the current classification, and loud labels proclaiming 'Flower Power!', 'Wham!' and 'Zap!'. As for the punters, they licked their Mr Whippy ice creams and drank their bottles of Pepsi as they browsed the shelves, as if they too had just come out of a Pop Art painting. Even in the loo, where the remainder of the paint must have been used up – each wall a different colour – you were pursued by the same imagery: piles of old *Beano*s and *Dandy*s teetered uncomfortably near, while mastheads from *The Eagle* soared up the wall.

The stock was equally quirky and the books were cheap, even by student standards. Jenny had said it was they who kept the place afloat, not just by buying there, but by offloading anything it wasn't worth lugging home. Yet this wasn't a recycling of their academic libraries, at least not of the textbook variety – perhaps those tomes commanded a better price at one of the second-hand shops in the centre of town. Instead, it was a complete mishmash of fiction and non-fiction read for pleasure as well as instruction, mostly in paperback. Even as I browsed, a girl arrived at the door with a bulging box of whodunnits, calling to someone behind her to say that she would only be a minute and then turning to the ageing hippy by the entrance to share a few words. No money was exchanged: it was as if the books were in the nature of a thank you for all the pleasures of previous years. She'd be back with more after Finals, she said, and swiftly disappeared.

I did a quick circuit to familiarise myself with the layout, and then enjoyed myself scanning the shelves. Within minutes I'd picked out half a dozen titles in a spurt of enthusiasm and happy accidents. Eddie's was the best – by a fluke there was the script of that comedy about a college reunion, *Donkey's Years*, whose premiere in London's West End had been the talk of High Table when I arrived. I also found Pevsner's guide to Cornwall for Rupert, and *The Pauper's Cookbook* for Hugh. Then I got stuck on Gloria and momentarily lost my nerve, thinking the whole idea presumptuous and silly; we hadn't been reading for entertainment, after all. But soon I had another four, and only Jim, Tyler and Loxton were left. They took me a little longer, havering between possibilities, wondering if I might cause offence with the wrong choice – *The Ragged-Trousered Philanthropists* for Jim, for example, which might be too close to the bone, or something for Tyler that might be misread. It took me over an hour to find something apposite for everyone.

My collection made for an embarrassingly large pile when I was ready to pay. 'Ziggy' – who even looked like David Bowie – must have guessed I wasn't a student. He took the pound notes, made a joke about poachers turning gamekeepers and opened an old wooden cash drawer with a ping of a little bell – there was nothing as infra dig as a proper till – to dispense change. It occurred to me that he might charge more to academics, on principle, but he volunteered that he operated a flat rate for almost the entire stock; as for the books in the glass case, they were priced individually, but he knew which of those I'd picked.

There was a lot of weaving as I cycled back, the books

lurching in my basket, my thoughts lurching happily with them. This was the bookshop equivalent of the *Whole Earth Catalog* – explosive and uncensored, once again a revelation! As soon as I was back in my rooms I called Jenny – receiver under my chin, one hand holding the scarlet box, the other lifting the flex over my purchases as I paced the floor.

'You know that crazy place we went to years ago, which we talked about with the guy with the balls?' I said, flicking the cord out of the way.

It took her a minute to work out what I was referring to.

'What, the hippy bookshop? God, that was a trip down memory lane – and I bet he still goes! Have you been again? Was the owner there? He was a real character . . .'

We chatted about Ziggy – apparently he'd been 'George' in her day, when he styled himself on George Harrison – and about the comics in the loo, even about the book I'd bought for Loxton.

'Did I tell you Dennis was a widower?' I asked as an aside.

'No, you said he was a bachelor don.'

'That's what I thought. But it turns out he wasn't. He had a wife who taught here, at your very own college, in the fifties.'

'Never!' I could almost hear her thinking it through. 'Hang on – she'd have been a trailblazer. You called him a crusty old boy.'

'I thought that too.'

'And what happened to her? Why "had"? Did she run off with somebody else?'

I did my best to recount what the Dean had told me. For some reason it got to me.

'Oh, don't cry, Sarah,' she said. 'That's not like you.'

'But it's so sad.'

'I can see. Two deaths – doubly tragic. But still.'

'And it's not just that. It's me misjudging him; it was so unkind.'

Her voice softened. 'You weren't to know.'

'But that's just it, I should have done.'

'I'm not sure how.'

'I could have seen the clues – he was such a hypochondriac.' I thought of Dennis and the pillbox by his bed.

'Don't be ridiculous. But your Reading Party may have made it raw.'

'I don't follow.'

'Going mixed. Those dates. Think about it. The daughter would have been the same age as the Finalists, wouldn't she? The girls must have been a constant reminder. No wonder he found it difficult.' Jenny had that knack of getting to the nub of things and not holding back. It was what made it difficult to confide in her.

'Mmmm.'

'Well,' she said, brisk again. 'You'll just have to make up for it. *You'll* feel better, even if *he* doesn't know.'

There was another pause for thought. 'Why not go over,' she suggested. 'There are portraits of women all over the place: on the main stairs, in those endless corridors and in the dining room. There must be one of Rose – there's probably one of Ivy too. I'm sure they'd show you, if you wanted to look them up. You could mention I sent you; see if they remember me.'

I didn't wrap the books. Instead I used the bags from my trips to the market – kept out of deference to Mum, whose squirrelling was easily a match for the Carreck Loose scullery. So when the Reading Party gathered, I was able to walk in with a tower of brown-paper packets under my chin.

The Middle Common Room was the kind of space that feels unloved when it's empty but fine when it's full. Generous and well proportioned, with views into both the front and the back quads, it was let down by cheap modern furniture and an air of transience. Low-slung armchairs and sofas sprawled across the carpet, interspersed with coffee tables. Dark fabric failed to conceal the wear and tear on the upholstery; a scattering of beer mats served perversely to highlight the marks on the veneer. Well-thumbed magazines and newspapers that had lost their shape lay wherever they'd been tossed; dirty plastic beakers littered the surfaces. All in all it had the air of a waiting room; a place you went to between doing other things, not a room that you chose for itself.

Some of this furniture had been shoved aside and the mess cleared to the periphery, to create a clear space in the centre. Loxton sat facing inwards, his back to the light, a few sheets of foolscap neatly set out by his feet. Hugh was cross-legged on the floor opposite him, knees sticking out like open scissors towards the edge of the carpet, jacketless for once; Lyndsey was next to him, chatting more easily again – perhaps Barnaby had been wrong about the dynamic between them. Tyler, who looked different – remote, not like the last time at all – was discussing something with Rupert in one of the two short window seats, their mugs resting on the bottom of the window frame. Mei and Priyam were helping themselves to tea, which had been left on the table against the back wall where the literature was laid out each morning. Eddie was prancing around at their side doing part of a skit from a show he was taking to the Edinburgh Fringe, the biscuits on the plate in his hand sliding dangerously close to the edge, ready to cascade to the floor.

'What have you got there?' Hugh stood up, arms held out, to help me unload.

'Aha! Wait and see.'

I put the bags to one side on a pile of stacking chairs, the open ends facing the wall where nobody could see in, and sat down on the nearest sofa.

Eddie paused mid-gesture to scrutinise, that arched eyebrow of his nearly as expressive as the Dean's. No wonder he always talked about acting. Maybe he would direct later, when he'd calmed down?

'That looks ominous, Sarah,' he said. He shook the biscuits back to the centre of the plate, took a piece of shortbread and passed the rest on, freeing up his hands to pull his chair into position. 'Like very fat exam papers. Are we being tough again? You don't have to hand them out, you know.'

They started reminiscing about their schooldays, arguing the toss: was it worse to have your teacher return marked essays to the class, naming and shaming the lazy or less able pupils, or to be forced to read them out loud to your tutor, even when they were shit? As the other students arrived, they picked up the thread, pitching in with ever-taller stories of embarrassment about academic performance. I was perplexed by the psychology of it; surely they would rather talk about something else with Finals looming – or did they avoid the subject the rest of the time?

Eventually Hugh detached himself and joined me on my side of the rug. It was too serious to risk being jinxed, he said, and asked instead for advice on his application to do a DPhil. He'd got an interview at the University Offices about funding for his research, but was having doubts: he'd wanted to carry on – thought he couldn't stop just at the stage where it all began to acquire meaning – but right now it felt as if the more you studied, the less you knew.

I said everybody felt that from time to time. Didn't his peers say the same?

He agreed they did, but it didn't seem to trouble them, and anyway there was also the business of spending so much time in the same place. Lyndsey was set on staying in Oxford, but hers had been a three-year course; Tyler was now having doubts, and he'd only done two. 'Your views are always refreshing,' he said. Should he take a twelve-month break, since he hadn't had a gap year?

That appeal for insight was troubling: I wasn't sure how to live up to it. And the news about Tyler was distracting. I didn't know what it meant.

Jim was the last to come in, still in that same pair of jeans – or very like. By now we'd formed a loose circle, which shifted to let him in between Barnaby and Martin. When he sat down, unwittingly the centre of attention, Gloria made a remark about living the life of Riley while the rest of them sweated. What did he *do* all day? There was an outburst of laughter, teasing faces turning to Mei.

Loxton started signalling to me – we were one short. Immediately I knew.

'Has anybody seen Chloe?' I asked. Blank faces.

Gloria put down her tea. 'She's split – not coming.'

I was shocked. 'Any explanation?'

But Gloria had nothing to add.

Register completed, Loxton was brisk, launching straight into the accounts. He reiterated the terms of the endowment, reminded us of the £1 a day cap and reeled out a meticulous record of what the kitty had spent. Remarkably, despite the general profligacy – presumably he meant the pub or all those Easter eggs – we had ended the week in credit. He had taken an executive decision to devote that to a celebratory gateau, which we could consume now; the remaining small change would be donated to the scouts' gratuities, given that they had so kindly supplied us with tea. He understood there was a small memento, which would be dispensed by 'my friend here' – that was me – before we all departed, but that was a private gift, not to be confused with expenditure from 'the pot'.

I hadn't noticed the cardboard box from the café, tucked behind Loxton's chair, which he was now showing round. It was a Sachertorte, so dark it was almost black; Tyler had hesitated over it when we had tea. I couldn't help but look to see his reaction. He caught my eye and smiled, then bent his head to speak to Lyndsey. At least we'd acknowledged each other. Had anyone seen?

Priyam cut the cake for Loxton – had she helped him procure it? – and dispensed neat slices that reeked of dark chocolate and the faintest whiff of apricot. Their mutual affection made more sense to me now: perhaps some instinct was at play there, a registering of absent family even if neither of them knew the details. No wonder she'd fussed about his celebratory meal and no wonder he'd patted her hand during the music – they were fond, like father and daughter. Now he was defending her use of napkins, saying that if we were going to look at photos we ought to keep our fingers clean, and she was beaming back at him, relieved. It was touching, almost painful to see.

And look at photos we did. How we kept the piles separate I don't recall – Mei, Tyler and Rupert had them, as well as Loxton and I, and the prints were pretty similar, although Rupert's and Tyler's were colour and one set was oblong not square. The best were those taken by Mei, who had done more snapping than I'd noticed. They were mostly of the people, taken at the kitchen table or when we were mucking about, and, as a record, had an air of completeness that the others' lacked. Tyler's weren't particularly illuminating – they were more about the place – though he did have a shot of Barnaby and me taken from behind on that final walk, against the backdrop of the cliff edge, which was evocative, and of course there was the one with Loxton and me, though that wasn't very good. Each batch prompted further exclamation and storytelling, a reliving of important moments, many of which I'd missed. There was even a photo of Tyler and me, heads bent together, talking over lunch – his finger raised to make a point, my spoon hovering over my soup bowl – which I didn't remember being taken. I tried not to linger over it and lost my place in mid-conversation instead. Was that one from Mei's set?

'So what about those paper bags, Sarah? The suspense is killing me!' Eddie never let up.

I collected the packages and plonked them by my side on the sofa, where they slipped against me, crinkling. I would have passed them round in batches, but Priyam urged me to do everyone in turn so they could all see what the others got.

'Okay. Martin, here's yours!' This was a guide to making real ale. Guffaws from all sides, and an offer to help with the drinking from Barnaby.

'Lyndsey, the Rossetti is for you.' Effusive thanks.

'And this is for Mei.' I looked around, forgetting where she was sitting. It had been hard to choose for the lawyers, especially her.

Eventually I got to Loxton. His was the only book I'd bought from the glass case, a volume of autobiography by Arthur Wainwright, with a picture on the jacket of a lone man standing at the top of a craggy peak. I was nervous that the image might offend, though it seemed apposite.

We watched as he eased it out of the bag and smiled gently at the lettering: *Fellwanderer: the Story Behind the Guidebooks*.

'Do you know, Sarah,' he said, raising the book in his hand for all to see, 'I began reading Wainwright when I was a young don, here at the College, helping Godfrey on one of his Reading Parties in the Lake District. He'd given me responsibility for organising the walks and I knew nothing about where to go. It was the year the first of those guides came out. That would make it . . .' – and he paused, returning the book to his lap and looking at the blurb on the inside cover, his index finger running down the text – '. . . that would make it 1955, when Rose and I had just got married. I have all seven of them, but I've never had a copy of this.'

There was a stunned silence, presumably because Loxton had never revealed anything so private before. Then Priyam started clapping – whether at the unexpected serendipity, the glimpse of Loxton's domestic life, or the two of us for hosting the trip, I didn't know – and others picked it up until everyone had joined in. It was a fine way to end.

Tyler came over afterwards to thank me for *The House of Mirth*. It was a little awkward. We had a brief chat about Edith Wharton, whom he confessed he'd never read, and Lily Bart, whom I described as the saddest of fictional heroines, tragically compromised. He promised he'd take it home with him to the States, which was confusing, – did he mean in the summer or was he indeed not staying on? – but also rather moving: after all, she was an American writer; he could easily get a fresh copy there. Perhaps he'd been touched in his turn by my inscription, which was perfectly proper but fond.

'Hey, good cake,' he said, readying to go. 'And that was right on,' indicating Loxton with that slight turn of his upper body that made the back of my neck tingle. 'You must have been pleased.'

And I was, I really was. I knew he'd appreciate it.

I worried about Chloe. The few students I felt able to ask were non-committal about her state of mind; she was living out, so I couldn't drop by to see her, and there was no reply to my note about her book. I didn't know who her current tutors were or who, if anyone, held the role of her moral tutor – an innovation that hadn't yet taken off. Loxton said not to fuss – students dealt with pressure in different ways and, mostly, they got through in the end – but he agreed we should alert the Dean in case something was seriously amiss. It was his role to follow up, not ours.

When later I came across him, the Dean was in 'on duty' mode, which meant he was patronising and pompous, just as I'd feared they'd all be when I first arrived at the College. He knew Chloe Firth from when she lived in as a Fresher, he reminded me; she was one of the women on whom he'd kept an eye during that first year. Consider it done. And he launched into a little homily about his thinking on pastoral care as the successor to being *in loco parentis* – all as if we'd never discussed it before. There were references to Adam Smith's invisible hand and to exercising the lightest of touches. Poor Chloe, I thought; poor women; and, most of all, stupid me.

It was unsatisfactory, but her well-being was what he'd have called 'his patch'. Besides – and I could see Loxton's argument – with so many students to watch over, you could only do so much. So I tried to stop thinking about Chloe and made only a mild overture to Barnaby, whose continued withdrawal concerned me. The rest of 'my' students – a notion now encompassing those from the Reading Party – I left to get on with it. A few took advantage of my open-door policy – Jim, for instance, which possibly meant more to me than it did to him, as there wasn't much I could say on the matter of his girlfriend, and Martin, who said he was surrounded by tension and needed to escape – but mostly they looked after themselves.

Perhaps I was just experiencing what my younger brother had talked about as a junior medic. It was that old trope that doctors had to learn to take an interest in a case history rather than in the patient as an individual. It wasn't just that they needed a little distance to do a good job; it was also self-protection – they couldn't function if they worried too much. There might even be something more: their progress up the career ladder depended on getting this balance right. Too clipped, and they were deemed to lack a good bedside manner; too concerned, and they were judged vulnerable. They all grappled with this conundrum, he'd said.

I could see why, as it was the same in academia. You were meant to take a professional interest in the students but not to let it get personal. Be close enough to develop trust, but not so close that you risked betraying it.

All of which was fine until you rocked the boat with an event like the Reading Party, which created new bonds and then deepened them all round. Tyler had joked in Cornwall that that was the point of it: it 'refreshed the parts that other beers didn't reach', as the Heineken ad said. Not an analogy for the likes of Loxton – or even, perhaps, for me.

I braved the question of balance with Loxton one evening when we chanced to sit next to each other at High Table. It was Friday and I knew his dissection of the issue would be accompanied by fastidious deboning of the sole on his plate, the debris from my poor reasoning put neatly to the side just like the offending portions of the fish. So I watched, fascinated, as we spoke. He began by removing the fringe at the extremities, so he had a neater shape; then he got down to the main body, lifting one fillet, then the other, so he could get to the spine; a quick look to check all was well, while I finished what I was saying; and then – *voilà!* – he lifted off the skeleton to reveal the two matching fillets in all their delicate purity.

Leaning aside as our waitress removed the plate with the filigree of bones, he asked if I might be confusing things. Firstly, as we had discussed before, the point of the Reading Party was indeed the reading. The social side, after as well as before the arrival of women, was at most an unexpected boon. Take that away, and the event would still have served its function, but take away immersion in relevant texts, and it would have failed. With a gesture to Martin's endless rehashing of *Monty Python* sketches, he even essayed a joke – the Reading Party would have 'ceased to be'; it would be 'an ex-Party' – and gave me a fleeting smile.

I waited as he paused to balance just the right amount of white flesh and spinach on his fork, and watched again as he retrieved his napkin from his lap and gave his thin lips a wipe.

Secondly, regarding those unexpected extras. If I didn't mind him saying so, this was surely another instance when it was important not to confuse roles and responsibilities. For the undergraduates, yes, the week might make or deepen friendships that lasted for years. But for 'you and me', the contact was necessarily fleeting. 'We' were there in the capacity of stewards, watching over the students' progress while they were with us, nurturing and guiding them as best we could, and then, just as we had welcomed them at the start, giving them a kindly send-off at the finish.

Here again there was a pause – not pointed; I'm sure there was no hidden meaning – that extended as he watched the replenishing of our glasses. He took a sip and leant back in his chair, arm still outstretched, the goblet slightly tilted so he could examine the quality, just as he'd shown us.

As we contemplated the wine, I found myself imagining Loxton towards the end of one of his lectures, at the moment just before he reached the fullness of his argument, when all the strands of thought he had unfurled would briefly, simultaneously, be on magnificent display, waiting to be drawn together and resolved into a single strong position. How was it that a man content to appear so austere and grey could conjure such colour out of mere ideas? It was like watching ribbons on a maypole rise into multicoloured brilliance before descending gracefully down again.

And, naturally, Loxton was about to draw it all together. The Reading Party, he reminded me, was only seven days – merely 'a pinprick in the timeline of their lives' – and it was important not to get it out of proportion. As tutors we hoped it would be important – just as we hoped our students' time at the College would later prove to be significant – but whether it was or not was largely outside our hands. We could only create the conditions in which the students might flourish; the rest was down to them and to luck.

He hesitated, picking at the capers left abandoned on his plate. On reflection, he said, he didn't like the word 'luck'. He preferred to call it serendipity, the unfathomable confluence of timing and ingredients that allowed something truly special to emerge. Hard to define, especially for a philosopher – there was a little smile here – but one sensed it viscerally when it was there. However, *our* feelings on the subject were not the point. What mattered was how the *students* reacted. And then he delivered his punchline: we might never know whether Cornwall, or indeed the years of tutoring, had had any real impact on a given individual – they might not know themselves, for a decade or more. That was life. It was another of the uncertainties one had to live with.

For a minute we sat together comfortably, saying nothing, looking over the long lines of the students beneath us, the twinkling lights on the tables, the pattern of the staff working their way up and down to remove the plates. It reminded me of that companionable moment when Barnaby and I sat on the clifftop, watching the waves, listening to the birds. There'd been a moment like that with Tyler too, lounging on the grass outside Carreck Loose one afternoon, absorbing it all, happy just to be.

As the gap in the conversation lengthened I realised Loxton was waiting.

'In that case, perhaps there are pinpricks and pinpricks?' I asked, unsure yet what I was referring to and whether the thought was merely a tease. 'Most are so small they are barely noticed; a few are large enough to make a difference to the picture overall?'

He looked at me with an air of pleased surprise, as if I were a pupil who'd managed to say something novel. It was a glance that would have infuriated me six months earlier, but now it struck me differently.

I decided to continue – 'in for a penny, in for a pound', as my uncle would have said. 'Thinking of my personal time-line – because of course we all have them – the Reading Party may prove to have been a pinprick of the larger variety.' And I qualified quickly, embarrassed to be revealing so much. 'Obviously – if we're going to pursue the analogy – I can only see the timeline up to the present day, and of course I don't know how long it will eventually be, but I suspect that in retrospect . . .'

He was waiting for the rest of the sentence, but I was faltering, in danger of trailing off.

I slid my glass back to its place in the trio in front of me and breathed in. 'The thing is, I can't help but think of it in terms of my own discipline. The business of identifying, even occasionally creating, the narrative thread that gives events their coherence is what makes History so fascinating. It's what I enjoyed most about writing my book – and again with the paper you were so nice about.'

In front of me the sea of students stretched out beneath the hall's lofty hammer-beam roof. The lights appeared stronger now that it was dark outside. Perhaps I was on the right track after all? I shifted in my seat and began again.

'As historians – that's not meant to be presumptuous; I know I've only just started – we're constantly trying to construct timelines, in my case for individuals, groups of people, most of whom have no idea they are part of a movement at all, even in retrospect. We have to develop a kind of sixth sense about our source material, a nose for what is and isn't likely to be important. Lawyers too, I presume, wading through all that detail, working out how to argue their case.'

Loxton was rotating his glass very slowly, examining once more, so I carried on. 'Every piece is helpful in assembling that vast linear jigsaw – or perhaps it's more of a tapestry, with lots of loose threads – but, very rarely, a missing piece turns out to transform the picture: it's a fact of such significance that it challenges our view of things. We couldn't function if we paid equal attention to every detail we come across, so I guess we learn to disregard the vast majority, because they're probably not material, but we don't forget them completely, in case they're needed later. Instead we focus on the tiny minority that catch the eye because there's something surprising about them, something that might prompt a rethink. And very occasionally we make real discoveries and have the wonderful thrill I had during my DPhil – establishing the links between all those ordinary women who'd fought for their rights and ours, knowing that future historians would see things differently because of what I'd unearthed.'

Loxton gently indicated the cheese platter, which was still stuck in front of me. I passed it on untouched.

'Nearly done!' I said, feeling self-conscious again. 'I suppose what I'm trying to say is that for me it *was* an important week, Dennis. I might even call it "seminal". So hard to explain, but a little like the glorious moments I had in those interminable archives, or recording all those interviews, when it dawned on me that I'd struck gold even though I couldn't yet prove it. Something about working out why it all matters so much; why I am here at Oxford, in this College, doing what I'm doing. Anyway, enough said – I'll embarrass both of us! Besides . . .' – and I gestured towards the Warden's wife, who was pushing back her chair – '. . . isn't that the cue to move upstairs?'

As we rose, I realised nothing had been said about the journal or Mrs Loxton or medical tragedies. All three had been uppermost in my mind when we sat down and, in their different ways, were important missing pieces. Perhaps Hall was too public a place. In any event, the moment was lost; by the time we'd reached the SCR someone else had nobbled me.

After that conversation I fretted a little less about the students, though I always noted whether Tyler's light was on when I turned in. I mentioned it playfully when by chance we met again and I wished him luck for his exams – it was in the garden, other people soon too near for comfort – and was taken aback when he said he thought mine had been on longer of late too. That wasn't true, but I liked the idea that he'd been looking. It made up for the shortness of the encounter.

I was always pleased to see the students from the Reading Party, though it didn't happen often. I was even busier teaching and, as my circle grew, went out more often in the evenings; besides, the Finalists weren't much in evidence. Lyndsey went completely to ground – I don't recall seeing her once after the reunion – though Hugh claimed she was okay and had made time to submit her poem for the Newdigate Prize. Priyam, who walked with me to the Lodge early one morning, was warm but so clearly preoccupied that I didn't try to detain her: she would have her revision mapped out; not my business to disrupt the steady progress. Still, there was time for her to spot that my eczema had flared again and to ask a concerned question; that was touching – roles again momentarily reversed.

Martin was an exception to the rule, being as visible as ever. You might find him chatting in a group of people outside the pub next to the College, where you could sit in the open, greeting whoever chanced to walk by, or lying on the grass in the gardens in the warmth of the sunnier days, his notes casually spread around. The first time I spotted him, I wondered if it was for show – but it happened too often and besides, that was the sort of calculation Rupert made, not him. I hadn't seen Rupert, who would have set himself the task of doing well; Martin probably didn't care.

As term went on – Finals started in Sixth Week, History on 1 June – you began to see more students in their *subfusc* as they walked or bicycled off to the Examination Schools or wherever they were taking their papers. The stark black and white of academic dress was in curious contrast with the other years in their summer prints and colours. Occasionally a mixed group would gather on one of the lawns, mortarboards strewn amongst the usual paraphernalia. The Finalists would stretch their black legs out across the grass, most of them still wearing their gowns, others having tossed them to the side. The rest of the students, in their gaudy t-shirts, flares and floaty dresses, revelled in the exposing of flesh to the sun.

Unsurprisingly Chloe was amongst those who treated their gown not as a badge of honour but as a symbol of all they disliked about the place. When eventually I caught up with her, returning from one of her exams, she already had it stuffed under her arm. It dropped out as she leant her bike against the wall, the crumple of drapes suggesting it had been used to mop up spilt tea – or perhaps it was beer: stains blotched the cheap black cotton and little bits of muck were caught in the pleating. Even her mortarboard – propped in her basket, its tassel hanging over the handlebars – seemed to have served an unofficial purpose: dust and ash despoiled the black interior with its proud label; the silk folds were losing their neat stitching where a cigarette had burnt through.

In the short gap since I'd last seen her she'd moved from Peruvian knits to punk rock. Her now jagged hair was complemented by a thick lock died a vivid blue. The white shirt, which gaped lopsidedly at her neck, was fastened by a single large safety-pin, tufts of thread still visible above and below, where the buttons had been pulled off. The smudge of biro across her collarbone might not be intentional, but the ripped fishnets were a blatant nod to Vivienne Westwood and Malcolm McLaren. Even the Dr Martens waiting in her basket looked suddenly all of a piece.

We spoke briefly while a couple of other students, also in impressive gear, hovered alongside with their copies of *Socialist Worker*, pedals at the ready; Eddie, with no such street cred, looked suddenly ordinary – and at a loss, being outclassed. Chloe ignored them, which I rather admired. The three hours that afternoon had been 'crap', she said, but she really didn't care, she just wanted to get through 'the whole bloody thing' and out of 'this fucking place'. She 'wouldn't say sorry' about missing the reunion: she hadn't been in the mood for a gathering of 'that extended dinner party', with 'Tyler and co.' exchanging *bon mots*. Cool choice of book, though (which at least was gratifying): they'd all read Pirsig in their first year – it was their route into philosophy, a Chautauqua of its own; *Zen and the Art of Motorcycle Maintenance* would be worth reading again. And she too liked to hang out at Ziggy's (as I'd known she would): she might do something like that one day – use grassroots power to fight the consumer society. Action was where it was at; commentary didn't change a thing.

She even mentioned my lectures. She'd have been a suffragette too, she said. She'd have chained herself to railings or set fire to pillarboxes; she was fed up with words. I should watch out – writing wasn't enough.

Needless to say she sang along with the Sex Pistols at the Silver Jubilee celebrations in the pub, refusing to drape herself in red, white and blue even as a joke, and sensibly she boycotted the Commem Ball – a showy affair with even more hideous music, altogether out of keeping with the tenor of the College – before she disappeared off the scene. I was nervous of finding Tyler there with someone else on his arm and attended it reluctantly, with the Mediaevalist as my partner in order to avoid the company of the Dean – who behaved like a complete jerk, dancing half-cut with anyone he could get his hands on. My colleague and I enjoyed a good giggle at his expense.

There was no sign of Tyler – I kept an eye out, uncertain which would be better: suddenly to come across him or endlessly to wonder where he was – but Rupert and Gloria were there, looking like Hollywood stars, magnificent in black tie and evening dress. They'd taken a bottle of champagne to the gardens to escape 'Shang-a-Lang' and the other Bay City Rollers hits, and were parked beneath the huge copper beech that spread its black purpliness over the lawn – Rupert leaning his back against the trunk, the textured panel of a dress shirt exposed above a ruby cummerbund, legs elongated, hand toying with a half-empty glass; Gloria lying sideways on a fluffy wrap, her body a voluptuous mound of shimmering satin, her sandals tossed off at a distance; abandoned napkins and glasses all around. She was helping herself from his plate, spearing mouthfuls of fruit tart with a fork and then pulling her hand away so the bait was just out of reach. It had the air of a game they were used to playing – might play repeatedly – until one or other of them got bored. Even as we watched, Rupert's attention was caught by somebody else, leaving Gloria, arm raised aloft, to eat the morsel herself. I would not have wanted that to happen to me.

Amongst the undergraduates I minded most about Barnaby, but I didn't get a chance to talk to him properly until the historian's Schools Dinner later that month, when it was all over. Even then it was difficult to get a private moment, my colleagues being endlessly attentive and the rest of the year too drunk to be tactful, but eventually we were left alone in a corner. He was clearly exhausted – barely able to find the words to speak coherently – and his relief at finishing was much more potent than that of his peers. He said he'd avoided the panic attacks but was still having nightmares about going into the wrong room – one empty save for line upon line of diminutive school desks, complete with ink-holders and bevelled slots for pens – and being stuck there with an exam paper printed in indecipherable hieroglyphs. I said we'd all had those nightmares; I still had them occasionally myself. Mostly we talked about Keegan's *The Face of Battle* – the book I'd given him – which he'd just begun reading 'for fun': he was fascinated by the archers' stakes at Agincourt, how so simple a measure could have been so decisive. We enthused about the historian's craft – if you could reinvent military history through details like that, what might you do in other branches? – and I agreed it was an inspiration. 'Like the tutorials with you,' he said.

He asked if Jim had said anything and, wanting to preserve confidences, I explained that I wasn't teaching him that term, so I'd barely seen him. It turned out Jim was having an even rougher time, having told Mei they couldn't carry on. Apparently it had been awkward when he went home after Cornwall, because his girlfriend sensed something had changed. Then there'd been a row on the phone and Jim had been summoned back to Wales to explain himself in person. After that he'd concluded the Welsh girl had the rightful claim – they'd been going out for years – but Barnaby didn't think his heart was in it. Jim kept asking after Mei, who was studying even harder when she wasn't planning her first trip back to Hong Kong. Everyone hoped they would work it out, as they were good together.

How lucky neither of them was doing Finals, I thought: it made their lives simpler. But all I said was that I agreed.

As for his own plans? Still uncertain. He'd enough saved up from a summer in a carpentry workshop to buy himself a bit of time. His parents were now on a base in Germany, so he would start his travels there; Mart would join him in Italy and then they were going to bum around the Mediterranean, crewing yachts where they could. He would take his sketch-book. If Mart made fun again, he'd get his own back: have him kill a few Greek chickens with his bare hands, to prove he could, or some such. Then, who knows, he might go back to the woodworking for a while, or, if they were still on speaking terms, follow Mart to Cornwall. There was a boat builder on the Helford and plenty of places to kip.

After the last of the Finalists' breakfast parties – I was invited to two or three, which was nice – there was a definite lull. Priyam came to take her leave when Full Term ended in the middle of June, bringing a present of Indian sweetmeats, but the others just disappeared, Tyler amongst them, without saying anything. No apology from him, no explanation, not even an excuse. Suddenly I realised they were truly gone, which put me in my place again, just as Loxton had warned.

Summer

Then, out of nowhere, there was a letter from Paris in my pigeonhole.

I took it back to my rooms so I could open it in private, and had to sit on the bed for several minutes before I could will myself to read it. But instead of the paper 'goodbye' that I was expecting, some wriggling out of an implicit promise, it was a friendly note apologising for the gap. He would be back by the time I received this, Tyler said, and it would be neat to say 'hi', if that was okay, now that purdah was over. He had a week before he got his flight home.

It took me the rest of the day to work out how to reply. Wariness, I suppose, not wanting to be disappointed again.

We met the following afternoon, just a few minutes from College in the University Parks, where we might reasonably have run into each other by accident should the likes of Gloria appear on the scene. I felt terribly self-conscious in light summer clothes, strands of pumpkin hair blowing everywhere; he didn't look awkward, just undeniably handsome in one of those sky-blue shirts he wore.

We tried pleasantries. I observed that he was brown – he must have had good weather in France. Tyler said he'd got it watching Wimbledon; I too must have been pleased about Virginia Wade.

This allowed us the odd glance as we walked, but the

conversation remained prosaic, like novice players attempting ping-pong – or tennis: *pop pop, pop pop*; occasionally *pop pop pop*.

We drifted towards the subject of work, still mostly staring at the ground, me in my sandals, bare toes peeping out, and him in his sneakers, which made his gait roll. I asked about the PPE papers and he seemed confident enough. He mentioned my article and I said it was off for peer review.

The sentences refused to turn into proper paragraphs. As for any chemistry, it lay submerged; you could sense it, but it stubbornly refused to surface.

Perversely, it was only when he confirmed that he was indeed leaving – off to Harvard Law School after all – that we both began to relax. It must have been knowing that he would never be a student here again; it put things on a different footing, the moral dilemma almost resolved. But then again it meant he'd be gone.

'Goodness, that's a big decision,' I said, working it through.

'Yeah, but the right one, don't you think?'

'Of course – you'll be a brilliant lawyer.' What else could I say?

He talked about the process. I suggested it would have been a formality, Oxford on a Rhodes Scholarship a huge advantage in taking up a provisional place. That made him smile in the way I remembered.

Then he said that actually the scholarship had been quite a burden. Surely the pressure to achieve was mostly self-imposed, I asked, and was rewarded with a Yankee chuckle. He meant the pressure to lead, to set an example, he said: sometimes it got in the way of having fun. So I joked that you didn't have to be a Rhodes Scholar to suffer from that. Look at me on the Reading Party, I laughed; it was a struggle to get the balance right. You did okay, he said, and grinned.

After that we chatted easily, bumping into each other more

than was necessary but not enough to be really noticeable, a bit like the walk up the hill from the pub. We talked about Loxton and the layers of his reserve; how much that might have to do with the war years; how much with being doubly bereaved; and how difficult it must have been for him to be surrounded, suddenly, by young women just the age that his daughter would have been, had she lived.

It turned out that Tyler too had only heard by chance about Rose, and what had happened, and had been just as taken aback as me. His parents had come over for his first Christmas and they'd all made small talk in Loxton's rooms. He gave a wry smile as he spoke about the occasion, calling it very English, very 'proper', as if he knew I would under-stand – which of course I did. I could picture the four of them in that same space, drinking from that same tea ser-vice as me, even eating the same kind of cake. Apparently it was a comment his mother had made, quite innocently, about all those silver-framed photographs. Loxton, put on the spot, had suddenly owned to the loss of Rose and then – odder still, given how private he was – to the unexpected complications.

It had been shocking to all of them, Tyler concluded. To die in childbirth, and the baby lost too; it was too much – something you didn't expect to hear said. No one had known how to respond.

This slowed us almost to a halt and a passer-by stopped to stare at us. We must look curiously intimate, I thought, compar-ing our initial horror and our continuing sadness about it. That wouldn't do, with so many people around; the Mediaevalist sometimes walked here and you never knew where the Dean might be. Besides, it would be a shame to get sidetracked, even by Loxton and his tragedies. We had to move on.

On impulse, I invented, just as Gloria would have done. It was another eureka moment.

'I'm going up to York,' I said, wondering whether a visit could in fact be fitted in.

'That's good,' he replied, still looking away.

We were back to the *pop pop, pop pop.*

'It's a beautiful city, much older than Oxford.'

'Yeah,' he said, gazing at something. 'So I've heard.'

I couldn't see his face. Maybe I'd misread him; he wasn't interested after all. Or was he misreading me?

I stared at my toenails, newly painted a plum colour. Usually I didn't bother. Even that morning I must have felt a kind of brazenness.

'If you're interested, I could offer a guided tour.'

There was a pause. The head turned to look at me: first the blue-grey eye, then the brown. The difference was still disconcerting.

'How long would it take?' he asked.

'What, the tour?'

'No, to get there.'

My confidence drained. York was much too far; I should have suggested somewhere nearer. 'It's not really a day trip,' I said. 'I did it once in reverse, for an interview here, when I was really short of time, but I wouldn't recommend it.'

But perhaps that was the answer he wanted. 'Not short,' he said, definitively. 'Let's make it three days.'

So we knew what was going to happen.

'We'll have to be careful,' I said, half expecting a 'Phooey!' in return.

'Sure,' he replied. 'Weren't we careful before? All those beds we didn't get into. And the one we did! We deserve top marks for being so restrained.'

And I had to admit that was fair.

Later that week Tyler and I had two nights together in one of York's quaint B & Bs, just outside the city walls. We didn't see much of the sights the first day – wouldn't have noticed them if we had – but we went to evensong in the cathedral, which for a pair of atheists was almost romantic, and we walked along the river at dusk, as lovers do. Just to be together was captivating, every moment a revelation. We didn't need anything else.

Back in our private space, I stood before him and at last he took my face in his hands. Our tongues roamed. We were like the birds we'd seen gliding over the water, following the familiar eddies, circling around the bends, occasionally delving; we could have swooped indefinitely.

Afterwards he spread his fingers through my hair. 'This is what sustained me,' he said, lifting up and sliding through, leaving my scalp tingling. 'I think I dreamt in apricot hues.'

No one had mentioned apricots before, the glorious blush of the ripening fruit.

'Do you remember those flowers?' he asked, stroking the freckles on my cheeks with the side of his thumbs, smoothing towards the ears. 'The ones in the market?'

I thought of the diminutive daffs, jaunty in his pannier, and nodded, uncertain.

'Their centres were almost the colour of your hair. I bought them every week until they didn't have them any more.'

And I had thought they were for someone else!

I smiled into his shirt, smelt the almond smell, slid my hands beneath.

There was a gusting as we lifted our arms, slipped our things off; then a realigning of currents, a moment of stasis as our skin touched and our bodies locked. His lips skimmed lower; the tiny kisses, the little puffs of warmth, descending oh-so-slowly as he bent to kneel, his breath hovering over the contours of my breasts, the inclines of my waist, until it reached the soft plane above my knickers.

'May I take these off?' he called up, gently. 'Are you the same colour down here?'

311

It was wondrous; beyond description.

The next morning we contrived to take a bath together, stifling our giggles in case the landlady was near. Afterwards he lay on the bed watching as I towelled my hair dry. He gave a running commentary on the changing colours, teased that if he'd been a poet he would have composed an ode to my apricot locks. When we set off down the road, he kept riffling through and I teased back, running in front and shaking my head until I had a lion's mane good enough to photograph. The jokes became a symbol of our ease together.

There were a few moments of tension, particularly when I showed him round the university, which we should probably have given a miss – we were demob happy and the campus brought it all back. Keeping our hands off each other was an unnecessary strain – I should never have suggested it, and I fretted about how to respond if we met anyone from the history faculty, which he said was ridiculous. In my effort to explain, I took him to that bench by the lake and the geese and talked about sitting in Oxford's water meadows, thinking of that very spot, debating the concept of 'allowed'. He said it helped to hear it all and acknowledged that for him the stakes had never been the same.

I had my own moment of taking offence, when we were on our way to an early afternoon tea in Betty's. It was only a little thing – an aside of his about the planning for law school – but it was a reminder that he would not be coming back. I wanted to say that he could change his mind, that the College would still have him, but instead I said he didn't have to sound so happy about going home. He held me tight, whispered that he hadn't meant to upset me and then, over the scones, talked me through his reasons for deciding against the DPhil. I didn't agree, but I pulled myself together.

Besides, there'd been no pretence that this could come to anything, no discussion of an 'after': it was just a wonderful folly, with no strings attached. There was no point spoiling it.

And indeed, after that episode, we agreed to ignore the issues that didn't have to be resolved there and then, and focus instead on the present – which we did, wandering through the old bits of the city, going back for a late siesta.

In the evening, we went out for a wonderful meal – I don't know how he'd found the French restaurant, but it was much smarter than any I'd ever been to – and we told stories about Cornwall and what people had said and done, and laughed so much we had to switch to other things, like the saga of our own collisions, though that too became equally comic. Later, we sipped our pudding wine, just as we had at Carreck Loose, only this time we could reach for each other's hands between the candles and we could hold each other's gaze. Not pinpricks – a whole evening of pleasure.

We were very tender that night and in the early hours.

The following day we rose even later. It was past lunch when finally we abandoned those crumpled sheets, the only pull the dread time of his departure.

I walked him to the station – both of us silent much of the way. Neither of us faltered as we said the goodbye we'd agreed upon, because the real one – the leave-taking that mattered – had been shared the night before. So we behaved as if it was nothing – shook hands, patted arms, as you might with a colleague or an acquaintance, and wished each other a safe journey home. No one could have guessed the hours we'd spent exploring each other's skin, our limbs entwined; we were entirely convincing.

Of course that made it all the more poignant. When Tyler loped off down the platform, I felt utterly bereft. The image of that departing back, the particular way in which his long legs seemed to operate from a hidden hinge, the pivot as he turned to wave, haunted me through the following days, in

York and when I returned to Oxford. I tried to focus on the other images, like his eyes smiling on the halo of my hair, but the desperate one dogged me. Memories like that take a long time to fade.

I ran into Loxton with the Warden towards the end of July, just after the last of the class lists were issued – they were standing outside the Lodgings as I came out of one of the staircases.

'Ah, Dr Addleshaw!' the Warden called out, his voice booming in the empty quadrangle. 'Dr Loxton and I need your informed opinion.'

So I went over to join them.

The picture overall was solid rather than exceptional: the women had done less well than expected, which made a difference, given that they made up a quarter of that year. Not a surprise in the science lists, where they were only a sprinkling anyway; disappointing in the humanities, where they were much better represented. The Warden had been listening to views. Perhaps there had been more pressure on the women than 'we' had realised, he speculated; maybe it was that old chestnut 'caution', the way they had been taught for so many years; and remember that there were always more 'gongs' in the sciences. But 'we' wouldn't worry about the Norrington Table: that had never been our motivation, given our academic record. If there was more the College should do, it would be for the women themselves, and the Tutorial Board could raise that with Governing Body. Meanwhile, he'd be interested to hear my views on the matter, if I would kindly give it some thought. Quite why he didn't want them there and then wasn't clear, but I suppose it was progress to be asked at all.

And how did the Reading Party do, the Warden wanted to know. Lyndsey Milburn was 'one of yours', was she not?

That was important: good, good. What about the men? 'Our favourite linguist', Rupert Ingram-Hall – wasn't he on the trip? His First too was no surprise. The Rhodes Scholar, of course. Always gratifying when 'one of ours' secured the highest marks for his subject; such a shame that Tyler Winston had dropped the idea of a DPhil – his sort didn't come round that often. Hugh Chauncey: a Double First thoroughly deserved; glad that he was staying on. As for the rest? Disappointing about Gloria Durrant. There were always a few who hovered on the cusp, and of course she'd been indigent – she had several regrettable propensities: they would have sniffed out any glibness in the *viva*. But the rebel, Chloe ... Chloe F–, Chloe Firth, that's it ... had not done ignobly and Barnaby Quick had pulled through for the historians – well done on 'our' pastoral care, 'our' faith repaid. Had he forgotten anybody important? If not, five Firsts out of nine Finalists wasn't bad. Congratulations, Dennis, and thank you, Sarah, for playing a crucial role: Godfrey would have been content – rather in awe perhaps (and here there was a little smile at me), but content.

Perhaps I would pass my probation after all.

Peroration over, the Warden disappeared inside. A few seconds later the reading lamp in his study went on, the green glass just visible through the window, translucent.

Loxton turned to me. 'Would you have a few minutes?' He looked at his watch and, barely waiting for an answer, set off around the quadrangle with only the faintest of glances to check I was with him.

I was reminded of the crispness with which he'd marshalled us by the front door at Carreck Loose, like a Scout leader with a bevy of young recruits.

We turned the corner by the Chapel, stepping aside to let a group of tourists pass in the narrow passageway, and walked across the lawn in the Fellows' Garden – no dawdling here and only the sparest of chat about the blues and purples of the flowers rising above the middle of the main border. Then there was a pause to negotiate the door to the Fellows' Private Garden, after which, thankfully, he slowed down. He seemed to be aiming for the bench.

I decided to broach the subject of the diary, before he got to whatever he wanted to talk about.

'I still haven't returned Godfrey's journal,' I began.

'Oh, don't worry, I dare say you have it in an archival box somewhere.'

'I do actually – how did you guess?'

'Ah. One observes.'

I couldn't imagine what he'd seen that might give rise to such an observation, but no matter. It sounded well meant.

'Anyway, I thought it rather wonderful – even if he was a dreadful misogynist.'

'Yes, I suppose he was, though we didn't notice that at the time.'

'And . . .' – was this wise? – '. . . did Mrs Loxton mind that he took such a dim view of married Fellows? Did you, for that matter?'

Loxton paused and for a moment I thought I'd blown it, but perhaps he was just considering his answer. I stood in the midst of all that calm, listening to the breeze in the trees and the muffled sound of traffic far away, watching him stare at the expanse of lawn as if fixed on a distant blade of grass.

'It was a nuisance, let us say. It made life a little trying. More for her than for me. People like Godfrey had such firm expectations. He was very old-fashioned: never acknowledged that she too had a doctorate and her own career.'

'She must have been quite a character?'

'So they said. She was also very lovely.'

Loxton was staring again, his hand caressing an iridescent blue frond – the raceme, he'd called it – that bobbed above an island bed. I thought of the picture I'd seen hanging in

316

the dining hall of Jenny's college, when I followed up her suggestion of a visit: the mixture of dignity and amusement in the expression, the sensitive but not exactly sensuous mouth. Would he have been allowed to tuck back the wisp of hair that fell from that French pleat? Presumably he must have.

'Shall we pause?' he asked, and I thought he might change the subject. On the other hand, we didn't need to sit down. The invitation was encouragement enough, though I decided not to mention the portrait – it might sound intrusive.

'I would have liked to meet her.'

'Yes, I have thought about that. The two of you would have got on.'

'We would? Do you think so?'

'Yes. She too was fierce, in her way. She was staunch about education for women, and co-education here; thought a lot of people like Ivy, who'd helped make it possible. You have to remember, no one dreamed of co-*residence* in our day: the fight then was over the limit on numbers – increased after the war to cope with the likes of Rose, returning from the services, but a limit nonetheless. She thought having a quota for women was wrong.'

He fingered the arm of the bench, rubbing a little burr, and then started again. 'I was proud of her. She went on battling when she joined the teaching staff – for self-governing status, for example. The women's colleges always had to prove themselves. It was invidious. I suppose that's why I could always see co-residence from their perspective: they'd been pioneers in their time and it threatened what they'd fought for. Someone had to speak up for them.'

This explanation of his reservations was new to me.

'I think I gave you a bit of a hard time about it,' I said. 'That discussion we had in the garden, or perhaps the one in the SCR, when we first met.'

317

'Really? I didn't notice. But there would have been nothing wrong with that.'

'Still, I may have been a little headstrong.'

Loxton looked at me, as if it mattered that I understood. 'There's nothing wrong with being headstrong, Sarah. Rose was headstrong and I admired her for it, even when she turned me down. She wasn't interested in marriage as an institution; that's why it took us so long. But in the end the pressure from others was too great.'

'So she was in a double bind – criticised for staying single and then criticised for drawing you away from the College?'

'Something like that.'

'And her own colleagues?'

'They were rather more accommodating.'

I didn't know what to say, but Loxton hadn't finished. 'Of course, it might not have worked long term. It was unusual then, two academics, but she never considered giving up her career and nor would I have wanted her to. Even if . . .' He trailed off, staring again at the grass. 'That is one of the odd things – one just doesn't know.'

'But it would have been good to have the opportunity to try?'

'Exactly.'

After that, it seemed superfluous to say anything else.

'Shall we carry on?' he asked, rising to his feet and putting out an arm so that I didn't slip as I, too, stood up.

We made our way to the raised path marking the boundary with the adjacent college. There were still a few elms in amongst the stumps of the diseased trees that had been taken out.

'Have you seen this?' He bent to show me a clump of delicate froth – bright green leaves and multiple tiny sky-blue trumpets – which had emerged from the mulched soil between the gravel and the shrubs beyond. '*Corydalis flexuosa*,

"China Blue". It was meant to stop flowering weeks ago – everything is late this year. The Head Gardener is very proud of it: came from the Botanical Gardens – rather rare. We're hoping that it will spread.'

I dropped to my haunches, trying to remember what I'd been told about the work of the Gardens Committee. I had an idea that Loxton sat on it too, although the cellar took precedence.

He carried on picking twigs off the surface of the mound, tossing them into the hedge behind us.

'It, too, is very lovely, don't you think?'

I mumbled assent and explained that I didn't know much about gardening.

'Oh you will, you will. Amongst life's great pleasures. Another kind of stewardship and serendipity – one does one's best, but one is never quite in control. Some things die, unfairly, like the elms; others take and flourish unexpectedly. You must come and see mine, before the summer is over.'

This too was astonishing. Not that Loxton kept a garden – that, now, made perfect sense. But that he wanted to show it to me – how bizarre!

We carried on down the path, chatting vaguely about the plants – or rather, me asking and Loxton explaining. Surely this wasn't why we were here, so I could admire the flowers and Loxton could tell me what was what. In the past I'd have suspected him of trumping me with superior knowledge, but we seemed to have moved beyond that.

As we completed the circuit he paused near a patch of pink-rimmed foliage. I waited to be told what it was. He was bending down again, his face invisible, somewhere else.

'So you enjoyed Cornwall, then?' It was more statement than question.

'Of course! How could I not?'

He was still looking.

Again the gap felt uncomfortable, so I filled it. 'I hope that came across over dinner, when we talked about timelines.'

Loxton straightened up, brushing earth from the side of his jacket where it had caught the ground. 'Ah yes.' And he quoted verbatim my line about 'pinpricks and pinpricks'. 'A good way of putting it,' he added.

'Thank you. It was an interesting conversation.'

'I look forward to many more.'

He gave me that little look of his, head tilted, like a bird.

'Be careful, Sarah. Once you start contributing to the traditions – sardines, the gift of the books – you too become part of the fabric!'

I laughed: 'Now that's not fair, Dennis. You can't make me responsible for the games we played that evening. Books, yes; sardines, no. That little romp has been enough of a liability already.'

'Indeed. I'm afraid it is already part of College lore; you will never be free of it.'

He gave up on his last twig and changed direction, leading us back towards the gate.

'I've been thinking about next spring, possible candidates. Would welcome your opinion.'

'Of course. Happy to comment.'

'And, if you don't mind, I was wondering . . .' He left the end of the sentence hanging, as if I should know what he was getting at. I didn't.

'If you mean the plan for the Dean to join you again,' I essayed, thinking how piqued he'd been, 'I don't mind at all' – and then registered Loxton's look of bafflement. Perhaps I wasn't meant to know.

But Loxton was still staring. 'The Dean? Well, it might be his plan but it is certainly not mine. I can't abide people who say "for my sins", let alone as often as he does – his sins must be very severe.'

He finished shredding his leaf and watched as the pieces fell. 'Whatever gave you that idea?'

I was still smiling at the thought of all the Dean's sins. Best not to try to explain.

The whole thing was too comic and too touching – like receiving a proposal of marriage when you'd assumed your suitor was enamoured of someone else. Pleasure suffused me, like a blush. Had Loxton's courtship of Rose been anything like this?

I started again. 'Are you asking, Dennis, if I would . . .' And I too left the sentence unfinished.

He creased around the eyes – perhaps a twinkle of recognition, complicity.

'Good. That's settled then,' he said and there was a quick pat on my back, as if I had passed the test – and passed well. I might even have got a First.

'I must let you get on,' he said. 'Don't forget to put it in the diary – Carreck Loose, the week after Hilary, starting on the Saturday, nine o'clock sharp.'

And he set off down the path back to the gate, leaving me to contemplate the glory of the delphiniums. They were, after all, magnificent: it was a good year.

Epilogue

Lyndsey Milburn seemed uncomfortable being the only woman with a gong in that intake, though she was certainly proud to win the poetry prize. *Isis* tried to interview her along with a few of her counterparts, but she refused. She's never been vocal about the representation of women within the University, seeing it as a distraction from her work, which is the only thing that interests her – as she says she realised on that trip, over Hugh. She's stayed in Oxford, becoming a College luminary and then one of the early female Fellows of All Souls. Over the years I've heard several men admit to thoughts of seducing her – the ghastly Dean, with whom I had that short and stupid fling, had the nerve to own to such fantasies – but their admiration must have passed her by: she's remained single. People speculate that she prefers women, but I think she just isn't interested. Anyway, who cares? Her friends – and there are some very loyal supporters of both sexes – say she's become even more reclusive since she had that health scare; meanwhile her renown in academic circles has stayed high. There are several of her books on my shelves. One of them is dedicated jointly to Loxton, me and Carreck Loose.

Hugh Chauncey continued to pursue her, doggedly hoping to win her over, and then gave up. He had a long, emotionally arid period in his late twenties and early thirties while he made his name as a classicist, moving eventually to Durham, where he has been much happier. It was there that he met the woman who became his wife, a Japanese student – not one of his – who is an accomplished violinist. This was a delightful story of 'love at first hearing', as he called it. They met at a recital for which he arrived late, so he had to sit at the rear, where he was quickly transfixed by her playing; it was only afterwards, backstage, that they were introduced and he saw her face – as he described it, a full moon of golden skin against the blackest of black hair. She is much younger than him so it was a while before he felt it fair to propose and longer still before they could marry. They have three children now; the youngest must be nearly ten. Hugh's a professor, but managed to fend off 'head of department', which he wouldn't have liked. He says he never expected to be so blessed.

Priyam Patel hasn't been so lucky, though she would never admit it. She spent that summer visiting relatives in India, reporting with some amusement that she was paraded as 'my great-niece Priyam, who has just graduated from Oxford' by the people she occasionally saw at family gatherings, and then went straight on to do articles at a City law firm in London. In time – she said it didn't help being a woman too – she became their first partner from an ethnic minority and, later on, a quietly compelling champion of pro-bono working, not least on behalf of the disadvantaged in communities such as her own. She kept in touch with Loxton, introducing him in her late thirties to a widowed businessman, also Asian and ten years her senior, with whom she managed to maintain a discreet affair for many years, unbeknownst to her family and most of their colleagues. He died of a brain haemorrhage before they'd gone public, leaving her bereft, but after an awful couple of years she began to pick herself up. She remains close to his daughter, who has two small children. They call her 'Nani' even though she isn't their grandmother, and are an even more important part of her life now that she's stopped working. She says she should have done it sooner; that it's wonderful to have time for herself and for her family, real and surrogate, at last. There are always people visiting.

Rupert and Gloria – for a few years 'the Ingram-Halls' – also got sorted before they left Oxford. He was taken on, during the milk round, by one of the old investment banks and embarked on a career in the City, while she took the Foreign Office exams and then, despite her cavalier approach to protocol, bowed to the demands of the diplomatic service and got on the fast track. They married a year after they graduated – a big wedding with a blousy marquee in her parents' Sussex garden – and, by the sounds of it, briefly revelled in the excitement of it all. Then it seems the strains of their burgeoning careers began to tell: the bank wanted him to travel but not where she was being posted; she balked at taking a lesser position elsewhere in order to be with him. They were on the point of calling it a day when she got pregnant – accidentally, or so she's always said – at which point they agreed to try again. It didn't work for long. She was frustrated with motherhood and a subordinate role, and perhaps he had a dalliance too many with the bright interns – he's never lost that eye for the next opportunity. They agreed to separate: Gloria picked up her career again and went back to being a Durrant; the twins were despatched to boarding school, which they turned out to enjoy; and Rupert moved into private equity and other things, including a new wife and, in due course, the grand house to which he'd always aspired, complete with a nursery for the second family. He's now a significant donor to the College development appeal – he's made a ludicrous amount of money – and the first batch of children are in their early thirties. Gloria is something lofty in public affairs, and is still deploying her skill in reading the runes.

Oddly, Martin Trewin kept in touch with them both. In the beginning he poked fun at their extravagant lifestyle, saying he preferred the country, the tang of manure. Later on he contrived to stay out of the marital squabbling, consulting Gloria regularly about his ramshackle relationships, discussing with Rupert how to make farming pay, never quite taking sides. When eventually he found direction, making organic cheeses, which he sold at the early farmers' markets, he was glad to call on their respective areas of expertise – contacting them separately, because by then the Ingram-Halls had long divorced. Rupert declined to invest seed capital – a decision he says he later regretted – but agreed to be a non-executive director; Gloria, meanwhile, gave informal marketing advice. When Martin sold a minority stake in the business, around the time he split up with his own wife, he bought a place on the coast – a spot not unlike Carreck Loose, as it happens – where, increasingly, Gloria joined him at the weekend to dig a vegetable patch and go for long walks. They still do that, though Gloria maintains a flat in Chelsea. Occasionally, Rupert visits to see how things are going, though what he is inspecting is never entirely clear. I assume Martin and Gloria are properly an item now, but that's their business. It's never wise to speculate.

Chloe Firth fell out with Gloria over the wedding – before rather than after, or even *at,* the event, which was a relief to everybody, especially Rupert – and she remained spiky about Oxford, and what she called 'the Breeding Party', for years. She said the weight of expectation could crush you if you let it, without revealing whether it was her own assumptions or those of other people that were so oppressive. She didn't go into journalism. Instead, after a difficult period when she 'came out', which included a patch in rehab, she joined a succession of NGOs – initially somewhat rickety, later of real weight – disappearing for long stints abroad, nobody was sure where, and going from one relationship to another, it wasn't clear with whom. Eventually her work brought her into contact with Priyam, whose firm was advising the charity on a dispute. Having ignored each other as students – Chloe used to dismiss her as prissy – they became wary allies. Priyam got to know the girlfriend and watched as Chloe stopped the frenetic travelling, settled into a steady relationship and returned tetchily to a few of the old friendships. When civil partnerships were introduced, Chloe announced that she and 'the doll' were getting hitched. Priyam, as well as Gloria and Martin, went to the party. A remarkable outcome, really.

Mei gave me a print of that photo of Tyler and me – if she suspected, she was discreet enough to send other snaps too, including a shot of me and Jim being tackled at football. The two of them were together again by Christmas and stayed an item throughout his final year. He did his teacher's training locally, so he could be near, and when she graduated and returned to Hong Kong, he saved up and went out to visit. It took a while – there was huge pressure on Mei, whose Oxford credentials had secured her articles with an English firm in that area they call Central, and who felt indebted in so many ways for the chance she'd been given – but eventually it was decided. A couple of years after she qualified she came back and they got married, very quietly, in the College Chapel. Barnaby and I were rare guests who weren't Chows or Evanses: she said I'd been like an elder sister, which was really touching – and, immigration sorted, they started life as a couple. They began their family soon after he became head of department and then, when he was offered a deputy headship, they upped sticks so he could return to south-west Wales. In the early years she channelled all her diligence into bringing up the children – they had three, fast, on very little money – and being a support to Jim. Once the brood were all at school and Jim was more established, she talked briefly about going back to the law – she'd invested a lot in it, after all – but it didn't happen. I suspect she was more interested in people; that she'd had enough of sacrificing family, of having so relentlessly to achieve. Besides, it took real work to establish a place for herself when she wasn't British, let alone Welsh – to become 'a pillar of the local community', as she's now been for years, on endless committees, organising and campaigning. She's very proud of Jim, who's done well: he made headship when he was only forty and his current school has consistently got top grades from the inspectors. Not that long ago she told me that he'd declined a final career move, to run a new academy in Bristol, because they were happy where they were and he didn't like the English model. They are an admirable family.

Like me, Barnaby still sees them both. He sees Martin too (he's less comfortable with Gloria, so Martin usually makes the trip). Their friendship helped get him through some bad times in the mid-1980s when the yard on the Helford river went bust and he found himself on benefits. That's when the deep fog of depression – which he always describes as the impenetrable green-grey of Cornish slate, but soft, asphyxiating – enveloped him fully for the first time. Eventually it lifted – he says it's hard to tell why it comes and goes, that the unpredictability is amongst the worst things about it – and he was able to work again. He's back on the North Norfolk coast now – has been in Cromer for a good twenty years – and has a small boat-building business, which 'washes its face' and provides cover for the writing, about which he's always been secretive. Jim and Mei used to take the children there in the summer and even at Easter too; nowadays they go as a twosome and do lots of walking – she makes sure they keep fit. Martin manages the occasional detour. Women reputedly come and go – Barnaby is still a ruggedly handsome man – but they've always been in the background, peripheral: there's never been a Mrs Quick. Mei suspects there's someone at the moment and hopes it will last, given how old we all are. I say Barnaby's okay and that's the main thing. More than okay, really. He's just finished his own work of oral history, on the disappearing fishing trades – encouraged, he tells me, by a comment of mine on an essay of his all that time ago, which is a lovely thing to hear. He let me read the proof a few weeks back: it's marvellous. I always knew he had it in him.

By contrast, Eddie Oakeshott sailed through the rest of his university years – acting, directing and doing very little academic work. By all reports few people asked what degree he got and for a while he affected not to remember; later, when he was beginning to be feted, he'd concede in interviews that he got a 2:2 – a Third would have been better, he used to say with a laugh – but it made no difference to his career, which drew more on his contacts, all the people he knew. He's currently running a small but influential theatre in downtown Manhattan that he likens to the Almeida in London. Tyler once told me that one of Eddie's early successes in New York was a long run of *Bent*, for which Eddie wrote the programme notes, revealing that he'd lost several of his closest friends to AIDS in the decade after Oxford, before anybody really knew what it was: a typically high-volume way of declaring your hand. He used to be quoted in profiles saying that he was astonished he escaped himself; that by rights he should have died many times over. Apparently he's still happy enough, on the surface; what happens below that remains impossible to tell. I've never come across anyone who knows whether the insouciance is real or not – years ago Rupert claimed it was shaken when he rejected a pass Eddie made at him in Cornwall during that game of sardines, but Rupert claims many things. If Eddie's nonchalance is an act, I guess it's so good it makes no odds now.

What of Tyler? That is the painful one. It took me an age to confide in anybody and it seemed no one saw us in York, or guessed from before, though of course I've never been sure. He went back to Boston, did well practising law in Washington, as you might expect, and I carried on with my own career. There were letters and calls in the beginning, although in those days everything passed through the Porters' Lodge and I still hated the idea of gossip, and gradually we reached an agreement about the business of 'after'. Bar one brief holiday together, which just made things worse, Tyler and I stuck to it: accepted what was and wasn't feasible, given our respective careers; didn't try to see each other; did our best to move on. I found it incredibly hard: broke down with Jenny when I got back from Venice, and was grateful for her support; took ages to recover. I used to wonder if I ever would.

A few years later he sent a Christmas card, mentioning the wedding. That too was a difficult moment, Jenny again in demand. It was weeks before I replied to the invitation and even then it was only a short note to wish them well. Still, it unlocked something. After that he and I went back to exchanging occasional letters – nothing too personal – and eventually we met at a conference at Columbia, where I was a visiting professor, around the time he began giving the odd lecture. And there he was, walking up to congratulate me, looking different but also just the same – older, of course, but the gestures, the mannerisms, even that pivoting gait unchanged. We had dinner with his wife a couple of days later and when he introduced me – he made a joke of it – he said that I'd been the only one he'd fancied on the Reading Party all those years ago. Of course I laughed too, and told a story about the students groping their way around the house in Cornwall and how disappointing it had been that no one groped me. And it was fine – they were clearly happy and anyway she probably knew the gist of the rest. You had to make light of it. We met quite a few times after that, mostly together, especially once they asked me to be godmother to their boy, and she and I too began to talk and write periodically. She's a fine woman, bright, attractive, and she soon became a good friend. Then she phoned to say he was ill and she thought I would want to be told.

It was cancer – an aggressive form. I saw him only once after that. Got a flight immediately after the end of term and stayed a couple of nights with them – she wouldn't let me stop elsewhere. Already Tyler was like an old man, curled up in foetal position under the bedclothes, one skeletal arm sticking out like an obscenity, and though he tried to smile, it was clear it was hard. So for two days I did my turn along with the family and a few others, holding that papery hand, talking quietly or listening to music with him. I took a disc of the Mendelssohn songs with me – it turned out he already had the Barenboim recording, but on this one the 'Duetto' was played at a kinder, slower pace – and occasionally I got the faintest squeeze back; even once, which was almost too much for me, a request to touch the apricot hair. He died not long afterwards – it was the anniversary only three weeks ago – and they played one of the songs at his funeral. I think of him often. Their son is very like.

Loxton died too, a little early perhaps, but at least it was more in the way of things. We led the Reading Party together for eight years and then he passed the baton to me, along with the safekeeping of Godfrey's journal. When he retired a few months later, Priyam helped me arrange a gathering in his honour of almost all the people who'd been to Cornwall over the years – Tyler was one of the few who didn't make it – and we all dug out photos and reminisced together. You could tell Dennis was touched. After that we saw each other from time to time. He enjoyed his role

331

as Emeritus Fellow, kept going with the Wine Committee and came in regularly to High Table or to read the papers at midday. We used to have Sunday lunch together – it was usually me to him rather than him to me; probably the quality of the cooking – and after we'd eaten we would do a tour of his garden and he'd tell me what was thriving and what was not. He died right there, suddenly, of a heart attack, when he was planting bulbs near the potting shed, and was found on the ground still holding his dibber. He would have liked that.

As for me, there've been other relationships, but never again with a student. I didn't marry, though I was with one man – nothing to do with the University – for nearly a decade, and I didn't have children; became a cliché of my own, in a way. At least, that's what Jenny once said, but then there was a lot I hadn't shared with her, so I probably deserved it. Mostly, she's been wonderful; she certainly stuck to a kinder interpretation with my god-daughter, focused on my books, which have always sold rather well, and my appearances on telly, which in the early days suggested a kind of glamour, rather than on that picture of a childless spinster. It's been a busy life: juggling so many activities, keeping in touch with so many young people, hearing tales of still more – they're almost family.

I stayed on for nearly twenty-five years, becoming the senior of several female Fellows; did my own stints as Dean and then Tutor for Admissions, graduating to better rooms – and a better bed! – on a staircase with other dons; and later, once they made me a Reader, using my 'living out' allowance to subsidise a ground-floor flat near that extraordinary bookshop until UEA enticed me away with the professorship.

The campus here is a marvellous place – still faintly radical, and I love the modernist buildings and the swathes of green – plus of course East Anglia has always been home to my parents, who are seriously old.

All the same, it was a difficult decision giving up the College and its batty traditions, abandoning my little garden – populated in the early days with cuttings from Loxton, and moving away from so many friends. But Oxford is a bubble, not quite the real world, and the barriers in the Faculty and the University can get to you in the end, though I'm told it's better than it was. Various people stressed the advantages of a change, not least my brothers, although Jenny said they had a vested interest, along with their wives.

Maybe recognition was just too beguiling after all that battling to shape things my way: Andy had been right about that – it *was* exhausting, demeaning even, trying to charm without losing credibility. Besides, the people who really matter come to visit me in Norwich. There is one man, a few years younger, as it happens, with whom I enjoy spending time. We choose not to share a house, but we sail a lot, do stuff together. He's perceptive and kind, and lets me get on with my work, even on the boat; and perhaps I stop him being too much of a loner – I get invited to endless events, so we're always going out, seeing people. Anyhow, we understand each other. I'm very content.

One of the good things I did when I'd settled in properly was to see about introducing a Reading Party. I'm an old hand now with 18–22 year-olds; they're endlessly stimulating. We've sorted the funding at last – Rupert has again been exceptionally generous, given that it's not his *alma mater* – and the School of History is selecting a dozen students from those who have expressed an interest and a good few who haven't presumed to do so.

Of course it will be different outside the collegiate system. Some of my old colleagues – even some of my old students – say not to mind if it doesn't work. I have more faith. Besides, it's important to try: young people need that sort of experience, especially when so much teaching has moved online. We've found a place in the Peak District, in the middle of nowhere and a bit wild. Loxton would have approved. It's nice to think it might be a success – and it would be another way of making history, another minor first. We'll see.

Glossary of Oxford terminology

bachelor set: A suite of rooms used as lodgings for a Fellow of a college who, being unmarried, found it convenient to 'live in'. (Until 1882, Fellows had to be celibate.)

battels: Termly charges made to a member of a college (student or Fellow) for board and lodgings.

a Blue: The highest sporting achievement, awarded after competing in the annual Varsity Match (often against the University of Cambridge).

Bodleian (the Bodleian Library): Oxford's largest library, founded by Sir Thomas Bodley. Its core buildings date from the very early seventeenth century.

Collections: College exams taken by some students at the start of term to assess academic progress.

college 'bible': Some colleges produced annually, for internal use, a printed list of senior and junior members with information on their subjects and so on.

Commem Ball (Commemoration Ball): A college ball held after the end of Trinity term, traditionally 'black tie'.

Dean: A senior member of the college, usually a young Fellow, responsible for supervising the conduct and discipline of junior members, i.e. students. The Dean sometimes had pastoral responsibilities.

don: A professor, lecturer or Fellow.

Double First: The highest class of undergraduate degree involving two examinations (as in Greats).

Duke Humfrey (Duke Humfrey's Library): The oldest reading room, built in the late fifteenth century. In the 1970s it housed the oldest and rarest books.

Emeritus (Emeritus Fellow): The title given at some colleges to a retired Fellow.

Examination Schools: An imposing building used as the venue for many University examinations (and for some University lectures).

Exhibitioner: A student holding a college 'Exhibition', or financial award; often a sign of academic distinction identified by college tutors, usually awarded for one year and lesser than a Scholarship.

Fellow: A senior member of a college. Collectively, with the head of the college, the Fellows comprise its governing body.

Greats: The four-year undergraduate course in Classics, correctly *Literae Humaniores*. The first five terms constitute Honour Moderations ('Mods'), followed by seven terms of Greats.

Hall: The dining hall for students and academic staff in a college (often large and high-ceilinged); also, the activity of dining at the college. Traditionally academic gowns were worn.

High Table: The long table in a college dining hall at which sit the Warden, Fellows and their guests. It is usually on a raised dais at one end of the room, looking down on the students.

Hilary: The second term of the academic year, eight weeks long, from January to mid-March.

Isis: A termly student magazine, first published in 1892, named after the part of the river Thames that runs through Oxford.

matriculation: Confers membership of the University on students enrolled for a degree-level course.

Michaelmas: The first term of the academic year, eight weeks long, from October to December.

Newdigate Prize: A prize for a poem of less than 300 lines. The prize was founded in 1806.

Norrington Table: A league table of colleges, published annually since the 1960s, showing comparative performance of undergraduates in Finals.

Oxbridge: Collectively, the Universities of Oxford and Cambridge.

PPE: The undergraduate course of Philosophy, Politics and Economics.

PPP: The undergraduate course of Psychology, Philosophy and Physiology.

Prelims (Preliminary Examinations): Exams set by the University. Undergraduates take them in their first year.

Radcliffe Camera: A circular library, funded by John Radcliffe and built in the mid-eighteenth century. Used particularly by the History faculty.

Rhodes Scholar: A recipient of the Rhodes Scholarship, funded by Cecil John Rhodes, which is an international postgraduate award for study at the University of Oxford. Very prestigious.

Scholar: A student holding a college Scholarship, or financial award; often a sign of academic distinction revealed in examination results, usually awarded for one year and grander than an Exhibition.

Schools Dinner: A formal dinner held by senior members of a college for junior members taking a given subject after their Finals (when undergraduates 'take Schools').

scout: A housekeeper employed by the college, originally responsible for making beds and cleaning student and other rooms on his or her allotted staircases.

set: A suite of rooms – variously including a study/living room/library, bedroom, bathroom and tiny kitchen – used as lodgings for a Fellow of a college who chooses to 'live in'.

subfusc: The dark clothes (black, with a white shirt or blouse) worn by men and women with their academic dress (a black gown, a black cap or mortar board, and white bow tie, black tie/ribbon) on occasions such as examinations.

Trinity: The third (summer) term of the academic year, eight weeks long.

tutor: Someone who teaches undergraduates one-to-one or in pairs, usually a Fellow of a college. S/he acts as teacher and academic guide.

tutorial: An hour-long meeting with a tutor, usually involving much background reading and writing an essay. Most undergraduates have at least one tutorial a week.

Tutorial Board: A committee of the head of a college and all its Tutorial Fellows, responsible to its governing body for all its teaching functions.

the Union (the Oxford Union): A debating society founded in the early nineteenth century; particularly popular with budding politicians.

the vac (vacation): The holiday between university terms (the long vac being the one in the summer).

viva (as in '*viva voce* examination'): An oral examination.

Warden: The head of the college (at some colleges; other terms are also used).

(With thanks to the glossary at www.ox.ac.uk and to Wikipedia.)

Historical note

Until the mid 1970s, female undergraduates at the University of Oxford had to attend one of its five women's colleges, opened between 1878 and 1893. Male undergraduates could choose between twenty-five men's colleges, the oldest of which had been founded in the thirteenth century.

Women were first admitted to the men's colleges as undergraduates in 1974, when five of them accepted a total of one hundred women. By 1985 all the men's colleges had gone mixed; by 2008 all the women's colleges had done likewise. Female academics first became tutorial fellows in male colleges in 1973, with the first woman heading a former men's college in 1993 and the first female Vice Chancellor of the university appointed in 2016.

In the 1970s there were Reading Parties at four of Oxford's male colleges. One had been taking students to a chalet in the French Alps since 1891; the others also went there or (in the case of the first of them to go mixed) to an Edwardian house on the Cornish coast.

With the exception of Dr Ivy Williams, all the characters in *The Reading Party* are invented.

Acknowledgements

Thanks are due to many people for help and support with THE READING PARTY, my first novel.

I am particularly grateful to Dr Ray Ockenden – who led the reading party at Wadham College, Oxford, for many years – for his early encouragement.

Various past and present members of the college kindly shared relevant memories with me, including Professors Quassim Cassam, Julie Curtis, Christina Howells, Sally Mapstone and Stephen Monsell; the late Dr Cliff Davies; Alexy & John Holden and Bekah Sparrow. Jason Leech's dissertation on the decision in favour of co-residence was a godsend. (There is also a wider study, '"Keep the Damned Women Out": The Struggle for Co-education' by Nancy Weiss Malkiel, published by Princeton University Press.)

I am enormously grateful to Lane Ashfeldt and Jenny Parrott, who gave me confidence when I first began writing and without whom I would never have got underway. Other early readers were generous with their time and hugely helpful: thank you Frances Ashcroft, Zanna Beswick, Janet Fillingham, Matthew Fox, Ruth Logan, Yvonne Milne and Frances Voelker. I'd also like to acknowledge the many friends who took a special interest, helped with research queries or kept me sane – notably Sally Bruce Lockhart, Margie

Campbell, Ivy Chau, Ann Marie Cooper, Sophie Day, Juliet Davis, Sarah Derbyshire, Julie Hage, Crispin Kelly, David Mitchell, Hugh Nineham, Hanni Randell-Bateman, Vicky Smith, Ayesha Tarannum and David Waller. The Gentleman and Freegard families were discreetly supportive: warm thanks all round.

The team at Muswell Press have been wonderful. A massive thank you to Sarah Beal and Kate Beal for their faith in THE READING PARTY, their editorial steers, marketing nous and friendship along the way. Thanks too to Kate Quarry, Jamie Keenan and Anna Pallai for meticulous copy-editing, evocative cover design and savvy publicity respectively.

Above all, I am grateful to the two people who put up with so much day-to-day: my husband Jonathan Freegard (second reader), who is astonishingly attentive, cheerful and kind; and our daughter Lucy Freegard (first reader), who laughs, comforts and teases a lot. They have always been generous about my need to retreat into my own mental space. My love and heartfelt thanks to you both.